"Move over, Bridget Jones—the new voice of twentysomething women has arrived."
—*Detroit News*

PRAISE FOR

CITIZEN GIRL

BY EMMA MCLAUGHLIN & NICOLA KRAUSS

"A satire about staying true to one's values while also staying employed, [*Citizen Girl*] is meatier and more engaging than *Diaries*—think *The Beauty Myth* meets *Sex and the City*. . . . McLaughlin and Krauss keep us amused."

—*Austin American-Statesman*

"Perhaps in the wake of the tragic events of Bridget Jones's love-life, women are ready for something a bit more serious, a bit more grown-up. And *Citizen Girl* . . . is it."

—*London Times*

"Young professional readers will relate to the degrading challenge of scraping for entry-level work in a lousy economy and the tyranny of clueless, selfish bosses. And McLaughlin and Kraus should be lauded for creating an old-school feminist heroine who knows where to draw the line."

—*The Washington Post*

"*Citizen Girl* takes shots at every single instance of one woman's confrontation with male society during the course of a few months. It does this while being wickedly funny and well written but not dogmatic or finger wagging."

—*The New Republic*

"The bestselling authors of *The Nanny Diaries* return with another mordant satire—this time they skewer self-important personalities of the twenty-first-century workplace."

—*Teen Vogue*

"The young authors have a knack for comedy, and there are priceless scenes here, some set at career fairs and in the halls of NYU, that will delight cubicle dwellers everywhere."

—*Hampton Family Life*

"The authors have conjured up a vision of America that's just this side of dystopian, and their funhouse-mirror worldview generates its own strange suspense."

—*Booklist*

"Many, many funny lines.... Girl's job-hunting woes will resonate with lots of readers."

—*Kirkus Reviews*

"[A] hyperventilating satire . . . witty and biting."

—*Publishers Weekly*

"McLaughlin and Krauss [have a] delicious sense of the absurd."

—*Entertainment Weekly*

ALSO BY EMMA MCLAUGHLIN
AND NICOLA KRAUS

The Nanny Diaries

Citizen Girl

A NOVEL

EMMA McLAUGHLIN

AND

NICOLA KRAUS

Washington Square Press

NEW YORK   LONDON   TORONTO   SYDNEY

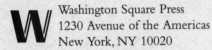

Washington Square Press
1230 Avenue of the Americas
New York, NY 10020

Copyright © 2004 by Italics, LLC

All rights reserved, including the right to reproduce
this book or portions thereof in any form whatsoever.
For information address Atria Books, 1230 Avenue
of the Americas, New York, NY 10020

ISBN-13: 978-0-7432-6685-7
ISBN-10:   0-7432-6685-4
ISBN-13: 978-0-7432-6686-4 (Pbk)
ISBN-10:   0-7432-6686-2 (Pbk)

First Washington Square Press trade paperback edition October 2005

10 9 8 7 6 5 4 3 2 1

WASHINGTON SQUARE PRESS and colophon are
registered trademarks of Simon & Schuster, Inc.

Manufactured in the United States of America

For information regarding special discounts for bulk purchases,
please contact Simon & Schuster Special Sales at 1-800-456-6798
or business@simonandschuster.com

"... I went to my adviser and told her of the fears that were choking me. 'You feel like an imposter?' she asked. 'Don't worry about it. All smart women feel that way.' "

—PEGGY ORENSTEIN

"I wanna be a cowboy, baby."

—KID ROCK

To Girl's Fairy Role Models: Shannon, Sara, Katie, Ally, and Olivia, who read endlessly, cheered tirelessly, and who, no matter what their twenties served up, always found the funny.

Citizen Girl

CHAPTER ONE

Doris Mindfuck

The ladies' room door squeaks open and I stop breathing, jerking my feet up on the toilet seat lid in an effort to work through my lunch hour in solitude. Rubber soles scuff along the honeycomb tiles as I bend to inch the remains of my lunch out of view, but my pen betrays me, rolling brazenly out of my lap and onto the warped floor.

"Who's in here?" my boss, Doris, shouts over the din of sweatshop sewing machines whirring up the air shaft. I consider not responding—maybe she'll think the pipes are now leaking not only asbestos but pens. "Hello-o?" She knocks once on the last stall door before rattling it forcefully. Her tightly permed gray curls appear below me. "Oh, Girl, it's you."

I will a cheery smile.

"You have your period again, don't you?" She stares up disdainfully as she turns a deep red from her inverted stance. "You know, Girl"—she takes in my research materials on the floor—"I've provided you with a perfectly good desk."

"Yes, thank you . . ." I try to dislodge my crossed legs without stepping on her face. "I was just taking advantage of the quiet to finish my presentation for the conference." I unlatch the door, and she abruptly shoves it in toward me, spraying the cup of coffee I'd balanced on the toilet-paper dispenser onto my coat. My new coat.

She arches her eyebrows over her multicolored Fimo clay bifocals. "You're a mess," she pronounces. "You really should make your lunch at home and bring it with you. You're not managing your finances very well if you buy those expensive sandwiches every day. But I guess that'd mean you'd actually have to get out of bed on time." She remains squarely in the stall doorway, indicating that I owe her an explanation.

"I should," I say with a nod, collecting the offending sandwich wrappers, along with my files, from the floor. She folds her arms across her ample chest and continues to stare me down. Before I can determine how to atone, the bathroom door squeaks open again, and Pam, deputy director of the Center for Equity in Community, waddles in.

"Oh, Doris, there you are." She approaches, hulking from side to side like a bloated John Wayne. "I'm heading uptown for that meeting on the Youth Center rally, and if it's anything like last week's, I'm going to be there till dinner—"

"Those. Are. Fantastic." Doris thrusts her pointer finger at Pam's purple clogs, which match her bright purple hemp jumper and the dark purple African lariat she has ambitiously combined with lilac Mardi Gras beads. Had an eggplant been available in her kitchen, she'd have donned it as a hat.

"Well, I saw Odetta's green ones, so I asked for a pair from Santa, but you know I'm still hunting for *those*." Pam gestures to Doris's black Nubuck booties.

"I'll never tell," Doris says coyly, turning her ankle. Doris's hemp and Nubuck ensembles are famously all-black, giving her a cosmopolitan air amidst the Center's menopausal sea of the waistband-and-ironing-board adverse.

"I'm just going to—" I point to the sink by the door and shimmy past them, dabbing at the pending stain on my coat with a sheet of toilet tissue.

"Look at this one." Doris grudgingly steps aside and jerks her thumb at me, letting Pam in on the latest Girl Headache. "Can't keep her coffee in its cup." She purses her lips, narrowing her eyes before continuing, "Girl, meet me in my office after you pull yourself together. I want to make an addition to the conference packet."

"Definitely. And I want to go over my presentation—"

But their pear-shaped figures are already disappearing as the door stutters closed. I slap my files down on the cracked Formica counter, yank the last paper towel from the cracked dispenser, and shrug off my assaulted coat. I *do* make it out of bed on time, thank you very much. And actually, since you ask, I'm working through my *unpaid* lunch hour. *For you.* And the fact that the *only* square inch of peace and quiet I can find in this swirling *tornado* of psychodrama is *on a toilet seat* should tell you *something* about the kind of outfit you're running here. *I'm* not the jackass. You. *You* are the jackass.

"Jackass," I level at the curling thirty-year-old poster for *Having Our Say: Teaching Young Women to Step Up and Speak Out!*, Doris Weintruck's iconic tome and the misleading cornerstone of my Wesleyan curriculum. She manages a dimpled grin, tilted with insouciance, to her raised smocked shoulder, her auburn curls teased into an empowering Linda Carter do. Gripping the lapel where the coffee stain is now indelibly entwined with the pink wool, I whisper my pronouncement to the Doris of the disco era, "I quit."

I turn to the door, heart rate escalating, mouth sandy. Just do it. Just march right in. Just march in and take a seat—no, stand. Yes, march right in there and stand and . . . and tell her that she's unprofessional . . . and a hypocrite and, and . . . and mean.

Or wait till five when she's tuckered. Or Monday when she's rested. Maybe don't do it in person at all: *Hello, you. This is me. I'm not coming back.* Hang up and that'd be it. Over. Done. No bloodshed.

No bloodshed but no closure.

I spin to the poster and search her flat eyes. Don't I owe Doris Weintruck, founding mother of the Female Voice Movement, the opportunity to throw her arms around me and wish me the best, so that we can move on, not just as colleagues but as friends? So, ten years from now, when we're cochairing the same board, and she can't get over how I look like a rocket scientist, sound like a rocket scientist, and am, in fact, a rocket scientist, we can have a nice long giggle about how she used to treat me like an asshole? I avert my gaze to the counter, where, inside my purse, my checkbook is barely covering the essential trinity of food, shelter, and student loans.

Fuck. Fuckfuckfuck.

I sigh, once again tabling the fantasy. Folding my coat over my arm, I pick up my paper, "Beyond Renouncing: Modeling Practical Strategies for Young Feminists," that I've been researching, on my own time, since Doris finally consented to let me deliver my first talk at her annual Having Our Say Conference. An event charged with activists at the forefront of the field, whose siren song brought me to the Center in the first place: *If women could just unite on _____, we could change _____.* And it's this opportunity to join the conversation that's the last anemic carrot toward which I'm running.

The next morning finds me literally up to my eyeballs in stacks of pastel photocopies. Mindlessly collating packets while the radiator cackles and clanks, I circle the table, lost deep within a vision in which I'm stepping down from the conference podium amidst warm waves of applause as Doris turns to me, her head bowed low in respect. "NOW wants you on their think tank, and Hillary would like to take a meeting," she announces, reaching to shake my hand. "I'm hiring an assistant for both of us."

"Girl! GIRRRRRLLLLLLL!" Doris screams me back to

reality from her office down the hall. "GIRRRRLLLL!" She fills the door frame of the overheated janitorial closet, retitled the Speak-Out Room. "What did you do with that number?!"

"Sorry, which number?" I bookmark the pile I'm collating from with my hand.

"That number . . . for the woman . . . with that program— *you* know!" Doris takes it upon herself to shift my piles to search for the number. Which I logically would have hidden beneath three thousand sheets of paper. I dive to save the lilac from toppling into the powder blue, but it's too late. "Come on, come look by your desk. I know you kept it." I swipe my coat before she jerks me down the long row of cubicles and back to the hot-flash-provoked arctic sector of the office.

"I'm sure we'll find it," I say, my breath hovering in little frosted cloud bursts as Doris stretches out my sleeve. "If you could just tell me which program she was—"

"Well, if I remembered that, then I wouldn't have to disturb you from your origami. I gave it to you this morning. Here, look around your area." She points at the child-sized school desk that's been allotted for my full and luxurious use. The very same desk on which I've had to store six hundred copies of fifty-three handouts because Odetta, the office manager, "just plain can't stomach people leaving all their junk" in the Speak-Out Room overnight. Reaching for the binder in which I've learned to keep a detailed log of every single phone message, I flip to today's date and run my finger down the list.

"Um, are you sure it was this morning?" I gingerly detach Doris's clam-grip from my now distended, coffee-stained coat. "Because I don't—"

"That's what I said, isn't it?" She drops to her knees and shoves herself between my legs to root through the garbage can. "If you would just keep things a little more orderly out here, Girl."

"Right. It's just that with all these conference materials—maybe it might be more efficient if, *maybe,* we could store them in the clos—Speak-Out Room. And I'm glad you grabbed me because I'm really eager to get your feedback on my presentation." I flip through yesterday's phone log. "Do you mean Shelly from the Oregon YWCA?"

She jumps up, knocking over the full can. "Yes! Yes, that's her. See, *I-told-you,*" she singsongs.

"Um, she actually called yesterday and I left the message right . . ." I walk into her office. "Here." I pull the Post-it off her computer screen and hand it to her as she shuffles in after me.

"Humph." Doris takes it with a slight blush.

"Super! So, have you had a chance to review my presentation?"

"Girl," she says sternly, "that's a premature conversation. I feel there's another issue you need to address first." She points with her nose to the sagging chair across from her, and my stomach sinks. "Go ahead, have a seat," she instructs firmly.

I detest this office; it has no windows and is covered with crumbling collages made by Doris's *Step Up and Speak Out!* adolescents of yore. I always end up eye level with the cutout of a woman carrying a big floppy hat from a Summer's Eve douche box circa 1979 pasted beside yellowed advertising copy that proclaims, *Sisters are doing it for themselves!* But even that is less cringe-inducing than the framed *Ms.* cover of Doris bleating into a megaphone.

"Girl," she says, "I want to share with you that I'm really quite troubled by something that I think would be a disservice not to bring to your attention."

"Oh?"

"You seem to be abnormally preoccupied with space."

"Sorry?"

"Space. Having it. Needing it. Wanting it. You talk about it all the time. I've told you on several occasions that we're operating with a commune perception here at the Center. I believe we've discussed, ad nauseam, that you need to make peace with your allotted area."

"Right. I'm, um, fine with my desk. It's just that these conference packets had only ten handouts for two hundred participants a week and a half ago. And I'm working with a lot more paper now, so—"

"See, Girl, I think it's pretty unhealthy that you choose to deflect responsibility for your own inadequacies right back onto me."

"Sorry?"

Doris leans in and places her hands on my knees. The Summer's Eve woman does a slow hula behind her as I lose air. "I want you to work on this. Maybe work on it in your own life. This is a sign of further—deeper—issues, I feel, for you. It's really why I don't like working with you young twenty-somethings—you're all just so . . ." She tilts her face to stare intensely at me over her bifocals. Instinctively I mirror her, leaning forward. We slowly continue to move in toward each other while I await my sentence. "Needy," she finally pronounces before nearly planting her face in my lap. She reaches around me to retrieve a stack of crumbling leaflets, momentarily suffocating me with her cleavage. "These should be added to the packets. I'm thinking fuchsia, lime green, and orange."

I stand up.

"Wait, Girl—not the light orange. I want the bright one."

"Okay. Sure!"

"No, no, maybe the pale orange is better. Make copies of both and bring them in for me to decide."

I glance down at the first thirty-year-old leaflet. "This one might be too old to Xerox. It's almost illegible—"

"Yes? And?" Doris smiles at my idiocy. "So, you'll need to retype it. Come on, Girl."

I check the rusted school clock above her shoulder. "I think

I mentioned this yesterday, but all these materials have to be in the mail by Monday. It's just that the copy machine has been kind of temperamental. So if, maybe, we could, you know, not add too many more—because so far I've only been able to make fifty out of the six hundred and twenty-two—"

"Six hundred and *thirty-four!* I just got a group from Des Moines!" Doris claps her hands like an excited child.

I dig my fingernails into my palms and don't roll my eyes. "So the six hundred and thirty-four packets—"

"Well, Girl, the point is the content. We aren't going to tailor a national conference around your social life now, are we? I'm not going to call the funders in Washington and tell them we can't do it just because you can't put a few more papers into a folder or two." OR SIX HUNDRED AND THIRTY-FOUR! Doris smiles coyly. "I think you had best plan to be here over the weekend if you're managing your time that poorly." The phone rings and I wait to remind her again about my presentation. Smiling out into space, she lifts the receiver to her ear. "This is Doris!" she chimes. "Hello, Jean. Before I answer your questions, are we getting Sunday coverage or not? Uh-huh, uh-huh. Well, I appreciate your challenge, Jean, I do, but if you set this as a goal for yourself—engaging with your editor is a growth opportunity for you. Reframe for him that this year's conference is going to be an *unprecedented* gathering . . . Oh, now, don't take me the wrong way, I'm only saying that when we silence ourselves, Jean, we suffer. And I know you know this. As I was saying, an unprecedented gathering of the preeminent thinkers in the field of teenage-oriented public policy and community outreach . . . I *may* have said that last year, I can't recall . . . No, I don't think my 'brand' of feminism is outdated . . . .Well, of course I'm participating. Why would you even ask that? . . . A different angle? What kind of angle? . . . *Where are they now?!* I'm right here! . . . You're questioning my *relevance?* That's an idiotic paradigm and a right-wing distraction tactic and I won't participate in it." Doris drops the phone and turns to me, her dimpled hands splaying across her hemp-swaddled belly. "Silenced, Girl. We're being silenced." She glazes over as she fingers her trade beads. "All my hard work getting this summit funded for the *back page*."

"Maybe this isn't really suited to *The Times*. Why don't we reach out to *Mother Jones, The Atlantic*? Or if you want local coverage, I can call *The Voice*—"

"Light orange. Definitely." She waves me brusquely from the room.

"I've brought you re-in-force-ments!" Doris singsongs the next morning from the hallway outside the Speak-Out Room, where I'm surrounded by piles of copies and boxes.

She sashays in wearing her black corduroy culotte and vest, looking every bit the Peace Corps elf.

"Great!" I reach for enthusiasm, praying she's pulled in a few of the other beleaguered, yet able-bodied assistants.

"Yes, our very own office manager has graciously volunteered to come to your rescue."

Wheezing, Odetta squeezes in around the far side of the table to join me, her polyester pants still stuffed into the tops of her snow boots. "She's not leaving her stuff in here overnight, is she?" she inquires suspiciously, as she heaves her girth up onto a stool. "I can't stomach that."

"Oh, no," I quickly reassure her. "I have a desk, my own desk, and it's all the space I need. I put all of this back in my area every evening. Because it's mine, my space, and I love it."

Doris rolls her eyes at Odetta.

"So what am I doing here?" Odetta asks her as she hasn't addressed me directly since I dared speak of the fax machine's penchant for not faxing.

"Start here," Doris instructs her with complete authority, while rearranging everything I've already arranged.

"Actually, Odetta," I finally interrupt after Doris has made a collating order that requires nine circuits of the table to fill a single folder, "maybe you could put the name stickers on. That would be super-helpful!"

"All right, boss!" Doris salutes me, and my fingernails find their way back into my palms.

Odetta then proceeds to laboriously center each sticker before applying it.

"Why is this orange?" Doris thrusts a paper at me as I squeeze past her.

"That's the color you wanted."

"Well, it's all wrong for this topic. Orange for menstruation? How about magenta? Odetta, what do you think?"

"You're the one who knows colors, Doris," Odetta coos.

"We'll have to decide later," Doris sighs, checking her Swatch. "Now, I have to run to a meeting in Brooklyn. I'll be back after lunch. Be nice to Odetta, and don't work her too hard—she's doing you a favor." She hustles out of the closet, and Odetta sends me a look that lets me know she's not putting up with any of my funny business.

"Thank you so much for helping out with this!" I beam, eager to boost her sticker per hour ratio. "The fax machine has been working *like a dream* lately. You really have a way with it. And I hear your plans for the Self-Esteem bake sale are going really well!" I collate around her immobile frame. "I'm so sorry I'm going to miss it—I'm presenting at the conference that day—"

"Nope. You're working the table from nine to noon." Before I can correct her, Odetta's cell rings and she pulls it from her stretched elastic waistband. "Thought you hung up on me . . . Well, you should carry more change. I was saying that I just don't feel like you've been there for me lately. You didn't call me on Christmas. Or New Year's. Hold on," she says, acknowledging my waving hands.

"Sorry, but I'm going to be in Toledo," I tell her. "I'm presenting this year."

Odetta shakes me off. "When my sister had that Pap smear, I spent a lot of time thinking about what's important in my life, and I have my husband, my cats, and us. You and me. I felt like I couldn't count on you at all this week—" I tap her hulking shoulder. "Don't touch me!" She puts her hand over the mouthpiece. "Yes, you *are* working the table. Doris signed you up yesterday."

"Yesterday?!" *No! Nonono!* With rising panic, I accelerate my collating, squeezing quickly past her mammoth butt with each orbit of the table. Odetta shrinks from the contact as she rails on to someone presumably in prison.

"When the cat's feet are acting up, it makes my rash come back. I've been awake every night itching and taking oatmeal baths. Well, I should be able to call you when I get to work and if you aren't there—I'm not saying you don't have things to do . . . no, I'm not saying that. I said I'm not saying that. If you'll listen . . . I'm saying that I had to take the cat . . ."

The radiator clanks aggressively, Odetta's motionless hand leaving a sweaty smear of ink on the forgotten folder, rendering it, and her, useless.

Trudging back from lunch, I unbutton my coat, prepared to do battle. My heart stops as I round the corner to find that my desk has been pillaged. "Shitshitshit." Every single thing has been moved; files are gone, piles have been rifled, my carefully constructed packing lists for the conference materials are nowhere to be found, and the binder with my notes on who's available to sub for me at the bake sale is MIA. I start to see spots.

"Um," I call out in greeting as I stumble to Doris's office, "I think my desk has been—"

"Cleaned. Yes, it was a disaster. I don't know how you were getting a single thing done out there. You've been whining about help, so I took it upon myself to make some order. You're welcome." Doris has my binder open on her desk, which is in its usual state of disarray. "I really don't know why you keep all these messages, Girl. It's a little neurotic. 'Not a baking enabler.'" She snorts and tosses the binder back to me. "What does that even mean?"

I consciously close my open jaw. "Right, I wanted to ask you. There seems to be some confusion with Odetta. She's under the impression that I'm working the bake sale while we're at the conference."

Doris just looks at me.

"So am I?"

"What?"

"Working?"

"Not at the moment."

"Right, no. I meant the bake sale."

"Yes."

"But that's the day I'm supposed to be presenting—"

"Your behavior hasn't really indicated you're ready to present. If you can't manage the assembly of a few packets . . ." She shrugs, helpless against my incompetence. "Besides, you never gave me a draft of your presentation, and we leave in two days. Did you see my note?" She reaches for the phone.

"What? Wait. I'm sorry, I gave you a draft on Monday. I can print you up another copy now—"

"I'm in meetings all afternoon. The note's on your desk. It came to me at three A.M., while I was peeing—you can forget about sleeping after you turn fifty—and I realized just what this conference is missing." The speaker at the other end of the phone picks up and I'm forgotten. "He-llo! Doris Weintruck at your service!"

I walk back to my desk, which looks up at me, sadly violated, trying modestly to cover itself with an article ripped from *Ms. Magazine* about teenage apathy. I sit down to stare at the flimsy toilet-tissue note paper-clipped to it, in which only an *A, S,* and

T are distinctly legible in the two-word message scribbled in bleeding felt tip. "Arrogant thrust? Apologetic trust?" Wait . . . is that an *m*? Carrie, another program assistant, squeezes by my desk, and I grab her arm. "Doris-speak." I hand her the tissue.

"*Absolute must.*"

"Thanks."

Carrie fixes me a quick look of desperation and jerks her head toward Odetta's cave. "Staple machine's busted again."

"Open with how much you love her and that you in no way consider what you're about to say to be her fault."

"Thanks." We exchange a nod, and she disappears around the corner.

"GIRRRRRLLLLLL. DID YOU FIND THE NOTE?" Doris's scream precedes her.

I leap up to catch her elbow. "Please, *please,* wait right here. I'm making a copy of my presentation right now—you could read it on the way home. Let's schedule a meeting tomorrow to go over your feedback." I grab her calendar. "I'll pencil it in on the way to the copier, you stand here—"

"Of course I can *stand* here," Doris mugs for a passing director. "You don't have to be so *dramatic.*"

First thing the next morning, having collated into the wee hours, I lure Doris to her desk with the aid of multiple cheese Danishes so she can review my presentation. She waves me back to work with the promise of a 'little helper.' And when he arrives, he is just that. The home-schooled offspring of Doris's friend, this germ-riddled assistant comes to just below my thigh. It takes his five-year-old hands eleven excruciating minutes to slide a single flyer into a single folder. Which is still faster than Odetta. Progress.

"Bor-ing. I want to play with the toys."

"Great! Fine! Go play." I wave him away to drip snot over the tower of training tools lining the walls of the Speak-Out Room.

"Hey, get that down for me." He points at the Tupperware tub of colored chalk.

"What?" I look up from where I'm stuffing double-time. "Yeah, okay." I pull the tub from the shelf and toss it on the floor.

"Hey! I want to play with the markers!" Followed by, "I can't reach the red things." And then, "See that yellow box? Get it—"

"LOOK. You're going to have to pick one thing here, mister. And *just* one thing. I only have one more reach in me, because, while it may not be apparent to anyone else in a twelve-mile radius, I'm actually *working here!*" His lower lip starts to quiver and, remorseful, I crouch down to his level. "So which would be your very, very favorite one to play with?"

He sneezes into my face before pointing to something high on the shelf that I have to balance on the conference boxes to get down. I toss him the container and try to make up for lost time.

"Aaahhhhh!" His orgasmic cries of passion startle me. "I . . . LUUUVV . . . STYROFOAM!!! I LOVE IT!" I pivot to discover a billowing cloud of sherbet-colored peanuts rising and falling in little bursts above the collating piles. "Ooooh! STY-RO-FOAM!" I inch around the table to find my helper supine beneath a pile of peanuts. Bits of mucus-covered foam cling to his ears, nose, and mouth. His eyes in a drugged-out half-mast, he rolls back and forth, smearing peanuts across his chest.

"Okay, you're done." In one move, I jerk him up and into Doris's office.

"He"—I deposit him in the doorway—"is not helping. Thanks, though."

"Well, you should have told me that right away, Girl. How can I help you if you don't communicate with me?" Doris rolls her eyes at Little Helper's mother before turning back to address him as if he's deaf. *"I bet you're very helpful at home, aren't you?"*

"I clean up the paintbrushes!" He sneezes, spitting pastel peanuts out of his mouth like a spastic Pez dispenser while my eyes fall on his mother's batik-covered lap. On which sits a very highlighted and underlined presentation.

That.

I.

Wrote.

"Justice, come here. We've been over this: Styrofoam is a killer of the universe and that means a killer of you." She pulls him to her, swinging her gray braid behind her. "Now play here while Momma finishes up her speech."

"Doris, can I speak to you for a sec in the hallway?" It's out before I know what's coming next.

"Excuse me, Justice, while I go in the hallway to be *spoken to.*" Doris curves the ends of her mouth down and raises her eyebrows. "Here, why don't you show Justice the pictures from our Guatemala retreat." She hands a water-stained envelope to Momma Batik and follows me outside. "Yes?"

"That's my presentation. That I gave to you to review. Why does she have it?"

"We're a team and you're sounding very accusatory." Doris rests her shoulder against the wall. "You should take a moment to listen to your tone."

"I respect that we're a team. But I don't understand. The research has taken me over a year and a half. I've spent weeks of my own time to get it written. When I interviewed with you—"

"When I *took a chance* on you, I made it extremely clear that you were committing to flexibility—"

"Right—"

"So, listen to yourself." She stares at me evenly, daring me to go on.

"I have done *everything* that you asked me to do, and I thought we agreed—look, don't you remember our conversation in August? When the air conditioner was broken and I had to ice your forehead? How you said my research would be invaluable to the conference participants, helping them mobilize young women for the next election—when choice and health care will be on the table. That my proposal was written with fresh eyes. Fresh. Eyes. Mine. That's verbatim what you said. We agreed that I was ready to—"

"You only hear what you want to hear. I never said—"

"But you did!"

"Did I?"

"Remember, you said that it was a great starting point for me, and if I wrote my findings up, I could do it."

"Do what?"

"PRESENT!" I feel as if I'm speaking Martian. Is she deaf?! Am I crazy?! Shaking, I point my paper-cut-riddled index finger in her pruny face. "Look, you! I know what I said. I said it and you said it and I'm doing it 'cause that's what we said I'm going to do. So just say that I said just now what I just said and you heard. Say it, I'm—"

"Fired."

CHAPTER TWO

Choking on My Parachute

The buzzer on my decrepit intercom rattles my tiny studio, rousing me from what is snowballing into a month-long power nap. I lift my head in the dusk-darkened room, pulling the phone from where it's embedded in my face. BBBBUUU-UZZZZ. After soliciting every remotely-public-policy-nonprofit-women-for-women organization in the tristate area, I passed out a few days ago while trying, in vain, to get through to my oldest friend, Kira, BBBUUUZZZ who's cruelly abandoned me to dig a well in some BBBUUUZZZZ Godforsaken country with one fucking phone and an inordinate number of water buffalo BBBUUUZZZ. I'm cosmically dumped, and everyone else is off on graduate odysseys BBBUUUZZZ while I stifle another sob and wait for whoever is torturing me to realize that they're pushing the *WRONG BUTTON.*

BBBBBBBUUUUUUUUUZZZZZZZZZ! BBBBUU-UZZZZ! BBBBBBUUUUUUUUZZZZZZZZZ!

Muthafucka.

I rouse myself from the futon, pull my bathrobe tighter, and shuffle to the door through a snowbank of pro forma rejection letters.

BBBBUUUZZZZ!

"Hello?" I ask tentatively, holding down the Talk button, blood draining from my head.

Static.

"Hello!" I cry into the wall.

Crackle. Crackle.

"HEEELLLOOO!!!!"

"It's me." Whoosh, whoosh, crackle, crackle.

"Who?"

"YOUR BROTHER! I'M COMING UP!"

Shocked, I press the button firmly with an added jiggle at the end, undo the multiple locks, and step out onto the landing, blinking beneath the bare bulb. I hear Jack trudging upward, thumping something heavily against every stair. He emerges, Cubs hat first, dragging our mother's ancient plaid suitcase, and looks squarely at me. "Been sent to rescue you." He flexes a hint of bicep before leaning back against my neighbor's front door to catch his breath. He lifts his cap off to run a hand through his chestnut mop.

"Rescue me?"

Jack gives my old bathrobe a once-over before raising an eyebrow with disdain. "Yup. Grace says you've stalled."

Following inside, I drag the suitcase down the path between the we-regret-to-inform-yous, lock the door, and do my best to scrape up some semblance of dignity in furry parrot slippers. But Jack's already thrown off his coat, chucked aside the empty Mallomars packages, and dropped onto my futon. "There're muffins," he says, clicking on the Knicks game.

"Jack! It's not safe for a fourteen-year-old to be wandering around this neighborhood alone. It's *rife* with junkies and pimps and . . . and . . . drummers." I kneel down to tug at the suitcase's chipped gold zipper to find two Tupperware bowls of Grace's oatmeal pecan muffins nestled between my grade-school skating trophies. I hold up my dusty *Twelfth Night* costume in disbelief. "*This* is what I need right now? Pantaloons?"

"Mom packed it. Said you needed to 'reconnect with your root accomplishments'—there's a note." I find a piece of torn paper bag marked by Grace's editorial red ink: "Get on with it." I bite into a muffin to quell the lump in my throat, swallow, and dial home.

"Chatsworth Writers' Colony."

"Hey."

"Hey, Chica," my mother's voice drops to an intimate timbre. "I only have a minute—that poet has locked himself in the pantry to 'rebirth.' It's nearly dinner. We're all getting hungry and grumpy, and I really don't think I can invite him back. Has Jack arrived?"

I watch Jack clicking through my meager seven channels. "Yes, miraculously he hasn't been sold for crack."

"Well, I didn't think he'd fetch much."

"I'm being serious."

"I know you are. You wouldn't let me come, so I sent an emissary. At fourteen I was—"

"On a kibbutz. Fifteen in Finland. I know." Jack gestures a gun to the head.

"*You* should go back to Finland. Remember when you were three—you loved the Northern Lights."

"So you tell me."

"Feeling any better?"

"It's not the end of the world," I lie.

"I know. Out here, we know that." I shut my eyes to the pile of homeless résumés, my unworn interview suit. "After you eat the muffins, I want you to celebrate all the incredible things you've accomplished. Put on the pantaloons."

"Right, a tenth-grade play is *exactly* what I want to look back on as my professional high point."

"And then I want you to get some perspective. Reread the opening to *Grapes of Wrath*. It sounds like you're getting a little dire over there."

"It *is The Grapes of Wrath*—nobody's hiring! I'm competing for unpaid internships with fifty-year-old PhDs who've introduced their own bills in Congress! *Nobody* is sitting out there tonight praying that some twenty-four-year-old with a whopping two and a half years' clerical experience will swing down their chimney."

"C'mon, chica, who was the five-year-old who had a booming business charging a nickel an adjective to the writers—"

"Mom."

"The fifth grader who got her idiotic school board to build a Women's History section in the library—"

"Mom—"

"The twelve-year-old who offered her own class in the barn when that ballet school refused to teach modern—"

"Grace—"

"Do I have to remind you that class is still running! You and I both know what you're capable of. As soon as you get in the door, you're going to knock their pantyhose off—" The televised roar of Madison Square Garden fills my tiny apartment, drowning Grace out.

I grab a balled-up sock and toss it at Jack's head. He gives a suit-yourself shrug before the basketball game audibly shrinks back to its nineteen inches. "Thanks, but there *is* no door. I haven't been offered a *single* interview." My shoulders slump. "I should've handled things differently with Doris."

"Oh, no, Missy May, we're not going down that road. You wanted to quit that job from day one. Now you're shot of it and can sign up for unemployment. It's a blessing—"

"A blessing that I spent eighteen months on research that may never be released? I dredged up *every single* outreach strategy dating back to the first suffragette! I went to the Smithsonian—on my own dime! And it's all going to have zero impact by the time she's done translating it into crazy to make it sound like she wrote it. All that work and it won't make a fucking difference to a single woman—"

"Language. G, I have about thirty seconds so here's my three cents." I see her pointing her red Bic as she speaks. "Start your own thing. If you can't function within the system, strike out on your own. Start your own organization—"

My head reverberates. "Oh my God. Mom, I'm doing everything I can just to get a desk. A desk and a paycheck. I just want my desk back. I want my paycheck *back*. I even want that fucking broken fax machine back—"

"Language. And that's system talk."

"I know! I operate *fine* within the system. I *like* the system! The system and me, we're like this!" I cross my fingers.

"So then get out of bed. I love you. Put Jack on."

"You're up." I stick the phone out to him.

"Yeah, uh-huh . . . yeah, Mom, *I know.* I will. Yes, a list. Heard you at the train station. Yeah, you, too." He hits the off button and drops the phone beside him on the futon.

"Oy," I mutter, my mouth full of muffin.

"When was the last time you changed these sheets?" he asks, distastefully lifting the duvet.

"You were eleven. Want one?" I hold out the rapidly dwindling stash.

"If I have another muffin I'll puke. Got any more Mallomars?"

I motion him to scoot over as I pass him a fresh yellow package. We sit and munch, glancing about at my living room cum bedroom cum kitchen cum shower, the two hundred square feet that, in a previous incarnation, was my neighbor/landlord's closet. Jack reclines, his baseball cap tilting up as he takes in the peeling paint, tattered ceiling, crumbling exposed brick, and duct tape that blocks the draft. "You're *totally* killing every desire I have to live in the city."

"If it's any consolation"—I reach for another muffin—"I'm killing my own, too."

"Ever consider working *for* profit?" he asks.

"Every day, asshole, every day."

"Language. So what'd Grace say?" he asks, licking chocolate off his fingers.

"She wants me to start my own organization."

"She wants me to start my own soccer league." He shrugs, passing back the package as he jumps off the bed. "She suggest a nonviolent coup?"

I smile, happy to be talking to someone who isn't a beleaguered receptionist. "This is nice." I tap the brim of his cap. "Ooh, I think I have a packet of popcorn left."

Jack looks at his watch. "Nope—no time." He claps his hands. "Hit the shower. We're goin' out."

"Out? *Out* out?" I stuff the remainder of the muffin in my mouth.

"Just get up." He tugs the duvet off and proceeds to strip the cloud-patterned flannels from the futon with me still on them.

I grab the remaining corner of the fitted sheet by its elastic. "Jack—"

"G, I am the emissary. I have the power of Grace behind me." He yanks the cotton from my grip. "You'll feel better when you're clean," he adds, unconsciously mimicking her.

"No, actually." I ball up the sheets he's tossed to the floor. "I'll feel better when I'm employed."

"*I'll* feel better when you've brushed your teeth."

Dumping the bedding in the hamper, I attach the hose to the kitchen sink faucet, turn on the hot water, and pull the step stool over. Jack turns away and tugs his Cubs brim low as I clamber gingerly into the old porcelain sink, toss my bathrobe, and pull the eyelet shower curtain closed. "So, did Grace give you a budget for this rescue effort? 'Cause I'm in the mood for Chinese."

"We're going to a job fair," he calls from the other side of the plastic.

"What! No—not tonight. Come on, let's eat Chinese and watch *Schindler's List*." I stare at the plastic, hoping for an answer. "Jack, I got six rejection letters this morning. Six. What do they do in person? Spit on you? I don't know if I can." I lather my hair. "So, it's what . . . in a gymnasium? With tables? What kind of jobs? . . . Jack?" I stick my sudsy head out to see him flipping disdainfully through my CDs.

He holds up the *Chicago* soundtrack and rolls his eyes.

"*Hello?* What kind of jobs?"

He waves a torn announcement from the newspaper circled in the familiar red ink. "We just have to go. It's a job thing. You need a job. I need a weekend, so let's get on with it. We have to make a list."

"Of what?" A rivulet of shampoo drips into my eyes, and I pull my head back under the water. "Why?"

"Grace," he answers definitively. I blow a raspberry to the chipped paint. "One: Find job," he prompts. I offer him my middle finger through the gap in the shower curtain. "Two?"

"Two: Start an organization. Three: Start a company. Four: Secede from the Union. Five: Cure cancer. And, uh, six: Free Tibet."

"Six: Free Tibet. Done!"

I coax the conditioner out with the last dribble of hot water. "Avert!" I climb down from the sink, wrap myself in a towel, and reach over him for my suit. He unfolds the extended liner notes of the Rolling Stones compilation while I get dressed behind him.

"How'd you get your old job with Dorisistryingtokillme?"

"Career Services," I say, smoothing down the hanger crease with my hands.

"So do that."

"Jack, that'd be like getting sent back to the 'start' square! If I went back to Wesleyan, I'd be conceding zero progress in two and a half years. No."

"Fine, free Tibet, then." He tosses the CD onto the futon before scribbling, "7: Career Services" on the list. He folds the paper down to matchbox size and slides it into his back pocket. "A plan of attack!"

We skibble out of my cheapie nail place an hour later, me waving my fresh manicure, *Essie's Pink Slip,* in the air, Jack tucking my pleather résumé portfolio under his arm and indicating the way with his hooded head.

"Wait. I need to buy a ponytail holder first." I glance around the narrow street for a pharmacy.

"The thing's going to be over before we even get there."

"Jack, I can't do an interview with my hair all down like this. It's not professional, I'm not projecting an image of—"

"Move it."

On Stanton, nestled between abandoned sweatshops-turned-dot-coms-turned-sweatshops, we locate what looks like a garage entrance. "Okay, where's a safe place for you to hang out?" I slide my portfolio from him and nervously smooth my hair back, while looking hopefully down the desolate street for an open library.

"Nice try. I'm coming in."

"I have to look professional. What'll they think? That I have a teenage business partner? That I got pregnant in fifth grade? No. You have to wait for me. How about over there?" I point to the flickering lights of the laundromat across the street. Jack tilts an eyebrow. "Fine," I concede. "But at least stand a few feet behind me at the tables. We'll start at the front and work around to the back."

Following the networking hum, we locate the entrance, no more than a rusted metal door cut into a corrugated garage wall. I quell my misgivings, while together Jack and I shove the door until it gives, spilling us into a noisy warehouse space packed with twenty-somethings shouting to be heard above pulsing rave music. We creep along the concrete wall, shrinking from the denim-and-Adidas-clad denizens angling so their messenger bags can hang. There must be five hundred people here. And not a single brochure-covered table in sight.

A young woman in a skimpy red camisole and jeans is released from the sea of Xtreme Networking to cheer from the sidelines with flushed cheeks. "Grab a Remy Red! Make a Bluelight connection!" she shouts, pointing to the crowd.

"Remy Red. Cool." Jack grabs a Dixie cup from a passing tray and quickly downs it. I give him a withering look. "G, gimme your jacket," he responds, hanging his down vest over someone else's on a precariously overstuffed coat rack. A gaggle of trendy Seven-clad women squeeze between us on teetering heels as I stuff my passé professional blazer inside my coat and hand it off. Triaging, I unzip my portfolio, hide it behind a stack of crates, and fold the résumés into my purse, scanning my Generic-Employee-Projecting-Dependability ensemble for quick-change possibilities.

"Jack, I need five minutes in the ladies' room." I point over the mass of heads at *toilet* ➤ spray-painted by the stairs. "Meet me by the arrow."

"Gotcha." He salutes with the empty Dixie cup.

"And you're already past your limit. I'm watching." He flips me off.

I race down the rickety stairs to the unisex bathroom, where I undo two more buttons on my shirt, ditch my stockings, roll my skirt, and rub Nars highlighter onto my brow and cheekbones. I go to wash the makeup off my fingers, competing for mirror space with a man appraising his goatee and a woman with pink highlights wiping away the day's mascara flecks. Our eyes meet in the reflection and Mascara smiles tentatively, stealing a furtive glance at my chest. Her vintage Pat Benatar shirt is adorned with a blue flashlight sticker. I glance over at the goatee stylist, who's sporting identical sticker-wear. Stepping back to give the person behind me access to the sink, I look pointlessly for something to dry my hands on.

"Guess it's an air-dry night!" Mascara remarks with an odd amount of cheer.

"Yup," I agree, as the throb of music filters down the stairs. We shake our hands vigorously while people squeeze past.

"So . . ." She smiles anxiously as Goatee joins in, hands flapping. "Who are you with?"

"With?"

"Who are you recruiting for?" They peer at me with laser interest.

"Oh, no, I'm—"

"Uch, you're not wearing a sticker." She wipes her hands curtly on her cargos. Goatee rolls his eyes before turning on his heel to leave. "You really should put one on, you know. There's *a system*." I roll my skirt one more notch and squeeze up past the queue of chattering people lining the stairs, smacking into Jack as I round the corner.

"You need a—"

"Sticker. I know."

He does a Vanna White across his sweatshirt. "Yellow Crown: recruiting people. Blue Flashlight: unemployed people. White Smiley Face: onlookers." He presses a blue flashlight over my heart. "That's all you need."

A Dockers-sporting Flashlight passes us, pausing his stride as he catches sight of Jack's Crown and then looks confused as he takes in the Flashlight and Smiley Face flanking it. He jerks forward and backward before ambivalently moving on, unsure if he's just blown it with the world's youngest CEO. Jack doubles over in hysterics.

"Jack, that's not nice," I admonish. "People here are fragile—"

"WHAT'S UP, YOU UNEMPLOYED PEOPLE?! HOW WE DOIN' TONIGHT?!" A whooping cheer goes out from the crowd as we strain to see the woman in the flimsy red camisole steadying herself, one hand to the wall, a microphone in the other as she teeters atop a bar table.

"WHAT'S UP, DEBBIE?!" A man beside me cups his mouth and belts into my ear.

She collapses in self-conscious giggles before tapping the wand, sending feedback splintering through the disco-lit air. "Can you all hear me?" Everyone claps. "Cool!" She grins. "Okay, so thank you all *so much* for coming out and making tonight our *biggest*-attended Blue Light event this year! And it's only January! We have over *ten thousand* members in the metropolitan area, and we're growing by leaps and bounds. Every. Single. Day." She dips down into one hip, as if skiing, her uncontainable excitement contracting her muscles into a downhill shoosh. "And big props to Remy Red for sponsoring this week's event! We would be *nowhere* without our refreshment sponsors. We're very excited to be trying the Passion Fruit flavor next week and the Avocado Guava next month! And especially, thank you to the recruiters who came out tonight!" Heads whip around in the crowd, searching for the coveted yellow stickers. "We're thrilled for last week's successful placement, Wendy Finn. If you want to swing by Dean & Deluca on Sundays or Tuesdays, Wendy will be happy to give anyone with a Blue Flashlight sticker free refills on tea. Now, she did ask me to stress that this is for tea only, no coffee beverages. And be sure to check out our mention in this week's cover article in *Time Out New York,* 'Unemployed and Loving It!' Thank you, *Time Out!* And *remember,* you're *all* Blue Light Specials! Now you only have forty more minutes in the Blue Zone, so hit the floor!" At that, the music level rises to an unhelpful pitch as a switch is flipped and all gradations of depth and color disappear, leaving the room a wash of phosphorescence, punctuated by blaring white.

"Great, a black light. I'm job hunting at a seventh-grade dance."

"Cool," Jack says, his teeth radiating, every fleck of lint on his sweatshirt standing out like electric rice kernels. I follow his locked gaze to the glowing bra of the woman on our left who clutches at her suddenly translucent shirt and makes a beeline for the coatrack. "I'm gonna see how many losers'll beg me to take their business cards. You're on your own."

"Don't leave with anyone, and don't drink anything." Nodding, Jack disappears into the throng.

All around me Flashlight stickers emit a neon blue beam as people do-si-do through the floor in search of a Crown. I jostle into the long queue for a free drink.

"Oh, Thirty-fourth Street is the best one." The woman ahead of me touches the arm of her friend's pulsing Union Jack shirt to emphasize her point. "They have couches *and* wireless connections. And they'll totally turn a blind eye if you bring your own sandwich. We should meet there. I'm serious about us starting this closet-organizing business."

"I'm still hung up on the book idea—your boss was as big an asshole as mine."

"We can decide Monday. How's ten?"

"Oh, that'll be tough. I used to have that hour between the *Today* show and *The View* free, but I can't miss *Ellen*."

"Huh." The Starbucks aficionado peruses her Palm Pilot.

"I could watch it at your place and we could work during the commercials," offers the *Ellen* fan.

"Can't. I just sold my TV on eBay."

"I got three hundred for all my bridesmaid dresses, but I can't give up my TV."

"I watch at the gym. Two, please." She waves her cigarette-free fingers at the bartender to indicate their drink order. "HR never cancelled my company membership and it's been, like, a year." She passes off a cup, but they remain rooted in my path.

"You know, I ran into a woman last week who's selling her used underwear on eBay—she's getting *over a hundred* a pair. *That's* how you really make money." They crane their heads. "See any cute Smiley Faces?"

Running an appraisal of my meager sellables—the roasting pan I don't have an oven for, the ancient laptop that sizzled to an ugly death, my lever-less toaster—I shimmy around them to grab my Dixie cup of booze. Jack leaps into the air from a nearby throng, waving a handful of cards over the heads of the legitimately stickered. Thus prodded, I down the free liquor, exhale, and plunge deep into the swarm, glancing at the chests of every passing soul. After a full loop of the room, I pause to get my bearings beside a thick-necked man whose lapels are sticker-free. We exchange smiles, and he flashes his leather jacket open in my direction, revealing a Crown sticker on the down low. "Hi!"

"What's up?" he asks, shifting his Dixie cup to shake my hand. "Do you produce?"

"Yes," I say definitively, swinging my hair over my shoulder.

"Really. What scope do you work with?"

"Multiple scopes! Big, small. Just completed a *massively* scaled production for an event in Ohio—it was a national thing. You know."

"Cool." He nods, the black light illuminating his bleached teeth through his skin, creating two macabre stripes. "We're looking for people who have experience instituting systems." He hands me a brochure from his breast pocket, and I catch a graphic of a satellite.

"I *love* systems. Yeah, I had to put together quite a system to get this Ohio thing to run smoothly."

He leans in to be heard over the music, enveloping me in his Remy-soaked breath. "How do you feel about Sun? Or do you prefer Microsoft?"

Um . . . "I'm really a paper person. You know, to-do lists, index cards, binders. But systems are really important. God, just so . . . important. For example, this production system that I set up for our Ohio materials—" He looks a bit lost. I switch gears. "I feel great about the sun, though. Just really good. Great."

Yup.

He scans above my head, prospecting greener pastures. I hold up the brochure hopefully. "So, I'll call you."

"Sure," he says, already past me, his jacket flapping shut.

"He's a dick." I turn to face an openly Crowned oxford, the pomaded Caesar and khakis placing him in his early thirties. "He just comes to these things to pick up women."

"Ah, good to know. How much of an epidemic is that? This is my first one."

"It's our third." Two women jostle in, unsolicited. "But this one is *way* better than last time, donchoo think?" They grin their toothy grins, and I reach for a second syrupy beverage from the tray passed over our heads.

"I've only been to a few myself," he confides. We lean closer to hear him over the din as two more women join the huddle. "Anyway, I'm Guy." His blue eyes smile warmly. "And I really am hiring."

Loud yucks from the ladies.

"Really Hirable, at your service." I slice the space with my hand, taking his in one firm up-and-down.

"And what are you looking to be hired for?"

Windowslaundrytoilets*anything*—"Well, I've been in the nonprofit sector for the past few years, but I'm looking to make a transition."

"Me, too, from unemployed to employed," the redhead guffaws. "We all worked for Priceline." They wave in tandem.

"How long?" Guy asks, cup at his lips, and we all lean another inch closer, forming a sound wall against the deafening Prodigy track pulsing around us.

"Since school. We loved it." They sigh. "There was a masseuse on staff."

"Yeah. Sounds great. Anyway," I say, "I want to gain expertise in the private sector and eventually bring it back to those who can most benefit from it in the public sector."

"Oh? And who are they?" Guy turns away to deposit his empty cup on a passing tray. "I bet the travel discounts were sick," he addresses the Priceline posse, momentarily derailing my response. A cluster of Flashlights, seemingly using this opportunity to vent their frustration by starting a mosh pit, pounds toward us, leaving a trail of elbow-rubbing casualties.

"Yes," I say as we collectively side-step, "so, my efforts thus far have specifically targeted feminist organizations—"

"Smack my bitch up!" a young man 'sings' along in my ear as he knocks a fellow mosher to the ground.

"—But I'm *totally* looking to branch out."

I extend a hand to the fallen woman, who stumbles to her feet. *"Smack my bitch up!"* She hops off, arms raised, throwing herself even harder against her toppler.

Guy, unjostled, is lost in thought. "Feminist. Cool." He reaches for cards from his breast pocket. "Ladies, My Company." The O in Company is the female symbol. We each hungrily take one. "It was a pleasure." He breaks into a magnetic farewell smile. "But I've got to spread it around." He makes it all of three feet before he's engulfed by another flock of Flashlights.

Half an hour later, as I'm whoring out my last breath to creatively package two and a half years of photocopying and becoming-one-with-my-nondesk, the black lights cut and everyone, their teeth restored to natural ivory, blinks up into the fluorescents.

I lift onto the balls of my feet, scanning for Jack, and lock with green eyes beneath tussled blond hair. "Excuse me, have you seen a fourteen-year-old trying to fleece people out of their business cards?"

He glances just above my head. "About yea tall? Wesleyan sweatshirt?"

"Uh-huh."

He breaks into a Dennis Quaid grin. "No. Never seen him." I follow his extended finger to where Jack is talking to the DJ.

"Thanks."

"Sure." We take each other in, smiling, the creases around his lovely eyes bringing a tingle. "Hi," he says.

"Hi."

"So," he says, glancing at my heart, "you're a Flashlight."

"Yes." I raise my eyebrows, feigning job-search enthusiasm despite his sticker-free chest. "Are you recruiting?"

"Nah, I just came for moral support." He slides his free hand down into the pocket of his Diesels, hunching his shoulder up. "My roommate's been laid off twice in the last year, so . . ."

"You're kidding." I'm shoved into him by the last of the tenacious moshers, and he reaches out to steady me, leaving his hand on my lower back as he takes a nervous swig of his Remy. He glances over his drink into my eyes. "You were saying?" I ask, flushing.

"Sorry?"

"Your roommate?"

"Luke, right." He leans in, his warm breath tickling my ear. "Kiss of death for any company. If you want to go under, hire Luke."

"Well." I slide back to smile at him. "There are so many companies looking to go under right now. He should definitely highlight that font on his résumé."

He laughs. *And* she's funny. "So, any leads tonight?"

"Not really. Did your friend have any luck?"

"He may. He left with a young lady who was seriously shit-faced." Charming.

"Come on, this is getting lame." Jack bumps my arm. "Let's go." He withdraws two fistfuls of business cards from his sweatshirt pockets and dumps them into my purse.

Green Eyes clears his throat. "What direction are you heading?" he asks.

"Thompson Square Park," Jack volunteers, pulling his sweatshirt tabs and closing the hood to a small puckered hole.

"Oh, I'm meeting some friends at the Slipper Room. I can walk you up," he offers tentatively. "Or not. I mean, I don't want to intrude or, uh, anything," he stammers.

"Uh, o-kay," I say.

"Okay," he says.

"Okay, whatever. Let's go!" Jack pushes his face back out from the confines of his hood.

We weave through the crowds toward the exit, stopping where the coatracks have toppled, leaving a heap of black wool on the Remy-sodden floor. "Shit," I mutter as I look down at an unaffordable trip to the dry cleaner.

Green Eyes squats amidst annoyed Bluelights and begins to rifle the wet cloth with gusto. "The most important thing is to check the pockets. Last winter, I got back from B-bar and realized I'd worn some lady's North Face home."

"So, what happened?" Jack asks.

"Well, her cell phone was in it, so I tracked her down"—and now she's your fiancée, great story—"but I never saw my ski parka again."

"I'm safe. No one else has a pink toggle coat."

"Pink?"

"Yeah, pink," Jack confirms, shrugging on his recovered down vest.

"This it?" Green Eyes thrusts his arm elbow-deep into the pile and surfaces with peony-colored wool.

"Thanks," I say.

"Now you can remember me as the boy who rescued your coat."

"I'm not shit-faced, so that should help."

His cheeks redden. "Ouch."

"Yeah. Kind of upsetting."

"I was just being a smart-ass. Not so attractive, huh?"

I shrug. "Not so much."

"Ah-ha!" He stands, victoriously raising a black pea coat in one hand and pulling a sheet of paper out of the pocket with the other. "Show me another man here who's carrying a flyer for Pinky Nail!"

"Dare I ask?" I pull on my own slightly damp coat, the sticky red Remy of my job search obscuring the coffee stain of my former employment.

"Just can't turn down a flyer." Now genuinely charmed.

As we shuffle with the exiting crowd into the stark cold, I instantly regret ditching my pantyhose. "Who're you?" Jack plods between us, chewing his drawstring.

"Buster," he says, fishing a wool cap from his pocket as we walk in tandem around the piles of frozen garbage bags. "Who're you?"

"Jack." He drops the tab out of his mouth. "Like Kerouac. G's brother. What's up?" He pulls his hand out of his vest pocket and swiftly swipes Buster's palm.

Buster pauses his gait to extend his hand to me. "Nice to meet you, G."

I smile as I slide my glove into his, warmth permeating through the layers of wool and leather.

"YGames," Jack acknowledges the emblem on Buster's cap.

"Yeah." Buster drops my hand as we resume walking. "I design for them. You played Zarcon yet?"

"You kidding?" Jack tries to cover his awe. "Hey, how do you get to Level Eight?"

"The bludgeon's in the third chamber. Past the droid."

"That is so f'ing cool. I can't believe you just, like, know that."

"I put it there."

Back to me—"Fifty bucks for the droid with the job behind it."

Buster laughs. "For hard cash, I'll see what I can do. Here's my stop," he says as we reach the no longer aptly named Orchard Street, the lines outside the grotty drag bars just forming. Buster swivels around in the glow of the Slipper Room's blinking lights. "Hey, why don't you two come in and warm up? On Fridays they do this retro show—it's a good time. And they make a killer hot toddy."

I hesitate, having not been on a date with Jack since the beach rental in Misquamicut. But Buster's lovely forehead furrows entreatingly, and the Brat Pack–styled lounge, a tonic to the earlier grungefest, glows behind him. "I could go for a hot toddy."

"Finally, some real nightlife," Jack mutters for Buster's benefit as we step into the swiftly moving line of platinum-and-ebony-haired women. They wrap their vintage furs close, stomping their combat boots to maintain circulation as we huddle above the steaming grate.

At the front of the line, I offer my Connecticut driver's license and the bouncer nods. "Not the kid."

"He's with me, Al," Buster says, bumping fists in greeting.

Jack's eyes widen at our escort's cachet as Al waves us into the bustling warmth of the dark gold-toned room. Scott Joplin tinkles above the heads of the mingling audience, while, on stage, a refreshingly robust young woman tap dances in a wholesome ruffled bra and shorts, the sailor suit on the floor suggesting the earlier part of her act. We follow Buster as he snakes past the ring of vinyl booths decorated with glossies of bygone starlets.

"My friends aren't here yet." His soft lips graze my ear. "Let's just grab a table." He pulls out chairs for us at a small café round and sets us up with two toddys and a cider. Meanwhile, Jack and I pivot to face the stage, our toes tapping to the syncopated beat. As the last few bars of "The Entertainer" peal out, the dancer slides down into a split, arms in a V.

I lean over to Buster, who's also grinning at the latter-day Shirley Temple. "Thanks for inviting us."

"Thanks for coming." He squeezes my hand.

"I'd heard about the show, but I had no idea it was this enchanting."

"They're reviving burlesque," he says, lifting his hand from mine to help pass our steaming drinks from the waitress. The next act begins, dimpled knees fanning in and out as she Charlestons her way across the stage in a flurry of ribbons.

For an hour, feather boas, playing cards, and pastel balloons flutter to the worn floorboards while I'm borne on a mellowing current of hot brandy. Between acts, a man in a zoot suit and fedora jumps up to the stage. "Thank you, Cindy!" People heartily applauding, Cindy peeks her ringlets out from the curtain for a final wave as Jack drops his head on the table and lets out a stream of bored air.

"What?" I lean over to him. He turns his forehead on the tablecloth to face me and rolls his eyes.

"Don't tell me you're not having fun," Buster says. Jack jerks back up, feigning enthusiasm.

"Well, *I'm* having fun," I say. Buster puts his arm around the back of my chair, his palm resting on my arm, and I find myself leaning in as if we're the room's oldest couple.

"Ladies and gentlemen." The man in the zoot suit takes center stage once more. "And now . . . the star of our show . . . Please clap your paws together for a little lady who needs no introduction . . . the delightful Rosie La Boom." A classic bump-and-grind horn-driven melody comes *waa-waa-waa*-ing out of the speakers as the next act struts on stage, her silhouette an exaggerated hourglass, immobile silicone straining beneath the sequined string bikini. Clearly we've made a departure from her sweetly-themed predecessors. Jack sits up pointer-straight as Rosie bends over.

Waa-waa . . . the horn peals out as she strips off her top, her tassled pasties circling in figure eights.

Keenly aware of Buster's touch, I look at Jack, who's utterly transfixed by the large breasts, largely exposed, before us. Then

I turn to Buster, who's glancing sidelong at me, as if gauging my reaction, which I haven't shown yet. *Boom-chicka-boom-chicka.* With a swift tug, Rosie jerks the G-string off her emaciated haunches and sends it flying toward our table. Jack's hand reaches up as if we're at Yankee Stadium.

"You know," I say, intercepting his catch as she does a spread-eagle, her thorough wax job laid bare before us. The sequins drop to the table, unclaimed. "I think Jack's a little tired."

"What?"

"You're tired." I kick Jack under the table. "Sorry, I didn't realize how late it had gotten."

Buster pulls up his sleeve to check his watch and shrugs. "Okay . . . guess I'll walk you out."

"Thanks," I smile nervously, pushing Jack ahead of me as he cranes his head, his eyes still riveted to Rosie's spread buttocks. I shuffle us out with Buster in tow, now trying to gauge his reaction.

"Busted!" Just in front of the exit, a guy in an army jacket blocks our path, leaning across me to knock knuckles with Buster. "Dude, we've been waiting on line for an hour, but it looks like we got here for the good stuff." He turns to where Rosie is bending over again, her nose job visible between her muscled calves.

"G, this is my colleague, Sam. Sam, G."

Sam nods, eyes locked on the stage, as a waitress pushes past, her tray laden with steaming mugs.

A young woman squeezes into our huddle, blowing on her red hands. Sam's attention still elsewhere, Buster makes introductions. "G, this is Camille, Sam's fiancée."

"Hey. Oooh—Rosie's on tonight! I fuck'n love her." Camille gently gyrates to the beat.

"We have a table." Buster points to the seats we just vacated.

Camille gives him a thumbs-up and edges over to be eye level with Rosie's snatch.

"Nice to meet you," I say to Sam, whose fiancée probably has an extensive knowledge of football, which she exhibits while smoking cigars and kicking his ass at Zarcon. Feeling deeply less than "down," I give Jack a final push out the door and Buster follows, hunching his shirtsleeves against the cold.

"Hope that was cool."

"Yeah, no, totally. That was totally cool." I nod like a Weeble. "Jack's just tuckered, so . . ."

"I'm fine."

"Actually, I'm tuckered. I went running this morning. Five miles. And then I went lingerie shopping . . . which I do, you know, once a month . . . just to be . . . not uptight."

"Where do you run?"

"Around."

"Well, Sam and Camille are really awesome. Maybe another time?" Shivering, Buster digs his hands deep into his pockets.

"Yes, definitely."

"What else you up to this weekend?"

"Mostly just camping out at Kinko's," I say, nodding into my scarf as I rub my bare calves together to warm them.

"Hey!" Buster points to a poster of Rosie promoting Monday's Martin Luther King Burlesque Brunch. "We could meet for brunch. YGames is closed."

"Oh, fun! Yeah, I'd love to. But." I inhale through closed teeth, exuding disappointment, as I scramble for any excuse to avoid sharing our childhoods over G-strings and granola.

"She's going to Career Services." Jack advances Grace's agenda once again.

"I am."

"How're you getting up there?"

"The train. I have to drop Jack back home for swim practice, and it's only a short bus ride from there—"

"Hey, I have a car. I could totally drive you. I know this great clam place in Bridgeport. We could grab lunch on the way back."

"Oh, that's so nice, but the train is really—"

"Gross," Jack interjects.

"Right, so let me drive you guys up." I get a split-screen flash of the return trip sans Jack; our entwined bodies passionately writhing in some sweet seaside motel; my mangled corpse bouncing along in his trunk.

"Okay, great." Sex wins.

"Cool. So, what's your address?"

"406 East 7th."

"Cool." He nods.

"I'll write it down." I fumble in my purse for a pen.

"Nah, I've got it." Buster breaks into another wildly endearing grin. "406 East 7th. So see you—?"

"Jack just has to be at practice by—"

"One," comes Jack's voice, muffled by the tightly corded fleece opening.

"So, nineish?" Buster asks.

"Great! Wow, thanks."

"Okay, well, have a rockin' evening. J, we have a game in development that could use test-driving. Think you and your friends might be interested?" Jack bobs his head wordlessly. Buster clicks his heels together, giving me a little nod. "G?"

"B."

"See you Monday at nine." He salutes.

Jack watches Buster return to the lounge, saxophone bleating out the door as he pulls it open. "Unbelievable. Un-be-fucking-lievable—"

"Hey, language," I mumble as I tear my eyes away.

CHAPTER THREE

Make Lemonade, Dammit!

"Un. Be. Fucking. Lievable." I bounce on my heels to keep warm as my watch registers 10:30, officially marking one and a half hours of standing in the freezing cold. I am furious. Furious at an epic level.

"Language," Jack calls to me from where he sits on his duffel bag, munching a steaming knish.

"Get up."

"Hey."

"Come on, Jack, we have to get going right now or you're gonna miss practice—"

He stands and sticks the last of his snack into his mouth. "Just because Game Boy flaked, this isn't my fault, so don't get all—"

"You!" I glare at the sporadic stubble above his lip. "Don't even—I can't even—let's just get a cab." He slings his bag onto his shoulder and follows me as I scurry over to Avenue A, weaving in and out of the street to flag a taxi. "Okay. Okay. So the upside, to borrow from our rainstorm-gets-your-clothes-clean mother, is that you're getting to witness, to see what it's like— what it *feels* like—when some man just waltzes into your evening and says, 'Oh, *yeah! Sure!* Lemme drive you some- where! Let's have clams! Let's watch a stripper!' With the, 'Oh, I have a flyer to a nail salon.' How original is that, Jack? I mean,

I have, like, thirty menus to the same two Chinese restaurants. Does that make me charming? Does it, Jack?" I throw his bag onto the backseat of the cab that's pulled up in a stream of slush. "Slide in—Grand Central—and then just not show up! Because you don't want to *be* this person, Jack. You don't want to leave people standing on a street corner at nine in the morning feeling rejected when it's TWENTY DEGREES outside!" I huff, crossing my arms in indignation as we snake uptown, the windows icing with the grime of civilization. I throw the door open at the station, jerking Jack awake as I toss a precious bill at the driver. "Can I have ten back? It's not like we *asked* him. It's not like I was *radiating* transportation neediness. So this is a lesson in watch-what-you-volunteer. Tell a woman she's going to speak at a conference, let her speak at the conference. You can't promise a ride and then have her make copies, Jack. You have to follow through. Raise your child outside the system, guess what she doesn't know how to start, Jack?! *Her own system!* Because pasties aren't art." We locate the train. "That seat in the front—"

"All aboard!"

"It's just no way to treat people," I offer my final thought as the doors slide shut.

Jack reluctantly pulls out his homework, his head slumping against the gray window. Making productive use of wasted primping, I borrow a cell phone from the businessman across the way, arrange for a ride from the station, and then feign napping to evade his expectant leer. Yes, as is the custom, in exchange for your electronic graciousness, I will now pleasure you.

By the time we roll into Waterbury, the Robertses, one of Grace's host of backups, are waiting in their station wagon, windshield wipers beating away the sleet. "Hey!" Jack's friend Xander waves from the car in a puffy yellow coat that makes him look like a hip-hop budgie. "Find her a job?"

"Nah, gonna take more than a weekend—"

"Thank you so much for the ride," I address Mrs. Roberts, ignoring Jack's depressingly astute observation. "My mom had a meeting with the trustees, so—"

"No, no problem. My babysitter has the flu, so I'm chauffeur today. Okay, Xan," she says, addressing the rearview mirror, "after swim practice, Dad'll pick you two up—if he's late, wait under the awning. Then you're all going to swing by the Changs' and collect Janie; dinner is pizza—remind Dad to pick it up and that Jack's allergic to peppers. Oh, and I'll get your new uniforms on the way home." I watch Jack and Xan nod along in the passenger-side mirror. Grace always did rely upon the co-parenting kindness of strangers.

When we pull up at the gym, the boys pile out to join their friends dashing from idling cars to the cover of the concrete awning. Jack nearly runs off without paying my hug toll. "Um, excuse me?" I catch him. "Come here, you." I lean through the window, wet snow falling on my hair, to give him a big squeeze.

"Okay, you're holding on tighter than Grace."

"Shut up. Listen, take it easy," I mumble into his hair. "Don't let her drive you crazy."

He pulls back and grins. "You're gonna be fine, G."

I nod, biting the inside of my cheek. "I know." He pulls away from me until I'm just holding his sleeve. "Okay, so good-bye, then. Thanks for getting me up here." He tugs free. "I LOVE YOU, JACK!!!"

He sticks an arm back at me, his middle finger flipping skyward, as he jogs to his snickering friends.

"Onto Chatsworth." Mrs. Roberts steers the car out the exit, harried in the middle of her daily routine, which clearly doesn't break for a national holiday.

"Actually, I'm going up to Wesleyan to tackle Career Services, so the bus station would be perfect if you don't mind." I stare out the window at the sleet slanting down the fogged glass, feeling the absence of my brother. "Thank you so much for this."

"Not at all." She loops her headset around her ears with her free hand. "Wesleyan's on the way to my client. Why don't I just"—she takes a chug of coffee from her travel mug before blindly returning it to its holder—"drop you directly?"

"That would be amazing, thank you—" But she's already on her cell. I nestle back into the seat as she confirms her client's address, a flower delivery to an in-law, a PTA fund-raiser, a transatlantic conference call, and a dentist appointment. This woman has a *life,* a *family,* and a *home,* which I'm wagering isn't predominantly held together with duct tape.

"What time will you be done?" Mrs. Roberts pulls to a rolling stop, sliding a sheaf of envelopes from her bag. "Would you mind sticking these in the mailbox for me?"

"Sure." I pass off the bundle into the squeaky receptacle. "Um, about four o'clock?"

"See you right back here at four!" She screeches out of the campus parking lot.

"Bye! Thanks," I call after her wistfully. Standing where the extremes of the Connecticut climate have warped the asphalt into small crags, I pull on my wool hat, insulating myself against the damp mist. As the fog eddies and swirls, the buildings of Wesleyan come in and out of view, an academic *Brigadoon.*

I recall sitting in my polyester cap and gown at graduation, imagining my return—the driver would help me out of my Town Car and I'd stride in, wearing a perfectly cut Gucci pantsuit, to give a lecture on a burning issue of global magnitude. At the very least, I'd arrive for my ten-year class reunion the picture of triumph—accomplished, secure, debt-free. Important. Nowhere in my fantasy was I wearing frayed corduroys and side-stepping patches of snow. Nowhere had I been flicked off the finger of my employer. Nowhere was I poor, irrelevant, and freezing.

Determined to leave with at least four solid job leads, I clomp across the grass toward Career Services, past students groggily clutching their plastic mugs of dining hall coffee. I hold one of Butterfield's side doors open for a cluster of girls dressed like Peruvians, who, come graduation, will be hoping their facial piercings haven't left visible scars and spending their disposable income on crap pantyhose with the rest of us. I follow them down the stairs to Career Services, surprised to find the steps lined with camped-out students. The waiting area is still painted the color of something left in the icebox too long, but now the wood-laminate bookcases hold dusty brochures from companies whose hiring freezes have made *The New York Times*. Despite the discouraging decoration, the floor is packed with eager collegiate mushrooms gripping the same questionnaire I filled out three years ago. Climbing between them, I take my place on line for the service window. "Excuse me?" I ask, leaning in toward a prim, matronly woman standing behind the counter, her tight pin curls secured with a slim grosgrain headband.

"Yes, dear, what time is your appointment?" she says with a smile, as she highlights the next name on her list. "Forgive us, but we're running a tiny bit behind today."

"That's okay, it looks like you have a lot going on."

The woman smiles, dropping her hands to the desk. "Goodness, do we ever. If you're in the two o'clock hour, you might want to go around the corner. We've set up some hot cocoa." Yes, that's exactly what this job search has been missing: hot cocoa. And heated dorm rooms, a meal plan, and dollar movies—

"So, what time?" she repeats, her pencil poised to check me off.

"Oh, I don't have an appointment . . ." Pleaseohpleaseohplease.

"Well, let's get you set up." Thankyouthankyouthankyou. She pulls out a large calendar. "Time permitting, we take drop-ins on Wednesdays and Fridays for quick questions, but if you want to see the binders you can come back . . ." She quickly flips several pages ahead. "How's the twenty-first of March for you? Four-fifteen?"

MARCH! "Actually, I came all the way up from the city today. I'm pretty familiar with the system, so if I could just poke my head in—"

Her expression quickens as she sighs through pinched lips. "You graduated."

"Yes, but only two years ago. I was hoping I could just take a peek—"

"No. Absolutely not." She shakes her head, crossing her thin arms over her faded floral blouse. "We placed you. Your career was serviced. Our task is to get you out the door, but it's your responsibility from there. Yet you alums come traipsing in here daily, thinking you can just storm the gates and we'll roll out the red carpet."

"Okay," I regroup. "Clearly you're working very hard and I appreciate that it's much busier than it ever was when I was here. And I've been doing everything I can, but I lost that job."

"Yes. I guessed as much. We're only helping undergraduates now."

"But I *was* an undergraduate."

She broadens her small shoulders. "And you had your shot."

The waiting room swirls. "That was not *my* shot. That was *a* shot. *A* shot. One." She puffs up indignantly and puts a finger to her lips to shush me, but I will not be shushed. "That 'job' you folks set me up with was with the boss from hell. *From hell*. I'm talking lying and stealing and—"

"Please, keep your voice down," she hisses, indicating the huddled masses behind me.

I wheel around to their frightened faces. "You think it's just about finding it and getting there?" I swipe a file folder off the counter and hold it aloft. "See this?! *This* will be your new best friend! *This* will be your working week and your Sunday rest!

So pick your color now, kids!" I feel my arm tugged as the door buzzes open behind me. "I was working on a *TOILET!!*"

Pin Curls jerks me inside. "There's no need to get bolshy. Fifteen minutes. But if a real student needs a binder, you *must* hand it over. I'm watching you."

Getting a grip inside the large, musty room, I perch at the humanities table, pull out my yellow pad, and grab a binder. Only a few pages in, I see that almost all the postings have big black check marks drawn through them.

"Excuse me? What do the black checks mean?"

"Filled. Sshhh."

"Filled?"

"Filled, young lady, filled. Thirteen minutes."

"Sorry, but why are the descriptions still in here?"

She squeaks her chair out and marches over to me. "I will kindly remind you to keep your voice down. You are a guest here. If they get unfilled, we reenter them." She returns to her desk. "So you'll know what you missed. Eleven minutes."

I roll up the sleeves on my sweater and dig for my real options. Fewer and farther between, they quickly blur.

Position: Administrative Assistant, Executive Assistant, Slave. Starting Salary: Nineteen thousand, Eighteen thousand, Unpaid. Responsibilities: Ordering new paper towels. Making coffee or coffee alternatives for our caffeine-sensitive employees. Arranging my travel, hair appointments, bikini waxes, and therapy. Held accountable for: paper-clip shrinkage, Xerox paper waste, coffee mug abandonment, FedEx, UPS, PMS, my marriage, and my weight.

Falling down a black hole of administrative misery, my eyes finally alight on a promising posting.

Position: Research and Policy Associate
Starting Salary: Negotiable

Responsibilities:	Working closely with Director to create female-constituent public-policy proposals
Held Accountable for:	Initiating and innovating organization's agenda

Weepy with excitement, I pull the sheet out of its plastic sleeve and run to the front desk. "This one's still available, right? There's no check."

Pin Curls slides on her glasses and glances down. "Yes, I rescanned that one myself." She types the code into the computer and the information screen opens. "You can't read over my shoulder," she scolds. "I have to print it out for you."

"Okay." I step back.

"No, collect your things and wait out there. *Quietly.*" She gestures to the anteroom.

"Okay!" I pick up my stuff and run out the door to meet her again from the other side of the window, leaning from hip to hip as the listing glides out of the laser printer. I reread the scanned-in description, eagerly scrolling down to the most important information.

Contact:	Doris Weintruck. The Center for Equity in Community
Posted:	November 15th

You've got. To be kidding.

Underneath, in her nauseatingly familiar scratch, Doris has delineated her idea of my perfect replacement. *Note to applicants: equal opportunity employer. Males* strongly *encouraged to apply.*

I somehow refrain from puking onto Pin Curls's wool flannel lap. "You scanned this *two* months ago? Are you sure?"

She purses her lips. "Of course I am. I suppose you don't even want it after all that fuss."

"No." Numbly, I slide the paper back through the window. "I just left it."

"You mean 'lost it,'" she mutters, as I hopscotch over the recoiling hopefuls, run up the stairs and out the fire door, gasping for air.

I sit silently as Mrs. Roberts drives through the revived sleet, so busily trying to scribble a grocery list on the back of an envelope while steering with her left hand that she misses the entrance to the train station altogether and has to pull a K-turn. She places her hand on my headrest before pivoting her body to back up, her fingers loosely brushing my hair. Tears spring to my eyes at the contact.

"Oh, honey." She brakes sharply and drops her hand to my shoulder.

"Sorry," I sputter, fighting the urge to drop into her lap, thankful for the restraint of the seatbelt. "I just, this is just, so . . . hard. I don't know why she—"

"You're taking this so personally." Mrs. Roberts looks me in the eye, the windshield wipers squeaking back and forth. She reaches down to open the glove compartment, springing a gaggle of toys, maps, and fast-food detritus across my lap. "Shit," she mutters.

"It's okay." I bend to help her shove everything back into the tiny space.

"Thought we had tissues. Will a Wet Nap do?"

I nod, dutifully blowing my nose into the moist antiseptic cloth. "I'm just so scared that I'm actually unemployable." That Doris was right. That I suck. "If I could just get an interview, or even a lead—"

"Of course you're employable—that's ridiculous. You know, maybe I can get the New York office to see you—they're still interviewing. I'll put in a call tonight."

"Oh God, I'd be so grateful—" The train clangs in across the street, forcing her to complete the ragged turn and pull, screeching, into the station.

"Gogogo!" she yells, already groping for the headset again as I unbuckle myself, slipping and sliding up the steps and into the ice-covered train.

Thursday morning finds me standing under the marquee of Radio City Music Hall, flipping through my Filofax to locate the address from Mrs. Roberts's message. The frigid wind bellows up Sixth Avenue, making my eyes tear as the fluttering pages reveal that I'm on the wrong side of five lanes of traffic. I scurry between steaming hoods of honking cabs to a tower soaring at least fifty reflective stories into the Midtown skyline. Pushing the revolving doors, I pause in relief under the blast of hot air, accidentally causing a hostile pileup of cashmere-clad businessmen behind me.

After a full cavity search at security, I'm directed to a set of elevators that promise to bypass the first lowly thirty-four floors. As the car hurtles upward, I reapply lipstick and try not to look nervous.

On thirty-five, the glass door clicks open and I'm let into a forbidding gray reception area dotted with birds of paradise and black-suited staff, giving the place a distinctly funereal air. After signing in, I run my hands down the back of my own dark suit and take a seat in the horseshoe of reception chairs. Surreptitiously glancing at the others also clutching leather folders to their chests, I try to imagine working in a place not illuminated by Technicolor hemp. I like it.

"Okay." A man with a clipboard appears, clearing his throat. "We'll take the next group; you, you, you, you, and you." I button my blazer and smooth my ponytail as our posse follows him into a windowless conference room featuring two concentric circles of chairs: Big Five does Dante. He pulls an about-face, prompting our group to stall in the doorway. "I'm Chip, and I want to welcome you to today's session." He pauses.

"Hi, Chip," we say, frighteningly, in unison.

"Great, so I'm going to grab the associates and we'll begin with a Group Exercise." I get a flash of us doing Tae Bo. "Why don't you go ahead and take a seat?"

Everyone seems to know to sit in the inner circle and slide their folders under their chairs. Despite their cagey glances, I imagine us in months to come reminiscing about this around the espresso machine; Chip will pass by, give us a thumbs-up. The few chosen ones will be my colleagues; we'll share our marriages, pregnancies, divorces . . .

Chip returns with his associates, who are our age but with the crisp air of the employed about them. They sit ceremoniously in the circle surrounding ours, while Chip hands out sheets of mint-green paper, a color that 'deeply troubled' Doris. SCENARIO is written at the top in bold letters. As I scan down the page, I learn that I'm now Sheila Smith, recently stationed on an 'engagement' for Teens Make Up Company, with the objective of convincing my team to 'reformat their strategy from explicit to implicit.'

"You'll have fifteen minutes for this simulation," Chip's voice booms to us from the two-foot distance between his circle and ours. "And . . . go!"

A man with overly gelled hair begins, "I have a proposed plan of action for which I think there are multiple reasons to consider its flexibility. I'd like to begin with our market share—" And I haven't got a fucking clue. Not a single one. All I know is that someone wearing way, way too much Polo cologne is scribbling notes behind me. Everyone in the group keeps interrupting one another using terms I've never heard before: 'emotional data,' 'tectonic client shift,' 'SMEs,' 'RFPs,' and a lot of talk about a 'multiboutique asset management model.' Then a blonde with dark roots announces, "I'm Sheila Smith, and I'm working at Teens Make Up Company—"

"Wait—you're Sheila?" Everyone stares incredulously at me. Sheila glares. "It's just that I'm Sheila." I turn to the circle surrounding us. "Is that right? Should there be two of us?" Everyone gasps.

Chip is the first to recover. "Well, we can't proceed after *that,* so we'll just move on to your individual case interviews."

Sheila's eyes well, and she spits at me under her breath, "Thanks. Thanks a *lot.*"

"Girl," Chip says, crooking his finger in my direction. "You'll be starting with Stu." I gather my folder and follow Stu down a long hallway to an empty cubicle, where we both take a seat. Stu pulls off his glasses and rubs his forehead fast and hard before refocusing his eyes on my résumé and then on the attached memo from Mrs. Roberts. "What other consulting companies are you meeting with?"

"None. I mean, this is my first. I'm just starting to look, so—"

"Right. How many years of internal consulting have you booked?"

"Well, I've been working as a program assistant over the last two and a half years, which enabled me to take part in a number of interesting research projects—"

"Uh-huh. So what *would* you do?" Stu tosses my résumé down onto the desk. "As Sheila, what would be your next move?" I think back to my mousy blonde nemesis with the tapping foot. Highlights with a semipermanent caramel rinse?

"Sorry, just to be sure, this interview is for the nonprofit division, right?"

"Good one," he chuckles. "*They're* not hiring. This is for Insurance, Property, and Assets."

"Oh! Okay, well, if you could just explain a bit more about this whole exercise, I'm sure I could give you the information you're looking for. Maybe you could just give me a quick overview of the kind of work you do here—then I could speak directly to that."

Chip pops his head over the cubicle wall, like a puppeteer. "Stu?"

"Yeah?"

"You ready for Monica to join?"

"Sure, yeah."

A brunette rounds the corner, her tailored shirt blousing perfectly over her pencil skirt. I look from one naked felt wall to the other, wishing there was at least a bumper sticker's worth of information about the company, instead of just its name pulsing from every surface. Insurance Property & Assets? Anyone? Anyone?! "I'm sorry, I was under the impression that I would be speaking with your nonprofit division—"

"Monz, Sheila wants us to give her some background."

"Yes, it would really help me to help you if you could just tell me a bit, say, about how you spend your days here?" I ask hopefully.

Directing her attention to her watch, Monica begins to talk. And talk. And talk. About markets, numbers, teams, and an *inordinate* amount of leveraging. Tons of leveraging. Leveraging is the sole verb in her presentation. Stu nods, tossing in statistics and acronyms here and there while I become enthralled by their enthusiasm, verbosity, and prodigious intake of Diet Coke, their watches that most definitely did not come from Chinatown. I marvel that we're the same age, yet they're going to jump into their all-terrain vehicles after work, park them in their two-car garages, and feed their big dogs. I plummet into wondering what, exactly, I've been doing these last two and a half years, farting around with public policy and thinking this sufficient. Just what has been so important that it's kept me from the vital work of learning how to leverage a single fucking thing?!

"I'm up." A woman peeks around the side before stepping in. "Whitney." She shakes my hand in one up-and-down move, light caroming off her four-carat emerald-cut diamond, splaying the drab space.

"All right." Her pink cashmere cable cardigan draped just so, she studies my résumé. "Girl." She eyes my hands clutched in my lap. "I see you haven't taken any notes. Do you have this completely memorized already?"

My face beats. "I was so absorbed by what Monica was saying."

"Right." She trades glances with her colleagues. "We're going to converse for a moment." They get up and stand just outside the cubicle, discussing me in hushed tones. Stepford employees, these people even know how to whisper perfectly.

"Girl." Whitney returns alone, folding her hands delicately in front of her chin as she sits across from me. "Here's the thing. We're just not getting from you that you're looking to make money. Money. As much as you possibly can. For yourself. Our clients. Us. We just don't see it." She leans in. "*Do* you want to make as much money as you possibly can? Do you *really* want to and we're just not reading you right?" She stares at me, and I detest her and every last thing about this whole event. I am, however, still sickeningly dazzled by her ring, proving that I'm officially going to end up as a starving forty-five-year-old Greenpeace petitioner drooling her days away outside Tiffany's. I take a deep breath.

"I want to make money—as much as I, um, can. You know, for you and me and the clients, and whoever. I just haven't really been able to get a sense of how you would like me to do that."

"Exactly." Whitney stands. "Okay!" she calls over the cubicle walls to Stu. "Who's next?"

I roll over to check the clock on the milk crate doubling as a nightstand, nudging aside the tiny stack of business cards I garnered at the 'job fair.' Eleven fifty-three. I inhale deeply, trying to slow my buzzing brain from replaying the phone calls I've put in to every half-baked Remy-stained lead. I exhale as I flick on the lamp and realize that my breath is coming out in steamy puffs. The pipes must be freezing up again. "I NEED A JOB," I yell at the waterbug making a relaxed trek across my floor. It skitters back into the shadows over a white card that's fallen between the wooden slats. Hunching the blanket around me, I reach over and jimmy it out, the thermographed women's symbol slick under my thumb. My Company.

Debating the air-of-desperation factor, I decide it's worth the risk in order to go to sleep feeling like I've made *any* headway. Getting on with it, I clear my throat and dial, preparing to leave a message that has the sound of a dynamic team player who's not even *remotely* desperate. I picture myself as Whitney. Whitney at eight o'clock in the morning, a flamethrower on her finger and a smile on her money-grubbing face.

"Yeah," a man's voice answers expectantly, catching me by surprise. I bite my lip. "Hello?" he asks again.

"Yes! Hi! Hi. Can I speak with," I tilt the card back toward the lamp, "Guy, please?"

"Yeah, this is Guy."

"Oh, okay. Hi, we met at the . . . networking event the other night—"

"Uh-huh."

"Sorry, I wasn't expecting you to be there this late—"

"We met at the Bluelight thing?"

"Yes!" I rerun our interaction and sickeningly register that we didn't talk about anything memorable. "I have brown hair, um, it's long, and I'm tall." Note to self: no more networking calls after dark.

"Yeah. So how's it going?" His voice drops a sexy notch. "You, ah, want to get a drink or something?"

"Uh, maybe. Actually, we spoke about my work with non-profit. I'm following up about your—"

"Righhhht." His voice returns to its original tone. "You were talking to the entertainment kid—he's such an asshole. You work with women." Ding, ding, ding!

"Yes! Yes, I do." Did. "I just wanted to follow up as you mentioned that you're hiring and I'm currently in transition, so I thought—"

"Great. Can you come in tomorrow afternoon at uhhhh . . ." I hear a few fast clicks on a keypad. "Six-thirty?"

"Definitely!"

"Very cool. See you then." He hangs up.

I stand and flick on the overhead in one deft move. Clicking on the stereo, I turn up the volume, letting Blondie tell me "One Way or Another" as I carefully iron and lint-roll the unraveling H&M suit. "Come on, baby, mama needs a new pair of *ev-e-ry-thing.*"

CHAPTER FOUR

The One, the Answer, the Reason

Having spent the day tap-dancing for overstocked, underutilized temp agencies, I zip into a public library to download everything I can about My Company. But confronted with a two-hour line of kids and dodgy-looking men in oversized raincoats, I hustle to Kinko's, cursing my fried laptop. At a disgusting dollar a minute, I pound in the URL and find myself before a pixilated collage of Gibson girls and *Vogue* covers. *"One hundred years of being female at your fingertips."* The cursor prompts me to enter a search item. Beneath Twiggy's awning of eyelashes, I scroll down through the options—predominantly beauty products—and click 'mascara.' While logos from Almay, Revlon, and countless other brands pulse in the margins, I'm told that there are two thousand, seven hundred and twelve matches. I open the first article from *Galatea*, a women's magazine of the suffragette era. *"Blacken the tips of your lashes with a simple paste of soot and cod-liver oil."* Yick.

Over ten dollars in but now handily equipped to make lipstick out of old candles and tartar paste, I click on the tiny hand-mirror icon for *Company History*. '*MC, Inc. is the award-winning designer of highly innovative search-engine software and proudly manages the patented on-line portal linking every major women's magazine dating back to the turn of the last century.*' Fifteen minutes later, I've burned MC's Web site and mission statement into my brain in case there's a pop quiz at the interview.

Heading west toward the Hudson, I burrow into the frigid wind like a salmon on a mission, silently pitching My Company to Grace as a conscionable use of my public-policy degree. I stumble, my big toe popping through my last pair of tights.

Oh, yeah. I'm going to Whitney this one so hard Guy won't know what hit him.

On Twelfth Avenue, I pass crews of construction workers transforming crumbling auto-body shops into art galleries, whose anemic interns steal cigarettes in the frigid sunshine. The gusts off the river sting my face, forcing me closer to the brick façade of my destination. "HEY, LADY! WHAT THE FUCK?" I jump aside as a loaded forklift backs out onto the sidewalk. The driver points belligerently, and I dart out of his path and into the cold copper lobby of the former warehouse, where the security guard is huddled like an ice fisherman over his *New York Post* and space heater.

"Help you?" he grunts.

"Yes, I'm going up to My Company."

"Ten." He jerks a thumb over to the elevator bank. "Gotta sign in first. And let's see some ID." In the elevator, an impressive roster lights up with each passing floor—clothes I'd love to wear, furniture I'd love to own. Anticipating glamour, I step out . . . onto an abandoned loading dock. Instinctively I get back in and re-press ten. The doors slide closed and then open again onto the same cavernous cement space. Confused and not a little concerned that this is how ladies end up on milk cartons, I step cautiously. Filthy eighteen-wheeler bays stand empty around a Mack-truck-sized hole in the floor, presumably where a freight elevator once was. I peek my head over the gaping chasm and see that it drops all the way to street level. This is not safe.

As I turn back toward the elevator, I'm relieved to spot the brushed-steel letters of My Company, Inc., the woman's symbol backlit as if hovering. I cross to the other side of the bay and peek in through the glass portals of the double doors, suffering an instant crush. On the far end of an open layout of at least a hundred blond-wood desks, floor-to-ceiling casement windows bathe the humongous bustling room in views of the star-sprinkled skyline above and the Hudson River below.

I want in.

I open the door, preparing to synthesize all I know about women's magazines (something) and software (nothing) with the determination to speak only in grand affirming statements. "I have a six-thirty with Guy."

The receptionist picks up her phone. In keeping with the Urban Outfitters vibe of the rest of the staff, she sports a Mickey Mouse T-shirt beneath her suit. "Okay, follow me." Anywhere.

After divesting me of my coat, she walks me across the room, past youngish employees in various stages of wrapping up their work week, messenger bags filling, bar names being volleyed. She deposits me in front of three steps leading up to a glass wall running the width of the room, which delineates a large office. I watch the man inside stoop to retrieve a Nerf ball while animatedly addressing the air over a speakerphone. I wait for him to hang up before I climb the steel steps and enter. "Hey!" Guy grins at me, his blue eyes twinkling as he tosses the orange ball in the air. "It's great that you could come in. It's great that you just called me up. I love that." He tucks the ball under his elbow before tugging lightly at his royal-blue cords and dropping into his desk chair. "How are you?"

"Good, thank you." I smile radiantly back. "How are you?"

He laughs, the air around him charged with the arrogant charisma of a man who has derived maximum mileage from his prep-school-crush good looks. Picking up a mug of filmed-over coffee, he gulps, wiping his upper lip swiftly as he sets it down. "I'm great, Girl."

Channeling Whitney, I stride over to the seat facing him and sit, unbidden. "Guy, first off I have to tell you that I'm a huge fan of My Company—I love what you do here: linking women to information. It's such an important service."

He smiles, his eyes locked on mine as he steadies the ball on his lap. "Pretty impressive, isn't it? Women of all ages log on every day with beauty questions, fashion questions, health—" He smacks his desktop with his hands, rattling the pens in their stainless-steel holder. "Yeast infections are our number one hit!"

"Really!" I match his enthusiasm.

"Want a Vagisil T-shirt?"

"Uh, sure—yes! Absolutely! I'd love one!"

"Great, you got it." We smile and nod at each other. "Cool," he says. "So now I want to take MC, Inc.'s success and leverage it—"

"Absolutely. *Everything* should be leveraged. Otherwise, why bother? I've spent the last few years conducting research on the needs of teenage girls and then *leveraging* that information to impact social policy. Really interesting work." I lean back and cross my legs.

"Huh." He nods. "So, the thing is, Girl, I want to tap this last corner of the marketplace that remains pretty stubbornly reticent. *Ms. Magazine.* My team tells me they've got some compelling journalism. I'd like to get their archive on the site."

"Of course!" Mascara and . . . female genital mutilation. "It's an obvious match."

"I think so. I brought you in because I have this initiative, a rebranding opportunity, and I thought you might be a good fit." He rolls up the sleeves of his blue-and-white-striped oxford. "I'm the CEO, so my plate's full. I need someone to run it, someone like you."

"Interesting." Initiative?! How many people involved? What, exactly, do you mean by *run*? Me? *Ms.*?! But questions do not inspire confidence. "Guy, I'm honored by your consideration." He smiles; I sweat. "And I have to say this sounds like an ideal match. First of all, I've been working with nonprofits my entire life. My mother runs the Chatsworth Writers' Colony in Connecticut, which no one's really heard—"

"Sure, didn't Plath write there?"

"She did." I smile, surprised as he doesn't strike me as the Plath type. "So, I've been helping my mother with grants, outreach, and administration since I was about as tall as your desk. I majored in public policy with a minor in gender studies, as you'll see from my résumé." I reach into my purse and pass it to him, trying to steady my shaking hand. "And, as I mentioned, my work at the Center for Equity in Community predominantly focused on serving the needs of adolescent females—"

"And, *you're* female!" He laughs.

"Yes." I'm female. I read *Ms. Magazine.* I've had a yeast infection. I'm a *Ms.*-toting, yeast infection–surviving, *unemployed* female.

"Excellent." Guy shakes his head slowly as he puts my résumé facedown. "I feel like you get it."

"I do," I say without hesitation. "I get it and I want it." Paid rent, restaurant food, new tights, I want it all.

"Shit, girl, I'm looking at you and I feel it, we have found the face of this initiative." Do not kiss him, do not kiss him, do not.

"Guyser." A golf club slides the door open, trailed by a very tall, very tanned man in his early sixties.

"Rex!" Guy stands and I follow, vibrating ecstatically as I turn 'the face' in greeting.

"*Qué pasa,* my friend?" The man tugs with his free hand at his cashmere slacks before sitting on the pony-skinned chaise.

"Have you heard back from the board?" Guy asks, nerves patently flickering across his face.

"Vote's in." Rex tucks the club behind his neck and dangles his wrists over the protruding ends, suggesting a stockade. "Apparently you really knocked their socks off." Guy beams as Rex continues, "Green light. But you're getting limited rope. They want a signed commitment from the client by May."

Taking a fax from Guy, Rex drops his club, which bounces off the carpet, narrowly missing my toes. Oblivious, Rex tosses his leonine white hair off his forehead, scanning the pages while Guy and I both stand awkwardly. Actually, I'm standing awkwardly; Guy looks as if he's ready to burst into "The Star Spangled Banner."

"*Now* I'm getting my money's worth." Rex swats at Guy's shins with the fax.

"I promised you, Rex. She'll meet with us."

"You prick!" The two of them beam at each other before the man cants his head toward me inquisitively.

"This is Girl," Guy explains while Rex looks me cursorily up and down. "I'm talking to her about our feminist rebranding. Girl, this is Rex, MC, Inc.'s chairman."

"Hello, Rex. It's such a pleasure." I step over to shake his hand, but he makes no effort to rise.

"So you've met the Guyser," Rex says as he squeezes my fingers, digging my rings into the bones. "My number one shark at The Bank. I'm proud as hell to set him loose on My Company—going to take this place to the next level, aren't you?"

"Keep you out of the salvage yard, Rex."

Taking my cue, "Well, I'm here to help you do just that."

Rex winks at me.

"Great, Girl." Guy nods down into crossed arms. "I'm very excited about this. Very excited." That's it—no Dante circles? No Cyrillic typing tests?

"Me, too. So when should I expect—"

"Yeah, I'll give you a call when I get everything lined up." Guy sits back down at his computer.

"Great! Do you have a sense of your time frame?"

"This is top priority," he says, already immersed in the screen.

"Damn straight," Rex mutters, rereading the fax.

I give official confirmation one last try, "So, I'm . . . ?"

"Just head back past the desks. Elevators are outside reception. Oh, wait! Don't forget this." He grabs a T-shirt from an open box and tosses it underhand to me. "Gotta fly the banner!"

"Okay, then, well, very nice to meet you, Rex. Thank you both for your consideration." I motion good-bye with the white cotton, effectively waving myself out with a five-inch Vagisil logo.

Lightheaded, I recross the giant room, past the remaining employees humming away at their tasks—tapping keyboards, working phones, flying banners. Holy. Shit. Run it—*run* it! Someone *like me*!! Relief begins to ricochet through my body, and I'm dizzy with what to do first. Call home, cry, buy something. I slide my coat out of the closet and tug my scarf off the hanger, but it's stuck. I tug harder, effectively tightening the noose. *Ms. Magazine*, rebranding—I snag a nail, ripping a long pink thread out of the knit—face of *what* exactly? I jerk the hanger down, ripping more threads.

"I have a seven o'clock with Guy." Alarmed, I dart my eyes at a striking brunette leaning against the receptionist's counter to pull off her calfskin gloves one finger at a time. She drops them into her quilted suede purse as I tug the scarf free. "It's Seline."

"Your last name?" The receptionist calls after her as she turns to sit down.

"Saybrook." She slides a thick sheet of paper out of an elegant leather résumé case but fumbles, sending it floating to my feet. I bend down, noticing *Ms. Magazine* lightly penciled on a Post-it, which nearly obscures the more alarming *Stanford* and *Columbia MBA*. No! This women's-information-initiative thing, this rebranding-new-direction thing, this Vagisil-gear-flying-the-flag thing has got *my* name written aaaalll over it. She clears her throat, and I pass the résumé back. "Here for the job?" she asks.

"I just had an interview."

"Well, good luck." Okay, I don't need it, Miss MBA. *I'm* 'the face.'

Downstairs I cross the street to take a last longing look up at the hulking building, and Guy's silhouette comes into view at the window. I replay the interview. No, definitely, I definitely have it. He loved me. I'm in.

A red light pulses in my periphery, a crimson hammer and sickle projected onto the sidewalk up the block. Bella Russe, a dinner befitting my triumph. Past Town Cars depositing their sunglass-toting, baseball-cap-wearing, don't-notice-me-notice-me guests, a doorman bundled in a Helmut-Lang-Cossack ensemble ushers me in. Moving out of the path of a weaving Hilton sister, I shimmy through the packed bar area in search of the hostess. "Welcome," she smiles graciously. "IMG has the private room. Rene will take you." She gestures to her colleague.

"I'm sorry, I don't have a reservation."

"Oh." Her energy drops. "Reservations only. We're booked."

"That's okay! Then I'll just take something to go." I lean in to be heard over the ambient music.

"We don't do takeout here." She recoils as if I've just asked her to supersize it.

"Really?" But having been forced in the last weeks to evolve into a human ball of unrelenting persistence, I persist. "Can you check with the kitchen?"

"We don't have, what do you call them?"

"Containers?"

"We don't have containers." This is ridiculous. I should just go home and scrape out the peanut butter jar. She returns to perusing her heavily marked-up seating chart.

But I can't. I can't seem to let this go. "How about aluminum foil? You can just wrap it up in that."

Sighing conciliatorily, she thrusts a menu at me. I quickly scan my options, my stomach sinking at the prices.

She taps her pen. "What do you want?" she levels at me snidely. "The egg noodles?"

No, Cerebus, egg noodles is assistant-to-the-assistant-color-folders-nights-over-the-copy-machine-working-on-a-toilet-seat. "Lobster."

"Fine. Wait at the bar."

"I'll do that."

Maneuvering around the six-foot Fabergé egg, I take a seat on a velvet ottoman to watch Cavalli-clad couples swill vodka out of melting ice glasses. I grab a handful of free dried cherries from a lacquered bowl and wonder how often My Company staffers hit the place for Happy Hour. On the mirror above the bar, someone's scrawled the wine specials in red lipstick. In the smoked reflection, my eyes alight on a certain choppy blond haircut.

Dennis Quaid grin.

Grinning at me.

A flush goes up the back of my neck. Shit. Well, I don't know who the hell he thinks—he's waving. I look down to my right heel. I study the mock crocodile for scuffs, twisting my ankle left and right. Pleasecomefoodpleasecomefoodpleasecomefood. I look back up—still grinning. I fix a flat smile on my face.

Buster picks up his beer and begins to maneuver over to my ottoman. Not a chance, no way am I going to—

"Hey! Kerouac's sister, what're you doing here?" He drops down to a squat and we are face to lovely face.

"Getting dinner," I say curtly.

"Cool. You meeting people?"

"Uh-huh."

"I didn't even know about this place, and YGames is only two blocks over. I was supposed to meet up with some friends at the diner. Didn't there used to be a diner here?"

I shrug.

"I feel like there was." He nods at his Campers. Whatever, fuckface. "So how's your brother?"

"He's fine. I'm fine. I'm going to go wait over there now." I gesture to a free booth across the room. "And you may be tempted to offer to drive me over there, but just sit with that, okay?" I stand.

Buster smacks his forehead. "Shit! Man, I'm sorry—this work thing came up—I spent the rest of the weekend at my desk. I wanted to call, but I didn't have your number. Are you totally pissed?" He grins and pulls me back down. "Seriously." He rests his bottle on the table and turns his face to me. "I'm sorry; it was shitty."

"It was."

He rubs his eyes and his energy drops. "It's just been a killer week—I've pretty much been chained to my monitor since a few hours after I left you. We're trying to fight a buyout. I've just been retooling and retooling and the reqs keep chang-ing—"

"Okay, *please,* no more jargon. I've filled my quota for, like, the rest of my life."

"Sorry. How's the job hunt going?"

I scan over his head for the hostess. "Killer week as well—I've pretty much been talking out of my ass since a few hours after you left us."

"Sucks all around."

"Yep." While my lobster remains MIA, the crowd conspires to part, giving me an unobstructed view of Seline Saybrook paying for iced vodkas. I glance down at my watch. Score! Only ten minutes—she blew it.

"Hey, why don't you ditch your dinner, come get a hot dog, and watch a game at the Piers with me? It'll be totally relaxing *and* jargon-free." I look back up as Seline flicks her mane of teak hair, clinks ice glasses with the man beside her, and downs her vodka in one shot. "Come on, give me a chance to make it up to you."

"Your lobster." The hostess, her expression vaguely contemptuous, waves a plastic bag under my nose.

"I have a lobster." The crowd shifts again and I catch sight of the blue-and-white-striped oxford of Seline's companion. Ohshityou'vegottobekiddingme.

"Bring him," Buster says, tossing blond bangs at the bag.

"That'll be forty-two fifty." Square red nails snap me to attention. "Cash only." *I should have had the egg noodles.*

Buster takes the bag as I pull the last few bills from my wallet to pay for the meal that's instantaneously morphed from celebratory feast to bank-breaking consolation prize. Out of the corner of my eye, I see Guy hold his finger up to pause Seline and cross through the restaurant to reject me in person.

Buster tries again. "So—"

I jump to my feet. "Great, yes, let's go!"

"Cool! Hang a minute while I run out and see where my friends are." He disappears toward the door, passing Guy in transit.

"Girl!" Guy jovially pokes me in the thigh before I can dive my MBA-less self over the crimson couch. "Fantastic place, isn't it?" His eyes sparkle. "I've been eating here five nights a week—almost sick of it. You gotta try the squab. Meeting people?"

"Yes, yes, I am. Doing some work on women's issues tonight. It's a brainstorming strategy sort of meal—you know how it is. We meet bimonthly actually." My vanquisher reapplies her lipstick at the bar. "So much information women need, so little time—"

"Solid presentation today. Just solid." Guy shakes his head, aglow from the two brunettes bracketing his evening.

"Thank you. As I said, I so admire your work and I think if you'll reconsider, I can add real value."

He glances back at Seline, giving her a nod. "Excellent, Girl. So we'll be in touch." His body is already beginning its orbit back to her.

"Great, yeah, I should get going, too! Thanks again for the interview! And the T-shirt—I'm really just totally looking forward to working for you, so, bye now," I call after him as I back toward the exit, smiling and nodding. "Just going to check for my women brainstorming friends outside. They might have gotten lost, so—"

The shiny red door is pulled abruptly shut in my face and I am, once again, out in the cold. I sigh deeply and look down at my shoes.

When I manage to lift my head, I find Buster leaning with two other boys against a parked car in an Abercrombie layout of distressed denim and calculated bed-head. "Ready to go?" Buster waves, swinging my lobster. Okay, so he's hot. And I can't spend the entire evening staring at the ceiling and obsessing over every little crap thing I said, everything I should have said not to sound crappy, and what Seline Saybrook is saying right this very minute to make everything I said sound like total crap. Plus, he's hot.

I smile at his friends, only to be met with clenched jaws. Buster steps over, his breath coming in steaming puffs. "Hey, these are two of my roommates, Tim and Trevor."

"Hello!" I give an encompassing wave.

"What up," they spit, already turning to head out. They set a brisk pace, which Buster matches effortlessly, leaving me scampering along behind while they stride in tense silence.

Catching up at the light, I try, "Hey, how's your coat?"

Buster grins. "Hasn't gone home without me this whole week—we're in couples therapy." Tim and Trevor turn around to give us 'nerd' glances.

"We couldn't find our coats last weekend," I offer.

"Whatever." Tim leaps up to grab the high crossbar of a lamppost, his Adidas swinging into my elbow as he lands.

"Dude!" Trevor says, hooking his arm around Buster's neck and pulling him away from me. I surreptitiously inspect the scuff mark on my beaten coat, which just can't seem to catch a break. "Sam called—he finally found a place near the thing." Ah, a place near the thing. He drags Buster along in a headlock while they talk about the merits of different places near different things. Watching them effortlessly vault the cement road barrier to the West Side Highway, I climb over, the seam of my skirt splitting as I straddle it, unassisted. If Buster were along with my friends right now, they'd be carrying him on a litter and feeding him grapes to make him feel included. With increasingly mixed feelings, I follow my rapidly chilling lobster across six lanes to Chelsea Piers, a stadium-sized sports complex built out over the river. We walk about a block through the dimly lit mammoth parking garage, until I step in an icy puddle.

"You know what?" I call out to them, my voice echoing.

"Yeah?" Buster yells over his shoulder, not even stopping.

"I think I'm gonna go. If you could hand me my lobster, maybe it's better if I just get a cab."

Buster trots back while his friends disappear into the building. "What? No! Come on, *hot dogs*. It'll be fun!"

"Thanks." I motion for my dinner. "But I feel like I'm crashing your date."

"No, not at all. Let's go inside—it's fucking freezing out here." He hides the bag behind his back and simultaneously reaches for my gloved hand to give it a squeeze. "Seriously, I'm holding the lobster hostage."

"Okay," I laugh. We ride, single file, up the escalator and into the fluorescent-lit lobby. My cheeks tingle from the welcome warmth as we cross the linoleum floor to double doors marked

Arena. Buster throws one open, and I'm immediately hit by icy air, colder than the winter we've just scuttled out of. Oh, sad.

"Ever been to the rink?" Buster grins. A player smashes into the Plexiglas inches away and before I can answer, a phalanx of helmeted gladiators rips him back onto the ice.

"Nope, can't say that I have."

I follow into the bleachers, taking a frosted seat between Buster and Tim, who scream war whoops of glee as the puck goes into play. Rebuttoning my coat all the way up, I attempt to set up my feast, resting the plastic in my lap and pulling out a lobster-sized aluminum swan.

Buster grins at me. "Claw?" I offer, catching the congealing butter with a napkin.

"Thanks, we ordered in burritos at work. Looks yummy, though." He wipes my chin with his thumb. I look down to hide the flush.

"It's already cold," I admit defeat. "I'll make it into lobster salad tomorrow." But Buster's eyes are riveted to the game. I stuff the remainder of my meal back into the bag and clear my throat. "So you guys all live together?"

"Yeah." He follows the darting puck as he speaks. "There're seven of us. That's Luke down there DOING A CRAP JOB!" He points indiscriminately at the pileup. "He's my boy—we all went to Chapel Hill together."

"Your boy?"

Buster continues to root loudly at the ensuing brawl another minute before returning his attention to me. "Huh? What did you say?"

"Luke, he's 'your boy.' "

"Not like *that*. Yo, Trev, pass me a beer!"

"Okay, 'cause I was picturing chaps," I mutter as a brown-bagged bottle is tossed just clear of my head. The opposing team scores, and sparse clusters of men seated around the rink cheer and boo. A slow half hour crawls by on frozen kneecaps, sans hot dogs, as advertised. While frost creeps up my stockinged legs, I pass the time flexing and pointing my toes to keep them attached.

Finally, Luke's team scores. "CUNT!" a large man behind us bellows, bringing the blood back into my brain. *"Cunt!"*

Jostled on either side by my screaming companions, I look up at the domed ceiling.

"Cunt! CUUUUUNT!" Budweiser spittle sprays the back of my neck.

I wait for Buster to flinch, roll his eyes, or in any way acknowledge the gynecological tirade, but his attention remains firmly on the puck.

The man behind us addresses his companion, "My son can't goal for shit."

I stand. "You know, I'm just gonna go to the ladies' room and thaw."

"Wha? Sure, fine," Buster says, effectively shushing me with his waving palm.

Fuck. You.

In the bathroom, I hole up under the hand dryer, letting several rounds of hot air bring circulation back into my blue fingers. So, where we going next weekend? Coal mining? Awesome, count me in. And we'll take your magic carpet? Fabulous. I'll be waiting!

Moderately warmed, I step back into the lobby as Buster bursts through the rink's double doors. "Okay, so, thanks!" I wave good-bye from across the rubber-coated floor.

"Hey." He strides over, his cheeks flushed from cheering, proffering my plastic bag. "You're not leaving, are you?"

"Yeah."

I reach out for my dinner, but Buster catches my wrist, holding me and the bag before dropping his voice. "Okay, well then how about I help you get this home and into a salad?" He grins that grin and I'm sure for him it's just that easy.

"I don't think we're quite ready to make salad together." I exhale. "Look, this has been an *insanely* long day on top of an *insanely* long week, and I just really want a hot shower—" I catch myself. "Which is more than you need to know. If you could just direct me toward a cab."

"Will you at least let me walk you? I'd feel better if I knew you got home safely." Knee-jerk-chivalrous-bullshit-signifying-nothing. But, facing a long trek through the desolate parking lot, I concede, letting him fall into step with me. We cross the highway and walk over to Eleventh, where we stare in silence down the empty avenue. Buster ducks his head. "I feel like I've totally fucked this up."

"What?" I ask, surprised at his acknowledgment. "No. No—it's not like this was a date." A glowing cab light makes its way toward us.

"I have fucked this up." The car slows to a stop. "You think I'm an asshole."

"I don't think anything. I don't even know you." I reach for the door, exhaustion officially setting in.

"Well, I'd like you to. Can I call you?"

"Actually, no."

Buster looks stricken as the cabbie raps his window impatiently. I slide into the backseat, the contents of my purse spilling out. "I'm sorry. But, um . . . here." I thrust the roll of cotton out the window. "Have a T-shirt!" He takes it from my outstretched arm as the taxi swerves from the curb.

"You have three new messages."

Beep.

"Message one received Wednesday at eleven thirty-four: Hi, this is Estelle from Tempting Temps. Again, we're not taking on anyone new right now. As it is, we have *no* assignments—"

★4

"Message deleted. Message two received Wednesday at twelve thir-

teen: Yes, this is Women In Action. With regards to the position, we'd love to hire you. We'd love to hire a hundred of you. But we simply don't have the funding—"

★4

"*Message deleted. Message three received Wednesday at two forty-three:* Hello, this is Stacey, Guy's assistant from My Company, following up on your interview two weeks ago. Our chairman, Rex, has just requested that you meet him at The Club today at four o'clock. That's Fifty-three East Sixty-ninth Street. Please call to confirm."

Running breathlessly up to the mansion, I bypass the liveried doorman loading an octogenarian into a Town Car and push against the trellised iron doors, falling into the imposing lobby of The Club. On one limestone wall sits a reception desk, on the other, beneath a portrait of Robert E. Lee, a wood-paneled coat-check, both abandoned. Following the sound of gruff laughter and clinking stemware, I race up the double staircase and down a Persian-carpeted hallway, past canvases of cigar-toting founders. Touching my fingertips to the mahogany doors, I propel myself into the dining room, where I'm met with the thick aroma of chicken pot pie and contraband Havanas. Through the smoke I spot Rex at a corner table overlooking Park Avenue, peering at a neatly folded paper while he eats.

"Rex, hi." Tilting like a cocktail bunny, I announce my presence, accidentally brushing the bald pate behind me with my purse. "Sorry." I spin to apologize to a gin-flushed face made even redder by my contact.

"Young lady?" a stern voice addresses me, and I turn the other way to find a phalanx of white-jacketed, dark-skinned men, armed with tongs and dish towels, poised as if about to snare a crocodile. The room has gone silent.

"Young lady!" The offended older gentleman is shaking a

freckled fist at me. "*You* are *not* permitted!" A host of heads-in-service nod emphatically behind him, while scores of liver-spotted wattles shake in horror.

"I'm so sorry," I say, mortified. "Was I supposed to sign in? I'm sorry, I didn't know. There wasn't anyone at the front desk." I turn to Rex, who's barely managed to pull his attention away from the editorials.

"Girl," he instructs, calmly laying down his fork. "Wait downstairs."

"I'm so sorry—the message just said to meet you here. I didn't mean to—" The headwaiter takes my arm firmly. A team in biohazard suits most likely en route, I'm escorted past recoiling members and their staff, who stare stonily at the floor awaiting a flaying worthy of their negligence. I'm led swiftly back down the staircase and released in front of the Ladies' Lounge.

"You may wait here," my captor announces into the tomb-like quiet. Shit. I sink into a tufted, quilted, ruffled, floral club chair and catch sight of my beating face in the mirror across the way. *Shit.* I grimace as I replay my entrance. Shitshitshit!

Half an hour perched expectantly in Rose Kennedy's wet dream later, and it becomes evident that I'm here for the long haul. I slump back against the tufts and pull my mail out of my purse. Bills, bills, bills, an aeropostale letter from Kira—*We finally got both tribes to agree on where the well should be dug. Only now they say we can't dig until they've consecrated the ground with—you guessed it—a rain dance, which, of course, is pretty fucking unlikely as we've flown six thousand miles to dig them a fucking well*—the taunting Pottery Barn catalog, and a handwritten note that must've been shoved through my mail slot.

Hey, Girl!
It's been totally rockin' having you live in our little Annex (hah, hah), but Zeldy sold a major piece this week (!) and she's finally letting me take

back the walk-in closet. We're gonna knock through at the end of the month, but please come over for the 'knock-through' party. Zeldy's gonna make her bourbon cake!
Lots of love,
Eva

I am not. Leaving here. Without a job.

"Can't," a Caribbean voice admonishes me as I head for the door.

"I'm sorry?" I glance around a potted fern to find an elderly cocoa-skinned woman in a maid's uniform, methodically folding hand towels.

"He said wait. Ladies ain't allowed in da building, 'cept for wife nights." Well, of course. I maneuver my chair to the doorway and stare intently at the bottom of the staircase. And stare. And wait. And stare some more.

Two elder statesmen shuffle themselves to the bench beneath Robert E. Lee to pull on their galoshes. "For my money, no one will ever top Connery. But the one we rented had that dark-skinned girl, what's her name?"

"A fruit. Berry something."

"Yes, that's the one. She put a bit of a crackle into the picture."

"Yes, Jefferson had the right idea."

I lock eyes with the woman folding towels, who remains stone-faced.

No, I think this is the *perfect* club for the chairman of a company catering entirely to women. Augusta with sheets. *Shame,* Grace's disgusted voice rings in my ears. *Shameshameshame.*

But, there's a wad of unpayable bills in my hand and Zeldy's artistic aspirations for my sublet.

As if a bell's rung, a throng of cashmere coats and university scarves suddenly swoops down the stairs. I dart into the hall, trying to pick Rex out from the faces stampeding to their pre-theater dinners. Headlights beam through the windows, and I run out onto the street. "Rex! Rex!"

He pauses, one foot already in his silver Jag, his open Barbour revealing squash whites.

"I'm *so* sorry," I say again as the doorman places Rex's racquet bag in the trunk. "I *really* apologize for my entrance up there. I didn't know about your," I swallow, "policy."

Rex smiles, chuckling to himself as the door is opened for him. "Girl, I saw everything I needed to see." He folds himself into the car, the glaring doorman slamming it shut.

I stare after the departing taillights, tears blurring their beams.

"Just fill out the form and take a seat." A stick-thin man draped in a nubby green cardigan sits beneath the water-stained STATE OF NEW YORK UNEMPLOYMENT OFFICE sign and slides a clipboard to me, along with a child-sized pencil.

"Can I just ask—I haven't received any checks yet. I've been trying to get someone on the phone, but I really, *really* need to get paid."

"Yes?"

"So when will that happen? Because in the booklet—"

"The booklet?"

"Yes, in the section about payment schedules—"

"Well, if it's in the booklet, then it must be right."

"So . . ."

"So, sounds to me like you have your answer." He slides a clipboard and pencil to the person in line behind me. "Just fill out the form, take a seat, and wait for the meeting."

"So, then you can help?"

He stares at me.

"Should I talk to someone?"

"You're talking to me." He arches a tweezed eyebrow without missing a beat in the next handoff. "Just fill out the form and take a seat."

"I need to attend the meeting just to talk to someone about getting paid?"

"Just fill out the form."

"Right, but I might not actually need to—"

"And take a seat."

We stare at each other.

He slides his Coke-bottle glasses up his nose before passing a clipboard and baby pencil to the next person on line. I shift my backpack to my other shoulder. "Okay . . . we'll resolve this later then! I'll just go on ahead and fill out the form."

"And then you can," he says, pointing over to where a group of people sit wedged into school desks, "take a seat. With your goddamn booklet," he grumbles.

Sighing, I do as instructed. Furtively surveying my fellow unemployed, I lock eyes with the dark-rooted blonde from the Big Five interview—the other failed Sheila. I blush and follow her head cock to the overtly gelled hair of the man who seemed to have the whole case exercise thing down. Apparently not down enough.

I smile meekly. Sheila glazes over.

"Hello," Nubby Cardigan drones as he stands up. "Hello," he repeats as we all look over. "Hello. This is my colleague, Mrs. Kamitzski." A frazzled-looking woman with glasses on a chain steps forward to give us a little wave as Nubby opens a binder and begins to read to us *sans* inflection. "Hello and welcome to the New York State Unemployment Office. You have been required to report in person today . . . Required to report in person today . . . *today*." He pauses, looking pointedly at Mrs. Kamitzski.

"February thirteenth," she delivers her line.

"Today, February thirteenth, for the purposes of a Periodic Eligibility and Employability Review interview. You are required to have been keeping a written record of all job search efforts with the dates, names, addresses, and phone numbers of employers contacted, the positions applied for, and the results. If you have not kept a written record of all job search efforts with the dates, names, addresses . . ."

The heat makes me woozy and I tune out, surreptitiously scanning the real-estate section of *The Village Voice* for free apartments.

"Can I just ask a question?" A large woman in a heap of crinkled velvet speaks up from my right.

"Apparently." Nubby pushes up his glasses at her. "You can."

"I'm a singer. I'm classically trained in opera and musical stage, but I've only been to a few gigs in the last month. I'd say three—no, four—wait." She digs into her overstuffed patchwork duffel, rooting out a desk calendar covered in photographs of red-eyed cats lounging on radiators. "Umm, I would say four, because even though the fourth was my cousin's bar mitzvah, they were going to pay for my transportation to and from the hall. And I've gone to tons of voice-over calls—do they count?"

"Do you receive a paycheck?" Nubby stares at her.

"Well, yes, if that's what you'd call it. Sometimes I just take the work for the connections. I got a great gig in Boca Raton from a car show last year—"

"Your question?" Nubby grips the white binder in front of him like a homicidal caroler.

"I don't have all the contact information for every call I went on and even though I put the time in and made the effort to go, which hasn't been easy, because my brother's been sick and I've been watching his parrot, who I sometimes take to auditions, but sometimes I just have to feed him. I'd go back to Boca if I could, but mostly I prefer the opera work, and there are just limited venues in Southern Florida for quality opera."

He blinks. "So?"

"So, should I not list those calls? Or do I list them? Or don't they count at all, because I think the work I do to take care of my brother's bird should count for something, because Lord knows that's work—anyone who's had to change a birdcage knows there should be some sort of salary for *that . . .*"

Sweet mercy at long last arrives in the form of Hair Gel Man, who extends his arm up into the air. "I just want to confirm that this meeting is an hour and a half." His tone is pleasant, as if, unlike the rest of us civil hostages, he's been getting a full spa treatment. "I have a pretty promising interview scheduled and would sure hate to miss it." He smiles winningly.

"Oh, yes, yes," Mrs. Kamitzski concurs coquettishly, turning back to Opera Lady. "We'll have to resolve your issue in private when the session is over."

After Nubby drones on for another forty-some minutes, we're instructed to bring our forms up as our names are called. Another half hour and it's down to me and Hair Gel Man, who covertly scrawls on the corner of his desktop.

"Girl?"

"Here!" I step to the front, hand over my form, and pull on my coat. "So, exactly how much longer do you think before I receive my first check?"

Mrs. Kamitzski scans the paper and then points out something in her binder to Nubby. Nubby smiles thinly. "Your claim was denied."

"What?" I break into a new kind of sweat. "How is that possible? I was fired."

"Record shows that you lost your position due to misconduct and that disqualifies you."

"What record? There was no misconduct. I was fired!"

"Well," Mrs. Kamitzski chirps, "you can always appeal if you want to get yourself a lawyer and register for a hearing, but you have to do that over the phone. If you take your seat, we'll get you the number, just as soon as I take care of this patient young man so that he can make it to his interview on time." Hair Gel Man waltzes up, debonairly straightening his tie. I wedge myself into his vacated seat, too stunned to protest.

"You sure have been nice to accommodate me with all you have going on here," he says sweetly, launching Mrs. Kamitzski into a fit of what I'm sure she believes to be girlish giggles as the three walk out together.

I start to see spots. I am utterly out of money. Game over. I'm going to have to move back home—and spend the rest of my miserable life enduring ceaseless 'Just start your own ____' pep talks while my chore list exceeds Cinderella's. I look down at my shaking hands, noticing Hair Gel Man's prescription for Mrs. Kamitzski, thoughtfully inked in a long column down the desktop. *"Mrs. Kamitzski, you fat whore, you need a cow's shlong shoved straight up your sagging ass—"*

"Here." Nubby thrusts a new booklet at me. "You were right. You didn't need to be here."

I grab it from him, dashing out to the frigid street, past the desperate souls lining up outside, and all the way to the subway platform before stopping to catch my breath. I lean against the cold tile wall, staring down the long hallway of the Fifty-ninth Street station. My breath is labored and my cheeks are wet.

"Shitshitshit," I mutter to my sneakers. Wiping my nose with my coat sleeve, I heft the thick booklet, at least fifty pages long in its explanation of the hearing process involved in contesting Doris. I eye the numbers listed on the back cover and walk over to the pay phone while digging deep in my bag to pull up a dog-eared card worn soft with worrying.

"My Company. How may I direct your call?"

"Guy, please."

"Hold on." There's a pause before another woman picks up the line. I clear my throat of all signs of sniffles.

"Hello, this is Stacey."

"Yes, is Guy in? I'm calling to speak with him regarding an interview I had with Rex. There was a misund—"

"Hold on, please."

I grip the phone with both hands, praying she returns within three minutes as I'm now out of change. I'm going to beg him.

"Hey, Girl." Guy comes on the line. "Yeah, so you wowed the fucking pants off Rex at your meeting. He *loved* you. We've been meaning to get a call out, but we're swamped with this client we're pitching overseas. Can you come in at uh . . . say, twelve-thirty on Friday?"

"Yes! Yes, I *absolutely* can. Um, sorry, for a second inter—"

"See you Friday." The call disconnects.

A bolt of sunshine cracks through sixty tons of New York City concrete and shines directly onto my head.

CHAPTER FIVE

By Any Means Necessary

Retracing my steps over the cracked cobblestones of far-west Chelsea, I nod confidently to the security guard, flash my license, and sign in. But when the elevator slides open onto the musty loading dock, my spirits falter. So help me God, I'm leaving employed or throwing myself out their perfect windows.

"Girl, hey." I startle as Guy strides up from behind, tossing a coffee cup into a nearby Dumpster.

"Hi!"

"Great." He continues past, his booming voice filling the dank air. "Glad you're here. We've got this thing I want you to be a part of." A welcoming Virgil, he holds the door open to his sunshine-bathed offices.

"Thank you. Yes, I'm happy to be part of a thing—" His cell rings and while he nods and yeahs into the minuscule appliance, I fall violently back in love with all that is My Company, filling with childlike yearning for every bonsai tree and brushed-steel recycle bin.

Clicking his phone shut, Guy stops abruptly just inside the doorway of a small glassed-in conference room, blocking my entrance. "Hey, folks, this is Girl. We're looking at her to head up the initiative." Squeezing in around him, I smile at the expectant faces as I roll out a mesh titanium-colored chair. "Girl, some key players to impress in the MC, Inc. family: Matt, design; Stan, I.T.; Angel, our office manager; and Joe here is the People Department, killing us with all the HR bullshit." Joe, his beard a soft gray, looks to be the eldest employee. "You made me a promise, Joe. All My Company policies should fit on one index card. Like running a hot dog cart." Joe laughs nervously, while the other men give me a halfhearted wave. "Let's just jump right in," Guy continues. "The issue on deck is what's going to bring in the *Ms.* woman; this is an incredible opportunity for everyone here. Incredible." He slaps the top of his chair arms. "Girl?"

"Yes." I nod enthusiastically, eager for details. "Absolutely."

"Right. Girl, take it away!" Everyone turns expectantly. I flash to the dream where I'm taking the biochemistry final, never enrolled in the class, and am naked.

"Well . . . I assume you're all familiar with the *Ms.* community."

"Me?" Angel asks.

"The Web site?" Matt asks.

"No, I mean real life, their readers." Blank looks all around. So totally butt naked. Guy's cell rings and he blessedly steps out, leaving me to flail unobserved. "Well, let's see, from what I know, their readers are politically savvy, socially active, and vested in gender equity across the board. So if you were them—"

"Who?" Angel interrupts.

"The *Ms.* readers."

"If we were women, you mean," Joe helps me out.

"Yes! Yes, if you were a woman who fit the description I've just given—"

"Did Guy say how long we had to be here?" Stan hooks a lackadaisical finger through the neck of the T-shirt escaping from his oxford collar. " 'Cause I have a dentist appointment."

Joe stands, his knees cracking, and lifts the whiteboard from the floor to the table with a thud. He writes *WOMEN* in squeaky felt-tipped strokes. The others stare at me.

"Maybe we should approach this in the reverse." I look from male face to male face. Stan glances obviously at his watch. "What aspects of My Company do you think would particularly appeal to the type of women I described?"

"The bathrooms!" Angel perks up. "We give free tampons."

"We do?" Matt asks. "We don't have anything free in the men's room."

"Maybe let's focus on content. How do we take all the information on beauty and health that our company has to offer"—my heart misses a beat at the proprietary 'our'—"and leverage it to capture the typical *Ms.* reader?" Silence. Matt shoots Stan a look. Perhaps they're fomenting a rebellion to get free condoms into the men's room.

"Okay, whadda we got?" Guy returns and swiftly takes in the empty whiteboard and silent group.

"Sorry, Guy, bit of confusion here," Joe explains. "Maybe it would grease the wheels if you speak to what MC wants from the *Ms.* woman." Thank you.

Guy sighs in exasperation, tugging at the skin on the bridge of his nose.

"Totally unnecessary," Stan says, suddenly animated. "As you were saying, Girl."

"Right," I scramble. "You know, examining what interests the *Ms. Magazine* crowd . . . culture, politics, social issues . . . basically the agenda of most nonprofits." Whitneywhitneywhitneywhitney. "So, *maybe* we could reach out to those nonprofits serving women, find out how what *they're* researching can benefit from our expertise." Whatever the fuck that is.

"Go on." Guy leans forward on the balls of his feet as I offer the one professional notch on my belt.

"I'm thinking My Company should sponsor a conference, get these organizations together, and . . . tap their brains." I flash to approaching Doris's wiry curls with an ice pick.

Guy claps twice and smiles broadly. "I love it." You do?

Taking their cue, Stan and Joe stand. "Awesome," Matt yawns.

"Awesome." Angel makes a beeline for the door.

"Yes." I smile, feeling the unfamiliar flush of acknowledged competence. "Let's leverage what they know."

"Sure, awesome." Stan follows Matt out, with Guy bringing up the rear.

"Excellent, just excellent," he says. "Thanks for coming. Got time for a bite? I'm starved."

"Yes, me, too, starved." For. A. Job.

"That was great," he says, dialing.

"Thanks, I couldn't be more intrigued by this initiative."

"Great. Let me just grab my coat."

Guy returns to collect me at the reception area, slurping from a Coke can and animatedly conveying a point into his cell. "Well, they're fucking me . . . No . . . fucking *me*. Their retention ratio has me grabbing my ankles . . ." For three avenues I walk beside him, getting a blow by blow on how the next quarter will relate to Guy receiving said fucking—in what positions, with which accoutrements, and whether his mother's going to be involved. He slaps his phone shut, returning it to his corduroy pocket as we cross Ninth Avenue. "So," he says with a grin, "like Italian?"

"Love it!"

"Didn't used to be a decent place to eat around here for miles, then a ton sprouted overnight." He holds the door to a little sliver of a restaurant, sleekly decorated with blown-up photographs of pasta against black-and-white marble. "Most didn't make it, though."

"Totally." I automatically match his tone of insider skepticism. We both order the special before Guy crosses his arms on the Carrara tabletop. "So, Girl, what've you been up to?"

"Oh, you know, I've just been—"

"Actually, I want an espresso—want one?"

"Sure."

"Waiter!" He flags him down. "Two doubles!"

"Yeah, I've just been *out there*." I steady my voice. "Trying to find the right environment for the skill set I've developed over the last few—"

"Bread?"

"Thank you," I say, nodding.

"Yeah, things are massively shitty out there, which is why I think it's so important that the MC, Inc. family helps the people at the bottom of the food chain, the people who traditionally get fucked when times are hard: women and minorities." With that he tears off a hunk of sourdough, drenches it in olive oil, and tosses the whole piece into his mouth. "People need resources, information. Or they fall between the cracks. My Company was built on giving women information. You have a problem? You type it in—bam! Information." Clumping mascara, the roadblock to civilization.

"And where does the profit come from?" I ask, taking a sip of ice water.

He explodes in hard laughter, tears dampening the dark circles under his eyes. "You just cut right to it, don't you, Girl? Great question. You're always thinking—I like that." He takes a long swig of espresso. "Advertisers. Plus the magazines pay us a fee to keep their archives current and accessible."

"And Rex?" I ask, 'thinking.'

"This is his baby; I'm just rockin' the cradle." Guy sloshes more bread around, spilling olive oil over the sides of the diminutive dish. "He was my mentor at The Bank, taught me everything I know about survival—"

"Rigatoni special?" the waitress asks, placing two steaming plates on our table.

"Thank you," I say as she extends the pepper grinder.

"Rex's one of the few to come out the other side who doesn't think entrepreneur's a dirty word. He brought me in to infuse this place with a little of my DNA." I nod, picturing Guy rubbing himself all over the office equipment. "Seriously, Girl, one million women click through his site *a day*. Rex and The Bank were sitting on a fucking cash cow with this subsidiary, but he had some *tool* running it down the recession drain, afraid to color outside the lines. No balls to leverage this company's biggest asset."

"Enter you?" I smile, sprinkling parmesan over my pasta.

"Yeah, I've got 'em. Big ones. Some say too big." He smiles from ear to ear. Is this another metaphor, or are we now actually discussing your testicles?

"Here's the vision, okay?" He wolfs down his meal while continuing, "And I'm letting you into the inner sanctum sanctorum—this hasn't been shared with the rest of the MC family *or* the public. We've just gotten it approved by the board, so this is between you, me, and The Bank. 'Kay?" I nod enthusiastically, and he shoves his empty plate aside, cheeks flushed as he slides his hands on the Carrara. "MC, Inc. has millions of women out there who we know naked. We've tracked their every move for months, giving us a shitload of hard data on what they want to know—what they're hungry for. Hell, I could even get back into their computers if I wanted to, which, of course, I don't." Well, that's something.

He wipes his mouth with his napkin and drops it on the table. "We're steering two million eyeballs a day to our advertisers. With the right manipulation, we could direct their attention *anywhere* we want." He squeaks his chair back, stretching to lift his hint of a gut above his monogrammed belt. "*I* stood on the fucking mountain, looked around, and thought, fuck, this is an opportunity *squandered*. MC, Inc. could evolve from tech shop to consulting firm. I know, I know, every consulting joint has gone belly-up, yada yada. But they didn't have our *prepackaged* knowledge base. A knowledge base that makes us extremely fuckable to companies with a large, feminist consumer base."

"Such as?"

"Nike, for one."

"You're going after Nike?"

"Well, we have a lot of irons in the fire. Getting the *Ms.* archive on the site would demonstrate an undeniable commitment to that whole thing. With the consulting industry in shambles, this is *the* out-of-the-box moment to compete at a boutique level. Whad'ya think?"

"Wow. I think . . . this sounds like an incredibly exciting time to join your crusade."

"I love your energy!" Guy lurches over the table to shake me by the shoulders. "That's what this place has been missing, some fucking enthusiasm!" He drops me to drain his espresso. "You've got the feminist pedigree, and we're on the same page. Took a while to get Rex on board—"

"Yes, the men's club thing's a little weird." I glance down to fold my napkin. "I didn't even know those were still legal."

He clatters his cup onto its saucer. "Got to have something left."

I smile fervently, overriding my instinctive grimace. "No, I just mean that it feels a little . . . antiquated." BACKTRACK! "But I'm sure people are entitled to, you know, gather with their peers and . . ." Guy nods slowly, and I trail helplessly off.

"Uh-huh." With each downswing of his head, the gulf deepens between us as he seems to be steeling himself for my pronouncement of reverent Wiccan worship. Oh, come back, *come back.*

"Sorry, I actually interrupted you. I want to hear more about your vision."

He appraises me for a nauseating moment longer. "You're a pisser."

"Thanks!"

He smiles tentatively. I grin winningly.

He leans in conspiratorially. "So, obviously, it's a competitive mess out there. Lotta sharks." I listen heedfully as he continues, my pulse recovering. "What I'm about to share with you is highly confidential, but I think you're going to be pretty damn happy to hear it." Adequately warned, I lock that smile in for the long haul. "The passion I feel about the feminist thing, that you feel about the feminist thing, MC doesn't show on paper yet. So we've decided, as a gesture of commitment to the female community, to offer up to a million in seed money to a nonprofit start-up who shares our concern for women." He beams, clearly savoring giving me this news, as well he should.

I still don't know what it is, couldn't explain it to a stranger on the street, but I want this job even more than I did an hour ago.

"That's incredibly generous. So then the nonprofit conference would be beneficial on two fronts. You'd get instant exposure to a number of potential recipients and demonstrate to *Ms.* that MC, Inc. has their issues at heart."

Guy leans forward to rest his chin in his hands, his energy draining away for the first time that I've seen, his face going slack as he runs out of show. "Great." He waves over my head for the check. "I gotta get back. You wanna come with?"

Still optional? "Of course, I'm very eager to get a jump on—" Guy's cell trills, and he claps it to his ear while shrugging on his jacket, leaving me to jog-trot beside him.

"Guy, accounting's waiting for you," the receptionist greets us.

"Okay." He claps his hands together. "Girl, why don't you, uh . . . generate a list of people you think we should . . . approach for this thing. And remember, the confidential stuff, that's, uh, confidential. For now." People smile up from their desks as he rushes past.

"Hi." I turn to the receptionist. "Where should I set myself up?"

"Oh, I don't do desk assignment. You have to see Joe, he's HR—I mean, People. I'll call him for you."

A few moments later, Joe shuffles out, hands stuffed deeply into the pockets of his sweater vest, a thick binder tucked under one arm. "Hello, again," he says, taking a seat beside me in the highly trafficked path between the staff mailboxes and the restrooms.

"Hello. I'm very excited to meet my desk."

"So you're official?" He cocks his head as he clicks open the binder.

"Aren't I?"

"Well," says Joe, nodding down at the first page illustrating fire-exit routes. "I haven't gotten confirmation on you just yet, although that's not unusual around here. I guess we should probably wait for me to do my spiel." He snaps the binder closed. "I don't want to get my wires crossed with Guy." He lets out a horselike flutter of his lips.

"Will I get a desk?"

"Yes," he laughs. "You remind me of my daughter. Yes, you'll be assigned to a desk cluster for total immersion. And hopefully enrolled in an orientation program I'm trying to restart. Supposed to meet with Guy about it all today, so I'll know more soon. But I can't put you in the computer till we get the go-ahead from him. I'm sorry, you'll have to sit tight."

"Okay," I sigh. "Thanks."

"I'll keep my fingers crossed." Joe looks out toward the windows, and I follow his gaze to the winter clouds tumbling over the Hudson.

"How old is she, your daughter?" I ask as a light patter of snow brushes against the glass.

"Seventeen. Just finished applying to schools."

"Urgh," I say with a shudder. "That's such a hard time."

"The waiting's the worst. Hang in there." He pats my knee paternally before walking back into the sea of desks.

Determined not to leave without written, signed, sealed, notarized confirmation, I pull out my yellow pad and address book to list all the connections I made over my time with Doris. By seven o'clock, I've written down not only the contact information and directors' personal quirks of every women's organization I'm thrilled to pester about something other than a job, but have moved on to writing long, hideously detailed letters to my peeps abroad. I'm completely engrossed in describing the texture of the receptionist's spiky sweater to Kira when a familiar voice asks the receptionist for Guy.

"Is he expecting you?"

"Yes, he is." Seline Saybrook takes one glance in my direction, shakes open her crimson shearling, and strides off across the office, her sleek hair swinging. And I'm up, tailing just a few paces behind her. Pushing Guy's door open, she drapes her coat over his empty chair, revealing yet another impeccably tailored suit.

"Hi," I say from the doorway.

She takes me in. "Hi."

"So you have a meeting with Guy?"

"He's expecting me," she says, rounding the desk to straighten his wall-sized *Metropolis* poster. "Why, do you?"

"I do. I didn't realize he was still interviewing."

"Oh, is he? I didn't know." We're interrupted by a flush as Guy joins us from his private washroom, wiping his hands dry on the front of his trousers. "Hi. Great. Ready to leave?"

"Yes."

"No."

He looks from positive her to negative me. "Seline, I need five. I keep putting off this fucking meeting with Joe. Girl, you all set?" he asks, looking down at the yellow pad in my hands as if it's papyrus with a derisive "Huh."

"I completed the list," I say, reluctant to hand it over for *her* initiative.

"Guy, Bella Russe won't hold our reservation." Seline checks her gold tank watch.

Guy tugs the list from my hands, slinging it onto a stack on his desk. "Oh, well, I have a friend who can get us into Smith and Wollensky later, no worries."

"Okay, then, lovely." She smiles broadly at him before pulling a folder out of her pebbled leather briefcase and sitting on the chaise to work. "Actually, I had sushi for lunch, so that's perfect. Take your time."

"What?" He looks up from his computer screen. "Yeah, great."

"So," I turn my back to Seline and lower my voice. "Joe says he's waiting on my confirmation so I can go ahead and—"

"Shit!" Guy leaps up and jogs out the door. "Shitshitshit." Shitshitshit.

"Hi, it's me. How's the call going?" Seline's voice downshifts into a professional gear as she curls over her cell. "Might as well patch me back in; I've got my notes right here . . ." I listen to Seline listening while I watch the lights come on in the apartments across the river.

"Can I just ask you?" I whisper, as it would seem this is a woman with a job of her own.

Holding a finger to her lips, she presses the receiver against her shoulder.

I click my pen and lean into a blank page of my Filofax. *"Are you still applying for the job?"* I write in large script and hold it up.

She motions for me to hand off the Filofax. She hands it back. *"No."* My whole body relaxes, and I give her a thumbs-up. She motions for the Filofax again, scribbles, and passes it back. *"Are you still interested in him?"*

"NO." She returns my thumbs-up and her shoulders relax. I'm holding, *"Really, never!"* over my head, Norma Rae-style, when

Guy darts back in, Joe's 'People' binder under his arm. I quickly drop the Filofax back in my bag.

"Hello, ladies. Shit—" He juts his head out the glass door. "Stacey, where the fuck is Joe? Don't let him leave—I've got to talk to him *tonight*."

A beleaguered woman, who looks to be maybe ten years older than me, nods from where she's packing up her beaten satchel, her owlish glasses matching her oversized vestments. "I need him in here!" She skitters away across the floor, and he follows with an impatient stride.

Seline flips her phone shut and slides it back into her briefcase to address me. "About five minutes into the interview we realized I wasn't a fit. So he asked me for a drink, and we've been dating ever since." She smiles, slightly smug.

Guy sticks his head in the doorway. "Give me five seconds to do this thing with Joe and we'll be outta here." He cants his head toward me. "Girl, there's a package for you at the desk. Take a look at it and, uh, we'll see you Monday."

YES, YOU WILL.

"*Thank you* for this opportunity, Guy. I'm very excited about creating this . . . with you."

I practically skip to the elevator as I rifle through the envelope. Tax forms and company brochures and contracts. Down in the lobby, I dump the whole stack onto the security desk, shuffling the papers around like a shell game. Finally, tucked a third of the way through, and detained by a paper clip, is my offer letter.

Oh. My. God.

Borrowing Guy's macho swagger, I stride out into the night to throw my proverbial beret in the air and tell New York I've arrived.

CHAPTER SIX

Show Her What She's Won

Monday morning I make my way, in my new Gucci coat, breathlessly purchased secondhand on Prince Street, around the now-familiar but no less dicey walkway to My Company. In the complementing bag jostles an exciting assortment of personal effects to decorate My Desk. The few divas allotted 'space' at the Center considered a yellowed *New Yorker* cartoon and decade-old Saltine box decor. But at MC, Inc., desks are feng-shuied with whimsical eighties action figures, the requisite Simpsons paraphernalia, and eco-challenge vacation snapshots. I've spent the sliver of the weekend not consumed by fruitless apartment hunting rummaging through Jack's artwork and photos of Kira, et al., to create the perfect installation that says, "I'm the colleague you'll want in your wedding party."

"Hi," I introduce myself again to the receptionist. "I'm official now. This is my first day."

"Hi. Girl, right? I'm Jennie—I, E." She extends her hand as the phone rings. "My Company?"

I wait until she's transferred the call. "Jennie, do you know which cluster I've been assigned?"

"Sorry, no, we haven't hired anyone in ages. Ages and ages . . ." She taps her pen on her message pad. "Let me see, Joe should be in any minute. Why don't you take a seat—"

Guy flies out of the kitchen, coffee splashing. "Shit!" He shakes off a scalded finger. "Girl, great, you're here."

"Hi! Good morning, I was just waiting for Joe—"

"Nope, let's not." I scamper after him. "Fuck, I'm getting a blister." He sucks his finger. "I let Joe go on Friday."

"Oh . . . I'm so sorry—"

"Don't be. Had to get your fancy salary from somewhere," he says, grinning. "Besides, that soft stuff was dragging us under. Stacey," he calls while we're still a few empty desks away. "I want Girl right here, in our area. Can you get her set up? And do something about the coffee—it's fucking McDonald's hot."

"I'll call Angel," she says, pushing up the sleeves on her large cardigan. "And I'll call Joe to—"

"Joe's gone," Guy says curtly, grabbing a pile of mail off her desk and leaning it against his chest to flip through. One eyebrow darts up behind Stacey's glasses.

"Would it be better if I was assigned to a cluster?" I ask tentatively, gazing at the honeycomb pattern of desks humming with activity at the front of the office. "So I can have total immersion?"

"Girl, I like the way you think. No, I want you close to me. I want to hear your thoughts before you even have them!" He claps me on the back with the mail. "Okay, Stacey, have I.T. get her hooked up with a computer and phone, ASAP."

Stacey nods, already speaking into her headpiece about setting up filing cabinets and "a gray desk chair, not one of the uncomfortable ones." She reaches a Post-it pad over to me. "Go ahead and write down your info so I can put in an order for business cards."

I savor writing my new title, *Director of Rebranding Knowledge Acquisition*.

If Doris could see me now.

Girl, congratulations on your new job! That is so wonderful! Zeldy and I couldn't be happier for you! Sorry about the time crunch, but the sledge-

hammers are rented for Sunday! Please swing by the party—come as your favorite power tool!

Having frittered away three weeks with delusions of real-estate grandeur, just seventy-two hours remain before my home is returned to its original incarnation as a walk-in closet. And just half my lunch hour remains before my first real meeting with Guy to shake him down for input on this conference I've been planning. Finally resigned that my new salary still won't afford me a Doris Day duplex, I hunch into a dirty phone booth—*got* to get a cell—on the corner of Twenty-third and Eighth to clarify the coordinates of my absolutely positively last-hope apartment listing.

"Hello?" a male voice grunts.

"Hi, can I speak with . . ." I scan to the bottom of my crossed-out list for the landlord's name. "Steve?"

"Yeah."

"Is this Steve?"

"Yeah." I can hear the beer breath.

"Oh, okay, great. I'm trying to see the one-bedroom sublet you listed this morning in *The Voice?*"

"How tall are you?"

"Sorry? The thing is that I think the paper got the address wrong."

"413 West 23rd."

"Okay, gotcha," I say, crossing out 431. "And it's still available?"

"If you want it you better come now."

"Okay."

"Ever done any nude modeling?"

"Um . . ."

"Just come alone."

Hemhawhemhaw. I put the receiver back and strain to see down the street to 413, a former tenement spruced up with flower boxes and a rainbow flag.

I dial my voice mail. "Hi, if I've turned up dead, I was going to see an apartment at 413 West 23rd, 3C, a man named Steve."

I spot a pair of cops emerging from the Krispy Kreme. "Excuse me!" I wave as they blow on their coffee. "Sorry to bother you, but I have to go see an apartment up there." I point to the third floor. "And the man sounded super-sketchy. Is there any way one of you could accompany me? I promise it'll take all of five minutes."

"We're not a babysitting service, sweetheart. If he sounds sketchy, skip it."

"I can't. It'll be really fast. You could even wait down here and just make sure I come back out. Please?"

"Call a friend." They stuff themselves back into their patrol car. I look up at the bank clock: twenty-three minutes till my meeting with Guy. My eyes land on the kiosk across from the phone booth, where a magazine cover tricked out to look like a Monopoly board asks, *"Got game?"*

I dial information and am connected to the closest thing to a rape whistle, working just a few short blocks away.

"YGames. How may I direct your call?"

"Buster, please," I say, my heart revving, as I give him a final opportunity to earn my number.

"I'm sorry, I'm new here. Do you have a last name?"

"No." No, I do not. What I have is one last apartment, a possible grisly death, a very attractive/attracted? boy, with *seemingly* good intentions, albeit questionable friends, and a penchant for fucking up the follow-through. "No, he's in the design department."

"Please hold."

I blow a slow stream of air out my pursed lips as techno music thumps through the line.

"Yeeeeaaallllo?" Unwarranted swoon.

"Hi. Buster?"

"Yep, how can I help you?"

"Hi, it's G—"

"Hi." I hear him whip his feet off his desk. "Hi!"

"Hey, how are you?" I steady my voice.

"Really enjoying the T-shirt."

Warranted chagrin. "Yeah, sorry about that. Listen, I'm sure you're busy, but you're also around the corner and I'm kind of in a bind."

"Yes?"

Is this a dating thing or a sex thing and if it's a sex thing, do we get equal booty call rights or am I signing on as your beck-and-call girl?

"G?"

"Right, so I'm being evicted, and I *have* to move this Saturday, and I finally found an apartment, but the thing is the landlord sounds like a perv. Only everything else I've seen is either already taken, or uninhabitable, or both. But I also don't want to end up in a snuff film and I have to be back at the office by two, but he said—"

"Okay, okay, I'm grabbing my coat. I'd been envisioning Antigua at sunset, but looking at a perv's apartment's good, too. What's the address?"

I hang up, giddy.

Minutes later, I'm warmed by the sight of Buster jogging down the avenue. "Thank you so much!" I call as he slows, his face flushed from running in the cold.

"Not a problem." He kisses my cheek, his lips lingering a moment against my skin. "I'm glad you called."

"Oh good, I'm glad you're glad."

He laughs. "Good. Well, that's cleared up."

Fighting the impulse to throw down in front of Krispy Kreme, I pull myself away to press the buzzer. The door clicks open into an old tile hallway that's been aggressively polished by an optimistic soul. Upstairs, Landlord Steve, a portly man in a stained tank top, awaits us, his face falling when he sees Buster.

"My husband," I announce.

"Whatever," he grunts. He gestures a hairy arm into the apartment, and I wriggle past, drawn like a lemming by the bales of sunshine. Buster stands guard in the living room while I swing through. There's a real galley kitchen, a roach-free bathroom, and a separate bedroom—with a video camera on a tripod facing a naked mattress.

"So?" Steve looks me up and down as I slump deeper into my coat. "You like toys?"

"No."

"I'll give you my number. You should call me. I'm subletting to raise some capital for a new Vivid Video series."

"*Honey!* Come take a look at the kitchen," says Buster, pulling me in while Steve stays back to dial my bank. Buster holds a cupboard open and gestures to sugar, nondairy creamer, and a crate of lube. "Think that comes with the apartment?" he asks, our faces close.

Steve sticks his head around the fridge, his smoker's wheeze audible. "Check's good. Rent starts Monday."

"I'm changing the locks."

"Whatever."

One last search for duct-taped women and we're back on the street. "Again, thank you so much."

Buster beams. "My pleasure. Hope I haven't thwarted your E! True Hollywood Story."

"It'll always be my road not taken," I shrug.

He glances back up the avenue. "So, you'll be right around the corner. There's a great wine bar where we go after work—"

"I'd love to—" I catch sight of the bank clock. "Shit, I have about two minutes to get back for a meeting with my boss." I throw my hand out for a cab.

"You got a job? So much happens when you don't keep in

touch." He pulls off his hat, leaving his hair rumpled like a kid just up from a nap.

"Yeah, I'm the new Director of Rebranding Knowledge Acquisition at My Company, Inc." I reach up to smooth his bangs. "You know, you're funny when you're not surrounded by sex and violence."

"Ah, sex and violence." Buster sighs nostalgically. "Just wait till you see what I'm building up to on our third date."

"Pestilence?"

"Listen, seriously, if you need help moving, my roommates and I can totally give you a hand," he says, pulling his hat back on.

"Really? That would be great." I wave my arm afresh at the oncoming traffic. "Wait. The ones I met at the game?"

"Yeah. They can be assholes sometimes, but they're good guys."

"Good, because I'm out of T-shirts."

"Gotcha. And I meant what I said the other night, about wanting to get to know you." A cab pulls up, Buster opens the door, and I step between him and the car, feeling the charge of his proximity. "I mean, I still don't have your number. But I understand. Just 'cause you're willing to give a porn king your social security, I shouldn't expect . . ."

"It's yours." I scramble for a temporary business card, surrendering to the current.

Emulating Guy's breakneck pace, I fly through the busy office, swipe my conference binder from my desk, and dash into his unlit den, slip-sliding to a flailing halt when I realize the floor is covered in a carefully laid-out grid of labeled manila folders. "Girl, urgh." Stacey winces from where she kneels on the other side next to a box filled with loose papers.

"Sorry," I cringe, stepping off the manila that banana-peeled me. "Where's Guy?"

"He's gone." She tiptoes between the folders to straighten the mess I've made.

"I missed him?" I cry, as she tugs papers out from under my forgotten heel.

"You didn't miss him." She pushes an errant chunk of hair out of her face. "He left right after you. Last-minute off-site."

"You're kidding. I really need at least *one* meeting before Friday to make sure I'm on the right track with this conference. Can't you see if there's anywhere at all to fit me in?"

I follow as she grudgingly returns to her desk to scan his schedule. "Not going to happen."

"Nothing?" My heart sinks. "Really? Not even ten minutes when I could brief him?" She shakes her head. "I mean it just seems a little crazy. I haven't really proven myself yet. What if my idea of a conference is getting everyone on the floor to play Jell-O Twister?"

Stacey rolls her cramping neck. "You can always try to catch him . . ." I follow her gaze back to his crowded floor. "I don't know. Maybe he just trusts you, okay?" She sighs again. Trying on the idea of being trusted, I chew the end of my baby pencil, courtesy of the Department of Unemployment. Stacey grimaces at it. "And by the way, the supply closet is the door past the ladies' room."

"Oh, thanks. Where do I get the key and who should I sign stuff out with?"

She looks back from his doorway as if I've asked for permission to pee. "Just help yourself."

"Oh, okay. Great." I watch as she steps wearily back inside. "Hey, Stacey?" I call. "I'm sorry about messing up your files. How about getting a drink tonight? Bella Russe has some fun wine specials."

"I don't drink."

My cheeks reddening, I back down the aisle. "Okay, well, maybe another night—for coffee!"

With one less wedding party to be in and an entire confer-ence riding on my sole judgment, I open the unlocked door into a supply *room*. There are shelves and shelves *and shelves* of Post-its, a wall of envelopes, and pens in every color and width, as if Tutankhamen was prepared for burial by Staples. Okay, I'm in a real office with real supplies and soon to be in a real apart-ment—and Guy trusts me.

I begin systematically to extract all the red folders, a color Doris deemed strident, embracing the control I've been given to design a conference I, to date, would only have been allowed to make copies for.

On the morning of the big day, I lean in toward the Marriott ladies' room mirror to pat concealer into the dark circles under my eyes. Stepping back, I give my new actually-lined, Seline Saybrook–inspired suit the once-over, Stacey pops her head in, glasses sliding down her nose. "People are arriving, and I have to get back to the office," she says. "Need anything else?"

"I'm all set, thanks." I follow her out into the garish faux-imperial decor of the hotel's meeting-room floor. My stomach jumps with anticipation as I see the arriving crowds. "Thank you *so* much for everything, Stacey. And have a great weekend."

She pulls on her quilted coat and tugs her eternally laden satchel onto her shoulder. "Sure," she mutters, rooting for her ringing cell.

"Seriously." I touch her arm, my eyes moist as I recall myself juggling a hundred thankless tasks for Doris. "I can't tell you what it's meant to have had your help. I've always been the one running around for everyone else, and the fact that you made time to support this conference, while balancing everything you already do for Guy just, really . . . means so much to me."

She nods distractedly while glancing at the number blinking on the back of her phone. "He must just be leaving the investor meeting now."

I check the time. "You're kidding. He's on in ten minutes."

She snaps the cell open to answer it as she races for the elevators.

"Okay, well, thanks again!" With another glance at my watch and a prayer for Guy's alacrity, I turn back to begin the day.

The entirely female crowd arrives in small sackcloth clumps, most in their mid-to-late fifties and all tilting beneath equally aged canvas totes proclaiming their allegiances to literate wildlife facing extinction on public broadcasting. Stationing myself under a large MC, Inc. banner, I direct each attendee to the buffet for coffee and pastries.

"Sorry." Stacey returns red-faced and out of breath. "I forgot to give you these—Guy wants everyone who attends to fill one out." She pulls a stack of questionnaires from her bag. "Bye."

I glance down the first page, my eyeballs slowly emerging from their sockets.

1. When it comes to undergarments, what kind of woman do you consider yourself?
   a) Victoria's Secret
   b) Frederick's of Hollywood
   c) Hanro
   d) Maidenform
   e) La Perla

2. Of the following companies, which one have you purchased from in the last six months?
   a) Victoria's Secret
   b) Frederick's of Hollywood
   c) Hanro
   d) Maidenform
   e) La Perla

3. Your lingerie makes you—

"Is Doris Weintruck here yet?"

"No," I say, looking up from the questionnaire I'd rather eat than hand out. "She's not coming."

"Yes, she is," the woman asserts, blinking at me from beneath her oversized Gorton's fisherman hat.

"No, she isn't." Not invited, not coming. "I'm sorry. Perhaps there's something I can help you—"

"Yes, she is. I spoke to her this morning." She plucks her hat off. "A conference is just stale bagels in a ballroom without Doris."

"My bagels are fresh," is all I'm able to manage before walking directly back into the ladies' room and locking myself inside the handicapped stall. I don't need this job. I'll collect cans, move back to Waterbury, join a cult. Anything is better than watching Doris tell Guy I'm a neurotic, immature codependent with a space problem.

No. You know what? Fuck her. Fuck her and the horse she rode in on. She's not running this show. I am. I'm running this show. She's just a guest. An uninvited guest, at that.

I emerge just as Guy comes striding down the hall, loosening his blue tie and ranting into his cell. And I love him . . . the ranting, the adjusting himself, the swearing, the clean masculine self-absorption of it all. I point at my watch and then into the conference room. He nods and waves me off. I hold up the forms and shrug questioningly. He turns his back on me. Yup, love him.

Unable to wait any longer, I take the lectern to introduce myself, the women pausing momentarily from schmearing their fresh bagels. ". . . And as Director of Rebranding Knowledge Acquisition for My Company, it's a great pleasure to welcome you today to this gathering—"

"Christ!" We all hear Guy from just outside the French doors.

"Between meeting your program goals and procuring the funding to pay for next year, you're all working, well, endlessly. You are busy. Too busy—"

"Rex could give two shits!"

"It's rare to have an opportunity to pause," I modulate louder over Guy's ranting. "Come together, and pool what we're learning about the needs of those we're working so relentlessly to support."

"Don't blow hot air up my asshole!" Guy's hand pushes the French door open, his voice hammering obscenities into the room, and Doris enters, waving and mouthing "Hello" to those seated nearby. "Sorry to disturb. Please, don't stop on my account!" My face beats as the room fluffs up and I'm unable to deny the stamp of legitimacy her attendance carries. She takes a seat by the exit, all the while staring me down, her gaze sending a familiar message: *idiot.* My eyes dart around for a safer place to land, and I find myself speaking to a striking fifty-something woman in a pale gray suit, who, uninterested in Doris's arrival, smiles encouragingly at me.

"With an eye toward a joint future, My Company is looking forward to providing you with a structured day in which to share your successes, findings, and organizational strategies. A day that will hopefully provide the foundation of a lasting, mutually beneficial relationship. We are confident that you will leave today secure in the knowledge that My Company is here as a resource for you and your sister organizations." Spread the word, ladies. "Now I'd like to introduce you to the Chief Executive Officer of My Company." I look to where Guy's Rolexed wrist still grips the open door. The women all follow my gaze, except Doris, who's fixed on me like a sniper rifle.

"No . . . I don't give a *shit* . . . No, I've been running numbers all week and I'm telling you *for the last time* to stop sending flowers and candy to the *fucking* fashion magazines. We've got to *cut them loose.* Focus every resource on this new account—"

"Guy," I say, my mouth closer to the mike, feedback piercing the room. A satisfied smirk creeps across Doris's face. OhdearGod, get your ass in here. "Guy!" I aim for perky. "You're up!"

"Right!" Trench slung over his arm, he strides to the podium, waving at the unimpressed room like a young Kennedy. Tossing me his coat, he pulls the microphone from its holder. "Women, thank you for coming." He slides an empty chair out from a nearby table and props a foot on the seat, leaning his elbow down onto his raised knee. "It's such a *thrill* for me to be here for this moment when My Company can begin to give back to those who matter most." Taking his time, he shares an impassioned story about his first gender studies class at UC Santa Cruz and how it awoke him to the struggles women face. Struggles he had long taken for granted as a 'privileged male.' "It's an incredible feeling, almost fifteen years later, to be able to devote my professional life to doing something about this unjust inequity."

He seems about to tear up; I glance around and am surprised by the sea of maternal smiles, with the exception of the woman in the pale gray suit, whose eyebrows are knit. Guy clears his throat and stands fully upright, gripping the mike with both hands like a choirboy. "I'm enormously proud of many things in my young life, but this moment in which My Company has achieved such success that it's able to give back to its oppressed clientele—this has to be close to the top. For three years now, MC, Inc. has helped women get their beauty and health questions answered. But *you* help women access information even more tantamount to their survival—" He surreptitiously glances down at the front page of the conference folder on the lectern. "Info on . . . housing and, uh . . . childcare, and," he stammers, "legal and . . . and civil support." He looks back to them. "The time is now. Let's stay connected!" Everyone claps. "And I want to thank Girl here for the incredible work she's done in preparing this great event." Doris rolls her eyes, but she can't quell the buzz of pride at my first public acknowledgment since they called my name at graduation. The applause dies down as the women turn to speak amongst themselves.

"Thank you," I say to Guy as he steps back from the podium.

"Have to run. Great. Fantastic work." He exchanges the mike for his coat.

I turn it off. "Can I just ask you about these questionnaires?"

"I need them."

"Okay, sure. They just seem a little off-point—"

"Girl." A cloud of annoyance passes over his face. "If I ask you to get 'em filled—get 'em filled."

"Of course." My heart speeds from his reproach, and I cast my gaze to the mike while I steady myself. "Guy, I know we haven't really had time to review our objectives for this conference, but I've structured the day so these women are going to leave speaking positively about My Company; an organization they otherwise wouldn't have known has a vested interest in their issues. It's just," no way in hell am I asking them about their underwear, "that I'd hate to have the group get off track."

"Uh-huh, uh-huh, I hear you." He nods at his watch before looking back to my face, which is fighting consternation. "Girl." He pats my shoulders. "You *single-handedly* threw this whole thing together—these forms are a cakewalk! A cakewalk!" He flips his phone open and jogs out of the room.

Inhaling the evaporating confidence fumes left in his wake, I flip the mike back on. "Okay, so today we'll be working in four groups . . ."

The morning session, devoted to current research and future goals, flies by.

After lunch, during which Doris and I avoid each other, I turn their attention to a session of obstacles and suggested solutions. Group One's obstacle sparks a lively discussion about a certain city councilman and guerilla tactics for fiscal triumph. Group Two focuses on union relations and is offering imaginative strategies when a pruney child-sized hand shoots up. "Parking permits," Doris interjects, apropos of nothing. "I don't think we've addressed that issue yet, Girl."

The room curdles with tension.

"Thank you!" I say. "I think we're trying to stay with the macro, but great work, Group Two! Which group would like to go next?" I glance hopefully at my silent audience, sitting stone-faced amid layers of marked-up poster paper. "Okay, I'll pick somebody! How about Group Four? What's your obstacle?"

"Since you brought it up, Doris, I'm just going to say how I feel." Group Four's elected speaker, Maxine, stands with her hands clenched in tight fists, her yin-yang earrings swaying menacingly below her small face. "When *some people* clamor for parking permits, and then *get* them, *they* should be prepared to give up a few of their *other* city perks to *those* of us who might really need them. Instead, *some people* use those parking permits to take staff to a certain *social activity* on Staten Island—"

"Those parking permits are *sanctioned* for social activities!" Another woman pops up like a demented prairie dog. "I suppose you prefer we twiddle our thumbs on the ferry!"

"I don't give a fig where you're twiddling your thumbs! *We're* not having parties on Staten Island or Roosevelt Island or any other island because *we're working!*" Maxine shouts, the room congealing into divisive resentment.

"Oh-kay, we're getting a little off track," I intercede shakily.

Prairie Dog is red-faced with rage. "That space was donated!"

I yell to be heard over the rumble of erupting hostility, "*I think we're losing sight of the incredible work you all do just to keep women, um, alive*—"

A third woman jumps to her feet beside Prairie Dog, spittle spraying from her mouth. "If SOME people would be more proactive in their fiscal planning, they wouldn't have to ask OTHER people for their parking permits when those

OTHER people have to go all the way to Staten Island on a *Tuesday night* when it's *below* freezing and those people still have to get *their* children from daycare in *Queens* and those people would begrudge me *A SINGLE GODDAMN PARKING PERMIT!!!*"

It's a face-off, the women eyeing each other, panting like patients in a psych ward. The room pulses with misplaced emotion as those still seated rock slightly in their chairs, frozen in collective trauma. "*I . . . Hate . . . You,*" Maxine hisses through clenched teeth.

Doris pulls her worn NARAL tote onto her shoulder, salutes me triumphantly, and slips out unwitnessed.

"If I could borrow your attention!" The woman in the pale gray suit steps to the center, making sweeping eye contact as she speaks. "For those of you who don't know me, I'm Julia Gilman of the Magdalene Agency, and the remaining time spent together will determine whether this day you've all taken from your programs was a productive one or a complete waste of time that none of us has to spare." Julia clasps her hands at her slender waist and smiles calmly. "If I may?"

I nod as those standing reseat themselves to look on with curiosity. Julia walks gracefully through the chairs to the front of the room, grabs a Sharpie, and scrawls on a fresh piece of poster board, "*In the next three years, we would like to unite with My Company to bring information on _____ to our target population.*" There's a grudging silence. She turns to me. "Is this all right?"

"Of course!" She steps back, allowing me to once more hold the floor. I take a breath. "So, let's each spend the next eight minutes generating as many ideas as we can. Go!" Ohpleaseohpleaseohplease. To my amazement, the rage dribbles away as the women drop their heads and begin to scribble as instructed. Within a few moments, everyone is fully absorbed in the task.

• • •

Having survived the long day, I slide towering boxes of materials back onto my desk, rolls of poster papers tumbling onto the floor with fifty unanswered lingerie questionnaires. In the soporific darkness, illuminated only by the red glow of the peripheral exit signs and a dim light spilling through Guy's glass walls, I step out of my heels and pull a Post-it off my monitor. "Bring me the forms."

Shit.

I look up at the large Nelson ball clock. Eight-thirty-three. I've *got* to get home; the move begins tomorrow at the ass crack of dawn and not a single thing is packed. Not a single solitary thing. Before Guy can spot me, I duck, grab my shoes and materials, and sneak through the maze of desk clusters to the ladies' room, my time-honored clandestine workspace. Only now I get to flick on a row of recessed halogen lights, drop my boxes on an immaculate sea-glass floor, and spread out my workstation beneath a row of polished stainless-steel sinks. Rummaging through the boxes for as many different kinds of pens as I can find, here goes . . .

4. What item do you buy most frequently?
   a) panties
   b) bras
   c) nighties
   d) tedd—

The door to the men's room opens on the other side of the wall. I freeze.

"They finally sent over the Valentine's sales numbers." I hear Guy, only slightly muffled by the thin plasterboard. "Through the roof across Europe. Some charity tie-in with thongs and deforestation." I hear spurts of urine.

"When'll Girl be back with the data?" Rex asks.

"What time is it?"

"About eight-thirty, and I need to get up to The Bank tonight—the board wants me to squelch some asinine harassment brouhaha before it blows up."

"Yeah, she should be back."

"BEEPBEEPBEEPBEEP!" Aaaaaahhhh! I throw myself over the box to muffle the shrill ring of a cell phone. "Beepbeepbeepbeepbeep."

"What the fuck is that?"

In stealth Cold War mode, I flick off the bathroom light with my foot. The door swings open just as I stuff both hands through the mass of papers, clamping my palm over the phone, and flatten myself against the wall. "Beepbeepbeepbeepbeep."

"Nah, there's nobody in there," Guy shouts from the hallway as the door swings shut. "Someone must've left her cell."

"Let's wrap this up. I promised Ashley we'd get to Greenwich before midnight," Rex says.

"Beepbeepbeepbeepbeep."

"Hello?" I whisper into the phone as I hear their retreating footsteps.

"Hello?" an older woman's voice speaks. "Is this the Marriott?"

"No, hi, I organized the conference."

"Oh, Girl, hello, this is Julia Gilman. I . . . addressed the melee over the little parking dispute—"

"Oh my gosh, hi. Hi! Thank you so much for this afternoon. I was about thirty seconds from committing hara-kiri with a scented marker."

"You handled it fine. You're whispering. Am I interrupting you?"

"No, I'm just—" I dare to return my voice to normal. "I was really impressed by your intervention."

"Well, I was happy to help—they're a rather contentious

crowd, aren't they? I'm sorry to bother you, but I just realized my cell phone was missing. It must've gotten mixed in with the materials I returned."

"I'll messenger it to you."

"Thank you, but I'm at INS, well the USCIS, but no one can get used to calling it that."

"Is everything okay?"

"Better than okay. They're *finally* being released. Of course, we've waited months, and then, with no warning, they just shunt twenty women out into the cold."

"Sorry?"

"The brothel in New Jersey that was raided last fall—you probably read about it—it ended up being part of a huge white slavery ring?"

"Yes, that sounded horrific." My addled brain reruns the afternoon. "Sorry, you said you're with Magdalene."

"I *am* Magdalene. This has been my first call to arms."

"Well, I can come to INS or the US . . . C—"

"No, no, I'm in Jersey now. I don't think I'll be back until Sunday." Her voice has an exhausted scratch to it. "At the earliest."

"Well, just call when you get back. I'd be happy to drop it by your apartment. I owe you that much."

"That'd be a real help, actually. I more than have my hands full. Thank you." Julia gives me her address and I hang up, scooting the forms over to where a thin beam of light is shining from under the door. Not letting myself take a breath, I dive back in.

abceaaebcd, acdebbebda, cedbeeadbe, deabbdceba, acdaebdabe, abcadabcad, abceaaebcd, acdebbebda, cedbeeadbe, deabbdceba, acdaebdabe, abcadabcad, abceaaebcd, acdebbebda, cedbeeadbe, deabbdceba, acdaebdabe, abcadabcad, abceaaebcd, acdebbebda, cedbeeadbe, deabbdceba, acdaebdabe, abcadabcad . . .

"Guy?" I step into the darkened room around a large rolling whiteboard, surprised by the late-night circle of accounting staff encamped at his desk, which is paved with take-out containers and glowing laptops.

"Yeah, Girl, over here." Guy's head lifts off the back of the Eames chair where he's slouched in the shadowed corner.

"Sorry." I turn. "I didn't mean to interrupt you. I just wanted to give you the forms—"

Rex's deep voice reaches me from where he's sprawled on the chaise nearby, stirring a nine iron in slow circles on the carpet. "Come here, Girl. We were just discussing women." But neither motions for me to sit, and I end up hovering awkwardly above their lounging figures as if about to slink into a lap dance.

"Folks?" Guy speaks to the ceiling, "Can you give us a minute here?" The men wearily pull themselves to standing, arch their backs like baseball players, and groggily shuffle out. "Oh, and turn the whiteboard, will ya?" One of the accountants reaches out as he passes, swinging it to the wall before I can catch the headings.

"So, here are the surveys." I pass them to Guy, praying I've made enough distinction in my fraudulent circles.

"Great." He hands the stack off to Rex, who begins to flip through.

"Sorry to be back so late. The conference was a great success. We hit a bit of a rough patch, but by the day's end I really feel we've secured a good place in their pantheon—"

"Cool, yeah." Guy waves his hand to the side. "We have a few things we want to discuss." He slouches farther, his chin hitting his chest. "We think what'd be great is if you hunker down and create a comprehensive pitch for this initiative."

Right . . . "Okay, just to be clear, when you say 'this initiative,' you're referring to attracting *Ms. Magazine.* When you say 'pitch,' you mean something similar to a grant proposal—"

"Oh, Christ. Haven't you talked to her about this, Guy?"

"Of course, Rex. We've covered this a number of times, right, Girl? A pitch! A pitch! A pitch for . . . a hypothetical target." Guy leans forward, resting his elbows on his knees.

"I guess—" His gaze tells me this is the only answer. "Like *Ms.*?"

"Yes, Girl, exactly," Rex says. "*Ms.* Write it for Steinem."

"Exciting stuff, huh?" Guy taps my calf with his outstretched loafer. "So we have a meeting with the board, and I'm gonna run your pitch by them first—you know, show them what you're up to. So if you could bring it to us Monday morning—anytime before 7:30 should work. Really talk up our history of feminist commitment. Great." He slumps back into his chair. Rex continues to draw silent circles with his golf club.

"I might need a little . . . background." As I have yet to meet with you or anyone else and, as far as I can tell, I *am* the feminist commitment.

"I can give you fifteen at, umm." Guy rubs his forehead. "Just give me a call on my cell tomorrow morning. Before eleven."

No problem, I can move all of my worldly possessions across the island of Manhattan while writing an initiativepitchwhatever for Gloria Steinem, as long as you give me fifteen minutes on your cell phone. That's like fourteen more than you've given me in the last three weeks, so I'm golden.

"We cool?" Guy looks up at me, and I can barely make out his eyes in the shadows.

I smile confidently in case he can see mine. "Cool."

Early the next morning, I stand on the interminable line at U-Haul, excruciatingly sleep deprived and caffeine-jangled. I just have to get all my stuff into the new apartment, grab a quick nap for an hour or two, and then pull a *pitch!* out of my ass in forty-eight hours. No problem.

"Next!" the man behind the glassed-in counter calls.

I scurry up with my ID and confirmation number. "Hi, Ireservedacargovan."

He glances at my info and snorts, punching leisurely at his keyboard, then speaks into the screen. "Nope." He blows his cheeks out slowly. "You'll have to come back Monday."

"What? What do you mean? I have a confirmation number—"

"We can't make people bring the vans back on time. Yours not back yet."

I flash to my van waking up in Vegas with a hangover. "Then I'll take a different one." I point behind me at the lot packed with vans just outside the window.

"Reserved. Can give you something bigger, but I'd have to charge you more."

"No way. That's ridiculous. I reserved a cargo van, and if you have to upgrade me—"

"Hold on, hold on. Lemme talk to my supervisor." He heaves himself up and strolls leisurely past the other teller windows. Buster and Co. will be standing on my stoop in exactly half an hour. *Pitchpitchpitchpitchpitchpitch*. I start to shred the corners of my confirmation sheet into tiny slivers.

"But I reserved!" A man in a leather bomber jacket at the next window throws a fit about his own renegade van.

"Of course, sir," the woman behind the desk acquiesces warmly. "We'll just upgrade you at no additional cost and give you an extra day free."

"My boss says we can split the difference." My service man shuffles back, gut first.

"What? Why's he getting an upgrade and an extra day *free?*" I point at the man getting the red-carpet treatment.

"No idea. Not my customer. Help you, sir?" he leans sideways to address the person waiting behind me. I square my shoulders, plant my Pumas, and stare at him through the thick plastic with a force that should make his last hairs fall out.

"Look, baby, make up your mind. I got a line behind you."

"Fine!" Beaten, I toss over my credit card and tap my sneaker on the floor while he processes it as s-l-o-w-l-y as humanly possible.

"Okay, that there's Jesus," he says, indicating a young boy who's leaning near the door, one Timberland against the wall. "He'll take you to your vehicle. Now don't be too long, Jesus." He winks. "I know she's a cute one."

Jesus leads me out into the vast parking lot, where the sun has risen to a blindingly crisp New York winter's day. I follow him to the far end, where he stops in front of a humongous truck and reaches out to offer me the keys.

"I'm sorry, I think there's a mistake. This isn't mine."

He smiles and tries again to hand the keys over. "No." I shake my head and point at the truck. "No. Too big." I extend my arms, shaking my head more vigorously to indicate danger. He points at the number on the keys and the corresponding digits painted on the truck. "Something this size should come with a crew to swab the decks and a lookout for whales! I can't drive this!" Jesus stares at me blankly. I give up, take his hand, and tug him back to the overheated office, where I'm made to wait in line a second time.

"Only size we got left." My service man shrugs. "What's a matter, don't like 'em big?"

I throw up my hands, and we run back out to the behemoth. Scrambling into the cab, I look down at Jesus, who has shrunk to ant-sized proportions, and give him a totally unwarranted thumbs-up. I maneuver gingerly out of the lot, trying to get a feel for the size of my automotive ass, and inch downtown, taking only wide streets in deserted neighborhoods. I alternately pray for Buster and his roommates to still be there, for them to have remembered to show up in the first place, and for all dogs, children, and elderly to stay inside. Finally, I touch down on Avenue B and double-park, over an hour behind schedule but blessedly accident-free.

I'm thrilled to spot Buster sitting on the front stoop behind the *Post*.

"Holy shit! What is that thing?" Buster calls, as he tosses the paper into the trash and jogs up to greet me.

"It's all I could get," I say, failing a graceful exit from the cab. He grips me firmly by the waist and helps me gently to the curb.

"How much stuff do you *have?*" His hands linger on my hips.

"About a Pinto's worth. But it was this or nothing." I step reluctantly back from his grasp to open the door to the building. "Where're the troops?"

"Oh, yeah. I may have, uh, overestimated their enthusiasm. But they said they'd meet us at the new place later and give a hand."

"Thank you so much for agreeing to do this. It shouldn't take very long." I lead the way up the stairs.

"How many years you been here?"

"Almost three. My friends moved me in the week after graduation." I unlock the door, remembering the hours it took and how afterwards we went to neighborhood bars to pick up unsuitable men.

"And where are these friends today?" he asks, surveying the many boxes.

"Abroad till June. I missed the boat. Everyone else figured out that with the job market apocalyptic this was the perfect time for grants and homework. We can start over here." I point to a large crate. "Let's get the books out of the way first."

"Yeah, it's a good time not to be doing the work thing." He crouches down, and I'm met with a flash of abs. We lift the box and trudge out to the stairs together. "How's the new job going?"

"Oh, ten times better than what I left. I have a ton of independence. And they have a digital copy machine with *eighteen* settings—" The full weight of the books pushes me against the flimsy railing.

"Here, let me go backwards," he says, and we do a slow dance to exchange positions. "Well, I'm glad you missed the boat."

"Hope you still feel that way when the truck's loaded," I say, the weight of the box shifting away from me.

It is a shockingly massive effort to remove all evidence of myself from one very tiny closet. We chit-chat at first, discovering a shared penchant for fried oysters, kickboxing, and Eddie Izzard, falling into the rhythm of a team so quickly that I get flashes of us moving our daughter into her dorm someday and sharing a private giggle over this memory. But as each five-flight trek makes only barely visible dents in the piles, we shift into silent just-get-through-it mode, jogging sweatily past each other on the stairwell with grunts of greeting.

"Only . . . four . . . more," I wheeze, meaning piles.

"Uh-huh." Buster powers on.

Eventually, I find myself leaning against the water stain I hid with the Audrey Hepburn poster Kira gave me as a housewarming gift, ready to bid farewell to the cracked plaster motif of my early twenties. *Pitchpitchpitchpitchpitchpitch.*

HOOONK-HOOONK! "Toss me the keys!" Buster yells up.

Happy to be relieved of steering the Death Star, I flout U-Haul regulations and exchange the keys for Buster's cell. "Hi, you've reached Guy. Leave a message, and I'll call you back at *my* earliest convenience."

"Hi, Guy." I pull on my seatbelt. "It's Saturday morning and I'm just calling, as we discussed, to talk with you about the pitch. Of course, I'll sell our *new* initiative, but that's fairly recent, so it would be really helpful to get more background on MC's feminist history from you or someone else on staff. I know you said it's confidential, but I think the strongest weapon in our arsenal is MC's plan to consult feminist-oriented companies. So, should I include this? I think *Ms.* might need additional incentive. I just moved, so you can reach me at my new number." I leave it for him, praying that when I plug my phone in I'll hear a dial tone. I hand Buster back his cell as he climbs up. "Still like me?"

"You have an insane amount of books. Insane." He arches an eyebrow and grins as we bounce onto Houston.

"Well, *I* like *you* more."

"Should have moved you sooner."

"As opposed to all the wining and dining?" I smile.

"I *asked* for your number."

"Duly noted. Hey, have you ever written a pitch?"

"Not really. But Luke worked for Ogilvy and Mather a while back. You should ask him when he shows up."

"I'm supposed to be pitching MC's feminist interest, which right now is one paragraph with my passport photo paper-clipped at the top."

He leans across me to check my side rearview mirror as we change lanes. "Feminist, huh?"

I tense. "Yup. Ever seen one in her natural habitat?"

He taps the steering wheel, both of us reverberating with the revving motor beneath us. "Without the protective glass?"

"Uh-huh."

He nods and leans over to turn on the radio, Dave Matthews filling the cab. I sink back into the seat as Buster slides his hand behind my neck and rests it there. I turn my head, nestling my cheek against his palm, and he gives my shoulder a little squeeze before returning both hands to the wheel.

When we pull up in front of my new building, I dart across the street to pick up breakfast for Buster's roommates, who, while not exactly brimming with enthusiasm, make short, testosterone-fueled shrift of my belongings. I try Guy again from the Krispy Kreme pay phone—*got* to get a cell—but he doesn't answer.

Upstairs, balancing four pastry boxes and seven steaming coffees, I'm delighted to find Tim and Trevor maneuvering my futon frame into the living room. Luke, who I recognize from the ice, is lugging a carton with my posters into the hallway. The crew nods hello, wiping their barely damp brows.

"Wow, you're like an assembly line!" I say, as I set breakfast down on a pile of boxes. "Please, everyone, help yourselves."

"Damn, you got a lotta naked chicks here." Luke, rifling my art posters with the same hostility he sliced the rink, holds up an International Center of Photography print for his friends to see, while Trevor lifts a lace thong out of the carton marked UNDERWEAR.

"That's a Man Ray." I tug the lace out of Trevor's hands. "Why don't you all have a doughnut while they're still hot?"

Buster emerges from the hallway and slides the last box onto a stack. "How about we help you unpack?" he asks, unaware that his friends have already begun.

"No. Thanks. But, please, help yourselves to some breakfast."

Buster joins us in the crowded living room, putting his arm around me as he reaches for coffee. "Isn't this place awesome?"

"Yeah. Not bad for a porn set," Luke smirks. "So they had the camera, what, like, there?" He points toward my bedroom. "Dude, we've got a pick-up game at one."

"Girl, this is Luke, our hockey champ."

"Yes, hi, we've met."

"Girl was wondering if she could tap your advertising acumen." Buster slides his hand around to my waist.

"Oh no, it's okay—"

"No, ask him. He's a genius."

"It's nothing. I'm just working on a pitch—"

"I'm sure you've pitched before." Luke eyes the Man Ray. "Busted, dude, let's go."

"Actually, I'm gonna hang here and help Girl get set up." Buster helps himself to a glazed.

"Whatever." Luke pulls on his leather bomber.

"I'll get the court next weekend."

"I said *whatever,* man—" Luke catches himself. "Okay, later." He wipes his face with a napkin, balling it up and lobbing it across the room onto the floor. The kids look from one parent to the other before shuffling out with sheepish smiles, Tim tripping Trevor to break the tension.

"Thank you so much! Please, please take the doughnuts!" Following them to the door, I angle myself from Luke's sightline as they pack onto the elevator. "Bye!" I lock the door and lean against it, turning back to Buster. "Okay, Luke's gunnin' for a T-shirt."

"Yeah, he's a little pissed about the game." Buster flexes the brim of his cap.

Forcing a shrug, I say, "I'm really fine here. Do you want to go?"

"No, I really don't."

"Good." My tuckered legs finally giving out, I slide to the floor.

Buster takes a doughnut from the box, wraps it in a napkin, and offers it to me. I bite it, reaching up to hold his other hand. We share the doughnut until it's gone, and then he traces my cheek with his finger, leaning his face down until his mouth is pressing mine. His lips are soft, and he tastes like honey glaze. He leans back, pulling me on top of his strong frame. He smells good feels good tastes good. "Let's unroll the futon," he murmurs into my ear, his hands under my shirt, our mouths connecting effortlessly.

"Okay," I murmur in return. He hops up and swiftly lifts me to standing, leaving me momentarily lightheaded. "I think it's in the bedroom." I slide my shirt back down.

He darts around the boxes, and I hear a loud thump. "Shit. Can you give me a hand?"

"Coming!" I wipe my hands off on my jeans as I weave around the boxes to find Buster tugging at the twine securing the heavy cotton roll.

"Maybe you could get some scissors?"

"Sure." I push aside a few cartons, awkwardness descending. Dust bunnies in his hair, he struggles to free the futon from its string confines. "Hey, I, uh, know you're pretty packed up here," he grunts, "but do you, uh, have anything?"

"Sure." I turn automatically to the piles to look for . . . ? Suddenly everything is happening in real time, bright Saturday afternoon Technicolor, soot particles suspended in the rays between us. "Buster?" I cross back with neither scissors nor protection to find him gnawing on the twine. "It's just, I've been awake for three days and I'm on this work deadline, and I still don't even really—"

"Know me from Adam."

"Yeah."

He lets the futon slide back to the floor in a swift hiss, his face falling with it. "I wore my lucky stuff and everything." He lifts his sweater to reveal a taut Vagisil splayed across his chest just as his phone breaks out into an electronic jingle.

"That's so sexy I can't see straight." I grin and sally over to him. He shoves his hand into his pocket to pull his cell out. " 'Sup? . . . Dude, I *am not* being lame." He pats my head like a puppy and walks into the kitchen. "What're you talking about? You met her for five minutes." He lowers his voice and I strain to listen. He laughs. "She's not a dyke . . . No, man. Look . . . I know you reserved the court." He sighs. "Fine. No, let's play. Yeah, I'll see you downstairs. Later." He slaps his phone shut. "I have to go."

"Oh-kay." Because I'm not ripping my dusty clothes off? He grabs his coat off the bathroom doorknob.

I cross my arms. "So, thanks."

"No problem. I—"

BUUUUZZZZZZZ. I step around him to hit the talk button of my intercom. "Yes?"

"Buster coming or what?"

"Hang on." I release the button. "Wow, you really better run along."

"Yeah—"

"So, if you're free this week I'd love to take you out for a thank-you lunch—"

BUZZZZZZZZZZ.

"Lunch . . . . .yeah . . ." Buster gives me a cursory peck on the cheek. "I've got a killer week. Maybe a drink?" With a "later," he hastily closes the door behind him. I stare at the hairline fissures in the cream paint.

What. The fuck. Was that?

I find the 'necessities' carton and pull out the loaned laptop and my phone so as to attend to the other boy in my life. I finally locate a jack awkwardly placed behind the radiator, but there's no dial tone yet.

"Guy?" I grip the Krispy Kreme pay phone.

"What's up, Girl?" he yawns. "Todd, man, I'll be out in five— so get the caddie to wait. Go ahead, Girl. I'm all ears."

"I left you a few messages—"

"Yeah, so what's up?"

"I just need details on what I should be pitching."

"We covered this yesterday. TODD! TELL THEM TO SET US UP FOR THE WHOLE EIGHTEEN!" I jerk back from the receiver.

"We did. I mean, I understand that it's for Gloria Steinem. It's just that we haven't really had a chance to talk yet about the other feminist aspects of MC—"

"Girl, I'm in a meeting, so I don't really have time—"

"I'm sorry."

"Look, Girl, you can do this! You've done all that nonprofit shit, so this should be right up your alley."

"Yes! No, I'm excited to write it, I just need some more information from—"

"This is a fast-paced business, Girl. I can't babysit you. You want to climb high? Then you gotta grab that mother, stick it in your mouth, and go for it, okay?"

". . . Okay."

The phone goes dead.

"Just a moment," Julia calls out to me Sunday evening as I slide my umbrella into the brass stand. Her elegant Sutton Place vestibule makes my box-furnished abode seem just one notch above dorm room. "Hello!" She opens the door, tying an apron over her caramel sweater, her shiny bob pulled back into a low ponytail, a wisp of pale blonde shot with gray framing her face. "Come on in. I was just about to heat up some manicotti— would you like some?"

"That sounds delicious, but I don't want to impose—"

"Not at all." She takes the phone from me with a smile. "You trekked all the way over here in this cold, the least I can do is offer you sustenance." At her prompting, I step into the softly lit entry hall and pull off my mittens as she clears a stack of files from the bench. "Go ahead and put your things down. I just want to get the pasta in the oven."

Peeling off my damp coat and scarf, I fight the urge to curl up on the toile cushion. Exhausted from packing, writing, unpacking, writing, boss-stalking, and writing some more, I follow her happily into the pine kitchen, where Pierre Deux prints bring the grandeur of the prewar space down to a cozy scale. "What's the weather doing out there?" she asks, as she adds the relocated files to one of many stacks lining the counters.

"Still sleeting," I say, sliding into the banquette.

"The drive back was a little hairy. Thanks for running the phone up; I've been under a pile of paperwork." She pulls off her oven mitts. "INS wants everything in triplicate, as if these women still had their passports." She pulls a bottle of red out of the wine rack. "And you? Tell me at your age you're having fun weekends."

"Well, this one was devoted to moving." I smile wearily. "My floor is completely covered in boxes. Yours is beautiful." I admire the marble black-and-white-checkerboard pattern that merges the entryway and kitchen.

"Oh, thank you." She gracefully slides the cork out with one swift torque. "It always feels so wonderfully Fred Astaire to me." She pulls out two glasses from the cupboard. "I was constantly traveling when I worked in finance. The floor's how I knew I was home—particularly on no sleep. Wine?"

"I'd love some. You were in finance?"

"Investment banking, primarily capitalizing on the fall of the eastern bloc."

"Wow."

"It sounds wow, doesn't it?" Julia laughs, pouring for us both. "It was mostly a lot of bad vodka and bugged hotel rooms. And yet they were amazed when I took early retirement!"

I laugh. "And now you're with Magdalene?"

"Now, I *am* Magdalene." She smiles, repeating the turn of phrase. She spreads her arms. "Welcome to Central Headquarters!"

"Thanks. Happy to be here." I grin as she clinks my glass. "You've started your own organization." I push aside the image of Grace pointing her red pen at me. "That's really amazing. How long have you been operational?"

"We just got our seed money about six months ago, but it's

something I've wanted to do for ages." Julia leans back on the counter. "I spent the better part of my career underwriting towns whose gross national product *was* their women."

"That's . . ." I falter.

"Shameful." She walks to the refrigerator and pulls out a block of Parmesan. "I was done with corporate life." She passes me the cheese and a grater. "Would you mind?"

"Not at all." I peel back the plastic wrap as she slides a bowl over to me. "MC, Inc. is actually my first venture into corporate life." I start sloughing the fragrant cheese against the metal grid. "I was working for Doris Weintruck—"

"The feminist-speak-voice-of-young-women—" She waves her hand, her antique gold stacking rings dancing.

"That's the one."

"What did you do for her?"

"Everything. Anything." I take out a spark of frustration on the cheese. "It was all a lot more administrative than I signed on for. But under her auspices, I was doing my own research, so that was good."

"Really? On what?"

"How to make female-oriented nonprofits more effective." I shake the grater over the plate. "I've been kind of motivated by the disconnect between how passionate the women I've worked for are about creating change and their actual ability to effect it. There's a real resistance to process."

"I know exactly what you mean." Julia dresses the salad. "In the last eight weeks, I've sat in on enough unproductive, let's-all-say-what-we-*feel* meetings to make me wonder if I should-n't have opened a tackle shop." She smiles; I swoon. "Whatever else I say about banking, those people know how to get things done—oh." Julia lifts a bucket from the sink and sets it on the draining board, her face soft with concern. "My houseguest must be washing her underthings. I'll have to show her how the machine works."

"Will she be joining us?" I ask.

"Goodness, no. Moldova's exhausted. She's been sleeping since I brought her home from INS." She turns from the sink. "I'm sure I'm breaking social service rule number one, but I found beds for twenty-seven of the twenty-eight girls and just couldn't leave Moldova behind. Let's have a seat while the oven does its thing." I follow her into the grand living room, where the mahogany dining table is serving as a workstation, coils of cord snaking over forms, neatly delineated by colored Post-its.

"Please excuse the mess; my home office seems to be migrating. And I can't get the damned fax machine to work for the life of me. That's where three decades of good secretarial help leaves you—utterly handicapped." Julia curls into a silk club chair.

I sink into the floral couch, as she cradles her glass in her lap, her eyes glazing over.

"You know," I offer, "I don't think there are rules, at least that I've observed. It really is a community of making it up as you go along, good, bad, or otherwise. So, you're probably not breaking anything."

"Thank you." She smiles deeply, her eyes crinkling. "I could have put Moldova up in a hotel with my own money." She rubs her temples. "But, by that logic, should I have invited them *all* home with me? Or do I sell this apartment? Do I move to a studio in Washington Heights, donate every last penny I have to helping? I'm still grappling." She smoothes her ponytail.

"Julia, I think what you're doing is *amazing* and admirable and a hell of a lot more than most people."

"No, *they're* the admirable ones. Barely teenagers, lured over here from the Balkans, thrown in a cargo container, and forced into prostitution in a godforsaken house on Long Island, which, by the way, was frequented by cops. Now that their work authorization has come through, I need to get them all employed to secure their Temporary Protection. In this economy." She takes a swig of wine. "Let's talk about something else. What's going on in your exciting young life?"

"Not much, unless you find Cloroxing an old refrigerator exciting. Mostly, I've been trying to write this big thing for my boss—"

"Ah, yes, your boss." She leans forward to push a sterling bowl of almonds toward me. "He put on quite a show Friday morning."

"I'm learning that he's quite the showman. He's given me the weekend to put together this pitch."

"For what?" she asks, popping a few almonds in her mouth.

"That's the thing." I drop my forehead in my hands. "I'm kind of having a crisis—" I whip up, appalled. "I'm sorry, not a crisis. I feel ridiculous calling this a crisis." I bite my lip, feeling very unsold-into-white-slavery.

Julia laughs deeply. "Don't. I feel ridiculous wondering if the manicotti's going to burn." She stands and walks past me. "Talk to me while I turn the oven down."

I watch her as she pads into the kitchen, weighing the risk of sharing confidential information with a conceivably not disinterested potential funding recipient. But my craving for a sounding board wins out. "He needs me to write a pitch to Gloria Steinem—he wants *Ms.* to join the other magazines on the site, part of rebranding My Company," I call after her. "And I'm carrying out these assignments—the conference, this pitch—with essentially no direction." I take a sip of my wine. "Doris didn't even trust me to alphabetize. So working for Guy feels great. It does. Just a little terrifying because I don't know what I'm going to do if this doesn't work out." Holding the glass between my knees, I stare up at the hunting print above the mantel, my eyes landing on the fleeing fox.

"Sounds like normal first-semester jitters," Julia calls out.

"Does it? I just have so many questions. Which *is* normal, I guess. I'm not invited to a single meeting, yet I can't help watch when they're happening because the whole office is glass. But Guy just shrugs and says they're 'outside my purview.'"

Julia leans against the doorway, running her finger absently around the rim of her glass. "He doesn't exactly strike me as an Einstein, and you seem pretty damn competent. I doubt you're missing out on much. Besides, there's always a learning curve. Look at me, I can't get the mass mailing doohickey to," she waves her hand, "mass mail."

"I can do that," I offer.

"Really?" She slumps forward, grinning. "I'd be *utterly* indebted. And I'm happy to take a look at this pitch of yours if you want to e-mail it."

"Actually, I have a draft with me. You wouldn't mind?" I stand to fetch my bag. "And I'll start by making your fax fax."

"We have liftoff!" I cry out victoriously as a fax goes through.

"You smart cookie!" Julia drops the pages in her lap from where she's nestled into her club chair. She pulls off her tortoiseshell glasses, laying them beside an empty sauce-drizzled plate on the coffee table. "You've done a bang-up job of eking every little bit of feminism from a, let's face it, less-than-feminist operation."

Holding the successful fax transmission report, I take the seat facing her. "Really? It doesn't feel flimsy?"

"Their offering is flimsy, but that's just the hand you're dealt. Do they really have data on NCI-sponsored experimental trials for breast cancer on the site? I logged on before the conference and I didn't see anything that useful."

"No, not yet. But the archives are there. I'm going to propose it first thing Monday."

"Good idea. But I'd lose the paragraph on the free tampons.

A thoughtful gesture but a bit of a flag that you're grasping at straws."

"Ya think?"

"Truly, good work, Girl. I'm impressed." Do not kiss her, do not kiss her, do not. "But you forgot to spell-check it."

"Julia, I can't thank you enough."

"May I ask?" She puts the tip of her frames to her lips. "Who'll be making the final decision on this funding?"

"Guy and the Board, I assume."

"I see. And what's the time frame?"

"I'm not entirely sure, but soon, I would think."

She pats the pages in her lap. "Well, let me just read through this once more."

"Thank you so much." I stand, picking our empty plates off the coffee table and bringing them into the kitchen. "Shall I just put them in the dishwasher?" I call out.

"If you wouldn't mind."

I happily rinse the bone china and slide it carefully into the machine. Bathed in gratitude and trying to remember the last time someone took more than two minutes to appraise my work, I step back out. "Julia, about your houseguest—"

"Moldova?"

"Yes, maybe I can help her. I could talk to Guy about getting her a job at My Company. I'm sure he'd like to help, especially if she's facing deportation. He's all about the people at the bottom of the food chain, the people who traditionally get, um, screwed, when times are hard."

"Anything you can do to help." She smiles.

"Can I use your powder room?"

"At the end of the hall off the foyer."

I walk back along the hallway, slowing where a soft triangle of light falls onto the cream carpet. I peek in the open door to see a sleeping teenager curled tightly on the daybed, every lamp in the room ablaze. Her overprocessed blond ponytail splayed beside her, she clenches one of the many throw pillows with her chipped red nails. I tiptoe past the door into the bathroom. After washing up, I step back into the hall, pausing to peer at a cluster of framed photographs, one of a young Julia wearing eighties linebacker shoulder pads, accepting an award, a room of dark-suited men applauding—

"YOU!!" I jump, startled by Moldova standing inches away. "You wake me! With your . . . bathroom! And your . . . flush!" She points her finger before slamming the door. "YOU! GO!"

CHAPTER SEVEN

Walking the Talk

With a grab, a grunt, and a nod, Guy retreats with my pitch into his dawn-filled office Monday morning. And I hear nothing. Nada. But embracing Julia's 'pretty-damn-competent' endorsement, I dive into a report on my top ten recommendations for funding recipients and don't lift my head until three days later, when Guy suddenly waves me into his office as he paces a semicircle around his desk chair, *uh-huh*-ing into the phone clamped to his shoulder. I return a take-your-time wave, sitting to give my report a last once-over while I wait.

"I'm confident it's the right move, Rex. She's ready and willing." Guy spins his chair like a top, smiling to himself. "I'm on it. Great." He tosses the receiver back into its cradle. "So, how's it going," he states more than asks as he drops into his seat.

"Terrific! It's been a very productive week. Writing that pitch was really helpful."

"Good." He rubs his stubble. I recognize yesterday's coffee-spotted oxford. "That's great to hear, Girl."

"Was it well received by the Board?" I find myself leaning forward, legs crossed at the ankles. "Did they give you any feedback for me?"

"Sure. Yeah, they loved it."

"Oh good, because it got me thinking about steps MC can

take to tweak its image, really leverage its attractiveness for the *Ms.* community and better position us to consult. The addition of the NCI link for breast cancer, for example. This'll give MC an edge on health info. I think if we add the same kind of links for a few of the more serious issues to the information menu, perhaps lupus or rheumatoid arthritis, autoimmune disorders that primarily affect women—"

"Whoa." He holds up a hand.

"Sorry, I'm getting a little ahead of myself. They're all outlined in my e-mail so we can talk about them, uh, when you're ready. Moving on! So, the first focus group is tomorrow night with gender studies majors at NYU."

"Focus groups?"

"Yes, I outlined it all in Tuesday's e-mail. So I can get firsthand understanding of the feminist MC user, really educate myself as MC makes this transition viable."

He glowers, the circles beneath his eyes deepening.

"But, of course, I'm open if there're other sources you'd prefer I—"

"The transition *is* viable. We don't need tests. Who signed off on this?" My stomach constricts as he puffs. "Did you run this past me?"

"I sent you e-mails—"

"This is fucking viable and I don't need a bunch of . . . gender cranks to tell me that."

I steady myself. "Guy, of course it's viable." I aim for a calm expression. "But this is a predominantly male office." His eyes widen as if I've just called him on a loud fart. "Which is *good!* It's good. Fine with me. I love it . . . But this pitch is extremely important to you, and I thought it only prudent to do a test run on, well, on young feminists who're familiar with your site, to get you some hard feedback—"

"Sound bites." He points at me like Uncle Sam. "I love it. *That* I can use—endorsements. Good, Girl, great."

"That would be helpful?" I ask, trying to nail down what the hell I said to finally get his attention and how the hell that translates into getting whatever the hell he wants. "Sound bites for Gloria?"

"Yeah, uh, Gloria." Guy slouches farther down, lifting up his loosened tie and centering it on his chest.

"If you let me know when you're meeting with her, I can compile some speaking points to go along with the written presentation."

"Speaking points. Fantastic. Sound bites, though, that's genius." He reaches out for an open Coke on his desk, shakes it, and tosses the empty can toward the garbage, missing.

"So when are you meeting with her?"

"Who?"

"Gloria."

"Right, right." He blows his cheeks out. "Next week sometime." He lifts his loafer up to his knee and wipes away an offending scuff.

"Great! So, to the business at hand, I've completed an analysis of the organizations who attended the conference and earmarked the ten I think would most benefit from our support." I reach it out to him with pride. "I look forward to hearing your—"

"Nope," he says firmly, lifting his hands in mock defense before sliding them behind his head, leaving me holding the unclaimed report between us. "This is your baby." He yawns. I drop the forty-plus pages back into my lap.

"Okay, then I'll just give you a brief summary of the organizations I've recommended." Please?

"Girl, seriously. I just—" Guy slaps both hands down on his desk, pushing himself up to stand. "Don't care. It's your thing. Pick one."

"Pardon?"

"Pick one. You've compiled all this shit. You know what there is to know. Pick one."

"I'm sorry, you want me to—"

"Pick one! You want to be a big roller, you gotta go from your gut. What does your gut say?"

"Well . . ." I get a flash of a Dickensian sea of soot-smeared faces, hands stretching toward me.

"I don't have all morning. If you'd rather, I can have Stan pick one—"

"Magdalene."

"Magdalene?"

"Magdalene," I sputter without conviction.

"What do they do, rehab hookers?" he asks, tapping it into his BlackBerry.

"They help young women caught up in international human trafficking—"

"Great, I trust you." He yawns again, circling around to walk me to the door.

"The other option would be to spread out the donation in smaller allotments. That way you could help more than one cause," I say, now Fagin, kicking nine of the ten urchins away from my ankles.

"Nope. One is plenty. That's it, Girl. I don't want to spend any more time on this."

"So what exactly is the time frame for this donation?"

"We're workin' on that." He smiles, his eyes watering. "But keep a lid on it."

"Okay. Um, also, Guy, the woman I e-mailed you about, Moldova, any more thought on hiring her for the Admin staff?" I ask his broad back as he pulls his shirt over his head and walks into his washroom.

I hear the tap running.

"What did she do again, clean houses on Long Island?" he calls out.

"Right! Yes, she was on Long Island, but she was . . . kidnapped and forced into prostitution. She was in a house, though. So, what do you think? She's really . . . passionate. And she's desperate to find legitimate work. It's a great opportunity to put our money where our mouth is."

I hear his electric razor turn on. "I'm giving you a million dollars I barely have, Girl," he yells over the buzz.

"She could just answer the phones." I walk hopefully toward the bathroom. "I'm sure she'd take minimum wage—"

Guy's half-shaven face reemerges, his nose nearly bumping into mine. "No, and I don't want to have this conversation again. It makes you sound . . . dissatisfied." He clicks off the vibrating shaver. "Are you? . . . Dissatisfied?"

"No." I step back, forcing a beaming smile of satisfaction from every pore. "No, not at all—"

"Good." He slides the door shut with his foot.

The following afternoon, I chug over to collect Stacey at her desk, lugging shopping bags filled with focus-group questionnaires. "Ready to roll?"

Stacey looks up distractedly as she pulls off her headset, dislodging her top knot. Her eyes focus in on me. "Can't. Guy needs me—last-minute accounting meeting." She nods at his crowded office before her fingers return to the keyboard.

"You're kidding." I drop the bags on the cement floor, papers sloping out onto my feet. "You're my neutral facilitator."

"Guy's orders."

"But there are supposed to be at least two neutral parties in the room for every fifteen participants—" I pedantically repeat Rule Twelve from *Focus Groups for Dummies*.

"Girl," she cuts me off with exasperation.

"Sorry." I've become the passenger complaining about turbulence to the flight attendant. "Okay, I understand." I quickly regroup. "Then I just need the cash for the participants."

"Accounting said all cash requests now have to go through Guy."

"Stace." Guy sticks his head out the door, a clover-leaf tie dangling, his piece of St. Patrick's Day flair. "How 'bout a round of water?"

"Guy, hey!" I flag him as she rushes off. "I need the six hundred for the focus group."

"Get it from Stacey."

"She said Accounting needs your sign-off."

He turtles into his office to snap his fingers at the accountant sitting over the Book-of-Kells-sized checkbook. "Here." He steps back through the door with a check made out to cash, adding a bank visit to my tightly planned itinerary.

"Thanks. Guy, who can you spare to help me run this focus group—"

"Gyirl! Gyirl!" We both turn as Moldova arrives for the cleaning job I finally finagled with Angel, wearing a skimpy crocheted sweater over her rather large breasts and Spandex jeans over her rather small hips.

"Moldova, hi! Guy, this is the young lady I've been telling you about."

"Nice." He circles around Stacey's desk, hand extended. "How's it going?" he asks.

She flashes a pretty smile, barely marred by Eastern European dental hygiene, while I check the clock to gauge what kind of teller line I'll be facing. "Did Angel get everything set up for you all right?" I ask.

"I nyeed to talk the job," she says forcefully to me, still holding Guy's hand and gaze.

"Sure. I'm just leaving, so why don't you walk me out?" I angle around them in the direction of the door.

She twists to face me. "I want work with you. I no clean."

"I'm so sorry, Moldova." I adjust my grip on the bags. "The cleaning position is really all that's available at the moment—"

"Yeah, no, that's great," Guy interrupts. "Girl, take her. I think it's perfect. Opportunity, that's what America's all about!" With a last eyeful of the opportunities in Moldova's sweater, he drops her small hand and turns back to his office.

"Oh, that's wonderful! Moldova, if you wouldn't mind waiting for me by the exit," I say, "I'll be right there."

"Thank you! You are very nice man," she calls over her shoulder to Guy as she sashays off.

"Guy, thank you *so much* for giving her a chance," I say as Stacey hands him a stack of messages and steps past us into his office with a tray of glasses. "She can help me today and then I promise I'll train her."

"Whoa, whoa, whoa, there." He flips through the pink squares, tossing the majority in the trash. "Just for today. I'm not paying your salary *and* some Russian hooker's."

"The Balkans, actually. And she's not—" Forget it.

As I approach the reception area, Moldova leaps from the bench, reaching to take the bags off my hands. "Thank you, Moldova, I *really* appreciate it."

She looks at me squarely, one overly plucked eyebrow arched. "See, I no clean."

Moments later, I'm leading the way against the early rush hour tide to the bank. Moldova keeps a brisk pace as I hustle to follow. Despite being half a foot shorter, she dangles two of the straining bags as if they were empty lunch boxes. When we finally cash the check and are able to flag a cab, I use our ride to NYU to explain the finer points of focus groups as I've gleaned them. "One of us needs to be taking notes, so it would be helpful if you could ask the questions. You can read them right off the sheet." She nods. I tentatively follow up, "Can you read English?"

"I have the Zen book, with the motorcycle. Back home American soldier customer gave it me. I learn."

"That's wonderful. That you learned it, I mean. So, right, just read the questions and stay neutral." I peer through tightly locked traffic in search of a building number.

"What *neutral?*" she asks, bumping me sharply with her elbow as she reties what I recognize as Julia's camel-hair coat, the fabric bulking up around her diminutive shoulders.

"Um, no opinion. Like, Switzerland. Uninvolved. Not . . ." I gesticulate wildly to demonstrate being partial, then flat-line my hands to show neutral, my gaze locking in on a young blond with Buster's build standing beneath a streetlamp, gracefully balancing his vertical skateboard with his fingertips as he flirts with a woman on Rollerblades. Suddenly he does a sharp three-sixty around her and zooms off, leaving her mid-sentence. The cab lurches onward, and I replay Buster's awkward departure. I'd replay his phone messages, but I can't. Because there aren't any. Which, combined with the fireman's exit and the lunch-no-drinks volley sends a clear signal, in the dots and dashes of the Boy Telegraph, *only available for sex—full stop.*

The flood-lit Washington Square Arch glows above the bare treetops as we arrive at the Silver Center for Humanities to find the classroom mercifully filling. Moldova, looking much like the incoming students with her pierced belly button and dark roots, flops down at a desk to read over the question sheet. She stares intently at her list, chapped lips moving, while I set the materials on the front table. With every swing of the door, the classroom looks more and more like a radio contest at the mall; at six in the evening, almost every student seems to have devoted the entire day to getting ready: there's the cowgirl, the pimp, the hip-hop star, more than a few Britneys, and a solitary Cher. And nary a backpack or sneaker to be seen among the leather, pleather, feathers, and fur, all arranged to most flatter the obvious implants and an impressive array of God's own nipples. Moldova stares slack-jawed, ogling those who've opted to do

Allure's four-step smoky eyes instead of last night's assignments. The only exception is, like everything else about this crowd, extreme. A cluster of women who look like they've just escaped from basic training take seats at the front, turning their scrubbed faces and bald heads in my direction. And just as I'm testing MC, Inc.'s tape recorder, the proudly token male arrives in a black body suit, his skin powdered a clownish white, his irises hidden beneath one red and one cataract-milky contact. Marilyn Manson, completing the tableau, bounds up the stairs, past rolling eyes, to the seat that requires stepping over the maximum number of female classmates.

Collecting my notes, I approach the lectern. "Thank you all so much for coming tonight. Before we begin, I just need to confirm that you are all gender studies majors. Can I see a show of hands?" Everyone. "Excellent. As you know from the flyer, tonight we're going to be discussing contemporary feminism and My Company—"

"To help the beauty site?" a woman with sparkling peach eyes seeks confirmation, as the other painted faces light up with interest.

"Technically? . . . Yes."

"Cool." They nod approvingly, while the scrubbed-face, shaved-headed cluster in front sighs and heaves out copies of *Memoirs of a Dutiful Daughter*.

One woman holds the book in the air.

"Yes?" I acknowledge her query.

"Just to check, you said on the flyers 'users' of the site. We haven't *used* it." She gestures to her friends, who nod emphatically. "Our professor showed it in our 'How the Media Is Fucking Up Women' class. Do we still get paid?"

"Absolutely. We're looking to attract a new kind of user, basically you, gender studies majors and *Ms. Magazine* readers." There is a marked shift; the midriff majority of the room exchange looks with one another, some crossing their arms over their wrap sweaters. The scrubbed, whom I'd lost a moment earlier, stick Simone de Beauvoir back into their messenger bags and return their attention to me. "First we're going to have a brief discussion and then I'm going to ask you to fill out these short questionnaires. Sound good?" They all bob their heads. "Great. Now I'd like to introduce my colleague, Moldova. She'll be asking you a few questions, while I collect data. Moldova, whenever you're ready."

"Okay-dokay." She approaches the lectern, clears her throat, and peers down at the paper gripped in both hands. "What is the num . . . ber one iss . . . ue you have as a wo . . . man?"

In the brief pause, I try to guess if they'll kick off with equal pay or choice. A student wearing a *Playboy* necklace over a *Playboy* T-shirt, cut just low enough to reveal the *Playboy* tattoo, jumps in. "Sexual freedom."

"Sexy freedom?" Moldova echoes.

"The right to have sex with whoever I want, whenever I want, however I want, without being judged by society and, you know, my roommate," she expounds, her tongue piercing catching the overhead fluorescents.

"That freedom?" Moldova's hand lands on her jutting hip.

"Moldova?" I lift a finger and wave it at her discouragingly.

"Americans chain women to bed!" she blatantly overrides me.

"For her own pleasure," Marilyn Manson asserts.

"You chain them for *you!*" she glowers.

"Dude, I refuse to be pigeonholed by your hate." He tosses his black-lacquered nails at his indifferent classmates. "As usual, no one here is paying consideration to the ugly truth that gender studies only studies *one* gender. I'm charged the *same* tuition as everyone else, and *no* space is given to the pain of the American male—"

"Oh, that is *it!*" declares a slight blonde in the front, hauling an enormous monogrammed tote over her shoulder, from which a pair of tap shoes is dangling. "Eight semesters! Eight!" She throws her hands up, the weight of the bag pulling her backwards. "You've followed me from class to class chattering on and on about *male* oppression and *male* bashing, monopolizing the whole discussion—you just talk and talk and *talk*. Listen, Jason, when you make eighty cents on the dollar, get thrown into a rape camp, or pass a baby out your ass, I will convene a special class just for *your* pain!" There is a round of scattered applause as she crosses toward the exit, the traverse requiring a few beats longer than her dramatic moment warranted.

"See?" Jason/Manson implores as the door shuts behind her. "See what I have to endure? Hypocrites and sexists and they don't even know it." All eyes roll to the asbestos tiles.

"Okay, thank you for sharing. Moving on," I encourage Moldova.

"Okay-dokay, I have question." She flicks her fried blonde hair. "Why Americans so fat?"

"Moldova?" I interrupt. "Neutral, remember?" I do my crazy arm dance, then level it into a smooth, gliding motion. "Just ask the questions."

"It *my* question." She glares at me. "What cur . . . rent wo . . . men's is . . . sues do you want more in . . . for . . . ma . . . tion about?"

"Abortion legislation," a scrubbed-face young woman in the front says forcefully.

A student in Hello Kitty pigtails rolls her eyes. "Puh-lease. I can't read another thing on abortion."

"Well, I support abortion," Jason/Manson pipes up. "I bet that surprises you."

Moldova shrugs. "Of course you want kill baby after you fuck girl with the chains."

"The questions, Moldova," I say through clenched teeth.

Hello Kitty braves on. "But I totally want more info on birth control in general, like, the pill, and lubes and toys and stuff—"

"Oh! Oh!" Jason/Manson splutters. "She wants toys, but I can't tie anyone up?"

"You, shove it," Moldova scoffs.

"No, you shove it," he growls back, his black hair falling in his face. "You don't know what the hell you're talking about!"

Moldova throws her shoulders back. "I know the fat American men in the brothel."

It takes only a moment for everyone to process the implications of her knowledge before a Juicy-fied J-Lo hopeful nods her head in approval. "Okay, so, see? You were workin' it. Ain't no shame in that game."

"I'm Chrissie and I think it's awesome," adds a tentative voice from beneath a feathered fedora, incongruously sporting the pimp look. "I just saw this really hard-hitting documentary about Nevada's Moonlight Bunny Ranch on HBO, and it's just so cool that these women are so in touch with their value. They love having sex and they love getting paid for what they love and—"

"Yeah," another student pipes in, as I step back to the blackboard to record their insights, struggling to maintain my own neutrality. "They make *so much* money bucking the societal constraints that say we should feel shame."

"Much money?" Moldova asks.

"Hell yeah. Six-figure salaries, all of them. Man, you might as well get paid for it."

"They all seemed so happy," sums up Chrissie. Practically every woman in the room is nodding along, elaborate dos cocked to the side, as if reminiscing about the finale of *Friends.*

The holdouts are the scrubbed-faced cluster in front, who clench and unclench their fists. "Yeah, I think you should look into it, Chrissie," one spits. "You'd make a great whore."

Moldova, her face knotted in confusion, steps from the podium and points at Chrissie. "Who happy?"

"It was on HBO." Chrissie shrugs.

"I go house on the Long Island," Moldova challenges her cable-fed congregation. "You take papers. And then chains." She pulls her cardigan sleeves up to reveal her scarred wrists. Her face impassive, she shakes off my hand. "And fat American men make the fuck." A few people stare intensely down at their platform sandals as the sound of traffic seeps in through the auditorium walls.

"Moldova," I say quietly, again attempting to gently place my hand on her small shoulder. "I'll take over for a little while. Why don't you go get some water?"

She throws me off, outraged. "No! I ask the questions—you pay me ask the questions."

"Yes, and you're doing a great job. I just thought you'd like a break."

"Pay for the break?"

"Of course."

She shakes her hair back, the color returning to her cheeks as she points her fingers like a pistol and clicks her tongue. "Okay-dokay." She shoots a farewell at the traumatized room.

I take a deep breath and sense the group wishing they were doing the nicotine-enhanced same. "I'm sorry that we've gotten off track. I'd really like to ask you about *Ms.* for just a few minutes." They look skeptical.

"The flyer said *contemporary* feminism," someone groans.

"Right, yes it did," I confirm. "So, which features of the magazine are your favorites?"

A girl on the aisle shoots up out of her seat. "My name is Lorelei? And I really resent being forced to sit here and listen to this crap? She had a choice and I resent being manipulated into retrograde feminist hype?" The lip-gloss brigade nods furiously, their arms crossed even more firmly across their chests.

"Actually, Moldova didn't have a choice," I say. "I'm sorry about the digression. That wasn't planned. So which features of *Ms.* are your favorites?" I ask, anxious to get them back on track or I'll be spending the weekend doctoring yet another stack of questionnaires.

The woman next to Lorelei chimes in to support her. "It's just, like, the whole magazine has such an ultranarrow view. The whole 'victim' thing is so old. Moldova"—she points toward the hallway—"supported herself. And I don't feel it's empowering to be so stuck in the negative—what we can't do, who we can't be—the *Ms.* thing is over."

Chrissie, the same soft-spoken student who cheered on the Bunny Ranch clears her throat. "Their sad stories make me want to crawl in bed and never leave my apartment." Her cheeks flush deeply to match the feather in her fedora. "I mean, I just really believe they exaggerate sexism to keep their readership. I kinda want to think of myself as more than just someone who's here to be raped—thank you, *Ms. Magazine.*"

"Amen," affirms Jason/Manson.

"I see. Well, then how many of you are readers of the magazine? Can I just get a show of hands?"

The women with the scrubbed faces throw theirs up.

Lorelei, apparently incapable of speaking seated, bounces to her feet again. "Don't read it? Don't buy it? Don't support it? No, thank you?" She plops down to a wave of applause, mostly from Chrissie.

"My Company is a much better model," Chrissie continues. "It's about women being out and about in the world. Taking it on. Taking *care* of themselves in a *can-do* culture."

"It kicks ass."

"Thank you, Jason. And how many of you call yourselves 'feminists'?"

The same four hands stay extended. Jason/Manson adds his.

"Why?" I ask. The unraised arms remain clamped across chests, firm in their position. "*Why* wouldn't you call yourself a feminist?"

"We don't hate men," says one with a shrug, speaking for the group.

I blink at them, my head filling with a dozen extraordinarily un-neutral tacks. "It's not at all about hate. Or an enemy." I grapple unsuccessfully for nonleading language. "It's about every one of you walking out that door, graduating, and leading a life where your gender doesn't determine your salary, your welfare, your health care, or your safety. And there's no reason that has to be at the expense of anybody else. Or your sexuality. It's not a negative movement . . . It's a positive one." I'm met with suspicious glares, and a heaviness takes hold in my chest. "Okay, well then, that'll do it." I force cheer and click off the tape recorder. "If you'd take a few moments to fill out the questionnaire, I'll give you your payment. Thanks, everyone."

I watch them scribble, pink fluff-tipped pens circling in front of their hunched-over faces. *Good news, Guy! We've got a bunch of half-naked Ms.-loathing, rather-be-labeled-Nazi-than-feminist gender studies majors just* dying *to be leveraged at the feminist company of your choice! And a whopping minority of four who'd rather stun-gun their soul sisters than have anything to do with you. No, it's totally viable. Viable central.*

Cigarette in hand, Jason/Manson bounds out of his seat, squashing exposed toes with his work boots. He shoots me his best scowling come-on as he takes his money and the women strut after him, cell phones beeping back to life and lighters primed. As the last stragglers file out, heaviness gives way to panic. I tug on my coat and hear a familiar voice call from the double doors. "Darling!" Professor Helen Wilcox exclaims warmly. "I was just speaking with your mother this morning, and she told me those flyers all over the department are yours."

Her winter-white coat open and ivory scarf dangling, she strides elegantly down the aisle to embrace me. "Have I missed it? My seminar ran late."

"Helen, hi!" I automatically kiss her cold cheeks and am met with a waft of Antonia's Flowers, also Grace's scent. "Yes, I cut it short after they disclosed their unmitigated contempt for *Ms.*"

"The discomfort is intriguing, isn't it?" She smiles, adjusting her overstuffed white briefcase under her arm. "They seem to think sexism is something we invented to depress them. You look gorgeous. I see the private sector agrees with you. Here, walk me out. What were you looking to learn?"

I follow her through the doors, scanning the corridor for Moldova. "I was hoping to find a bevy of women who could help me figure out how to transform a beauty site into a feminist venture."

"Yes, Grace said you're peddling Avon for Ann Coulter." She switches her briefcase to her other hip with a wry smile.

"Oh, no, not at all. No, I'm heading up a philanthropic rebranding initiati—wait, sorry, she said *what?*" My eardrums ring with adrenaline as my brain tries to repel Grace's characterization.

"Darling, a little rebellion's good—"

"Helen, I'm not rebelling. Does Grace think I'm rebelling? I'm not. I'm working." The bag strains against my fingers. "There aren't a lot of job offers right now for 'come, change the world.'"

Helen lets out a small peal of laughter. "Oh, darling, I know. Don't mind your mother. She makes all the tough choices on paper. If she wants someone to have a job, she only has to write it in the margin." She pulls her scarf up and around her neck.

"She wants me to start my own organization—"

"She wants me to assassinate the dean." Helen kisses me good-bye as I pull the heavy plastic bags up against my chest.

"But I'm content just to keep serving up heaping portions of depression for the third wave. Will I see you at Chatsworth's Joe Conrad egg hunt this year?"

"I'll try."

"Do. Take care, love." She turns into the stairwell, and I manage to summon up a farewell smile before starting toward the elevators. I spot Moldova down the hallway, tugging a bunch of brightly colored flyers for computer classes off a corkboard.

"Going down!" the elderly operator announces as I get in his car, decked out for St. Paddy's Day in green streamers.

"Moldova!" She leaps on, her eyes devouring the Doris-hued bouquet as the car drops. We jerk to a stop on every other floor, the metal arm clanging back and forth in time with the low thud of panic growing in my temporal lobe. *It must be viable. There* must *be feminist consumers out there.*

"So! Gyirl! Tomorrow I begin."

"Begin what?" I gulp cool smoke-tinged air into my lungs as we step onto crowded Waverly Place.

"Work with you." Moldova grips Julia's coat in both hands, the flyers jutting out of one pocket. I run my fingers over my eyebrows, returning to her and the jostling street. Guiding her elbow, I move us into the park, past the dry fountain, through wafting clouds of pot, narrowly dodging a string of after-dark skateboarders.

"I'm sorry Guy wasn't clear, Moldova." I touch her cold fingers. "But the cleaning job is all that's available right now."

"No! I *no* clean," she scoffs, twisting away. "I in cargo, no breathe. I go America work secretary and chain to bed. I no clean. I *no* clean." She slaps the back of her right hand into her left palm for emphasis. "Where you go from the clean? How you—?" She shoots her hand up in a diagonal, like a departing plane, speaking in animated Slavic before catching herself, searching my eyes. "Like your *Dynasty.* Like Joan Collins. I need good job. To be respect, to—" She repeats the takeoff gesture, holding her hand up in the air. "I have to. For my family. I have to! I no clean!"

"I understand. Moldova, I understand about the cleaning. I want to help you, but I don't make the decisions at—"

"You got me cleaning job! Get me real job!"

"I'm so sorry, Moldova, that is the 'real job.' I had to pull strings just to get you the cleaning—"

"Gyirl, I no clean!" She jerks me around with her rough nails. "I do many jobs! I very good work with the people!" She shoves me back into the lamplight, Julia's coat falling in a heap on the dirty cement.

"Look." I raise my hand to loosen her grip so that I can bend to retrieve the coat. "I don't have that kind of power—"

"Fuck you!" she spits, slapping the coat from my extended hand.

"If you're Irish, I'll fuck you both," a male voice notifies us from behind a peeling tree.

Moldova bites the insides of her mouth as she lifts the camel wool and shakes it off.

"Moldova, I'm so sorry." I take her arm, trying to move us out of the park. "I'm sorry—"

"Fuck you!" She jerks her elbow free. "I in your country—I come for work. I want real job."

"Moldova, *I* want a real job! I'm rebranding a company I know nothing about, run by a man who won't even talk to me, for women I don't even like!"

"Thanks, Gyirl." She holds her palms up. "I no want to make you the trouble." She takes off running, followed by a stadium wave of catcalls from a line of hooded heads perched on steel railings.

"Moldova! Wait!" But she's quickly gone from view.

Fuckfuckfuck.

I drop the bags, lower my face into my hands, and breathe

deeply before gathering myself together and moving toward Sixth Avenue. Aware only of my sore feet and the frost swirling up my skirt, I find myself turning into the warm glow of Babbo and shrinking into a corner of the bar by the window. Ordering a Scotch, I stare out at Waverly, watching weary commuters and students with dorms in prime real estate make their way home through the cold mist. How is Moldova even going to get home? I drain my glass and head downstairs to the pay phone. Gottogetacell.

"Hi, you've reached Julia Gilman and the Magdalene Agency. Please leave a message."

"Julia, hi. I just wanted to let you know that Moldova came down to NYU to help me with a focus group and . . . she left from there. The thing is I'm not sure if she has a MetroCard or even cash. I mean, I'm sure you've taken care of that. But I thought you should know. So, if there's a problem, please call me at home. I'm so sorry I . . . let her leave without figuring out her transportation. I shouldn't have . . . So, I hope everything is going well, and okay, bye."

The door to the ladies' room opens, and a couple spills out in a peal of giggles. His horn-rimmed glasses slightly askew, he devours her with his gaze as she straightens his tie, her face glowing beneath the heat of his attention. A last kiss and they undulate together back up the stairs, the force of their attraction encompassing the restaurant in its magnetic waves.

I feel Buster's hand snaking up my spine, cupping the back of my neck.

That's it. I need a boy-sized dose of distraction. My head needs a *night off*, my body needs a *night on*. So, I can a) get wasted and take on the bartender. Or b) just go get what I'm gonna get from this boy. He's made it clear what he wants. He's made it clear what he's available for. And I'm a Scotch, a failed focus group, and a whopping dose of maternal judgment into making this his lucky day.

I dial his cell. "Sam!" Buster shouts to be heard over the competing music and laughter on his end. "Sam?!"

"It's G!" I shout back, because one does.

"Sam?!"

"No, G!"

"Dude, I got nothin'! The reception at my place is shit! Tlel the cab it's Three forty-*seven* Allen! Four A!"

"It's G! I wanted to see—"

"You're gonna miss your own party, dude! And yeah, bring whoever you want! See you soon!"

Yes. You. Will.

I dial him back, but his voice mail picks up. "Hey, it's G. We just spoke, but you thought I was Sam. Anyway, I'd love to see you, and it sounds like you're having some people over, so maybe this isn't a good time. But maybe I could just stop by for a drink, and if it isn't a good time then I could just, you know . . . wait in your bedroom. Or you could leave the party for five minutes, I mean, five minutes, *tops*. It doesn't have to be a big deal. No strings. No talking." No way. I press 2 to discard the message.

I throw down some cash, knock back a second Scotch, and grab a hunk of sourdough as I depart, undaunted, to trek down Broadway. *Notgonnaoverthinkitnotgonnaoverthinkitnotgonnaoverthinkit*. I'm on my way to make something happen, and I'm not leaving Buster's building until I've obliterated all my current anxieties with a whole new host of anxieties and see if they kill me. I'm going to throw myself into some inappropriate, ambiguous something with someone—Buster or a roommate or the building superintendent—that will keep my brain occupied for at least the next forty-six hours.

I round the corner to Houston, past a group of men staggering in bright-green bowler hats. As I delve into the Lower East Side, more revelers tumble onto the streets, brushing against me and flicking my hem as I pass. Then, at the corner of Delancey, a boy in a yarmulke, shamrocks painted on his cheeks, projectile-vomits green beer onto the sidewalk, narrowly missing my pumps. "Suck it, bitch," he croaks before the next heave. All hail, St. Pat: local patron saint of sexual harassment.

Grateful that the front door is propped open with a brick, I dart inside Buster's lobby and press for the elevator. Behind me a woman in a trench coat and sneakers wheels in a small suitcase, a bungee cord precariously holding a boom box on top. "Phew." She blows a red curl off her face. "What a night. I hate working St. Patrick's—" Her cell rings. "Hey, honey. Uh-huh, uh-huh . . . Well, put him on." She pulls a tube of lip gloss out of her pocket and swipes it on, rubbing her lips together as she leans back against the wall, her voice softening to a comforting semi-whisper. "Hi, Christopher, now be a good boy for Daddy, and go have your dreams so you can tell Mommy all about them." She wheels in next to me, and we both reach for the 4 button. Transferring the phone to her shoulder, she opens the outside pocket of her well-worn case and pulls out a pair of gold stilettos. "Only three more. I'll be home around four . . . No, Ed's sick . . . Honey, please don't start. They'll send another bodyguard when they can, but I can't wait any longer or I'm gonna lose this gig. I'll call you after." She shoves her sneakers in the suitcase and grimaces as she slips swollen feet into the platform heels. The elevator stops and the door rattles open.

We start down the hall in the same direction, the highly audible moans of either a deeply pleasured or deeply pained woman growing louder with each step. *"YES! YES! YES!"* Oddly, we both stop in front of 4A. She presses the doorbell, then unties her coat, goose-pimpled skin popping out over her tight vinyl top. *"GIVE IT TO ME! DO IT! DO IT!!"*

"Dude, he's got both fists up her ass!" Boisterous male voices spring at us through the door.

"He's up to his elbow! That's fucking insane!" I hear Luke laughing. "Hey, who wants to fist the stripper?"

Exchanging silent glances, we both step back. Whipping her coat closed, the woman reaches for her phone, her finger hesitating over the send button as the door swings open with a fresh burst of male cheers and Luke appears, ringed by a cloud of cigar smoke. He looks us up and down before calling over his shoulder, "She's here!"

The woman drops the phone in her pocket and fixes Luke with a steely gaze. "Only dancing. Just like at a club, no touching. Got it?" He nods, and she braves a wide smile. "Okay, boys," she yells out, rolling into the dark apartment and taking a deep breath as she leads the way for both of us. "Who's the groom? I want to party all night long!" I place the kid in a tuxedo T-shirt, wearing an inflatable ball-and-chain around his neck, as Sam from the Slipper Room. "Where should I plug this in?" She holds up the boom box.

"Just get that ugly-ass coat off! Let's see what we got!"

I scan the room for Buster but am caught by the television screen, where a shaved vulva looks to be in the final stages of birthing a large man, with only his forearm left to expel. Buster enters from the bedroom, examining a plastic bong. "Dudes, it's tapped." He sees me and blanches.

I turn on my heel as the boom box fires up.

"Shit! Wait—"

Buster slams out after me, catching up as I pound for the elevator. "G! What're you doing here?"

"I don't even—I can't even—" I throw my palm up in his face, unable to look at him.

"It's just a bachelor party." He shrugs incredulously.

"Fine! Great! I'm leaving." The elevator door opens and I escape, but he slips in after me, quickly pushing the black PH button.

"Jesus, *wait a second*." He lifts his baseball hat to roughly tousle his hair as the car jerks upward. "Can we just talk about this? I didn't know you were coming over—"

"And that makes this okay?" I uselessly jab at the L button.

"You have nothing to be jealous of—"

"*Jealous?!* That you can pay someone to fake wanting you for money to feed her child? *Jealous?!* Yes, two fists, please. I can never get enough. God, let me off this elevator—" I shove past him onto a stairwell, slamming through the exit door to a dormant roof garden. I pace a large lap around the barbed-wire perimeter before I realize there's no other exit.

"Look," he calls across the roof. "I helped you find a place! I hog-tied my roommates into helping you move! And now you think I'm an asshole just because I'm having fun with some guys and there's some stupid porno on, which we're barely even watching. Well, if you think I'm an asshole, then there's nothing I can do—"

"Except not be one!"

"*It's not my party!* And she's just dancing, there's no child! Everyone has bachelor parties—I don't understand why you're so pissed at me."

"Because I am!" I stride back to him. "I don't want you to be this boy! I just spent the afternoon listening to coeds fight for the right to fuck you, trekked through an onslaught of disgustingly personal commentary from the general male population, and arrived here to see a woman getting her anus torn, a woman who may or may not be doing it of her own volition—"

"Jesus! That tape was Luke's idea! I wasn't even watching it—"

"And fisting the stripper, were you going to be around for that? Oh, sorry, am I keeping you? You don't want to miss the ceremonial donning of the latex glove."

"Luke's just talking smack. They've been here drinking for

hours. She's just gonna dance. She's gonna dance for twenty minutes and go home and I'm gonna clean up after all of them—"

The wind gusts, my hair cutting across my face as I lose steam, his defense weakening my conviction until I'm nothing but an uninvited harridan shrieking on his roof. "I don't know what I was thinking," I lie, all hopes of a bottle of wine and mind-obliterating sex vanishing. "I shouldn't have come. I don't know you."

He blows out a long breath. "But I want you to," he says quietly, sticking his hands deep into his pockets. "I'm sorry. I really don't want to . . . upset you." Fighting against a tide of so much conspiring to upset me, his lanky frame swims into view, borne to me by the floodlight. He shivers in the darkness.

"What's going on down there—I'm not okay with it," I say quietly, clear on this much.

"I hear you." He reaches out for me, gingerly taking my hand. I look in his eyes as his thumb runs delicately over my skin. "I really feel something here."

"I do, too. And I hate that we can't seem to get past . . . this."

Pulling me to him, his other hand slides up my arm to my cheek. He takes my bag off my shoulder and sets it down. "I'm so glad you came here—that you just came over. I felt like a shit for running out of your place. It's been an insane week, and Luke's freaking out with the whole unemployment thing, and I kind of have to look out for him—"

I stop him, taking his face in my hands, forcing him to look at me as I try to gauge his sincerity.

He smiles softly, staring into my eyes. And then we're kissing—backing up toward the brick wall. "Let me not be that boy," he says, before pressing his mouth onto my neck. My fingers find their way into his hair as his warm hands slip under my skirt and I'm filled with the resolution to obliterate the past fifteen minutes from my memory right along with the rest of this day.

"Um, Buster?"

"Yeah?"

"Could you not be that boy at my apartment? 'Cause it's freezing up here."

CHAPTER EIGHT

The F-Word

"Guy, hi. Hope you had a good weekend. I e-mailed you the findings from the first focus group and wanted to schedule a time to go over them in person as they were slightly different than we anticipated. I'm free so, uh, whenever is good for you."

"Hey, Buster. Good for me? Thanks for asking. Yes, very. And I'm sure my futon is recovering nicely. I'll pass along your concern as soon as I have a chance."

"Hi, Guy. I'm calling because I see you haven't had a chance to open my e-mail so maybe we could schedule a lunch date. I've completed four more focus groups now, and the results are pretty static. I'm e-mailing them over so . . . I'm here, whenever you're free."

"B, of course I'm free. If you get the movie, I'll pick up the wine. Say, eight-thirty? My futon sends its regards."

"Guy, I'm just going to send along a revised plan for making us more appealing to feminists, in case you didn't read my e-mail yesterday. I think this document would be a better use of your time. Again, just a few changes MC could make. I'll be at my desk. Look forward to your feedback. Sorry, it's, ummmm, Thursday evening."

"Girl." Guy leans over the MC kitchen counter the next evening, drumming a cabinet door, pa-duh-bum, before tipping back out of sight. "Let's catch up."

"Coming!" I abandon my search for a plastic fork and skibble into his office after him.

"What's the status?" He opens his steaming take-out platter. "Where are we?"

"I'm not sure what you've read of my e-mails . . ."

"Skimmed 'em." He tears open ketchup packets with his teeth.

"Well, overall, the focus groups have been really informative. Essentially, MC has a significant following."

"And?" he asks, mouth full.

"It's more of a 'but.'"

"Cut to it, Girl."

"These women don't associate themselves with *Ms.*, to the extent that adding *Ms.* to your site could turn off a large proportion of your users."

"I thought you were polling the feminists?" he asks, sticking a fat french fry in his mouth.

"I tried. But, unfortunately, it seems that self-identified 'feminists' are primarily localized to an older generation more represented by the women you met at the conference. And they're generally a skeptical bunch—a very savvy, "Killing Us Softly" group of women who don't leap on a product bandwagon just 'cause it rolls by. Suspect of advertising, suspect of the media, in a manipulative marketplace, they put significant value in Gloria's brand. Bottom line, they might come, but only if they're following her. And even then there are additional changes we need to make for the site to be palatable."

He coughs, his Coke going down the wrong pipe. "Palatable?"

"You okay?"

He waves me on.

"I've outlined them in further detail than was in yesterday's e-mail." I study his face for signs of recognition. "We have some sound bites." His brow lifts. "Sort of short and sweet and not really from Gloria's camp—"

"Kill Gloria," he interrupts, wrapping both hands around an overstuffed cheeseburger and biting into it. He chews, wiping his ketchup-covered mouth with a napkin. He swallows. "What else?"

"Well, I've covered all the college campuses in the five boroughs. The results were pretty consistent. Sorry, kill Gloria?"

"Good. Consistent is good." He wipes a glob of ketchup from his chin. My stomach growls as I remember the pasta growing cold on my desk.

"Yes, but I only found a handful of young *Ms.* readers—"

"You're getting way too hung up on this *Ms.* thing. I want a, you know, young feminist appeal, that's all. You're overthinking."

"But I was only able to find a handful of young feminists. That was really the overwhelming—"

"Overwhelming?" He cocks his head at my hyperbole.

"And they don't like the MC site. At all. Guy, I'm concerned that without the *Ms.* archive, we don't have a whole lot to hang our hat on."

"Don't be." He reaches for his Coke and takes a swig.

"Okay." *Why?* "So, why, exactly? I mean, if you're not able to get Gloria to—"

"Jesus! Fuck Gloria." He stares across the desk at me. "I don't want to talk about her anymore." He wipes his fingers and tosses the napkin in a long arc, just missing my head and, yet again, fully missing the trash can behind me.

I reach down to retrieve the sticky wad and deposit it into his wastebasket. "I'm sorry. If we could just take a tiny step back. You asked me to help you get the *Ms.* archive on the site, to rebrand—"

"Ms., Ms., Ms." He scowls at me like a petulant child.

"You did say *Ms. . . .*"

"Girl, I'm not going to have a conversation where we're quoting each other back and forth because I don't have to."

"Okay," I say, fumbling for footing. "So what should I be working on?"

"I don't know."

"I can take these issue-oriented site additions directly to the designers. And I'm happy to reach out to the breast cancer organizations—"

"You know what? I do have a homework assignment for you." I click my pen open. "Stop thinking."

"Sorry?"

"Stop. Thinking," he repeats in frustration. He stands and arches his back. "Shit, is it seven already?" He runs both hands through his hair. Panic swirls up through my pumps.

"Okay, I'll just . . ." I feel myself shrinking, Alice-style, until he'll be able to pick me up with his fingers and blow me into his wastebasket. And most likely miss. "I can work on other things for you, Guy."

"I gotta go." He tightens his tie knot.

"Did you ever have a chance to read my pitch, because it's all spelled out there—I'm just concerned about where we crossed wires."

"So am I." He tugs a ream of files from his bag, tossing them forcefully onto the desk. "I talked till I was fucking blue in the face. I offered your *Ms.* Steinem the fucking world. That woman has no vision and no sense of humor. Have I even read her magazine?" He flushes at the memory. "As if you don't get the whole fucking sob story from the first three pages." He whips his headset off the desk. "*She's* not selling them anything—what kind of bullshit is that?! Everybody's selling something. And if you think you're not, you're totally fucking deluded. Complete waste of my fucking time. Both of you."

The blood drains from my face.

Must stay composed. Must pick up bag. Must take all I can.
Download files. Turn off computer. Lock emptied desk. Wave.
Smile. Leave.

On the street, I flail madly for a cab in a flurry of fat
snowflakes, my terror coming out in an interpretive dance per-
formed for the oncoming traffic. A cab pulls up in a torrent of
slush.

"Where to?"

"First stop Twenty-seventh and Seventh and then we're
heading uptown. Thanks." I look over at the dashboard clock,
in complete disbelief that instead of fleeing home to implode, I
have three minutes to pull my shell-shocked self together for
Buster and our first formal outing as a 'couple.' I run my fingertips in deep circles over my forehead, trying to stave off the
budding migraine.

Buster hunches against the snow in the doorway of YGames,
bouncing slightly to keep warm. Spotting the cab, he folds in,
reaching for me. A surge of hormones rush my brain, battering
at my professional insecurities. "How are you?" he asks, his cold
lips still close to mine.

"Getting fired."

"Shit." He tilts away to look in my eyes, the snowflakes at the
tips of his eyelashes melting. "How do you know?"

"Long story." I pull him back to me, determined to preserve
the lulling buzz.

"Next stop Eighty-third and Second, please," he calls up to the
driver before whispering into my hair. "Tell me what happened."

I weave my fingers through his, my mouth finding his again.
"Do we have to go to this party?" I mumble.

"I said we'd stop by. It's my college crew, and I want you to
meet the rest of them."

"Let's just go to my place." I grip his thigh, roving higher.
"I'm not in the mood to talk."

He clamps his hand down on mine. "I've made it a whole"—he glances at his watch—"twelve hours outside your apartment. I'd like to see if I can go at least another three, if you don't mind."

"Okay," I say, unsure how to take that.

"Look, I've slept at your place every night this week—"

"Because you have seven roommates who don't like me—"

"Seven roommates who think I've fallen off the fucking planet. I've gotta check in." We crawl up Sixth Avenue. Outside the blurry window, maintenance men toss salt at the ankles of the last straggling office workers. "Besides," he says huskily, sliding his hand across my stomach. "It would be a shame not to take this dress out for a spin."

"Hey, dude!" The cashmere V-necked host throws open the door, music blowing over us as he tugs Buster into a bear hug.

"Chris, this is G, the one I told you about."

"Ve-ry niiiice," Chris says, slapping Buster on the back as he blatantly appraises me. "Drinks are in the kitchen, smokes on the balcony, and yeah, just help yourselves!"

"Pleasure," I lie and follow Buster inside the boxy apartment, where, between the scuffed parquet floor and smoke-tinged stucco ceiling, beer memorabilia is holding its own as the only attempt at decor. In addition, all the lights have been extinguished for that junior-high-rec-room ambience, save the kitchen, which is interrogation bright. We weave through cliques of Buster's former classmates and the people they've picked up since college, catching sight of Tim and Trevor on the seventies leather couch, their hands performing reconnaissance under the skirts of the women beside them. Luke raps on the balcony door from where he crouches in the snow with the other smokers, waving at Buster and managing a contrite smile in my direction. Progress.

"Hey, Jill!" Buster exchanges cheek kisses with a brunette in a frumpy suit who steps back to let us into her circle. "Jill, this is G."

"So nice to meet you." I take her hand.

"Jill dated Tim senior year," Buster fills in.

"Dating is such a nice way of putting it." She grimaces, making me at least thankful that I'm not at some Wesleyan ex-fest right now. "This is my group from Bear Stearns." She gestures to her companions, all decked in their drab corporate finest.

"How's that going?" Buster asks.

"Moderately less hellacious. We're taking the red-eye back to Pittsburgh in the morning for week five of due diligence. And you?" She addresses me as Buster excuses himself.

"Oh, I work for My Company," I say, mustering the conviction of a woman who is not a *complete fucking waste of time*.

"The Web portal?" One of her companions looks down his thin nose over his plastic cup.

"Yeah."

"Ooph," Jill sucks in air through clenched teeth.

The other one pats my shoulder. "They came out of the bust really strong."

"MC was one of my top picks two years ago, but . . ." Jill reaches out to examine a pretzel from a wooden bowl as they all shrug. I gulp down the rest of my whiskey. "Although I heard they've had a change in management and are shifting direction—trying to go up against the Big Five."

"Still Five? Isn't it the Big Two?" The wrinkled Brooks Brothers crew crack each other up. I rattle the ice cubes in my cup. Someone should go up against the Big Five, with their money and their Diet Coke and their money.

"What do you do there?" Jill asks. *Where* did Buster *go?*

"They're moving in a more feminist direction—"

Jill snorts. I barrel on, "Well, the plan was to bring in *Ms. Magazine,* so it made sense—does make sense. It's viable. There are millions of women who use the site and I've been, you know, running focus groups and conferences and I . . ." *Am a complete fucking waste of time.* "Will you excuse me?"

I snake toward the bathroom, coming upon a less intimidating clump of dreadlocks and Rage Against the Machine T-shirts in the hallway. I slow, spotting one of Kira's old roommates among them. "Hi!"

She turns her face, revealing the left side to be tattooed like a Maori warrior, and I realize my mistake. "Sorry, I thought you . . . looked familiar," I say with a shrug. She turns back to listen to the story I've interrupted.

"Wow, man, that's heavy." A snarly beard nods in empathy.

"So after I helped her deliver the afterbirth," a woman says with quiet intensity, twisting a dreadlock, "we managed to get her back to the village before the guerillas resumed fighting." She eyes my dress and heels. "Are you with Busted?"

"I am." I extend my weary hand in greeting. "Sounds like you've been on an amazing trip—"

"It wasn't a trip. I was *working* there. What do *you* do?" And it's time for a second drink.

I'm emptying the last drops of crappy Jack Daniel's into my cup as a traveling clique arrives in the kitchen for a refill. "So, I told my boss this afternoon there's *no way* I can get this project down to twenty-five million," says a petite blonde wearing a tight quilted jacket over the Nanette Lepore dress I've been coveting. "He's going to have to get them to cough up the extra five. Um, excuse me?" I make myself flat against the damp Formica so she and her squillion-dollar budget can pass. She pours herself a seltzer with her tiny ringed fingers. "And if he wants Mary Kate and Ashley, then *forget it,* unless he can get them for scale. It's just been the *shittiest* week." The crowd nods appreciatively. I look out the pass-through to the balcony and lock eyes with Luke, who somehow manages to leer at her and me simultaneously. "Losing Ron Howard was just such a blow."

She shakes her head, her blonde bob brushing my cheek as she sighs.

I down another drink before pushing out of the crowded kitchenette. Weaving a bit, I steady myself against the wall, dislodging a taped *Deer Hunter* poster before I feel my way to the coat-covered bed, curling up in a fetal position beneath the flickering neon Heineken sign and letting the room swirl away from me.

The keys still in the door, I swipe twice before my hand finds the switch. Blinking as the garish overhead illuminates all the boxes still stacked against the wall, I flip the light back off.

Buster gently peels my coat from my slumped body and walks inside. He pauses to look around, then drapes both coats over a box containing the yet-to-be-assembled IKEA dinette set. Unable to move from the front door, I stare at my strange apartment, the piles of laundry, the take-out containers rinsed and piled by the sink, the new sheet packaging sticking up out of the trash can. And everywhere boxes: half opened, half unpacked.

He holds out his hand from the living room. "Care to join me?"

I nod but remain rooted. He comes around me to lock the door before bending down on his knee to lift one of my feet, then the other, gingerly out of its heel. My bare feet sink down onto the wood as he stands back up, wrapping me in a slow bear hug. I lean against him and breathe in his now familiar smell of Downy fabric softener and boy.

Then tears are streaming down my face and soaking into his sweater. "Hey. Hey, now," he murmurs into my hair. I pull back from him, my hands covering my face, my shoulders shaking. "Okay." He reaches to hold my elbows, ducking to see between my fingers. "No more parties for you."

"No. It's not. It's not that. It's just—"

"It's just that you've had too much to drink," he says gently.

"No. Well, yes, probably that. And I miss my own fucking friends so much I can barely breathe. But it's that I'm going to *get fired . . . again.* I was doing great at what I thought he wanted and now he says he doesn't want that and if he won't *do* any of my suggestions then it'll only be rebranded in my head."

"G, it's Friday. You don't have to worry about this tonight—"

"I can't bear the firing, not again. I can't—" I wipe my nose on my hand, unable to finish the thought aloud.

Buster leans into the kitchen. "Tissues?"

"Cupboard to the left of the sink."

"Gotcha." He reemerges with a box of Kleenex. "You got a permit for all those paper products?" He pulls one out and hands it to me.

"My mom's strictly for the environment," I sniffle. "So it was only one disgustingly overtaxed cloth napkin per customer in our house. This is kind of my I'm-a-capitalist-and-a-grown-up-now splurge."

"Well, in that case." He reaches for a roll of paper towel. "Live it up." I laugh for a moment before the tears return. "You should go in on Monday and make your case."

"My case?" I look up at him over my tissue.

"For why they'd be assholes to fire you. Here, let's make some notes." He flips on a lamp.

"Now?" I ask halfheartedly. "I thought we were going to hang out?"

"It's cool," he says, shaking his head. "I'll make coffee and camp out in the bedroom. Then you can come find me when you've got it on paper. Sound like a plan?"

I sniffle again, looking up at him, his dirty blond hair surrounded by a halo of bright light from the floor lamp. "Really? Is it really cool?"

"Yeah, I'm beat. I could use a nap. As long as you give me a little flash—I'm good for an hour or two." Red-nosed, I untie my wrap and shimmy my dress open as he sighs deeply and then banishes me to my makeshift desk with his hand over his eyes. "Too hot. Much too hot," I hear him mutter as he opens the freezer for the Lavazza.

At first my fingers just wiggle in space over the keyboard as I stare at the pulsing cursor and will the whiskey cloud to thin. I pull the old pitch from my purse and flip through its pages . . . Feminist, he said *young* feminist. I drum my fingers on the plastic cover . . . Hello Kitty . . . Playboy . . . What would make them want to stick with a feminist site? . . . How to keep them comfortable? . . . Attach the word 'feminist' to the existing content that validates the commercial norms they embrace. I snort, envisioning articles on *feminist* tanning beds, *feminist* crash-dieting, *feminist* boob jobs . . . I stare up at the ceiling, letting out a slow stream of air . . . Okay, Guy, feminism for the new economy . . .

Then, very slowly, I start to write the pitch that would entice those students to reimagine the history of lip gloss as a saga of empowerment. Better yet, reimagine empowerment as the history of lip gloss. Soon, I'm speedily pounding out paragraphs on HBO feminism, sifting through my notes from the sessions and quoting anything that might help me get back in. My dress still open, my body hunched over the laptop, I don't once lift my head, not even to sip the coffee Buster left on the box beside me before padding to bed. Once I've finished, I comb the text, Grace's red pen looming.

An ambulance wails by on the street below, stirring me to look up to where steel-blue light breaks over the building across the avenue. I stand, crack my back, and take a gulp of freezing coffee before pressing print. The pages slide out, wafting into a pile on the floor, where I crouch down to reread them before shuffling the proposal neatly together.

I squint to check the clock on the laptop screen: five forty-one; I hesitate for only a second before clicking print a second time. Suddenly, I need this thing out and over so badly I can barely swallow. Not another minute can tick by with these men stuck under the illusion that I'm expendable. Do not pass go, do not collect nothin'. Leaving Buster in deep slumber, I grab my coat and run for the elevator, heels in hand.

As the cab pulls away from Guy's Tribeca condominium, I stare at the remaining document in my lap with heightened certainty. After 411'ing from a barely functional phone booth—*got*togetacell—I take the cab up to Rex's town house on East Sixty-fourth and, with a deafeningly pounding heart, slide the second copy through the mail slot of his black lacquered door.

I skip giddily down the slate steps, holding the wrought-iron fence open, and take a deep, deep breath in the chilled early East Side morning. Stepping back into the waiting cab, I pull my coat tighter around me, wrapping it around my naked legs as I lean against the frosted window and drop promptly to sleep.

Alone on Sunday night, relaxed after a weekend finally spent putting my apartment to rights and enjoying some daytime hours with Buster, I light a few pillar candles on my newly assembled IKEA dining table and carry one into the bathroom with me, killing the overheads as I go. I turn on the shower, letting the steam blanket the tiles as I slip out of my robe.

The hot water is rinsing away my conditioner when I hear the squawk of the buzzer. I slide my towel off the toilet seat and pad into the hall, securing it around me as I buzz in the Chinese food deliveryman. I unlock the door and pull my wallet from my purse, counting out singles in the candlelight—

"Who *THE FUCK* do you think you are?" Guy shoves past me, the frigid leather of his jacket scraping my naked shoulder as he storms into my apartment. The shaken deliveryman grabs a twenty from my paralyzed hand and shoves a plastic bag at me before taking off down the hall. "You're here what—two months—and you think you have even the *slightest* fucking clue?! To go to *my boss* and tell him I don't know *what the fuck* I'm doing?!" he spits, red-faced, as he circles like a caged Dober-man in the flickering candlelight, his hands balled into tight leather-gloved fists. "What the fuck is *wrong with you?!*"

"I—"

"I did you a favor here, Girl. I went out on a limb for you—you have jack experience and this is how you thank me? By *fucking humiliating me!!*"

I recover a shaking voice. "Guy, no—that's not at all what I meant—"

"Nobody gives a fuck *what* you meant! OR how you feel! I say 'stop thinking,' then fucking do it! Don't go tattling on me to Rex like a spoiled fucking brat!" He faces me in the dark-ness of the kitchen doorway, his voice a low growl. "It's unpro-fessional, Girl. It's amateur shit, and it doesn't speak well of you. *At all.*"

"I'm sorry—"

"You want to participate, you're going to fucking partici-pate."

"Thank you." Icy water slides down my spine and forms a puddle at my bare feet.

"Thank Rex. If it was up to me, you'd be out on your ass." Guy pounds his right fist into the door frame, dislodging the Man Ray still leaning where Luke left it. His gaze follows the nude outline of her body. "*Nice,*" he hisses, stepping past it, then me, the door rattling shut behind him.

CHAPTER NINE

I Love L.A.

Proceed to checkout?

I click to an enlarged picture of Martha Stewart's garden boots, racking up another half hour of company time to the two weeks I've spent on-line, sexing up my résumé, and flat-out job hunting. Since the "stop-thinking" directive, followed by the "if-it-were-up-to-me-you'd-be-out-on-your-ass" communiqué, and despite the endearing promise of "my-fucking-participation," nada from Guy. Guy, who hopped a plane for L.A. promptly after leaving my apartment, who I haven't heard a single word from since, and who hasn't fired me—yet—even though he wants to. *A lot.* That Guy.

I glance over my screen for the billionth time at the occupied honeycomb of desks by the front. But no one—*no one*—is taking any notice. I'm physically so far removed from the MC action that Jenna Jameson's latest offering could be moaning from my speakers and *no one* would venture over.

I give Grace's birthday present unnecessary scrutiny, as it may prove to be the pinnacle accomplishment of yet another afternoon spent searching for the panacea to quell my Guy-induced Doris flashbacks.

Yes, I click. I want to *check out.* Of this fear. This job. This economy.

As has become the daily routine since Guy's departure, Stacey bounds across the office in her sagging raincoat, arms full of dry cleaning and mail, a shopping bag swinging from each elbow. While he's forced me to idle, Guy has her running all over the city like a coked-up jackrabbit.

"Hi, Stacey." I click back to a blank spreadsheet. "How's it going?"

She passes my desk, pressing his loot to her chest as she fumbles in her pocket for his office key. "Here, let me help you." I jump up.

"That's okay, got it." She scoots inside, shutting the door.

I follow, leaning into the doorknob. "Are you sure I can't give you a hand?"

She whips her head up. "You're not supposed to be in here. Guy doesn't want you involved with paperwork right now." She scoops up a stack of files and slides them into the cabinet behind her, locking it.

My cheeks sting. "When did he say that?"

"Last week. Look," she ushers me out the door, relocking it, "he's pretty stressed managing L.A. I wouldn't read into it."

"Did he say anything else?"

"No."

"I mean anything. If he said anything you can tell me."

"I just did." She sighs, moving away as she slings on her bag.

"Stacey, I already know he wants to fire me," I admit to detain her. "I just don't know when."

"Well, he hasn't said anything like that to me."

"Oh. Okay. I guess that's a good sign, right?" I dart my eyebrows hopefully.

She picks the shopping bags back off her desk, bouncing them up against her chest. "Look, I have a hundred things I've got to get finished for him today. I've gotta get going."

"Okay," I say quietly, feeling the corners of my mouth start to twitch.

"Girl," she softens, "he's not really a hesitater. If he was going to, he would have."

"Right!" I say with false buoyancy.

"Okay," she huffs, winging back out.

And I'm back to being a good forty feet from humans again.

I stare through the glass into the empty museum of Guy's office. Pacing the length of the transparent wall, I fight the reflection to make out anything that will reveal my fate—ideally a memo that says this is all building up to a surprise party in my honor—but Stacey has cleared every surface.

Back to Hotjobs.com. Casting my career net wider, I'm squinting at the ten-point font enumerating the requirements for joining the army when my message light blinks on. This is it. He couldn't even face me. With a sinking stomach, I dial my code.

"Hi," Guy spits through the earpiece. "We need a binder on the stuff you've got. 'Kay? Great. Bye."

"Yes!" I thrust the receiver victoriously in the air. I'm getting *actual* tasks—work I can *do*—stuff that I've got! A whole binder of it! Yesyes*yes!* Okay, the stuff I've got, the stuff I've got . . . the *stuff* I've got? . . . *The stuff I've got??!!* I punch the air with my fists. *?!?!?!?*

Torn between being the soon-to-be-fired asshole who sends everything and the soon-to-be-fired asshole who sends nothing, I dial his cell. Which blessedly he doesn't pick up. "Guy, hi! It's *so* good to hear from you. I hope you're having a good trip. Hope the weather's good. I'm totally happy to get you *whatever* you need. Would you like me to include the focus-group findings, or Magdalene's prospectus, or the suggested changes for rebranding MC? Or are there additional materials you're interested in? Just let me know and I'll get right on it. Right on it! I'm at my desk. Thanks!"

In the minute it takes to assess the contents of my file cabinet and all the "stuff" he could mean, my message light winks at me again.

"Hi. Yeah. I don't know how to make myself any *clearer*." Guy's contempt is barely contained. "I want *signed affidavits* from *Magdiwhatsit* saying we saved their *fucking* lives. I want happy pictures of you presenting one of those *big cardboard checks*. I want a *full breakdown* of what my money is fucking *accomplishing* over there. Got that? All of it. Supplies, coffee, fucking taxi receipts, all of it. Bye."

What his money *is* accomplishing—*is* as in present tense? Just kill me. I dial Guy's cell again. Again he shunts me over to voice mail. "Guy, I would love to do that. Last we left off, this donation had not been made. Have you, um, made it, or am I now authorized to do so?"

In a matter of seconds, the light blinks again. "Fuck, Girl, yes."

I drop my head to my desk and pound it lightly before calling back. Voice mail.

"Sorry, sorry. Yes, you've made it, or yes, I should make it? Sorry." I cover my eyes and peek out between the slits in my fingers.

Bling! "You," he grunts.

I dial again. Voice mail. "Thanks, Guy! Great! No problem. So, as soon as you tell me who to pick the check up from, I'll head right out."

Hands clenched, I bite my lip and fix myself on the red light. Bling! I jam in my code and am met with a sigh of disgust. "*Not the real check.* Jesus, we're not giving the actual donation *now*. Just go pledge it, and get me some heart-fucking-warming presentation. *Okay?* Can you *handle that much?*" I slam the phone back in its cradle, my heart fucking warmed.

"Girl! Hi!" Julia pulls back the door to her apartment, balancing a large accordion folder on her hip. Glasses low on her nose, wisps of blonde escaping from her loosened ponytail, cheeks flushed, she waves me in to complete what may be my last MC, Inc. task. "What a lovely surprise! I'm afraid we're having a rather mad day." She gestures to the boxes filling the entryway. "Supplies just arrived. A load of paper products from Philip Morris. Which is fantastic, but what we need is food to put on those plates. Guilt funding is so fickle."

She walks away, leaving me to set down my prop-laden shopping bag and lean the absurd Ed McMahon–sized cardboard check facedown against the wall—the check I practically had to dance atop the counter at Kinko's to get on a two-hour rush, then practically had to blow a New York City cabbie to get in the cramped cab. I step around the cartons and follow her into the kitchen, which has been similarly overtaken. "That's okay."

"I've essentially adopted thirty daughters, only our first family get-together revolves around immigration hearings." She flips through piles of papers on the counter.

"How's Moldova doing?" I ask.

Julia sets down the accordion folder. "I'm paying for a room at the YMCA. It got to be a little too much over here, what with running operations from the living room." She pulls her glasses off and squints. "I do appreciate the cleaning job though. How does she seem to be doing?"

"Her shifts are after hours, but Angel tells me she's doing just great." I steeply upgrade his grumbles about finding her constantly on the computers instead of dusting them. "Julia, I'm so sorry about letting her run off without—"

She makes a wiping motion with her hand in the air to stop me. "She's run off from me on more than one occasion. Don't give it another thought. She's a handful."

"Well, I felt really awful that I couldn't get her anything clerical."

"She seems to be tolerating the cleaning." She smiles at me, acknowledging her overstatement. "And she's already taken on studying for her GED."

"That's great! Good for her—"

"Julia?! Where did you put the pro-bono list?!" a woman calls from the living room.

"Green folder! On the mantel!" She grins at me. "Quite a PA system."

"Actually, do you have somewhere we can speak alone?" I ask, eager to live out at least one moment of the fantasy that was this job.

"Other than the bathroom?" Tucking her long bangs back with her glasses, Julia motions for me to follow. I do, through the barely recognizable living room, where her elegant furniture has been replaced by three efficient workstations. Two young women and a young man, engrossed in their various calls and tasks, nod hello as I squeeze by into the long, box-lined hall.

"I just need a minute, folks," Julia notifies them over her shoulder before we step into her beautifully appointed bedroom. She closes the door. "We'll have to sit on the bed. It's the only un-Magdalened corner I've left myself."

I take a seat beside her on the pale-blue silk duvet. Feeling an anticipatory rush, I turn to face her, one knee sliding up on the quilted fabric. "So I came to tell you that I, well, Guy—My Company has decided to award the funding to Magdalene."

She shakes her head as if she hasn't heard me. "Sorry?"

"The million dollars."

"*All for us?*" Her eyes widen. And I nod, smiling. "Oh, *Girl!* Oh, *God!*" She wraps her slender arms around me in a tight hug. "Oh, that's *wonderful!*" She pulls herself back to hold me at the end of her outstretched arms, tears breaking in her eyes. "Thank you. Thank you, thank you, *thank you!* You have no idea how much we—" She shakes her fist in the air, her ivory bangles clattering together. "There is a God! And it's you!" She hugs me again, her infectious high making me laugh for the first time in well over a week. "Come!" She pulls me by the hand and leads me briskly out to the living room.

"Everyone," she announces, "this is Girl, Girl this is everyone." They wave tentatively. "AND SHE'S GIVING MAGDALENE ONE MILLION DOLLARS!" She throws her arms up, and her staff jumps to their feet applauding.

"Oh no, please don't," I say blushing.

"I must open a bottle of champagne!" Julia claps once more and dashes to the kitchen. "Now we can sign that lease! And buy food! And hire lawyers! What time is it? Can I still make it to the bank?"

"Oh, Julia, I don't have it with me," I call to her.

"Right, let me get you our wiring information." I hear the clink of glasses being gathered.

"No, this is just the pledge really, not the actual, um, donation."

She appears in the kitchen doorway. "When will the funds be available?"

Four expectant faces stare. "I don't know." If I'll even get to be here for that.

Julia looks across the crowded space at me, but I can't read her expression. Then she smiles. "Doesn't matter. It's still good news. We'll have a toast."

"I'm sorry," I say, as the phones ring.

"It's Sasha." The young man reaches the receiver over to Julia. "She's had her bag stolen at the shelter."

Julia trades the glasses for the phone, her face clouded with concern. "Sasha? Where are you?" The man walks the flutes back to the kitchen, the toast forgotten, as the two young women resume working. While Julia talks Sasha through her options, I look over toward the black-and-white-marble-tiled entryway where my five-foot check awaits its photo-op.

• • •

The following morning, as I jostle my way off the M23 crosstown and plod up Eleventh, armed with every bit of gratitude-evidence I could shake down from Julia, I continue to ruminate. *It felt great—Julia's face—everyone clapping.* I give the security guard my morning nod—*then awful—the forced photos—the uncashable check.* I squeeze onto the elevator. *And now it just feels desperate.* The door opens on ten. *Because it is. This has just got to be the binder to end all binders. It has to knock Guy's fucking socks off.* I push into the bright office. *And he will not fire me. I will give him no opening, no opportunity, not a single window to point his pruney finger in my face and hiss—*

"Girl."

I bolt around to find Guy glowering in my face. "Hi! How are you?! You're here! You're back!" I slide the bags onto my desk, shakily stepping against it to distance myself from his glare. "So, good flight? Good trip? Good business?"

"You're being—"

"Guy, I've gathered everything you wanted from Magdalene," I breathlessly preempt him. "I've got the presentation right here. You sit right down. I'm going to—"

"Promoted," he spits.

"Sorry?"

"To Vice President," he continues in the same jarringly hostile tone. "That's a twenty percent increase effective today."

"Promoted . . . thank you—"

"Fifteen thousand bonus if you stay on for thirty more days."

"I don't know what to say—"

"Don't say anything. I want you in this meeting immediately." Guy stalks off to his office, the sun reflected off the river giving his figure a nuclear glow. Sucker-punched, I drop my coat and reach for my yellow pad, locking eyes with Stacey.

"He did say 'promoted,' right?" I ask, his words and tenor jousting in my head.

"Yes," she says curtly, still typing.

"I wasn't expecting that." I sit down in a daze onto my coat.

"Uh-huh."

Vice President . . .

"I know," Stacey continues, "it's not like you've done all that much."

"Sorry?" I look back to her as she studies her screen with a pinched expression.

"To be promoted, I mean."

"Well, maybe not in the last few weeks, but I've had a lot on my plate since I got here."

"Of course." She nods, swiveling her monitor and torso away from me as much as her desk will allow.

I have. I have had a very full plate. And I've hit every mark he's asked me to, and he did behave totally inappropriately, and why the hell not?! Why *not* Vice President?!

"Girl! Now!" Guy yells.

I charge my V.P. self up the three steps and into his office, where I find him angling around an impeccably put-together man, late forties-ish, seated at the table by the window, his legs crossed primly at the knee. "Still have your place in Southampton?" Guy asks, as he struggles with the blind cords. "Seline keeps nagging me about driving out to nab a rental for the summer."

"Oh, no, *much* too crowded." The man widens his taut eyes, their youthfulness betrayed by his budding wattles. "I got the house on the Vineyard when Mother died, so Tad and I are up to the family crest in renovations."

The wooden slats drop open with a crash. "The Vineyard—yeah, of course," Guy recovers. "This is Girl." He indicates my presence without turning around and, even though I stand here as Vice President and am wearing the most powerful of my new power suits, I still feel like I'm dripping in a towel.

The man places his subtly manicured hands on the table, his

gray summer-weight wool suit sleeve pulling up to reveal a David Yurman ensemble of cuff links, watch, and ring. He smiles politely, looking me over with a sniff. "Hello," I say, taking a seat across from him.

"This is Jeffrey." Guy joins us at the table. "Friend of Rex here to lend a hand." Jeffrey's face flattens into a tolerant cast.

"Oh, great." I lean back, cross my legs, and square my shoulders, instinctively needing to take up more space. "Welcome!"

Jeffrey smiles wryly, his eyebrows rising enough to lift his meticulously tussled salt-and-pepper hair. "Thank you, Girl," he murmurs with the slightest undercurrent of sarcasm.

I hate him.

"Jeffrey's here to make sure this whole thing stays on track. He's *the* brand man—"

"Eighty-six the intro," he says, the vestiges of a New England lockjaw audible beneath his Beverly Hills locution. "Let's just get on with it, shall we?"

"Sure. So, Girl, let's get an overview."

An overview . . . Let's see . . . I'm an unfireable, incompetent psychobitch who shouldn't mean/feel/think anything. And Vice President. "Yes. From which juncture?"

"From the beginning, Girl," Jeffrey says, his nostrils flaring to accentuate his equine profile.

"Of course." I begin to recite the original *Ms. Magazine* pitch, while carefully trying to avoid using the actual words *Ms. Magazine* and triggering the implosion of Guy's head. "After years spent answering women's beauty questions, My Company wanted to rebrand from serving a solely commercial purpose in the female community to carving out a niche with the feminist activist. We began to explore a plan to align with a certain . . . someone—"

"I don't care for it." Jeffrey wrinkles his nose at Guy. "Too strident. Do you do anything else?" He turns back to me.

Burp the alphabet? "Sorry?"

"Any other bits?"

Guy, his face curdling, tosses me a copy of my 5 A.M. attempt at job salvation.

"My proposal. Okay." I flip it open. "I began by conducting focus groups in the metropolitan area. The attendees fell into two camps. The first were self-identified feminists who feel alienated by the MC site as it stands, perceiving it to promulgate a commercial agenda, such as keeping women preoccupied with their weight rather than with their status and rights. The second group, the vast majority, frequent the MC site and have reinterpreted liberation—"

"This is the proposal?" Jeffrey looks at Guy.

"The bottom line, Girl."

"Um." I awkwardly scroll through the document, my mouth going dry as I confront what I proposed to save my own ass. "Essentially, we could bring the second, larger group content that validates the commercial norms they embrace so enthusiastically, reconfiguring and relabeling what some would call sexist content under a feminist banner, thus encouraging them to embrace the term . . ." And I continue nauseously on, uninterrupted. On and on and on, through a list of ideas, which, upon hearing them out loud, should revoke my NOW card. Jeffrey slowly removes his glasses, sliding one tip into his mouth and nodding at me as if watching TV. Guy puckers his lips and nods along with him, staring down at the table, elbows perched on his knees.

Jeffrey's hand pats Guy's. "She's perfect."

This shuts me up.

Jeffrey places his glasses gently on the table and fingers his open collar. "Perfect. Wherever did you find her?"

"Thanks, yeah," Guy fluffs from the praise. "Some networking thing."

"Divine find. You certainly have the lingo down. And a size

four, am I right? Just a few tweaks here and there and we'll have an excellent show."

"Jeffrey, man, you're like a breath of fresh air!" Guy stretches up.

Sickened, I scramble to undo the damage. "But, Jeffrey, there's a much more direct way of reaching our goal. I don't know if Guy's shared with you, but I've created an action plan for making the site *genuinely* compelling to actual feminists—"

"Yeah, no. So," says Jeffrey, crossing his slim arms, his attention fixed on Guy. "What do women want?" he asks rhetorically, his eyes tracing an arc across the ceiling. This coming from a man whose life would clearly thrive without impact should every woman on earth simultaneously drop dead. "Fun," Jeffrey pronounces as he clasps his hands in an affected prayer. "They want fun, Girl. So no more of this dreary activist poo." Guy leans down and pats him on the back. "Just that part about the commercial stuff from now on. Nix the rest." Jeffrey slides his sleeve back to look at his silver braid watch. "Anything else for her in New York, Guy?"

"Nope. Jeffrey's office is in L.A., so we'll be heading back this afternoon for some major prep for the big client pitch. Cool?"

"So, there's a client?" I ask, trying to recall the potential companies he mentioned at our first and only lunch. "Nike came through?"

"Close. It's an entirely female-run company, right up your alley." Jeffrey winks at me before turning back to Guy.

"Sounds wonderful. Which company is that?"

"Let's not get ahead of ourselves," Guy retorts, fighting to keep his reigning title as King of Vague.

"Well, then." I stand. "Have a safe trip."

Jeffrey smiles indulgently. "No, Girl, you're coming along. Be ready to leave by noon."

"Oh." My eyes dart out the window to the Nelson ball clock.

"And Girl," Jeffrey calls after me, "don't forget your little yellow pad."

One flailing trip home to stuff wrinkled summer clothes in a suitcase later, I twirl the spiral phone chord around my fingertip. Overwhelmed with self-loathing about what I've set in motion, I watch the cord cut off my circulation and will Grace to pick up.

"Chatsworth."

"Mom! Oh, I'm so glad to reach you!"

"Okay, so you're fired. Once again, not the end of the world—"

"What? No—how do you—"

"Jack said your 'tush' was hanging in the balance."

"Gi-irl!" Jeffrey calls out in a singsong from the front door. "We're wai-ting!"

"Chica?"

"No, I've been promoted—and I got a raise."

"That's *wonderful!* Congratulations."

"Thanks, yeah, I'm really excited."

"And what do they have you doing now?"

I'm Vice President of Ann Coulter's Crack for Minors Division. "More of the same, you know."

"And what does that mean, exactly?"

"Gi-irl! Come on!"

"Mom, sorry. I'm heading out to L.A. for work, but I just wanted to give you the good news. I know we haven't talked in a while, but I'll call soon. I promise."

"Okay, I really would feel better if I knew what it is that they're paying you all this money to do."

"*Gi-irl!* For goodness' sake!" His back turned, Jeffrey is no doubt rolling his eyes at Guy, as if we're heading out clubbing and I'm the roommate changing her bra for the third time.

"I've got to go, Mom." I release the chord, my fingertip numb.

"Oh, be sure to check out the Getty—what's today? April . . . twenty-sixth? I think the Henry Moore show just opened."

"Yes, I'll try—"

"We miss you, Chica."

"Me, too. Love you, bye." I hang up the receiver, hating my-self.

Lightning cracks as we roll and scrape our luggage out of the building onto the dampening sidewalk. The limo driver hastily comes around the car to help us load in our bags before the sky opens. "Ugh, the one thing I do not miss about living in New York is this ghastly weather." Jeffrey pulls his Burberry trench tight around him, flashing a watermelon pink custom lining. I catch the driver shake his head derisively as he opens the rear door.

"Girl, you'll be more comfortable in front," Jeffrey offers as Guy slides in.

"It's okay. I don't mind squeezing on the bench opposite."

"Not okay," he counters. "I think you should sit in front." I wait while the driver leans in and swipes empty coffee cups and soda cans to the floor. The hours-old V.P. in me bristles, but keeping in mind that Jeffrey's the only one at MC who thinks I'm 'perfect,' I smile graciously and do as instructed.

"Which airline?" the driver asks, readjusting his mirror and turning on the windshield wipers.

"American, domestic terminal," Jeffrey calls up before raising the opaque partition. "I need a little tête-à-tête time with my Guy."

The smoked glass slides into place, effectively excommunicating me from My Company, and the driver gives me a sadly mistaken knowing nod. "Fruits," he mutters in a thick Greek accent. I huddle down in my seat as raindrops pelt the windows, wishing he were right, that they wanted privacy to get it on, rather than shut me out.

When we arrive at JFK, I follow Guy and Jeffrey to the Business Class counter attendant. "Oh no, Girl, that's you." Jeffrey points over to the endless line of plebes shuffling their way in minuscule increments toward the Economy check-in. "Try not to miss the flight."

The last one to board, I pass Guy and Jeffrey reclining in wide-seated, full-leg-roomed splendor, drinking champagne. Jeffrey raises his flute to me and smiles. "See you in L.A.!"

See you in hell.

Dropping into the cramped seat, I remove my blazer and fan my boarding pass to cool down, my mind falling over itself to catch up with the day's events. *Still employed—promoted even—making more money than I ever anticipated—in this economy—*The plane taxis to the runway, rain streaming down the small oval windows, blurring the lights from the tarmac into yellow pom-poms. *So they took my idea—my awful, awful idea—not that a million people aren't having the same awful idea—*I rest my forehead against the cool plastic as the plane picks up speed, hurtling down the runway, a small jolt in my stomach as it makes that first bounce off the earth before we lift off completely. *A female-run company—that's probably doing great stuff—really great stuff—stuff that will negate this sellout—*I take a deep breath as the plane dips and circles back over Manhattan, finding its course west. *Maybe even—*

"Traffic?" an apple-cheeked young man in the seat beside me asks.

"Sorry?"

"You barely made it. Were you stuck in traffic?"

"Oh, no. Just the airport." I settle back. "My boss didn't account for how long security lines are when you're not flashing a business-class ticket."

"Raisinet?" he offers, as he clicks his seatbelt open to grab his Hudson News bag.

"Sure." I accept the handful he pours and pop a few in my mouth. "Thanks."

"I hear ya. My boss has no sense of the whole space-time continuum. He asks for work in hours that takes weeks and gives us *months* for something that requires one phone call."

"I've worked for her." I watch the city falling away as we climb higher, breaking through the cloud cover to the burst of unexpected sunshine hidden above—*I have. I have worked for her. And this is not that. Where did Doris ever take me? Not even Toledo.* Heartened, I stare out the window, watching the country pass below us as we keep pace with the sun.

"Don't let your boss get you down."

"Sorry?" I turn back to my companion, addressing me from behind his copy of *Barely Legal*, whose cover proclaims in fluorescent block letters, OUCH! EYES TOO BIG FOR HER COOCHIE!

He drops the magazine for a moment. "Life's too short."

"Welcome to Los Angeles. The local time is 4:12. Local temperature is a balmy 82° Fahrenheit." By the time I make it off the plane, Guy and Jeffrey are already waiting at the baggage-claim exit. Guy leans against the glass, unwittingly tripping the sliding doors, which glide open and close, bursts of warm air from the palm-tree-lined arrivals sidewalk wafting over us. "Hi, I just have to pick up my luggage." I gesture to the dormant carousel.

"You checked it?" Guy tugs his tie off and stuffs it into the pocket of his blazer.

"I had to." That's how it works in Coach.

"Well, four's a squeeze anyway." Jeffrey steps through the doors, blowing a kiss to a buff male lounging behind the wheel of a silver Porsche, hazards flashing.

"Here's the address of the hotel." Guy tears off a sliver of the first page of his itinerary, giving it a careful once-over before he hands it to me. "Find me at the pool after you check in." He plods out on his loafered heels to Jeffrey, who swings the car door open, the sun bouncing off the chrome finish, blinding me.

In the semicircular driveway of The Standard, a porter effortlessly lifts my suitcase from the trunk and wheels it inside the lobby, where customers and employees, equally gorgeous in a made-by-Mattel way, weave around an artistically arranged obstacle course of dangerously sharp, knee-high plaster sculptures.

On the unsettling Miró-blue Astroturf patio, I locate Guy sitting pretty amid a thonged-bikini ass-scape. "So I'm all checked in," I say, stepping into his Ray-Banned line of vision. "What's the plan?"

"Oh." He looks up, or rather, over me, his greased face registering a beat of disappointment. "Of course you don't have a bikini."

"No, I—sorry, will the client be joining us here or—"

"Nah." He shuffles the papers in his lap before flipping them against his hairy chest. "That's tomorrow. Relax. Have the concierge send you somewhere." He waves his fingers toward the horizon. Outer space?

"What time tomorrow?"

He sighs. "Christ, I don't know. Not everything can be planned to the minute just because you're a little anal. You've got to *relax*." He taps my thigh with his pen to make his point.

"Okay. Well, I'm in room 411, so just call." I turn away, then swivel back, nearly raking the preening toes of a tanning wishesshewas. "Guy, isn't there anything I should be preparing? I can put my proposal into PowerPoint."

He slides off his Ray-Bans, leaving a little white ring where the sunscreen congealed on his skin, his pen dangling from his mouth like a cigar. "The big pitch isn't till Friday, so I just need you relaxed. Jesus, this is L.A. Loosen up. *Re. Lax.*"

"Okay!" I salute him. "You got it! I can definitely relax," I cheer. Guy closes his eyes and drops his head back, effectively finished with me.

The automatic doors slide open into the lobby, where I'm surprised to find Seline at the deserted concierge's desk, hair pulled back in a ponytail, nervously tapping her Gucci lacquer slide against the marble floor. She looks equally "relaxed."

"Seline?" I call. "Hi, you may not remember me—"

"Sure, you're doing that charity initiative for Guy." She smiles distractedly as she flips through the concierge's Zagat.

"Were you on the plane? I didn't see you."

"I came out yesterday." She adjusts the mother-of-pearl disk in her black bandeau top. "Guy invited me to spend my birthday with him." She looks toward the pool where the setting sun is bathing the valley in a pink glow, Guy's flat feet coming into view as he angles his chair to catch the last light. "We really needed some time together."

"Yeah," I nod in agreement. Time with Guy . . . who can get enough of that?

"Huh," I exclaim as my gaze lands on the glass tank set into the wall behind the concierge desk, displaying, not fish, but a real-live scantily clad female lying eerily still on a bed of bright-green Easter grass, her breasts pointing suspiciously skyward.

"Don't worry," Seline says dryly. "It isn't a design element carried through the rooms." And she's funny. "It can't be a bad job, though," she continues. "You don't have to talk to anyone. No one talks to you. You just have to look hot and sleep. Where is he?" Seline taps the service bell. "I just want a massage."

"A massage? Oh, wow, yes, me, too."

"I'm sorry to keep you waiting," the concierge returns to his post.

"Hi, yes, we'd like a massage," she says, taking charge. "I'm in 602 and she's in . . ."

"411," I add.

"I think we're fully booked for today . . . Wednesdays are always hectic." The concierge shakes his head as he peers into the computer. "But let me see what I can do. In case I can arrange it," he leans in, "would you prefer a man or a woman?"

"Either," we say emphatically.

"Okay, I'll see who I can rustle up."

"Thank you." She gives him a courteous nod. "See you later," she tosses over her shoulder as she strides out to the aqua Astroturf to rejoin her Guy. He leaps up at her approach, offering a fresh citrus-colored cocktail to her outstretched hand.

Despite not yet having any actual "business" on this business trip, it's so far been a raging success. Following a soothing soak, I don a fluffy robe, recline on Frette sheets, sip a supple brandy from the minibar, all while contentedly clicking through CNN, CNBC, and FOX News on my flat screen. All that's missing from this Donald-Trump scenario is the cigar. A *knock-kn-knock-knock* at the door announces the private sector perk-de-resistance. I gingerly pop a steaming scallop into my mouth, return the room service cover, and pad over to let in the masseuse.

"Nine-thirty, right? The last customer kept me late." The stocky man speaks to my feet from a squat so as to balance multiple suitcases. Dressed in a golf shirt and warm-up pants, he instantly reminds me of my eighth-grade gym teacher. Looking up with annoyance, he readjusts his grip. "You want to let me in?"

"Oh. Right." I set down my brandy and pull the door wide as he drops the suitcases next to the bed with an unceremonious thud.

"Watch your feet."

I stand aside as he sets up the table, puts out the lamps, lights a candle, and saturates the air with noxiously fragrant essence. "Patchouli." He drops the little glass vial by the sheeted table, walks wordlessly to the bathroom, shuts the door, and leaves me standing in the near darkness feeling suddenly weird. A few minutes pass before I decide to knock.

"Everything okay?" I ask tentatively.

"What?"

"Um, you okay in there?"

He opens the door. "You want to get undressed and hop on the table?" he gestures with an unmistakable, 'duh.'

"Oh! Sure. Sorry, I thought—yes, I'll just lie down." He closes the door. I pull my robe off, freezing momentarily as I get down to my underwear. Panties/no panties? As I've already revealed my hotel massage virginity, I'm now inexplicably compelled to demonstrate my confidence in his services, and opt for no. Hopping on the table, I squiggle under the towel and plop my face into the headrest.

Yeah, I'd just plain feel better if I was wearing underwear. I start to hop down, but the door opens, and I freeze like a relaxed person. While he circles round me in preparation, I focus on making minute adjustments to the position of my face so as not to choke. Which I am. Very quietly.

Suddenly, flute and cricket music blasts into the room so loudly my pelvis lifts off the table.

"Shit." The crickets are lowered. "Damn thing is busted. I haven't had time to get it fixed, and it keeps jamming."

"No problem!" I say into the sheet-covered doughnut. He oils his hands and presses firmly onto my back. Ahhhhhhh. Good-bye Guy, good-bye Jeffrey, good—

"So where you from?" Wha? Huh?

"Um . . . New York."

"Oh yeah? My cousin lives in Queens. Cool. You here on business?"

Don't want to talk. "Umhmm." He slowly works down my arm until he gets to my hand. Stroking my hand. Holding my hand. Crouching down to peer up at my face and HOLDING MY HAND! Deep breath. Deep breath. Maybe he's just checking the table, maybe—

"You're real pretty." He runs the fingernails of his free hand up my neck. "I hope next time you ask for me special." His voice takes on a suave, oily tone that, despite its rehearsed quality, *freaks me the hell out.*

"Well, yes, that's very kind," I affect my best Shirley Temple. "So kind of you. My husband's with Special Forces, so I'm really just looking forward to getting home to him." I strain my neck and smile like a stewardess. "You know, catching up with him, celebrating our eternal love. That kind of thing." I drop my head back down, heart pounding. He stands, silent. Shit—I've pissed him off and now he will hurt me. "Feels great, though!" I cheer.

He slides the sheet all the way down, allowing an air-conditioned breeze across my upper thighs. Okay, I should just sit up and say something.

Before I can move, he reapplies the patchouli stank to my goose-bumped skin. "Man, this has been a whacked-out night! My last customer was a pain in the ass. This dude just kept grabbing at me! I don't know what gave him the impression I was like *that,* but . . . phew." He kneads my lower back.

"Well," I chatter, overjoyed to be off the topic of my next special trip to L.A., "sounds like he was looking for more than a massage, which is crazy, 'cause who wouldn't be totally, utterly satisfied with a good old-fashioned, classic massage? I know I'm loving this one!"

"I just prayed he'd fall asleep and Jesus listened. Jesus listened to my prayer." I count a few beats and then focus on quietly snoring. Soon, I'm devoting all attention to the host of sounds that would indicate my journey into deep sleep, complete with carefully timed dream twitching. He goes to readjust the sheet, and I practically jump off the table.

"You fell asleep."

"Yes, I'm just so relaxed!" I lie back down, and he pulls the sheet up into a wedge and stuffs it around my right butt cheek. I'd give my left one to have my panties back on. He works his way onto my upper thigh, his hand inching higher in slow circles toward my private sector. "So, did you dream about me while you were sleeping?"

"Oh, no. No, I was dreaming about food! I dream about food all the time. Love to eat pasta." I nod rhythmically into the headrest for emphasis, so uncomfortable I could cry.

"Yeah, pasta's good." A buzzing noise plows over the crickets. "I'm gonna use this vibrating massage tool. I have to tell you that, you know, by law."

"Okay," I say meekly, beginning to leave the room altogether. I'll just float down to the lobby and have a drink, come back when he's done with me.

He rolls the device down my rigid lower back and clamped thighs, while I get him—not a monumental challenge—to tell me about the screenplay he's writing on werewolves falling in love, blow by intricate-plot-twist blow. "And I'm thinking Nine Inch Nails for the closing credits." Suddenly the buzzing is deafening. I open my eyes to a vibrator gyrating inches from my face. His head comes into view, his lips moving.

"What?!"

He turns it off. "Are you *sure* I can't finish this for you? I do a nice release. Only twenty bucks extra. I add it as a towel charge."

"No. No. Thanks. Thanks. But no. No, I'm all set with my towels. Me and my towels, we're just really . . . set."

He drops the wand to the floor, announces he's done, and disappears to the bathroom, instructing me to "take my time." Jesus listened! Fully dressed with every light on and the front door ajar in a minute flat, I knock on the bathroom door. "Okay, thanks! You can go now!"

He lounges against the door frame. "That bread looks good."

I follow his gaze to my now tepid dinner. I dart to the tray, stuff the rolls into a napkin, and dangle it out into the hall as if he were a puppy. "Take them!"

"Cool. You gonna drink that wine?" He saunters over to lift the untouched glass from the tray.

"I guess not—" He gulps it down, wiping his mouth before moving in exceedingly slow motion to pack his equipment. "I'll just leave these here." I bend to put the napkinful of rolls on the hall floor, retrieving a note half-shoved under the door. "I need to call my husband at the base before it gets much later so . . ."

He continues at his leisure. "What happened to your friend anyway?"

I slit open the envelope. "Sorry? My friend? Oh, she's getting a massage in her own room."

"Oh. Okay." He stands from his final zip and nods at me in revelation.

"What did they tell you at the front desk?"

"Two ladies requested me."

"For a massage." I open the card. *Meet me out front at noon—Jeffrey.*

He lifts his suitcases, pausing by the bed. "You want these?" He points to the turndown chocolates on my pillows, stuffing them into his pocket. "Thanks. You can tip me on the bill."

After hours of watching four crappy movies simultaneously, I finally feel "relaxed" enough to click off the TV. I stare for a while at the slim shaft of boulevard light twitching where the curtains meet over the air conditioner before sliding my hand from the covers to dial Buster's number, loneliness overriding any guilt about rousing the roommates. The phone rings repeatedly out into the ether until his machine picks up.

"Hi, everyone. It's me in LaLa Land—just wanted to say goodnight to Buster. I guess it's kind of late. Or early. I left a message this afternoon. I'm not sure if he got it—"

"Girl?" his sleepy whisper beeps on.

"Hey! Sorry to wake you."

"Don't be," he says groggily. "It's good to hear your voice." My heart clenches, and I want to crawl in next to him. "I missed you tonight. There was a party. It looks like Atari's gonna buy us out."

"Oh, Buster—"

"Yeah, but we all get to stay on staff. And they're not gonna relocate us, so we're pretty psyched." He yawns. "You okay? Get out there all right? Meet your client?"

"Not yet. Congratulations, Buster, that's really wonderful." My voice sounds loud in the empty room.

"Yeah, I didn't want to worry you, but I heard rumors of layoffs if we sold."

"Buster, you can worry me," I whisper. "I want to know if you're stressed—"

"Nah, it's gonna be okay now. Shit, I miss you," he mumbles, his breathing getting heavier.

"I miss you, too. I'll call you tomorrow night, okay?"

"Yeah. Don't forget. And, G?" His voice perks awake, I half sit up. "I like you a lot."

"I like you a lot, too, Buster. 'Night."

" 'Night."

In the morning I'm told breakfast is served on the unnaturally, oppressively blue patio, where Guy sits in a linen suit before an untouched plate of French toast. Across from him, I recognize

Rex's long legs sticking out beneath the pink pages of *The Financial Times* spread like a wall in Guy's pinched face.

"Good morning," I say, affecting chipper, productive, and, above all, relaxed.

"Morning, Girl!" Rex folds his paper to reveal a cleaned plate.

"Hey," Guy says.

"Hey," I reply, as Rex continues to read. "So, where's Seline?"

"Sleepin' in." Guy fingers the base of his coffee cup. "We had a late night."

"That's my boy." Rex drains his espresso. Ew.

Guy seizes the opening. "Look, Rex, I can lead this meeting. I've done way more prep on this than Jeffrey and frankly his whole . . ." Rex's face is impassive. "I just think he's going to overhit it. He's too much drama—"

"I told you what I want." Rex slips his tongue forward to suck something from his teeth before continuing coolly. "And yet we still seem to be having this conversation." They stare at each other.

Guy breaks the gaze, picking up his fork and fiddling with an orange slice. "Right. If you felt you needed to have the prep meeting as a one-on-one with Jeffrey, if you didn't need me there, that's cool. That's . . ." He nods with too much enthusiasm. "That's great."

Rex drops both hands on his chair arms. "Great," he echoes as he pushes back from the table, reaching his paper to Guy and sliding his blazer off the back of his chair. "I'm choppering out to Pebble Beach. Jeffrey has my schedule." Guy nods again. "Girl." He slaps me on the back as he passes. "Excellent proposal. Excellent catch."

"Thanks! Thank you, I'm glad to help," I call after him as he struts into the shadow of the lobby.

Guy throws his fork across the table, and it clatters like a skipping stone, dropping soundlessly onto the Astroturf. I stand stock still. "What?" he exhales quietly, turning to me with a slackened face. "What do you need?"

"Oh." I take a breath. "Is everything okay?"

"No, it's not," he says, his voice low. "I've been working twenty-five hours a day for the last eighteen months since this was just the seed of an idea I had in the shower." He rubs his face. "This is my thing. Mine." He lets out a grim laugh. "It just blows, ya know?"

"I do."

"Right," he scoffs. "I'm sure."

And . . . back to hating him. "I got a note from Jeffrey to meet him out front at noon."

"So, can you do that?" He opens the pink paper with a snap and begins to tensely flip through it. "Or do we have to psychoanalyze it first?"

Lettingitslidelettingitslidelettingitslide. "I can do that. But I am going to need fifteen minutes to take you through the PowerPoint."

"I don't have fifteen minutes." He hastily folds the front section and opens Markets. "Just go meet with Jeffrey. He's the brand man. He wants to work on yours."

"My brand?"

"Lighten up, Girl. It's just an expression."

"Okay. So I'll . . ." He stares at his paper. "Guy, given all your feedback, we need to be on the same page before I go in front of the client."

"*Jesus,* Girl, just meet with Jeffrey and don't give him any trouble."

So then I shouldn't put gum in his hair?

"Oh yeah, hey!" he recalls me. "Do me a favor and have room service send up some breakfast to Seline. Pancakes or something. Something birthday-ey. Oh, and have them stick a rose with it." His cell rings as he heaves his briefcase into his lap.

"Jeff, yeah man. What?" His face darkening, he angles away from me, and I take my cue to head back up, order birthday room service, and stare out the window at four lanes of traffic and one lone palm tree.

Promptly at noon, the silver Porsche glides up to the lobby with Jeffrey yapping away in the passenger seat. "No, no, that's all wrong!" he cries as I squeeze in back.

A disembodied voice retorts, "Jeffrey, you always order four shrimp platters—there's no need to yell."

"On speaker," mouths the same surfer-gorgeous blond who picked them up at the airport as he gives me a wink from the driver's seat. "Tad, Jeffrey's 'assistant.'" Offering back his right paw, he steers us out with his left.

"Hi," I mouth in return.

"Don't take that tone with me. Last time you ran out halfway through, so I'll yell if I damn well please," Jeffrey says testily, disconnecting the call and dialing his office.

"Jeffrey," Tad intercedes. "I can handle this crap. You don't need to micromanage."

"It's not that I don't trust you." He pats Tad's thigh. "It's that they're only scared of me. Now be a love and put me through to the florist—I've changed my mind, I want bamboo."

"Jeffrey, about my brand," I begin in the pause.

"Not now, Girl. You'll have my undivided attention as soon as we get out of the car. Yes, hi, it's Jeffrey Wainwright. About the bamboo . . ." Thwarted, I slouch back and take in the city as the traffic slows to a crawl beneath the beating sun. Steaming vapor trails from the tar roofs along Sepulveda, while Jeffrey's ceaseless patter of charm and derision fuels us across town. Pulling into Fred Segal's, the infamous department store/celebrity haunt, Tad jogs around the Porsche to let Jeffrey out onto the radiant asphalt. "Girl, we're here. Chop chop. Tad, I'll ring."

I follow Jeffrey through a blast of cold air and techno into the labyrinth of upscale boutiques, each one painted a different Lifesaver shade and trolled by a different desperate demographic—wife, waitress, starlet, star, and stylist. Yet, despite the differences in status, all the women have the same too-blonde hair, too-tan skin, too-wide eyes, too-full lips, too-small noses, and too-pert breasts. They are all in some form of midriff-and-calf-bearing ensemble. Only the range of accessories—from gym bag to cheap bag to free bag to custom bag to twelve bags—distinguishes them.

"Come along!" Jeffrey turns back like Orpheus to make sure I haven't been waylaid by a oncewas. "People are waiting." We arrive at the reception area of the bright pop-art salon. "Hello, yes, I have an appointment with Jean-Claude," he informs the receptionist, who wears a white retro smock over a black turtle-neck.

"Hello, Jeffrey," she confirms, batting her black awning of fake eyelashes like Edie Sedgwick. "You're all set."

"You're up, Girl." He indicates the woman holding out a folded robe. I look skeptically from her to him. "Up. Up. Let's get a move on." He pulls off his Prada wrap shades. "Didn't Guy tell you our plans?"

"No, and I'm not going 'up' until *we* have a conversation—"

"That man. Whatever shall we do with him?" He smiles, straining for conspiratorial as my protest arouses the attention of the other customers, prancing the white floor in their Ugg boots, denim minis slung so low that they seem designed to barely cover crack on either front. He lowers his voice to a purr, "Dear, you're in L.A. now. And out here it's ninety percent show, ten percent go."

"Go?"

"Go." He flits his hands, the Pradas snapping open and shut. "Content. Ten percent content. Goodness, just *relax*."

"God, I'm relaxed! Look, you want to give me a free makeover, I'm game. But I think I deserve an explanation of what my appearance has to do with selling our services—" I'm interrupted by the stylist I saw earlier passing between us lugging an armful of shoes.

"Shit, *I* don't know which pair," we hear from the other side of a shoji screen. "The network has a teen demographic, so I want something that says, 'Young.' But experienced. Humorous. But with a sense of the dramatic. And a flair for writing cop dialogue."

Jeffrey swoops his shades in the direction of the shoes about to take a meeting. "In this town, every detail tells a story. We want yours to tell the right one."

I take the robe and lean into his face. "Fine. But my details aren't getting implanted. And I'm leaving here a brunette."

"Let's move." He maneuvers me through the sonorous whir and snip of the salon, past a long wall of framed gratitude-inscribed magazine covers, to where a man with a platinum goatee is waiting behind an empty chair.

"Girl, Jean-Claude." Jeffrey drops his voice to address him. "What we talked about." They nod in agreement. "I'll be on my cell, should you need."

Jean-Claude waves Jeffrey off with diamond-laden fingers. "Zo," he says, running said fingers along my scalp. "Beautiful." He takes my face in his hands and turns it side to side. "Tall, zin, could be model, no? But you need to be brightur. You're dark, so darrrrk." He lifts a chunk of my brown hair with derision. "Your clothes are darrrk. Your hair is darrrk. You New Yorkerz, you need your *soulz* lightened. *Tout de suite!*" He claps his hands to have my soul whisked to the color station. And I let him.

Several hours later, my hair is a long-negotiated caramel, my toes deep pink, and my fake tan is rapidly developing. I'm Malibu Me. Fingering the racks, I wend my way through Red Carpet, Black

Tie, Luncheon, Cocktails, and Beach House, bopping along as Prodigy pounds from the loudspeakers. Arms filled with Marc Jacobs and Marni, soon I alight on the still-coveted Nanette Lepore jacket, which I parade before the mirror, trying to analyze the story I'm telling. "Here, try this," the stylist says as she passes with another armload. She reaches deep into her pile and hands me a short-sleeved blouse, gathered at the shoulders.

"Thanks! I'm going for feminist, but relaxed and bright, and no . . . um, dreary activist poo." I fan my hands along my silhouette. "Are you getting that at all?"

"Then wear it with irony. Switch the shirt out for a tank top and find a baby pink leather cuff bracelet."

"Thanks!" Having more fun than I've had in a very, very long time, my Anistoned-self skips over to the jewelry department to find a cuff.

"Girl!" Jeffrey descends on me as I ogle the Me&Ro case. "Fabulous. You look perfect. Well done. Now, come on." He trots me back to the dressing rooms.

"I'll show you what I picked. I think you're going to be really happy." I pull my pile off the woven dune-grass counter.

"Mmmhmmm . . ." He chews the tip of his glasses again as he stares the Nanette Lepore down. "Yes, yes, and yes, but with a tank top and it needs a leather cuff—baby pink." I proudly extend my cuffed wrist out of the sleeve. He pulls out his Corporate AmEx. "Okay, so you're squared away for the meetings. This is for tonight." He hands over a small velvet jewelry pouch.

"Oh my gosh. Wow."

"Go try it on. Then come out and show me."

I return to my changing cabana and gingerly untie the ribbon securing the pouch. I cup my left palm and shake out . . . a ball of gold string. What the? I untangle it and hold it to my throat, tying it loosely and leaving the slightly thicker bits to dangle like a deconstructed Chanel flower choker.

"Ta-dah!" I hop out of the dressing room.

"Not on your neck." His eyebrows dart up as he gives me a withering appraisal. "It's a bikini, you idiot."

"What?!"

He tugs at the threads. "Girl, it's a pool party—a little ice-breaker thing with the client." He balls the fabric in my palm, gripping his fingers around mine. "*Everyone* will be in swim-suits. We want you to be comfortable."

"Comfortable?" I cock an eyebrow, pulling back from him.

"Now don't get all uptight," he says with a smile. "Just go put it on properly." One arm supporting the other elbow, he waves me back.

"Not a chance, Jeffrey," I say, laughing at the idea.

Jaw set, residual charm evaporated, he bears down on me, lowering his voice to a tight hiss, "Wipe that smile off your face. I can have you fired with a phone call."

"I—"

"You're lucky to even be here. We've paid to have you made over by one of the premier salons in the business. We're about to buy you a whole new wardrobe, for fuck's sake. So just go try on the goddamn bikini." His eyes sparkle anew. "Hop to it!"

I shakily teeter back into the little room. Seconds later, he throws open the sailcloth. "Come on, let's see! Oh, fabulous! Per-fect!"

I tug at the minuscule triangles to try to cover something of my breasts. "Jeffrey, this is *work*. I'd really prefer a one-piece."

"Oh no, they don't stock those." Jeffrey shudders as if I've re-quested a Victorian bathing costume. "It's a *pool* party—loosen up! This is a winner!"

"Do you have a sarong?" I furtively ask the passing salesgirl. She looks to Jeffrey, and he shakes his head. He whispers in her ear and she nods, taking his station in my cabana.

"Honey, what're ya gonna do about the bush?"

"Excuse me?" I ask, distracted with trying to keep my nipples covered.

"Waxing, sweetie. Ya gotta wax."

"I am waxed." I cross my arms. "I have a boyfriend. I'm waxed."

"Honey, this isn't Vermont. *Any* hair ruins the lines of the suit. People'll be looking."

After a second, chafing, *way* too up-close-and-personal visit with Jean-Claude, I'm directed to Tad, who's waiting for me in the Porsche. "Hey," he says, shoving my three shopping bags in the backseat. "Hop in. Jeffrey had to run. Here's our address." Tad tears a sheet from the dashboard notepad as we pull out of the parking lot. "Be there by seven." Absorbed by the traffic, he pumps up the nine speakers to clubbing decibels, forcing me to fume silently all the way back to The Standard.

In the quiet refuge of my room, the techno bass still throbs in my ears as I wriggle back into the suit, tugging it this way and that in front of my goose-bumped reflection.

Jesus, no. I am just naked. I am Cinemax-After-Dark naked.

I shut off the air and open the window wide, the rumble of Sunset Boulevard rolling over me with the humidity. Increasingly uncomfortable—with Jeffrey's demands, my complicity, and mostly the irritating residue of hot wax————I pick up the phone and dial Chatsworth, counting on Grace to give me a one-sentence cyanide pill.

"Yeeelllllllooo."

"Jack, hey, it's me. I'm in L.A."

"I heard. Also heard you got a big fat fuckin' raise."

"Language."

"Gonna buy me a car?"

"Gonna learn how to drive?" I lean out over the sill, the sun penetrating my chilled skin. "Okay, here's the thing."

"Always a thing."

I puff up my cheeks, blowing out the air as I try to decide which of the nineteen things Wrong With This Picture I should mention first. "My boss, but not really, took me on this shopping trip but ended up stripping me down to a bikini for this work thing tonight—"

"A swimming work thing?"

"I guess."

"Well, if it's a swimming work thing, you should be in a bikini."

I look down at my copiously exposed breasts. "I just feel weird."

"You *are* weird."

"That's helpful."

"Dude, you worry about everything."

"Not everything." I reach back inside the room to pull a cigarette from the emergency pack I copped in the lobby.

"You thought you'd never get a job."

"Yeah," I say, lighting up.

"And you got a job."

"So?" I exhale, blowing a strong stream of smoke into the smog.

"So, you're in L.A. and I'm cleaning out drainpipes in the pissing rain. And there's this man in the tower room writing a book about Chernobyl. And we can't get through a meal over here without a little mutation talk. And if we're really good, he brings pictures."

Smiling, "Point taken. Love you."

"Yeah. You need mom?"

". . . I don't know . . ." Reaching around, I smash the cigarette against the outside wall. "You're right. I'm in L.A., in a four-star hotel, with a celebrity haircut and a tan. It's not the end of the world."

"Uh-huh. So you want to talk to her or not?"

"No." I gaze out at the *Baywatch* billboard. "Just tell her I'm okay."

The setting sun rapidly cooling the air, I step out of the taxi, straightening my Juicy terrycloth strapless minidress and folding my jacket over my arm. After a brief, but moving, memorial service for the bikini, I revisited the shopping bags with a fresh eye, pulling together the 'perfect' pool-party-work-thing story. My chandelier earrings swinging, I pass through Jeffrey's neurotically symmetrical Zen garden, careful not to catch the heels of my new Sigerson Morrisons. A Thai gentleman in a white Mandarin ensemble beckons me from the door and takes my jacket. "Welcome. You Girl? Friend of Mr. Jeffrey and Mr. Tad? Please, come in." I follow into the slate-tiled entryway, its interlocking slabs flowing uninterrupted through the glass-walled house and out to the crowded pool.

"You change here?"

"Sorry?"

"Change now?" He gestures to the powder room off the entryway.

"Oh, no, thanks. I'm all set."

His previously courteous tone insistent, he says, "Please, wait heh." Left at the teak bench by the door, I rub my arms in the chilly hallway. Outside, space heaters are ensuring maximum skin exposure from the almost entirely male crowd, frolicking amidst the ubiquitous bamboo.

"Girl!" Tad's voice echoes as he slides the patio door open, bossa nova beats momentarily reverberating in the stone space. He shakes his head vigorously, droplets of water darkening the slate before he bounds over in a Gucci ball-hugger that highlights his role in Jeffrey's household. "Hey, so, uh, where's the suit?"

"Yeah, it didn't fit. It's okay, I don't plan on swimming."

"Okay, well, we'd really like you to. So, we're just gonna get you another suit. Jeffrey'll be here in a minute, so, uh, why don't you pop a squat in . . . uh . . . here!" He backs me into the teak powder room and hunkers in the doorway. "You look really hot with your hair that color."

"Thanks," I say, looking behind me and realizing the toilet lid is my seating option. "I really don't need a suit."

"Lady, your champagne!" The butler passes a flute over Tad's shoulder, complete with a strawberry sliced onto the rim.

"Thanks."

"You not allergic strawberry, ah you?"

"No."

"Good, good." With the other hand, he holds out several more of the small velvet pouches. "Mistah Jeffrey heh soon."

Cornered against the toilet bowl, I look to both entreating faces as they squarely block the doorway. "Gentlemen, I appreciate your interest in my comfort, but I swam at the hotel. I'm not swimming tonight," I say definitively, gauging if we're on the verge of a smackdown.

His lank, sun-streaked hair draped like puppy ears around his face, Tad simply begs, *"Please?"*

"Where's my Girl!"

"In here!" At Jeffrey's voice, I squeeze between my captors back into the front hall as he glides in through the glass living room door, clad in modest yellow Vilebrequin trunks. He tugs a young Sharon Osbourne manqué along on his arm, the mellifluous sounds of Dean Martin crooning in behind them. "Here's someone I'm *dying* for you to meet," he calls as the mid-thirties-ish woman eagerly frees herself and alights on a passing server.

"Hey, you, with the crabby things!" Her Manchester accent ricochets off the stone as she unabashedly loads up her mendhied palm.

Jeffrey's face curdles as he takes in my suitless self. "Girl, this is Kat, president and cofounder of Bovary." He pulls her attention from the hors d'oeuvres as I try to recall any reference point. *BovaryBovaryBovary?* "Kat, meet Girl, the feminist backbone of MC, Inc."

"Well, it's about time." Kat lights up beneath her electric-red pixie bangs, saving me from having my ignorance revealed. "I was starting to think all that crap you've been shoveling about a female face was just that—crap." Jeffrey looks tense until she breaks into hearty laughter. Nervously, he joins in a second later. Okay, clearly it doesn't behoove him to have the 'feminist backbone' exposed as knowing diddly. Her chuckles subside as she smiles warmly at me. "I love this dress. You look enchanting." She darts her index finger under the elastic smocking between my breasts. Oh-kaaay.

"Yes, Girl has a great eye," Jeffrey coos.

The butler retreats, followed by, "I'll be out there if you need me . . ." Tad points to where wet male bodies undulate in the glow of the tiki torches.

"Yes, go," Jeffrey excuses him.

"I'll come with you! I haven't made it out to the pool yet." I step after him, but Jeffrey slides his arm around my waist. This is not good.

Kat chews enthusiastically. "Have you tried these?" She swallows. "They're fucking brilliant. Dead sinful but brilliant." She winks, wiping her fingers on her camouflage-print capris.

"Oh, no, dive in! They're baked with low-fat tartar," Jeffrey chimes, prompting me with an eyebrow.

"Yes, I haven't tried those yet—"

"Oh, good God, well, let's get him back!" Kat exclaims. "Better yet, let's stake out the kitchen."

Jeffrey nabs a server to request a fresh tray of crab cakes as Kat lowers her voice to a throaty, conspiratorial timbre. "My girlfriend and I, we just checked out the library—not many books but enough naughty-boy tapes to open their own shop." She licks her shiny fingers, her nose ring sparkling *fuck* in tiny diamante letters. "So, Bovary—what're your thoughts?"

"My thoughts . . ." Jeffrey, his attention returned, squeezes my side. Anyone? *An-y-one!* Jeffrey breathes on my neck unhelpfully. "I . . . I'm a . . . a firm believer in the female-run organization." She nods. "It's the very essence of action-oriented feminism."

"Yes!" she chimes. Jeffrey squeezes again.

"Female management is the key to change." I eye her matching camouflage bikini top. "As long as it's done in style, of course."

"She's fab! Jeff, you're spot on—she does have the Bovary look."

"*And* she thinks your brand expansion from bedroom to poolside is genius! She picked up one of your suits this afternoon at Segal's—loved it."

I'm remotely aware of Jeffrey twittering as the hairs on my neck stand on end.

"Loved it?" Kat asks, holding my gaze.

"Loved it," Jeffrey answers in his singsong.

"And I *love* this." Laughing, she points at two Adonises tussling atop their friends' shoulders in the pool. *"I love L.A.!"* she sings, stretching her arms wide as she spins to the windows. "The board wants U.S. headquarters in New York—you know, fashion capital, quick hop over the pond, and I'm like, fuck no. I want sunshine! I want palm trees! I want *movie stars* fucking in my knickers! *My* bras hanging over the bar at the Whisky-a-Go-Go. I want a starlet found O.D.'d with *my* slip up over her head. Glamour, baby." No, Mom, you had it all wrong. I'm not Ann Coulter. I'm her panties.

"Hate to eat and run, but we have that blasted thing in the

Valley." Kat motions a finger to her throat. "Darling, a pleasure! What's your size?"

"Small, of course," Jeffrey says, giving my waist one final squeeze that threatens to bring up my lunch.

"Fab—I'll have a bunch of samples sent to your hotel. See you in the bright and early!" She swivels my numb face to plant glossy kisses on both sides.

"Come along, Girl, your car's here, too."

"I need to find Guy."

"Let's get Kat to her car and then I'm all yours."

Glowering in the dark, I wipe away her lipstick imprint with the back of my hand. The gravel crunches beneath our feet, mixing with the grating chirp of cicadas. Kat slides into a Town Car, nestling herself beside a slumped platinum blonde, who limply flutters her fingers at Jeffrey. "Bye, darlings," Kat calls, pulling the door shut.

The car rolls away down the drive, Jeffrey flagging the next one in line as the butler approaches with my things. "She's such a spark plug," he says, smiling to himself.

"Why didn't you give me a heads up on this?" I demand, tugging on my jacket.

"Oh, didn't I?"

"*No!* No, you didn't!" I'm getting that speaking-Martian feeling.

"Oh. Well, I'm sure I must have mentioned something."

"Fuck, Jeffrey." I feel the blood flood back into my face. "Putting aside what that woman even does—that was *completely* unprofessional! This is a job. I work for My Company, Incorporated. *They* pay me to think and execute—which requires the necessary preparation—preparation that has nothing at all to do with my pubic hair!"

He sucks in his cheeks in distaste. "Your pubic hair is absolutely in my purview, little miss. This is working. Not shuffling pathetic little grants around to save the whales. Success takes every hour and every inch. All of you. You think I'm throwing this party for my own amusement? You think I wouldn't rather drape myself in velour and drink beer and get fat in front of the TV?" He sniffs. "In the real world you work twenty-four/seven and you use everything you've got."

"Maybe your working isn't my working."

"Obviously."

"I need to talk to Guy." I stride past him toward the house.

"Anything you have to say to him you should say to me."

"No, Jeffrey. It's between me and Guy."

"And I'm telling you, anything you have to say to him you might as well say to me."

I turn to his faceless silhouette, backlit in the headlights. "*He* hired me."

"He wasn't even invited tonight." Moving out of the car beams, Jeffrey stares me down.

"Fine. I quit."

"No, you don't," he says, laughing.

"Yes, I do." Marching back, I reach around him to pull the car door open. "However 'normal' this all is," I wave my free hand back in the direction of the borderline orgy in his pool, "I quit."

"No. You don't." He shuts it, the force snapping the handle hard against my fingers. "Look, that makeover, from which you're obviously having some sort of posttraumatic episode, was a one-time deal. You had an edge. It needed to be softened. Kat, for your information, is the Paul Newman of intimates. Bovary's the second-biggest fund-raiser in the U.K. behind the Princess Trust. They've given millions of pounds to women's homes, political refugees, the cancers—" Tad thumps down the gravel toward us, clutching a thick black dossier across his torso like Adam's leaf.

"Then why didn't you tell me any of this earlier?"

"I'm telling you now." He opens the door for me. "Tomorrow morning, MC, Inc. is pitching to orchestrate their U.S. launch. And I'm about to do you an incredible favor." He shuts it and leans in the open window. "I'm going to forget the last five minutes ever happened. I won't let you blow this opportunity just because you're being ignorant and reactionary and, frankly, unprofessional." I flush as Jeffrey passes the binder in and lays it over my lap. "This contains all of Bovary's pertinent stats. Make it your bible. Tad'll pick you up at nine-thirty sharp. Knock 'em dead. Kat loved you." Before I can even form a response, he raps the roof with his knuckles, and the car takes off down the drive.

Two A.M. finds me staring into an empty coffee mug at a booth in the hotel's diner-style restaurant. Having abandoned trying to make sense of Jeffrey, I'm still trying to make sense of Jeffrey's dossier. Sliding the cup onto the orange Formica, I shut the binder and rub my tired eyes, ears tuning to the low hum of CNN from the bar TV. I glimpse documentary footage of Sierra Leone as the screen casts a green glow over the beautiful few slumped in postparty exhaustion at nearby booths, their drunken chatter mingling with the grim report.

Taking a deep breath to revive, I flip the binder back open and reread, for the fourth time, the final paragraph of the last article. No, it officially ends mid-sentence. I stare again at the blank page behind it. Nothing. Each article, after enumerating the reams of charitable causes Bovary has championed, seems to end at the point of addressing their U.S. launch.

The door at the far end of the Gulfstream-styled room swings open, and Seline shuffles in, swathed in one of Guy's blue-and-white-pinstripe shirts over jeans. She walks to the bar and peers at the bottles behind it, running two hands through her bed-tousled hair.

"Hey," I call to her. It takes a moment to register who I am before she nods hello. "Can't sleep?" I ask.

She nods and slides in across from me, tucking the cuffs into her palms. "Working?"

"Prepping for tomorrow's meeting."

"How'd you get out of dinner?" She holds her finger up to catch the bartender's attention. "A glass of port, please."

"I was at Jeffrey's."

"Oh, then I guess my evening could have been worse." She picks up the small plastic snack menu and gives it a cursory glance.

"Yeah, it was probably my first and last gay pool party."

"At least you didn't spend your evening being force-fed shot glasses of slime at Asia de Cuba while your boyfriend licked his boss's ass." She grimaces. "Oh, God, are you watching this?" Her left hand still balled beneath his cuff, she points at the scarred limbs flashing from the screen above us.

"Help," is all I can muster.

"Can we switch it to something lighter?" she asks the bartender as he places the sherry glass before her. He points the remote.

"Mmmmm, the Style Network." My shoulders sink in relief. Seline pulls her feet up and I do the same as the screen fills with the transformation of real people and homes into momentary ideals of perfection.

"How was your massage?" I ask, the respite from genocidelingeriegenocidelingerie perking me up. "Was your masseuse . . . under the impression—"

"Guy was on the balcony talking on the phone the whole time, so." She swivels her forearm, dislodging a bracelet stuck near her elbow, and I catch site of a Whitney-worthy diamond solitaire that definitely was not there yesterday.

"That's . . . wow," I say, my eyes widening.

"Two weeks ago we walked past this store. I said, 'Gee, that bracelet's ugly.' " She twists her wrist, making the moonstones glint. "Guess we know which part he heard." The lady from Shabby Chic is perusing a flea market on the big screen.

"Sorry, I meant your ring. Congratulations."

"Oh." She tucks her hands back into his large shirtsleeves, the fabric obscuring the diamond. "He just proposed tonight, so I haven't really had time to . . . Thanks."

We both stare at the television. Yeesh. I search for a comfortable topic in our extremely limited parcel of shared experiences.

"I didn't really expect this." She glances up at the ceiling. "You just . . . never know with him. I mean . . . if he's going to break up with you or . . ."

"Promote you?"

"Yeah," she laughs, pushing up her sleeve and looking down at her four-carat promotion until her eyes suddenly well and she blinks, her lashes wet. "He's a great catch, and this ring is fucking huge, and then we . . . and then I tried to go to sleep, but my heart is just racing." She holds her hand over her chest and takes a shaky breath. "Some birthday."

"That's right, happy birthday!"

"Thanks." She takes another steadying breath and looks out the darkened diner window, where a group of porters playfully jostle one another in the drive. "The big three-oh."

"How does it feel?" I ask, eager for a report from the front. She shrugs.

I lean my head against the cool window, imagining a future of self-assertion. "I'm gonna be a festival of boundaries by then, so help me."

She flags down a refill. "You think?"

"I hope."

"I still let a lot slide. I mean, not at work, or with my friends, but . . . I'm the girlfriend who lets a lot slide. Maybe he's looking for the wife who does the same. Or not. I don't know." Seline tosses her hands up. "I didn't expect this. I'm just not . . . prepared." Her eyes are fixed on the screen, where a bed frame is being meticulously repainted, and it's unclear if she wants me to prompt her or let it drop.

"*It's about a lifestyle of comfort, relaxation, and beauty . . .*" the nasal British voice drones, and there's only the tiny motion of Seline's sleeved fingers clasping and reclasping the small glass.

She drains it. "The thing is there are hundreds of women who wouldn't bat a mink eyelash that he cancels dinner an hour after he was supposed to pick them up."

She pauses and I temper my impulse to eviscerate him. Do not diss him. Do not diss him. Do not. "He does seem like . . . a busy person."

"He is. But when he's there for me, he's so there for me it's electric." Her whole face breaks open into a soft smile. "He's amazing with my family. He loves kids. We both love black Labs. He so wants to be 'the man,' 'the husband.' I can just so easily picture him as the soccer dad. And I can so easily picture him never coming home." Her expression once again clouds. "But does anyone come home anymore?" She looks to me to weigh in.

"I don't know. I think so. I hope so."

"God, I could use a cigarette."

"I have some in my room," I offer.

She flattens her forearms on the Formica. "It's shocking there isn't a clearer line here. I can't believe I'm staring at thirty and I still don't know what's worth overlooking."

"He's confusing." He is. I'd say that to his face.

"They all are. I've definitely put up with a lot worse," she says with a smile. "There are a lot worse out there. I could do a lot worse."

"You could." He could be an asshole *and* a homicidal maniac.

She nods down at her hands and then up at me. "This is a good thing."

"Okay."

"It is. So, I was taken by surprise—that's how it's supposed to be, right? That's what makes it romantic."

"Yes." Every time he takes me by surprise I come over all aflush.

Seline slides out of the booth, the ring sparkling in the dim spotlight over our table.

"If you wait a minute, I can pay and then get you that cigarette."

"Oh, I'm okay. I just need a good night's sleep. Thanks, this was really useful. Just put everything on my room. Good luck in the morning."

"Thanks." You, too.

The Porsche pulls in behind a nondescript stucco building on Melrose, and I climb out at Tad's prompting, this time fully clothed in my Marc Jacobs capri suit. "Just take the back door, there. One flight up."

I walk past the Dumpster to the black metal door and take a deep breath, ready to knock 'em dead.

"Gi-irl!" Jeffrey greets me as I step out of the stairwell into the industrial-carpeted hallway, lined with racks of short garment bags marked Bovary. "Perfect. Right on time. Kat's been asking for you. Now I want you to come into the conference room and do your bit. Sell the charity stuff, sell MC's feminist commitment, but keep it light. Light and bright!" He grabs the handle to one of two large steel doors, and before I know it, I'm staring down at a dozen people seated casually around a large Plexiglas table that's shaped, painted, and strung like a corset.

"Everyone, this is Girl," Guy, swiveling in his seat at the left breast, announces jovially to faces I watched partying in minimal Lycra scraps just a few hours ago.

"Girlie Girl!" Kat, in the buckled Dior blouse from *Elle*'s April cover, hails me from the right breast. "Sleep well?"

"Yes, thank you," I fib.

"And this is Liz." Beside her sits the buxom blonde from the Town Car, in a low-cut white jumpsuit that does little to brighten her hungover pallor. Slumped, she avidly clutches her coffee mug.

The rest of the assembled, Jeffrey's minions and Bovary's backup singers, are all androgynously decked in their *Wallpaper* hippest, making Guy the only nerd without a leather cuff.

"Hi." I give a collective pink-cuffed wave and drop my bag on the floor. "I'm here to take you all through the nonprofit component of what My Company brings to the table. Or corset." I reach into my bag for my laptop. "So, if you'll give me a moment to boot up—"

"Girl, everyone has the sheet you prepared—it's page *sixteen*," Jeffrey says, passing me a binder with a fluorescent arrow marking the place.

"Oh! . . . Okay! Right." I open to page sixteen to find a revamped version of my NOW-card-revoking proposal, only my queries have become assertions, extensively supported with fallacious quotations from nonexistent coeds, *"As a gender studies major, I depend on My Company for daily reports on improvements in the plastic surgery revolution!"* Like confiscated letters filtered through the communist Russian propaganda machine, every other word in this bogus document is *revolution.* "In the future, the feminist *revolution* will best be served by the *revolting* women who can adorn themselves in the *revolutionary* war paint of our sisters—Avon, Revlon, Estée Lauder . . ." I flip the page over and then flick numbly through the packet. Botched fragments of my ideas are everywhere—phrases stolen from my desk and laptop completely reconfigured, as if edited by Chrissie and her glitter-eyed cohorts. And smattered throughout are my fake lingerie questionnaire results backing it all up. My eyes shoot across the table, locking with Guy's.

He clears his throat. "Yeah, before Girl continues, I want to take a moment to say she's just done a stellar job of pointing our team in the right direction, getting our compasses set to Bovary. Let's give her a round of applause!" There's an awkward smattering of claps. "Yeah, Girl, go ahead." Eat me.

"So . . ." I struggle against derailment. "My Company's commitment to women is both . . . philosophical and philanthropic." For fifteen minutes I spew everything, from how Guy's first gender studies class at UC Santa Cruz awoke him to the female struggles he'd long taken for granted as a privileged male, to the script's upbeat version of human trafficking. "So, thanks to Magdalene, and the money we've given them, after a little rough patch, these young ladies are getting their lives right back on track! To conclude, My Company has the female mind-set in its hardwiring and women's interests at heart."

"Bravo, Girl!" Kat throws her thumbs up. "But, Jeffrey, darling," she pouts, putting a hand on his forearm. "That's really what we've *been* doing."

Perking up, Liz, in turn, puts a protesting hand on Kat's thigh. "To great success, Kat."

"But this is a new country, new market, new frontier."

"Thank you, Girl, that will do." Jeffrey taps my binder as Guy grows palpably agitated. "You can meet us back at the hotel—"

"Oh no," Liz protests. "Can't she stay? *Please?* Please?"

Guy makes room next to him at the table's cleavage.

"I mean," Kat continues, "that's only been our brand because Europeans are so bloody serious. But if we're going to launch in the U.S., we want to do something much more *fun* and really *expansive*—rebrand ourselves a bit. Bovary as *lifestyle*." Kat looks around the table at the sycophantic nods. "Fabulous. Now, while we're over here, our goal is twofold. One, find an American firm to help us think American and appeal to the American consumer. That's why we're meeting with you and your larger competitors. And Guy, after several meetings, I see now that you were spot on about one thing at least: What MC lacks in experience, you make up in personal attention in a way that a bloated behemoth like McKinsey can't." She puffs out her cheeks like a blowfish. "But we're not above nicking *their* point, which is that, as a new brand in a crowded marketplace, this launch stands a much better chance should we align with an established noncompetitive product to give ourselves all the benefits of brand recognition. Are you with me? Fab. Let's show them the video." She points at a faux-hawked boy hunched over a keypad. With a few punches, a soft whirring brings a white screen descending over the windows, and the lights extinguish. Kat, illuminated like Evita in the rectangular spotlight, speaks with great passion into the darkness. "So here's what we've been obsessing over: working women. We feel working women have lost touch with the fun. They're *so miserable.*" She slumps her torso over the table for emphasis. "Liz and I've been leafing through your *Fortune* and *Crane's*, and we've been meeting with all these banks over here and it's the same thing whenever a working gal's at the table. Utter, utter misery—"

"Totally," Guy gives his heartfelt agreement.

"—Long faces, blah boxy suits, and dreary, dreary, dreary. They look *exhausted*. And the few free bits of their brains are all taken up with Johnny's soccer practice and little Suzie's piano recital. *Where's the fun?*" She looks around the darkened table. "It's a tragedy. And we want to do something about it. Video, pretty please."

Rock music comes on with a commercial I instantly recognize from late-night channel surfing. Shot after shot of dangerously inebriated coeds lifting their tops to expose their breasts. "Chicks Gone Senseless!" Kat screams as the title flashes over two teenage girls, uninterestedly making out, their bloodshot eyes rolling back.

Kat leaps up and strides to the front of the room, standing before the screen, the distorted angles of the topless twosome projected across her torso as she speaks. "This man, Jed Devlin, is a bloody genius—fun and spirit and liberation all in one brand! He's got the videos, the parties, the restaurants, the respect of all these celebrities—he'll have a cereal in another week." She points the remote and whizzes along the tape. The ads segue into an interview clip from *Primetime*. Jed Devlin reclines in the backseat of his stretch Hummer, his dimples and skater attire make him look all of twenty, but his smug demeanor ages him another decade. "Here, listen to his philosophy."

"The rape charge is total bull(bleep). She was all over me, man—"

"Oh, that's not it, hold on." Kat fast-forwards.

"The lawsuits are total bull(bleep). I get subpoenaed every time some spring-breaker's old man freaks out to find he's whacking off to his own piss-drunk daughter—"

"Nope." She aims the remote again until Jed puffs up, openly glaring into their rolling camera.

"Yes, I'm conducting business." He spits the last word, punching the ceiling of his Humvee. *"I'm a businessman. I didn't just wake up one day as the Chicks Gone Senseless Billion-Dollar Emperor. I wasn't just lucky. I'm so sick of hearing that. I made this happen. And it's pure genius. Look at Hefner, look at Flynt, look at their overhead. I get this material without paying a cent of royalty. And I get no (bleep)ing props."*

"Kill it." She points to Faux-hawk and the projection disappears. "He doesn't get props. And he should. Jed Devlin's billion-dollar market is contriving the moment of innocence lost, popping the cherry, if you will. I get fifty spams a day, as I'm sure we all do—'barely legal,' 'hot teens,' 'wet virgins,' blah, blah, blah. Young and innocent is hot. The hottest. Yet *your* dominant brand, Vicky's Secret, markets a gal who's waaay too knowing. She exudes over-the-hill-kept-woman-Zsa-Zsa-Gabor with one good inning left in her. They're ignoring the psychology of the *tremendous* market that Jed Devlin's tapped into with Chicks Gone Senseless." Dear God, are you listening? I'm in a small white stucco building on Melrose with a certifi-

ably insane, albeit well-dressed, woman. And if you could just, I
don't know, start a fire drill or something—

"So first we outfit his coeds in unicorn knickers and rainbow
bras and then once we've established our brand, we take the
revolution to the next generation. Bottom line, I want to walk
into any boardroom in America in six months and have these
forty and fifty-year-olds"—Kat points back at Faux-hawk and
Chicks Gone Senseless reappears life-size across her petite
frame—"want to flash me their tits like a bunch of crazy, carefree teens!"

"Close your fucking mouth," Guy growls low in my ear.

"Oh, Kat, it's . . . ," Jeffrey gushes, "it's so new and just so . . .
so"—WRONG?! *Wrong, wrong, and WRONG?!*—"fresh. I
think the working women of America have been waiting for
just this type of revolution."

I recover my voice. "Do you plan to continue your European
business model here? Giving a portion of the proceeds to
women-based charities?"

"Maybe." Kat shrugs.

"No, no, definitely," Liz enthuses.

Kat shoots her a look before reaching over the table to grab
a handful of Skittles. "Honestly, though, what's more fun than
childhood?!" Liz darts her eyes about woefully. "Well, for most
people, darling." Kat pats her silk shoulder. "We're going to take
career women back to their preteen years!" Skittles fly as she
waves her arms. "And that's the Bovary charge. Think you're up
to it?"

"Unquestionably," Jeffrey says, slapping his Smythson note-
book closed. "We'll draw up a timetable for the rollout and fax
it over to you by the end of the day."

Everyone stands and my hand is shaken repeatedly, with the
bonus accolade of a cheek-kiss from Kat.

"You're all fab!" she cries as she struts out of the room. "I *love*
L.A.!"

• • •

I walk in tight circles around my hotel bed, fists clenched, freezing every few minutes as scraps of the meeting come back in torturous flashes. I sit to kick my shoes off but stand back up. I begin to take my earrings out but stop halfway to my lobe. I reach down for the phone and stare at the keypad. To call whom? Hello, is this the U.N.? Yes, I'm calling from Sunset Boulevard to report the SETBACK OF CIVILIZATION! I toss the portable onto the bed, and it bounces off the pillow, deflating the duvet.

I'm so—

I just—

I can't—

"FUCK! Fucking fuck." I slide onto the floor in a rage. I never signed up for this. Not even a little bit. I picture Grace giggling with Chatsworth's benefactors, tugging up her shirt. Or Julia. I'm sure flashing her boobs is exactly what would help her with INS. Don't we *ever* get to grow up?!

I lunge for the phone, tugging it from under the bed where it's landed.

"This is Guy. Leave me a message and I'll get back to you at *my* earliest convenience."

"Hi, it's Girl. So quite a meeting today—interesting direction. We should, um, talk—" I erase and start over. "Hi, we need to talk about this—this new direction. Today's meeting has really thrown into question your—and MC's—mission—value—ethics—just how evil your—it's so evil—" Erase again. "Yeah, I was wondering if we could work out a system? Because I actually work best when I'm not being lied to all the time. LIIAAARRRR!" *Erase! Erase!*

The phone rings still in my hand. "Ma'am, this is the hotel operator. You have a message waiting from a Mr. Jeffrey Wainwright."

"Thank you." I look down at the red light on my phone,

blinking like a beady little Cyclops. I can only imagine: *Girl, meet me out front at noon with a gag in your mouth and a dirty diaper on your head—Jeffrey. Girl, meet me out front at noon with cymbals strapped to your knees and a kazoo up your ass—Jeffrey. Girl, meet me out front at noon with Gloria Steinem's still-beating heart in your hands and your integrity on a spit—Jeffrey.* I slam down the phone and hunch my shoulders as tears of frustration stream out. Crawling into the bathroom for a tissue, I drop my wet cheek down to the cold white tile and am comforted by the melodramatic alignment of my position and predicament.

Rolling onto my back, I stare up at the egg-white crescent the toilet bowl makes against the metallic ceiling. Desperately in need of advice, I spy the phone hanging just above its seat and reach up to dial . . . ? Kira? God, if only. Grace? Way too much. I need baby steps.

"What?" Luke answers.

"Hi," I sniffle. "Can I speak to Buster?"

"Maybe." We have an audio stare-down. "BUSTED, PICK UP THE PHONE!" I yank my head away.

"Yeah, got it." Buster picks up.

"You mean 'getting it,'" Luke sneers to his audience as he hangs up.

"Ignore him. Hey, what's up?"

I roll onto my side under the towel bar. "The account we're trying to land is a lingerie company, only they want to rebrand as some Chicks Gone Senseless lifestyle thing to make every woman in corporate America feel like a twelve-year-old and flash her breasts at her boss—"

"Chicks Gone Senseless?"

"Yeah, and somehow I wrote the script for the whole thing."

"And this is bad, right?"

"Buster, this is *not what I was hired to do!* As soon as the plane lands in New York, I'm quitting."

"Whoa, whoa, quitting?"

"Yes, I can't be a part of this. I can't."

"Girl, you make more than my parents."

I sit up. "And that makes this okay?"

"No, but you've been out there. It's *really* bad right now. Luke's unemployment ran out. He's moving back with his folks in Binghamton. You think that was his plan?"

"No."

"Everyone's compromising. My aunt lost her entire retirement fund last year, and my cousin can't go to college now. It's worse than it's been in our lifetime."

"But I, I—"

"Listen, we're heading out for send-off beers for Luke. Can I call you later?"

"Please, I need to figure this out."

"Don't do anything rash. Miss you crazy."

"You too, bye."

I pick myself off the floor and rummage in my purse for the last of my emergency cigarettes. Pulling the kazoo out of my ass, I dial the room's voice mail.

"Hi, this is Jeffrey. I'm calling to tell you what a stellar job you did today—Kat just *loved* you. Now, she may seem a wee bit over the top, but just like the runway is the fantasy version of what hits the racks, her ideas will be toned *way* down for the real marketplace. You hear me, Miss Doom-and-Gloom? Brainstorming means talking in extremes, and I want your assurance that you're not going to go pull the emergency brakes. In fact, and this is an honor for someone of your experience, Kat actually requested that you be assigned to her starting Monday— and Liz loved your refugee thing! There could be some extra money if you play her right. Soooo . . . treat yourself to a fun meal, and I look forward to seeing you in New York!"

I call back, but there's no answer.

• • •

Five A.M. and the phone has been stubbornly silent. Picking it up, I dial Chatsworth. "Happy birthday to you," I sing softly into Grace's answering machine, hoping she might pick up. "Thinking of you, Mom. I love you . . . Bye." I grab my toothbrush off the counter, zip it into my toiletry bag, and close my suitcase. Maybe he drank too much and wandered off from his friends . . . Maybe he hit his head and stumbled over to the highway . . . God, what if he fell into the river! The phone rings, and I leap across the bed. "Hello!"

"This is your wake-up call. Good morning, the current time is—" I clang the phone down and shrug my trench on over my suit. What an asshole. I hope he hit his stupid head and drowned in the fucking river.

I drop onto the beanbag chair, sinking into the silver vinyl, my knees squeezed in slow motion up to my chest. I look over to the wastebasket, piled with wrappers from my minibar dinner, and out beyond the fluttering curtains at the flashing *Baywatch* billboard across the street. Leaning my head against the wall, I can feel the tension and two nights of lost sleep mix a rancid cocktail in my stomach. Rolling the last bottle of water on the floor over with my foot, I pick it up, unscrew the top, and take a long swallow. It has to be—what, at least eight there now?

Might as well call. Make sure he's not drowned.

"Hello?" A groggy male voice answers.

"*What the fuck?*"

"Shit! Who is this?" I recognize Trevor.

"Sorry! Sorry, sorry. Um, is Buster there?" The phone clanks, and I try to determine whether it's been dropped or if I've been hung up on.

"They're not back yet."

"What?! Are you sure?"

"Yeah." The phone goes dead.

"Hello? Hello?" I hang up. And cry. Cry as I do one last

sweep around the room, cry as I get into the elevator. Cry as I check out.

Guy wheels past me to the Porsche. Despite the dark indigo sky, he's donning glasses as well, his bride-to-be apparently not on our flight. I scrape my suitcase outside and squeeze it with me into the back where Guy's seat falls against my knees.

Jeffrey, already fresh from the gym, drives us in silence down Hollywood Boulevard as the sun creeps up. We pass homeless men and women pushing intricately packed shopping carts, while straggling hookers duck down at each stoplight to see if we might be their morning clientele.

I awake as the plane bounces onto the runway and skids through streaking rain along the Long Island Sound. Fighting to surface from a deep haze of exhaustion, I groggily follow the tide of passengers down to baggage claim, where I spot Guy beside a capped man dangling a sign for MR. MAI C. OMPANY.

We weave out of JFK in a halting stop-and-go as Guy listens to his cell phone, jaw set. "No, Seline, that's *not* what I meant . . . What do you want me to say? . . . *Hello?* Are you still there? . . . Oh, well, you weren't saying anything . . . Seline, are you there? . . . Then why don't you say something? . . . Because, I know it's not fine . . . No! Don't say *fine* when you don't fuck-ing mean it . . . Okay. Okay, then it *is* fine." He tosses the phone down, and it hits me sharply in the thigh. He gazes out the streaked window, pursing his lips. "So, Girl." He drops his head back against the seat. "How you holdin' up?"

"Tired," I say, staring through the rain as we exit the Mid-town Tunnel.

"I hear you," he says. "Got a relaxing Sunday planned for yourself?"

"Hope so."

"We've got some crazy work ahead of us . . ." His voice trails off, and I feel a little prickle of opportunity.

I face him, careful to keep my eyes tired and my tone relaxed. "So, Jeffrey's really . . ."

"Yeah," Guy snorts.

"Will I have to keep reporting to him? Now that we're back?"

He sits up. "Who said you were reporting to Jeffrey? Rex? Did Rex say that to you? Has he been talking to you?"

"No! Guy, no." He urgently studies my eyes. "Not at all. Rex hasn't said a word to me." I fight the impulse to pat his hand reassuringly. "Jeffrey just implied that I, that he—that I should discuss things with him, that's all."

Guy nods slowly at me as he shrinks slightly down into himself, resting his chin in his hands in a childlike posture.

"But I want to talk to *you*." I swivel on the seat to face him fully, leaning closer. "What do you see my role being moving forward? How exactly is this whole thing with Kat supposed to work? What does the whole V.P. promotion mean? What are *your* thoughts? God, I'm so glad we're talking."

His phone rings again, and he flips it open. "Seline, I'm sorry . . ." His face slackens as he listens. "Well, if that's how you feel." He darts his eyes at me. "I'll come over later and we can . . . I see. No, that's fine. Fine, then leave the ring with my doorman. I gotta go." He slaps the phone shut, glowering, and I focus very hard on the passing streets, debating the level of injury if I jumped out right now. I sense him puffing up beside me. "Your neediness is pathetic, Girl." I whip around to his flaring eyes. "Stop looking to me for every fucking little answer. You show *me* why you're an intrinsic part of keeping this company alive."

We pull up on my block, and the driver hops out with an umbrella to get my luggage from the trunk. The windshield wipers strike back and forth. I feel for the handle. "I'm sorry about Seline."

His lids swiftly shut and open. "And you need to start keeping your notes, or whatever, on your laptop or a BlackBerry or something. It's pretty fucked up that you work for a software company and organize your shit on school paper."

The driver pulls open my door, and the sound of the downpour floods the tense space. "See you Monday." He deflates, sinking once more into the polished leather.

"You too," I manage before stepping from under the umbrella into the drenching rain. As the car splashes out into the traffic, I turn to find Buster slumped on my front stoop, soaked to the skin behind a proffered bouquet of hopeful white tulips. I blink through the downpour at him, but it's just so clear, so clean a gesture in the midst of all this crappiness that I'm wrapped in his dripping arms in seconds.

CHAPTER TEN

You Want Me to What?

Breathless, I stare in the darkness at the red eye of my alarm clock counting down the hours until I report back to MC, Inc. To Kat. To Guy. To *show me why you're an intrinsic part of keeping this company alive* . . . I put my hand over my chest and force my lungs to fill, blowing out quietly to the ceiling while I focus on the rain-splattered swish of traffic below. I can't tell which is causing the harder palpitations—being a part of keeping this wrongwrongwrong company alive or the prospect of not being one.

Careful not to wake Buster, whose tulips were merely the overture to a weekend spent "making it up to me," I slide slowly out of bed. Tiptoeing around my still-packed suitcase, I pick up his soft sweatshirt and zip it closed, carefully shutting the door.

I pour a glass of water, sipping it in the shadows from the streetlights refracted through the kitchen window. My heart gradually slowing, I nestle on the futon in the living room, and turn on the first hours of early Monday programming. I click past several infomercials—abs, abs, abs, abs . . . acne—before landing on *Cheers* and sleepily follow a righteous Diane as she clings to professional dignity amidst a sports bar crowd. Then I'm back under for a fitful hour, surfacing as Julia Roberts is teaching Mr. Gere how to drive stick, working the pedals expertly with her thigh-high patent-leather boots . . . Mmmmm, and then it's all so lovely in a movie-set-perfect kind of way when she finally crawls over to service him in their Beverly Wilshire penthouse.

I startle awake to the sound of a male voice rising above the soft patter of the rain. It takes a moment to place the jaundiced film illuminating the room—Jack Lemmon tirading at a hotel concierge while Sandy Dennis looks on. *"Give me your name. You'll be hearing from my lawyer."* I push myself to sit, stretching Buster's sweatshirt over my tucked-up knees.

Soon I'm giggling out loud, remembering watching *The Out-of-Towners* with Kira when we first moved to the city, how perfectly it captures the constant sense of assault and indignation that comes with taking on this make-it-here-make-it-anywhere town, or as Kira called it, *Survivor: Manhattan*. I rest my chin on my knees, captivated anew by how a hapless Ohioan, here to nail down the Perfect Job, takes every single obstacle so personally—the lost luggage, the cancelled hotel room, the mugger, right down to the garbage strike and the pouring rain. And alongside him, for contrast, is his wife, beatifically making the best of things as he battles the relentless urban challenge. He's so . . . so . . . insulted.

I grip my arms around my hunched-up legs. I'm tired of being the Jack Lemmon of My Company. Exhausted.

I stare intently at the television. What if Bovary is nothing more than a downpour or a garbage strike? What if I stopped reacting as though this job is such a personal violation? What if it's *just a job?* I feel a rusty shift in my thinking, and as the credits roll, my stomach fully relaxes for the first time in weeks.

I slip off Buster's sweatshirt as I pad back to the bedroom. Pulling a corner of the warm duvet over me, I slide my fingers into his, and even though he's deeply asleep, he squeezes them. Within seconds I find myself falling into blessed unconsciousness, my hand held loosely in his.

"G?" Buster nudges me. "Phone."

Squinting, I reach over him for the receiver as dawn floods through the slats of the blinds. "Hello?" I murmur.

"*Darling,* sorry if I've woken you, but I simply *must* see you. Jeffrey gave me your number."

"Kat?" I croak, half sitting up as Buster rolls away from me and pulls my pillow over his head.

"Darling, I'm downstairs. It's a *massive* favor, I know, but just throw a mac over your nightie and meet me out front." Dial tone.

"You okay?" Buster asks, reaching a hand behind him and half patting my thigh, half patting the mattress.

"I don't know," I say, now sitting fully up. "The client—that woman, Kat, she's downstairs."

"Okay," he says, his breath already deepening.

The low sun is drying the sidewalk as I shuffle outside, tying my coat closed over my slip and wriggling my heels fully into sneakers. Weaving between the evaporating puddles, I approach the white stretch limo, double-parked, its idle the only sound on the deserted street, save the chirp of hungry starlings.

I squeeze in the tiny space between two parked cars, and the limo door swings open to greet me. Tucking my hair behind my ears, I lean down to peer in. "Kat?"

She angles out into the morning light, the sun electrifying her hennaed hair as she reaches up to kiss me on the cheek, a waft of woodsy cologne lingering. "Darling, *so* good of you to come down. I know I'm being a pain, but I've just made the *most* amazing discovery. Here, Brit, slide over." Kat tugs my hand, and I duck into the dark interior, tucking my coat under my thighs.

"Hi." I give a collective wave to the four other women reclining on the red velvet benches. Wrapped in evening silks, they lounge in varying levels of luxurious repose around a swell of slipped-off Jimmy Choos. Their glowing skin sweat clean of makeup, their manner relaxed as if sitting in a sauna, they sip from small bottles of fresh orange juice, while in the far corner Liz sleeps against the tinted window.

"O.J.?" Kat reaches into the deli bag ballasted by the abandoned heels in the center of the upholstered car floor.

"No, thanks."

"Bagel?"

"That's okay," I demur, as Brit tears into hers, licking errant cream cheese off the corner of her mouth. "Sorry, you wanted to tell me something?" I stifle a yawn.

Liz stretches awake, her hands landing on her Versace ribbon-bound chest as her head drops back on the seat. "Muffin! MuffinMuffinMuffin*Muffin!*" She savors the word.

"No, thanks. I'm not really hungry yet."

The women erupt into deep laughter. Kat just smiles. "No, darling, not the food—the *lifestyle,*" she murmurs.

"The philosophy," Brit declares with a sweeping gesture, the large diamond butterfly on her right hand given the illusion of flight.

"The revolution!" Liz cries. "Have you been?"

Okay, first syllable—sounds like? "I'm not sure . . ." I squint at Kat, who, seemingly more sober than the rest of her party, presides regally.

"It's a soiree—" the others all begin to explain at once. "A carnival! A movement!"

Brit's pedagogical voice rises above the rest. "It's a celebration of the goddess, taking us back to the ancient rituals and rites that once celebrated *us*—our bodies, our power, everything that got taken away by the Judeo-Roman tradition—"

The woman next to her jumps in, her strands of uncut aquamarines rustling together. "There are no shoulds, no shame, no sanctimony."

"You can be purely, wholly yourself," croons another, pulling a small jar of Jo Malone vitamin E cream from her python clutch and passing it to her left. "Dancing to Madonna and serving in the religion of your pleasure."

"Ooh, put Sarah McLachlan back on," Liz pleads, motioning her fingers at the panel by her seatmate's elbow. "Surfacing" wells up and the women shimmy in their seats, humming contentedly, lost to themselves, like a *Vogue* spread in motion. Kat continues to smile at me as if she and I are sharing a confidence.

"Okay, so," I say, still hopelessly unclear. "That's really great that you found this. And that you stopped by to, uh, share it with me. I guess now you know where I live, and that's . . . good. So . . ."

"Girlie Girl." Kat leans over to me as the others continue to dance. "Look at them. *This is it! This* is our American brand! It has mystery and texture and . . . Bovary opportunity written all over it."

While Brit mists herself with Evian, Liz twinkles her bordeaux toes out in front of her. "We're dropping that dreadful Jed Devlin."

"Chicks Gone Senseless is a one-trick concept," Kat continues, electrified. "There's no reason to align with him when there's—"

"*MUFFIN!*" everyone else cries ecstatically.

I grab Kat's arm, amazed that my first fifteen minutes of Not-JackLemmon consciousness could prove so rewarding. "No more Chicks Gone Senseless? That plan's over?" No more wanting to walk into any boardroom in America and have forty and fifty-year-olds flash you their tits like a bunch of crazy, carefree teens?

"Over. Dead. Now go get some kip. We have a big day ahead of us." She reaches over me to open the door as she joins the sing-along, *"Building a mystery . . ."*

At an infinitely more civilized hour of the same morning, I proudly set my new cell phone next to my new, took-the-entire-weekend-with-Buster-to-master-this-fucking-thing Palm Pilot. I sit down in my desk chair and open my laptop. Even the MC, Inc. logo stuck above the screen feels less offensive. It's going to be a good day and a good job. I can do this.

"Your phone's been ringing off the hook since you left," Stacey mutters, as she passes with a tray of pastry.

"Sorry," I apologize automatically. "Good to be back!" I call after her. She circles her head in a manner that suggests some eye rolling, but that's o-kay.

I look down to retrieve my messages.

"*Girl!*" Julia's ebullient voice greets me. "*Hi, it's Wednesday. I've found a space! It's perfect, but I need to make a commitment. Do you have a delivery date yet? Call me.*"

"*Hi, it's Julia. You may have already left for the weekend, but they want me to sign the lease on Monday. Do you know when the money will be coming through? Thanks. I'm on my cell.*"

"*Hi, Girl. Not to be a nuisance or add to your juggernaut, but I'm a little concerned that I haven't heard from you. I don't know if I should read into that—*"

"Girl, they want you." Stacey swooshes her finger toward Guy's office.

I hang up and head in, Palm first.

"You're going to love this." Jeffrey sidesteps me to get to Rex, who's reclining majestically in Guy's chair. Displaced, Guy paces in front of a row of shrouded easels. Without so much as turning his head, Jeffrey passes off a packet of markers to me.

"Guy." I drop them on the table. "I need to tell Magdalene exactly when we're wiring them the money."

"Uh-huh." Guy pops his jaw in annoyance.

"So what's the date? I need to run out and call them before we get started on this . . . Guy?"

"*This*, Girl?" He swings his hands in large quotation-mark swoops. "*This* is us trying to get the money for your little charity, so just chill out with that for, like, five minutes." Five minutes . . . and . . . go. "Okay, Martha Stewart," he snipes at Jeffrey. "Kat's gonna be here any sec; let's just see what you've got."

While the two stare each other down, I offer myself a seat and take it. "Hold these." Jeffrey picks the markers off the table and puts them pointedly back in my hands, shining his focus on our reclining leader. "Rex, I was thinking along the lines of the work I did in Miami, keeping in mind Kat's much further left." Rex nods, not looking up from an invoice with Wainwright, Ltd. scrolled in purple ink at the top. "So, we need her to approve the design, the concept, the execution, the budget," he ticks off on his fingers, "and, of course, commit."

Rex's face clouds. "Billing double overtime for your entire team this weekend—that's steep."

"You wanted the best," Jeffrey retorts dryly.

"Guy." Rex drops the invoice on the desk. "The Bank's reached the end of its patience."

"Well, I'm ready to cut to the chase." Guy shows us his palms. "I've been ready since February—"

"We can't bully this." Jeffrey sighs, adjusting the tassel on his Tod's loafer with the tip of a metal pointer. "I've worked her type before. This is an ego you need to coax."

"Bullshit, just let me talk to her—"

"All right, keep moving." Rex waves them on. "I'm curious to meet the lady who has your collective balls in a sling." He props his hands behind his head.

"Hullo, boys." We turn to find Kat standing in the doorway clad in a bouclé trouser suit over a sliced and liberally safety-pinned T-shirt declaring, *This is what a feminist looks like.*

"Kat's here," a flustered Stacey announces on her heels.

Jeffrey leaps to give her a kiss. "Kat, darling, you're early."

"I know." She shrugs, exchanging stares with an immobile

Rex before stepping past everyone to plant red lips on my cheek. "It's one of my foibles. Well, better early than late, I always say." She pats her uterus for emphasis and plops into the seat next to mine. "So, what are we up to, Jeffrey?"

"Well, first and foremost, I'd like to introduce Rex, Chairman of My Company."

Rex stands a tad too slowly, causing Kat to blatantly swivel her torso away from him to turn her glow on me. "Did you get back to sleep?"

"Uh, yes." I dart a stern, squash-the-budding-fantasies look at the hetero side of the room.

"Jeffrey, I've only got a half hour here. Let's get a move on."

Guy tilts his eyebrows at Rex, telegraphing over Kat's head: *Told you she was a bitch.*

"Absolutely, let's get started." Jeffrey claps. "Girl, take notes on the whiteboard." I take my station, me—marker holder, note taker, Vice President. "Since our Friday meeting, we've been working round the clock to mine MC's extensive database of user preferences for a launch campaign that would unite Bovary's brand with Chicks Gone Senseless." I look to Kat to update him, but she remains mum. "The *facts,* brought to you by the million women who pass through MC's site each day, are consistent. The *younger* the model in the ad, the *more* hits the product gets. Yet Bovary wants to take the revolution to the older, more-established corporate woman. With that in mind, we propose that these lovely ladies . . ." He flips back the shrouds dramatically to reveal ad mock-ups showing barely pubescent bodies frolicking in spring break settings, seamlessly superimposed under Catherine Deneuve–like fifty-something heads.

"Hmm," Rex murmurs, ogling #3, an eleven-year-old physique spread-eagled off a diving board, a gleeful looking dowager Photoshopped above.

"We're going to pick up where Calvin Klein left off," says Jeffrey, savoring each word as he gestures to the body of Kate

Moss's kid sister pushing her hipster swimsuit down to hint at her hairless mons, her head eligible for Medicare. "By breaking new ground for older women—" Jeffrey's pitch grinds to a halt as he registers Kat's souring expression. "But, of course, everything is flexible."

"Well, it's not *exactly* what I'd been thinking." Squeakily I write, '*Not what Kat's been thinking.*'

Guy looks furtively to Rex. "Now, Kat, at this point we've put considerable resources into your interests," he addresses her as if admonishing a petulant child, "and I want something firm."

"Oh, boys." She tears her eyes away from the cardboard chimeras to wag her finger. "You're trying to put on the thumbscrews!" Jeffrey and then Guy break into forced smiles. "I told you, as soon as the Bovary board makes a decision, I'll let you know. I'm really at their mercy for the moment. So let's just keep moving forward *as if*. For the time being, keep *beavering* away." She snorts with laughter just as her cell bleats. *Hey, Julia, baby, it's me. Just keep moving forward 'as if.' 'Kay?* "Feeling better? . . . Well, I told you tequila was dumb after all that wine . . . I'll wake you when I get back." She drops her phone into her bag. "Liz is retching her guts out—we went to the most amazing party last night, and that's what *I* want to talk about. The more I think about it, the more I'm put off by the notion of getting my revolution into bed with such an arrogant sod as Jed Devlin. So new brand: Muffin."

"*New* brand," Rex repeats.

"Yes. *New* brand," Kat asserts. "I've been thinking, Chicks Gone Senseless—it's the now, which means it's the past. Muffin is the future. They throw these parties that cater entirely to an empowered reenvisioning of women's sexuality. *That's* who Bovary should get aligned with—my product in every goodie bag and promoted on their Web site—"

"Yeah, fine, great, Muffin." Rex tosses his hands.

"Pardon?" she bristles.

"Muffin, fine."

"*I'm* totally on board," Guy rushes in. "The future. Parties. Women's sex. Sexy women. Yes." He nods, fumbling. "We can totally work with that—"

"Do we have a deal or don't we?"

"I'm sure what Rex means—"

"I can speak for myself, Jeffrey. What I mean is, you're being a cock-tease, young lady. And I think you're enjoying it. We've given you significant time. We've made your ideas viable. We've proven ourselves." Rex shrugs as if there's nothing else to say.

"Have you? I wasn't aware you were in a position to be quite so forceful," Kat manages to purr.

"Well, we're all grown-ups here," Rex continues, as Guy nervously clicks his pen. "We can be frank. It's shit or get off the pot."

The room goes quiet. I look to each of them: Jeffrey, mouth pursed, eyes rolled to ceiling in disapproval; Rex, smug smirk, hands behind head; Kat, forehead rigid, cheek being sucked slowly between teeth; and Guy, drained of all color, pulls at his collar, a trickle of sweat sloping down his temple.

"Kat." My heart quickening, I reach across to her. "We can make this w—"

Kat swipes her handbag off the floor. "Girl, it's been a pleasure."

"My, my, Rex." Jeffrey infuses the tense silence with a laugh. "How you talk."

"Kat, let me walk you out." I stand.

"Thanks, but this cock-tease can find her own way." Without a backward glance, she sashays out of the office. Taking my pledge with her.

"Get her back."

Jeffrey turns from the doorway.

"*Get her back,*" Guy says again, his constricted face turning a deep red. Rex, surprisingly calm, bends for the golf club.

"Please," Jeffrey corrects drolly.

"Not you. Girl."

The door to Kat's Mercer Hotel suite cracks open, and a mascara-flecked cheek appears. "Hello?" a small voice croaks.

"Hi! Hi. Remember me? From the limo?"

The door recedes, and little Liz, wrapped in an oversized terry-cloth robe, peers at me, rubbing glitter out of her blood-shot eyes.

"I'm from MC, Inc. Sorry to disturb you, but I'm looking for Kat."

"Oh, yeah, I know you," she says in her upper-class childish singsong. "You're Girl. The lovely one." She shuffles away, and the door swings at me. Catching it just before it clicks shut, I push into the darkened room. The curtains are drawn, and the air is thick with the fetid smell of stale smoke. I pick my way through the velvet sofa cushions strewn around the candle-wax encrusted coffee table.

"Please, have a seat. Drink?" Liz plucks an open bottle of champagne off the TV, which has been duly swathed with a silk scarf.

I perch on the edge of the bare sofa frame. "No, thank you. So, are you expecting Kat soon?"

"Yeah, she just popped to some spa place with a lovely kind of peaceful sex name." Liz trails her fingers through the air.

"Bliss?"

"Yeah!" She tosses her skeletal arm toward the ceiling. "That's it. Mind if I take a bath?"

"Uh, no, of course not, please go ahead."

"Splendid!" She turns to the white folding doors behind her and pulls them open, revealing the bathroom. "Isn't this fab? Americans are so social—I love it." The rectangular marble tub runs the length of the opening. She turns on the water, gener-ously dumping in most of the blue salts from a jar on the rim.

"You know, I'll just wait in the lobby." I stand up.

"No, no, talk to me." Liz flitters around and alights in the bathroom from the hallway door. "I've been up here for days, feels like." She drops her robe and slides her tiny bruised body into the massive basin. "Oof, I get so banged about at these dance things."

I inch down onto a floor cushion and try to clear my head from the bungle of instructions shouted at me by GuyJeffrey-Rex as I was leaving. "So . . . you founded Bovary?"

"Oh, I started making knickers for friends when I was at the Royal College. Kat was my dad's assistant, and we just kind of fell madly. I had the trust from Mum's family, and she had the business whatchamacallit." She snaps her fingers in the air absently.

"Acumen?"

"Sure!" She holds her nose and dunks under the water, leaving me momentarily alone.

"Your charity work is really admirable," I say as she surfaces.

"I know, I'm really proud of that." She alights on a bristle brush and starts scrubbing her small feet. "Twenty-five p off every sale goes to something. Can you pass me that bottle?" she asks, holding out her arm.

I retrieve the warm champagne from where she left it on the coffee table and hand it off to her. "Thanks." She takes another deep swig, patting the rim of the tub for me to sit down. As my skirt absorbs her splashes, I speculate if my next MC, Inc. errand will be conducted in stirrups. "I think that's really what it's all about, but, well, Kat's really the, the, the—"

"What'm I?" The door opens and Kat strides in.

"The brains!" Liz calls gleefully, having found her train of thought. "I was just telling Girl about our philanthropy. Good rub?"

"Yes, dear." She kisses Liz perfunctorily on the forehead as I stand up quickly. "So, the old fart sent you."

"No! What? No. No, I'm here because . . . uh, yeah. Yeah, he did."

Kat pulls down her trousers, and I back away from the bathroom as she flops down to pee. "I can't say I'm sorry to see you."

"Rex really regrets getting off on the wrong foot," I say to the drawn curtains.

"He's a fuck. And don't tell me you think any different." A pause as Kat presumably reaches for the toilet tissue. "Look, Girl, I've been the slave. You know Liz's dad, Robby Switch, he produced all those crap pop groups in the nineties?" I nod from back on the metal couch frame. "Well, he was my first gig out of university."

"I told her," Liz says petulantly from the bubbles.

"Well, did you tell her that among other assorted tasks I had to take this bird he'd knocked up for an abortion 'cause he wanted to make sure she went through with it—I mean, way fucking above and beyond." She snorts in disgust at the memory, while Liz finishes off the champagne. "So I don't need to take a step backward, thank you very much."

"But you're not working for Rex—I am. Look, he'll get the hang of answering to you—just give him a chance to get used to it—"

"He'd rather cut his balls off with his money clip."

"But there's an amazing opportunity here!" I stand to plead, modulating over Kat's flush. "He's pledged to donate a million dollars to a charity that's saving victims of white slavery—"

"I like that bit," Liz says, combing conditioner through her hair. "That's a really good cause, Kat."

"It is!" I stride back over to them as she zips up. "But we'll only be able to help them if you commit. It's so Bovary—the money would go to—"

"*That* was just a way to distinguish ourselves in the saturated European market." Kat tosses her hand as she rifles through her vanity case. "But, I'm sorry, Girl, Liz, Americans do not shop for a cause. They buy knickers to get laid." She pulls her diamond Rolex from the suede folds and slips it on. "So how can we help them get laid?"

"Kat, you're so *crass.*" Liz steps out of the tub and reaches for a towel. "We have an *obligation* to help those less fortu—"

"Please, spare me the sanctimonious crap. It's wonderful they taught you charity at that posh boarding school, but *I'm* running a business where nearly every fucking cent goes to the government for socialized *this* and socialized *that,* so I really think *I'm fucking doing my part!*" She hurls the bathroom door shut, barely missing Liz.

"How *dare* you?!" Liz throws it open, struggling to follow Kat through the cushion-strewn floor to the bedroom. "Without me you'd be *nothing.* You'd have *nothing*—"

Hearing the distinct sound of a slap, I start toward the front door. "Pull yourself together," Kat hisses. "You're high as a *fucking* kite. It's pathetic."

"Kitty, Kitty, I'm sorry, I'm sorry, wait!" Liz sobs.

Kat marches out of the bedroom, pulling me with her as she passes. "Come on."

"I should check on her." But I stumble as Kat tugs me out into the dimly lit corridor.

"No," she says, pressing for the elevator. "She just gets like that when she hasn't slept." She rolls a shoulder back and huffs. "Liz is a very passionate person. She's not really cut out for business."

The door to the ebonized elevator opens, and we descend in near darkness to the lobby. Kat unfastens her bag, extracting a lip gloss, which she applies carefully in the reflection of the button panel. I watch her through a haze of loathing as she smiles at herself, tilting her face side to side, before running a finger through her hair to reinvigorate her spikes. By the time the door reopens, her gleam is returned. "Look, Girl," she says, facing me in the deep mauve of the lobby elevator bank. "Europe's market's in shit shape, too. There's a lot more riding on this launch than there was a year ago. It has. To be. Spectacular. I want Muffin. Their members are our target consumers—they'll deliver us directly into the black. Mark me, *this* is the next sexual revolution." She shakes her hair out. "And I hear the cha-ching."

"Cha-ching that trickles down to Magdalene?" I ask evenly, as she struts through the lobby.

"I think we're on the same page." Smiling at the doorman holding open a limo door, she stops short of him, cocking her head at me. "I like you, Girl. I liked your presentation. I liked the bemused look you have on your face around those useless sods." She squints, taking me in from head to toe. "You have a quality, something I think Bovary's missing."

A conscience?

She pulls out her sunglasses. "Whatever happens with this deal, I want to work together. Do you?"

A swarm of tourists engulfs us, buying me a moment before they pass. "Kat, I'm flattered, really. But what I want, what I need right now is to get Magdalene the funding Guy promised. *I* promised. I just—this has *got* to happen."

She swoops her hand in a circle around me, as if encompassing my aura. "I like that. Meet me tonight, and you can tell the boys I'll come to a pitch tomorrow." She scribbles an address on the back of a business card. "Party's at eleven. See you outside."

"Have some cheese; it's the house specialty." Julia slides over a plate of Ritz crackers gobbed with orange smush. I pick one up, surprised that the Harvard Club, bastion of the intellectual and social elite, specializes in something that so closely resembles Cheez Whiz. Julia polishes off her Reuben. "Well, there's no denying it must have been awkward."

"No."

"But it's over."

I raise an eyebrow.

"This Kat character's given you a second chance. What you're helping Magdalene accomplish can't be overstated—"

"Julia, maybe I'm not doing it justice—Kat full on slapped her."

"I'm not saying it wasn't uncomfortable. I'm just saying, add it to your record book. Mine's long enough: meals around the samovar with the kitchen staff while my male colleagues are being served out front, lap dances for all," her voice echoes in the wood-paneled room. "What meeting haven't I conducted with a hand on my knee?" Our retired crimson-clad cohorts glance up from their chowder.

"It's just that suddenly my mother's in that hotel room with me. I already feel like this job is letting her down on just about every principle she ever instilled in me and now—"

"She's in a different milieu. I challenge her to step into your shoes and do anything differently."

"She painted, 'Tell me who you walk with and I'll tell you who you are,' *over my crib. She* would have duct-taped Kat to the Eames chaise and talked at her until Kat 'let go of the anger.' "

"Which would have gotten you where, exactly? Honestly, Girl, what does Kat's anger have to do with what you're trying to achieve?"

"Nothing."

"I look back at those women, whose protests I stepped past to get to work, and where are they today? They're foaming at the mouth over parking permits in a ballroom at the Marriott—it's performance art. So keep Grace out of this. Business and mothers don't mix." Julia wipes her mouth neatly with the linen napkin.

"You make it sound so easy."

She breaks into a deep laugh. "Do I? It's not. It's ridiculously hard. But I can't feel sorry for this Liz—she sounds like a drug-addled brat, who, thank God, still has the conscience to want to do good. Which is fortuitous, because I'm managing three suicide attempts, an ectopic pregnancy, six HIV-positives, and a bed shortage. So . . ."

"I know," I say quickly. "Thank you for taking the time to talk me down when your hands are so full."

"Of course." Julia flips open the leather case to check the enclosed bill.

"Oh, please, let me, it's the least I can do." I reach over for the check.

"Don't be silly."

She calculates the tip, while I look down at the chipped plate, embossed with a scarlet H, as is everything in the room. Pushing the sound of the slap from my mind, I concentrate on counting the ubiquitous H tie clips, jaunty red scarves, and Veritas earrings, so unabashedly prevalent as to suggest a prime layer of H tattoos, jaunty red thongs, and Veritas piercings.

"So, Girl." Julia places the pen into the fold of the leather case. "You'll go to your party, I'll go to my fund-raiser, we'll both do our work. And, God willing, Magdalene will have its coffers lined by the end of the week. Okay?" Julia returns her gaze to my fretful face. "You didn't instigate it, you didn't stay for it, so don't obsess. Just get on with it, okay?"

"Okay," I say.

Julia offers me the last cracker, but I push the plate toward her.

"Suit yourself." She pops it into her mouth.

That evening the cab snakes down Seventh Avenue, and I'm committed to getting on with it. I straighten my tank that says JUST BROWSING in Swarovski crystals and lean down to untuck my jeans from where they've wedged between my heel and the sole of my stiletto slides. *Ring-ring, ring-ring, ring-ring—*

"Hello?" I fumble open my new cell.

"Did I do it? Am I your first call?" Buster's voice comes to me in patches.

"Yes!" I grin. "Oh, this is so exciting, I'm talking to you from a cab, on my very own phone."

"You're such a nerd," he says, laughing, "Where're you headed?"

"I'm going to this party thing with Kat—Muffin?"

"Shut up. That's so fucking cool. Wait till I tell Sam. Camille goes all the time—she's a *member*."

"I see, very impressive. So what are you up to?" I tug a loose thread from the hem of my tank.

"Yeah, well that's why I called. I'm out with this kid from work, it's another bachelor thing, and I just wanted to give you a heads up about it."

"Okay," I say, not sure where this is going.

"Cool?"

"Cool to what?"

"This is ridiculous," he mutters. "I can't believe I'm standing out here having to call you."

"Out where?"

"The Hustler Club."

"You're calling me from outside a strip bar?"

"You're going to a sex party!"

"Buster I don't understand, are you looking for me to give permission?"

"I don't know, I'm communicating," he mutters.

"So I'm informed that you're about to spend the evening paying women to act like they want to fuck you. Thanks for the update."

"You're being a total hypocrite right now."

"How long have you known about this bachelor party?"

"I don't know—a few weeks."

"And you're telling me now? What would you have done if I hadn't gotten a cell?"

"The point is, I'm telling you. I thought that's what you wanted." He sighs. "Look, I've got to go. Let's deal with this later. I'll meet you at your place."

"Fine," I say, plate full.

"Fine, so we're cool?"

"Fine, so we're not going to talk about this now."

"Fine."

I flip the phone closed and slip it back in my clutch. NoroomonmyplaterightnowNoroomonmyplaterightnowNoroomonmyplaterightnow.

Smoothing back my hair, I start to feel very sixth grade: The fast girls are about to sneak me into my first R-rated film and I'm expecting . . . I don't know what I'm expecting. Really happy women. Peaceful, ecstatic women. Women who are redefining comfort. And a check for a million dollars.

Under the lingering stench from the nearby meatpacking factories, Kat and Liz are waiting in matching mini satin trenches. "Hello," I say, awkwardly brushing their proffered cheeks just below sparkling painted butterflies.

"Ciao, darling! Wait right here." Kat, clearly having moved on from the events of this afternoon, deposits us in the queue hugging the brick wall, then marches along the barricades to the front of the line.

I turn to the subtly vibrating Liz. "How are you doing?" I ask gently.

She stares at me with every ounce of her attention.

"Feeling better?"

"Oh,yeahyeahyeah." She nods rapidly, her eyes like blue pupil-less saucers in the glare of the few bare bulbs signifying the entrance. "Yeah,I'mnotdrinkingtonight,justhadsomemethandthatshoulddome,youwantsome?" she rattles before sucking on her water bottle.

"No, thanks."

"Okay, let's roll!" Kat reappears to grab Liz's ass and propel her past the line, which is packed with a confusingly large number of men.

"*Dude,* you'll never guess where I am," a passing male voice cheers loudly into his cell. "I'm at *Muffin* . . . I know! I get laid every time I come here."

Kat reaches back to take my hand, and we clear the ropes. Stepping inside, Kat stares on impatiently as Liz shows her Muffin card, painstakingly counting out balled-up fifties to grandfather me in as a member. "This way, darlings!" Kat parts the velvet curtains and the music blasts us as we pass into a disco-lit, glitter-strewn club peppered with clusters of other early birds. On stage the MC, a lithe, heavily made-up man, paces in a cropped top and low-riding red vinyl pants. He surveys the scene, his microphone poised beneath his sparkly mouth. *"Come on, you horny godesses, let's get dancing!"*

"Woohoo!" Kat, her right hand still positioned on Liz's ass, uses her left to lift mine in a celebratory cheer, which is shared by the other small bevies of twenty-something, Agent Provocatuer–clad guests.

I follow up the stairs to a roped-off VIP area behind the speakers. "Ah, the cofounders of the revolution!" Kat screams in greeting to a raven-haired couple who look to be about my age. Thin, beautiful, and utterly androgynous, both offer languorous waves from the leopard-skin couch where they loll amidst magnums of champagne. Kat slides down her trench and then tugs off teetering Liz's, revealing matching sheer tops and minute denim skirts barely grazing their gartered thighs. In turn, I remove my own jacket and rest it with theirs. Below, people are starting to flood in as the volume of the hip-hop music rises, the women rapidly peeling down to bare breasts, while the men lounge comfortably in suits. *Déjeuner Sur l'Herbe:* the music video.

"Drink, darling?" Kat helps herself to a mini-bottle of Piper from the sterling ice bucket.

"Sure," I reply, staring out at the revolution that so far looks strikingly similar to the regime.

"Romy." The pixie-cut woman nods up at me by way of introduction. "And this is my brother, Remus." He takes my hand with a limp, clammy grip.

"And this is my Girlie Girl." Kat insinuates herself into the small space between them on the couch, leaving me to drag over two heavy ottomans from the neighboring banquette. Liz perches on the edge of hers for all of a minute before hopping up to dance frenetically by our table.

"Did you get the package I sent over?" Kat asks.

"Ooh, yes," Romy giggles, looking at her nodding brother for confirmation. "We loved the crotchless ones—*very* Muffin. I think they could sell really well here."

"But, of course!" Kat thrusts both thumbs into the cork, popping it to the ceiling.

"You work for Bovary?" Remus addresses me, as he passes over a second Piper.

I hold up my barely touched first. "No, we're wooing Bovary to consult their stateside launch."

"Oh, you're a McKinsey minion."

"I work for My Company." The twins exchange glances.

"You're not still dating *them,* are you?" Remus asks Kat, his black eyebrows knitting together. "I mean, no offense, but they don't know dick—"

"Or Muffin." Romy giggles, her small breasts momentarily shaking loose of her cocktail dress.

Suddenly the audio of an interview being projected on screens around the room supplants the music. "Well, I'm a . . . sexual person." Al Goldstein holds a mike to a garish redhead's mouth. "I really just . . . love sex." She sniffs, running a taloned hand under her red nose. "I shot a double anal today," she says vacantly.

"Wow," Al smirks into the camera. "That's a double I'd like to get in on."

"It was really . . . fun."

"Sounds it," he leers. "I bet you cum all day long."

She blinks her false lashes. "I do. I cum just pulling into the studio parking lot."

"I bet you're cuming right now."

"What? Oh, yeah, yeah, I am. I just love sex. I'm just . . . a very sexual person."

"Hey, when're your next auditions?"

She blinks into the bright light, her Muffin tube top sliding down to reveal the upper crescent of her distended, saucer-sized nipples. "I'm just . . . a very sexual person. I just . . . love sex."

"And sex loves you. We'll be right back with video legend Ginger performing *live* from Muffin in New York City, so stay tuned!"

"Cable access. New Muffin frontier," Remus says.

"Speaking of which," I ask hopefully, "when is Muffin starting?"

"Right," Remus says. "Excuse us for a moment." They skip down the stairs and over to the stage, where the MC hands over the mike. "Testing, testing!" Remus shouts, grinning devilishly as his voice booms over the expectant faces. "Welcome one and all to our First Annual Liberated Lips Party!" Whoops and cheers explode from the exuberant crowd. "For those of you for whom tonight is your first Muffin Extravaganza, we are a cross-platform production and entertainment company for young heterosexual women that represents a contemporary female sexual lifestyle!" Awkward silence. "And we're here to get you hot!" Robust cheering.

"Isn't it fab?" Kat's lips find my ear. Isn't *what* fab?

"Tonight we're taking the revolution to the lips that are cut no slack in our culture of shame!" Romy holds a slender arm aloft beside him for support as he continues. "We want you to use your lips to express your freedom and individuality. Let's have some lip service, everybody! Use your mouth to shout your name!"

A raucous cry of names goes up in shrieking sopranos. *"Kaaaaaaaaat!"* she deafens me.

"State your Muffin rights!" he commands them.

"To strip! To slap! To cum! To go!"

He breaks in to deliver his final instruction. "Now . . . *grab a dick!"* As Romy mock-lunges her small hand toward her brother's crotch, the MC rolls out a round table displaying a three-foot-tall dildo, presented in the manner of a wedding cake. A frenzied uproar breaks out on the dance floor as the coiffed, panty-clad women rush the stage, like someone shouted, "Fire!" at the Victoria's Secret runway show.

"Suck it!" shouts the MC, who's reclaimed, if not his sexuality, at least the mike. The men in the crowd are wildly agog with delight. They thrust their pinstriped pelvises out, offering up their vessels of liberation. One of my eyebrows has darted so far up it's on the back of my neck. Romy and Remus weave out of the escalating melee and skip back up the stairs. Reaching for fresh bottles, they plop back onto the couch, once again bookending Kat. *OnemilliondollarsonemilliondollarsonemilliondollarsNotJackLemmonNotJackLemmonNotJackLemmonBusinessandMothersDon'tMixBusinessandMothersDon'tMixBusinessandMothersDon'tMix—*

"See, Kat," Romy resumes discussions, all traces of giggles gone, her expression steely. "You don't need some has-been beauty site posing as consultants. You don't need consultants, period." Whoa, whoa, whoa! "Kat, selling sex isn't brain surgery. Women *want* to buy that *this,* the most commercially accepted of routes, can change the world," she pontificates, clearly getting turned on by having a captive audience for her marketing philosophy. "We sell them that liberation is performing sexually and publicly for a male viewer. And they should feel *righteous* about it."

"Who doesn't want to conduct the revolution on their backs?" Remus adds matter-of-factly. Me?

"Get him off—change the world," Kat murmurs appreciatively, while around us, in darkened nooks, bobbing heads seem to be doing just that.

"Exactly. If we could sell them *that,* Kitty Kat, we can take Bovary's brand national inside five months."

"But the deal is quid pro quo," Remus picks up the thread. "We let your brand align with ours to launch stateside and next year Bovary launches Muffin in Europe."

Romy slides her hand onto Kat's stockinged knee. "We're already in Miami and Vegas; we're opening L.A. and Chicago next month."

"Look around—" Remus points at the dance floor, which has evolved into a Bergdorf's bacchanalia, manicured fingers grasping Frederic Fekkai highlights, deep St. Bart's tans bumping against sweaty torsos, drunken tongues slurping the red soles of the Christian Louboutins held aloft. "This is hardly an administrative crowd. Muffins think nothing of dropping three hundred on a bra—they'll eat your stuff up."

"*If* we tell them to," Romy adds, licking her feline lips as if a canary feather might float out of her mouth. "I mean, who'd have thought we could get them to buy glass dildos?" Remus erupts into laughter and drops his head into her lap. She runs her fingers through his dark curls as she enumerates. "He bet me I couldn't do it, but we sold *over two hundred* on-line. *Glass! Dildos!*" Her free hand still on Kat's knee, Romy's fingertips begin to play up Kat's thigh.

"That's hilarious! I could make dildos," Kat says, tugging a bouncing Liz down by the scruff of her denim mini before she topples over the railing. "I could put the Bovary label on anything. And, as I've said, I want to see the corporate powerhouse woman at the party. There's a huge, untapped market out there, just waiting for us."

Remus straightens up to lock Kat in his gaze. "*If* you're ready to drop the charity boulder you've been tethered to." He tosses his head in Liz's direction. Her back turned as she sits facing the dance floor below, only I see her squeeze her eyes tightly shut as he continues, "Tell My Company and the rest of your consultants to go fuck themselves. Bovary and Muffin will align our brands for your launch and introduce America to our kind of liberation—a highly lucrative one. Do we have a deal?" Remus flicks his hand, and a naked waitress appears with small beakers of clear liquid nestled in ice. "Shall we drink to it?"

"Oh, Remus." Kat tsks her finger at him. "You're trying to put on the thumbscrews!" Apparently a pathological commitment-phobe, she clinks her glass against his. "To monogamy! In the bedroom, if not the boardroom."

"Don't waste our time, Kat," Remus admonishes in a stern déjà vu.

Kat takes a lingering sip of her drink, prolonging her last moments as a free agent. I hold my breath. Liz's hands grip the black velvet, her eyes still clenched shut. "Remus, you have a deal." The room lurches.

"How divine!" Romy claps her hands together, lunging to embrace Kat as light lip kisses are exchanged amongst the new triumvirate. The VIP rope opens to allow an oiled female dancer to shake herself between me and the others, her thong serving as the engine car for a long train of women. Steadying myself on the ottoman, I feel Liz's cold hand grip mine. The twins rise off the couch like inflating hot-air balloons to join the slithering samba line.

"Cheers!" Kat knocks back her drink and follows her new playmates.

Suddenly Liz and I are alone, forgotten, our hands clasped tightly together. "We should drink," she speaks first as she reaches into the ice bucket.

"What?" My voice sounds strange to me. I feel a striking

sense of falling, a falling worse than being fired. No client for Rex, no money for Julia.

"Liz, I need that million dollars. Do you think you could—"

"Here." She shakes a beaker in front of me. "Take it. Drink it." We both down one, then another, and another, still holding hands as the music washes over us. When I let go, she pulls back to curl into a ball on the empty couch, lips moving over the lyrics like whispered rosary prayers, wild eyes following the darts of colored light spraying the dance floor.

I crouch down and bring my face near hers. "Liz, you have the power to do a really good thing here."

Her eyes focus on me, then close slowly. "I've come down," she says so softly I can only see her small lips form the shapes. Tears stream out from her lids, smudging the painted-on pretense of the butterfly, her diminutive frame shaken by her over-sized emotion.

The vodka hits my bloodstream. "Liz!" I take her shoulders. She shudders. "I'm *done*," she says tearfully, opening her eyes and pulling herself up to sit. "She wants to buy me out, *fine*."

"Buy you out?" I blink as she splits into three fuzzy images of herself.

She nods, rubbing away the tears. "She gave me the papers in L.A. I didn't think she meant it."

"That's perfect then! You'll have a fresh start, do a new thing, and Magdalene would be a perfect—"

"You don't understand a *fucking* thing, do you?" Swerving to stand she roots around for her trench, tugging it out of the couch in lunging jerks. She stumbles down the stairs and into a throng of Muffins lap-dancing their men.

I follow after her into the crowd, but she's gone. Searching, I weave through the dancing mob toward the exit, a remix of Madonna's "Erotica" pounding my skin as I'm enveloped by women sliding their sweaty, sparkling limbs against me. They reach out for me as the alcohol opens a funnel in my brain for the music. *"Give it up, do what I say, give it up and let me have my way."* Fingers slide up into my hair. I shut my eyes, letting my mind tumble backward, my pelvis swaying with the lyrics, falling deeper and deeper into the music. I feel soft lips press against my neck, sending waves up my spine. And then I'm kissing. We're kissing. And it's not Buster. And I want to go home. I open my eyes and pull away.

From Kat.

I stumble back. But she writhes off, borne away by the current of throbbing bodies.

"Wait!" a cherubed hip-hop boy calls as I plow through the velvet curtain. "Your goodie bag!" He presses the silver handle into my palm, his feathered wings slapping against my shoulder. I burst onto the sidewalk, gulping the air and nearly tripping over the cardboard sign of a kid curled next to a sleeping mastiff. As three giggling blondes abandon a cab, I throw myself in, toppling as we swerve out into traffic, too drunk to ballast myself.

Home, struggling with the key, I shove open my apartment door and careen into the darkness. Finding the bed, I climb on and straddle the comforting shape under the covers that is my boyfriend.

"Wake up," I say, kissing his ear. Buster's mouth responds before he's even fully conscious.

"You taste different," he says, but I'm already pulling at my clothes in a frenzy of alcohol-sodden atonement and lust. We roll over, the silver souvenir sack digging into us. "What's in the bag?"

"Don't know," I murmur into his neck, tugging down his boxers.

He pulls out a black silk rope and smiles at me. "Tell me what it was like tonight."

I stare drunkenly at him. "No, you tell me." In a swift move, he rolls me over and ties my hands behind my back. I'm starting to laugh, nervous laughter into the pillow, not even able to formulate if I want it like this or not, feeling as if everything done to my body is being revealed to me minutes after it's happening. And I'm catching up. And I'm catching up. Catching. Up. Catching. Up. I blink in and out, my face pressed into the pillow, his breath on my neck; it is faceless, wordless, loveless.

Shaking violently, I withdraw to the bathroom, where I curl up in the shower, crying under the water, unable to surface or sober up or know what just happened to us in there.

CHAPTER ELEVEN

Hang On, You Know What You'd Be Perfect For?

I hover in the reception area, gripping a dented coffee cup and bracing my splitting temples with my free hand. Ugh. I begin to make my way across MC's cement floor when I'm caught up in a shifting migration as every employee abandons his or her desk and converges on the far corner of the office, where I see rows of folding chairs have been set up. Ugh. I allow myself to be borne along by the current and deposited on a metal seat in the back row, where I hunker down once again. I feel revolting, so morning-aftered I had to disembark the bus twice to relieve the nausea. But my resolve to convince Rex to shake down The Bank for Magdalene's funding propels me. That and the specter of a loudly snoring Buster sprawled across my mattress.

"All right, people! All eyes up here!" Splintering my eardrums, a kinetic Jeffrey toots a gym whistle to grab our focus. With little concern for those of us seated facing the floor-to-ceiling windows, he wrenches the blinds open, the sun revealing Muffin paraphernalia beating from every surface. My toast repeats on me.

"Time to look lively! Take one and pass them over. Take one and pass them over." Jeffrey glides down the narrow makeshift aisle, handing out index cards. I try to focus my dry eyes on the small print, which begins with a list of 'Muffin-approved' lingo. "All right, *people!* I understand that you haven't gathered in a number of months, so I expect your *full* attention. We've called you all together this morning to show our new client, Bovary, that MC's greatest asset is *you,* its workforce, its brain trust. To that end, I've given you each a list of speaking points about Muffin. Please memorize them immediately." Everyone nods uneasily. "We're going to brainstorm when Bovary arrives."

About that. "Jeffrey?" I raise my hand, flinching as I'm assaulted by my own voice.

"Later, Girl. The brainstorming shall proceed as follows: I'll enthusiastically look to you for 'input.' You are to contribute the 'idea' written on the card you've just been handed. Now, every time I straighten my tie, that'll be the cue to jump *right* in. If you have an A on your card, you're to speak in the first quarter of the hour, B's speak in the second, and the C's are backup for the first and second quarters. Now, I want everyone to look at their watches and make sure they're set for nine-oh-seven. Annnnddddd, go."

"Jeffrey, I think you should know—" I put my hand back up to circumvent this festival of desperation.

"Not. *Now.*" His hiss immediately derails any Vice Presidential impulse to march to the front of the room, where, let the record show, I would either be a) handed a packet of markers, b) stuffed in a bikini or c) beat about the head.

Fine. Suit yourself. While my colleagues' faces pucker in confusion, I rest my throbbing eyes. Within seconds I'm slipping into unconsciousness, chin dropping, my mind spiraling back to my bed, the rope chaffing against my wrists as I squirm, lips pressed into the pillow. *Catching. Up. Catching. Up.* The cotton warms into skin and I'm pressed against Kat, a Toulouse Lautrec crowd of male faces leering in.

"Christ, where is she?" Guy's voice startles me awake, and I check my watch. Almost ten o'clock. Noting that both neighbors are covertly playing Centipede on their Palms, I glance over a mass of restless heads to the front. Guy scratches his aggravated shaving rash. Jeffrey does not look pleased.

"Girl!"

"Yes?"

"Stand, I can't see you." Jeffrey waves in my direction.

The sea of heads turns to me as I pull myself up. "She's not coming."

I fold back down.

"What? Why?" Jeffrey asks, pulling off his spectacles.

"Why?" I repeat.

"*Why?*" Guy asks more forcefully. "Where is she?" Having an incestuous threesome?

"Let's talk about this in your office, Guy."

"You were with her last night." Eyebrows shoot up at the MC geisha. Titillated murmuring.

"Guy, let's not—"

"*Oh, Christ, just answer me,*" he blows.

"Fine. Kat and the Muffin people really hit it off—"

"Well, great then!" he interrupts, throwing his hands up as his mood lifts manically. "So let's get her on the phone and get started!"

"Guy, I really don't think—"

"Jeffrey, do it."

Finefinefinefine*fine*—your fucking problem. Jeffrey turns to us. "Ladies and gentlemen, our client seems to be running a little late—"

"A little?" snorts someone behind me. *Our client?* I snort to myself.

"So, we're going to conduct this meeting via speakerphone. Same rules and instructions apply, only now we won't be inhibited by her presence, therefore I'll be able to point to each of you directly when I want you to *participate*." Guy drops into a chair facing the crowd as Jeffrey taps a number into the voice conferencing contraption that looks very much like a miniature UFO.

"Mercer Hotel, how may I direct your call?"

"Room 612," Jeffrey leans over to instruct.

"Hullo?" Kat's voice crackles, acid floods my system.

"Good *mor*-ning, Kat!"

"Who is this?"

"This is Jeffrey and Guy and the whole My Company family. We're just so excited to talk to you about your Muffin that we figured if you couldn't come to MC, Inc., MC, Inc. would come to you!" He grins at the UFO while Guy anxiously drums the table. "Yes, we've gathered the *entire* company—and I wish you could see this, Kat, it's pretty impressive—"

"Let's hear it," she mutters humorlessly into the room.

Jeffrey chuckles as if she's just made a funny. "Now, this would, of course, be more organic if you were with us—"

"Like you promised yesterday, Kat," Guy interjects, scowling in my direction.

"Neither here nor there!" Jeffrey breezes over him. "Anywho, we've all gathered together to tackle making the Bovary Muffin campaign. Rex couldn't be here, but he's standing by, dying to know what you think of our plans."

"I'm sure."

"And, Kat, you should see it, the room is bubbling, just *bubbling over* with ideas. Okay, okay, one at a time now, everyone will be heard. Yes . . . you!" He violently beckons a woman seated a few rows back, sending her racing to the front, gripping her flashcard.

"Hi, I'm Marsha. I . . ." She scans the card. "Have a doctorate. A doctorate?" Jeffrey glares. "A doctorate. In marketing and . . . human sexuality?"

Jeffrey proceeds to orchestrate, pointing at different employees, who must scramble over each other to make it up to the table, where he pushes them inches from the speaker to perform stilted recitations of his 'ideas.' The floor rapidly descends into muffled chaos as everyone readies for Jeffrey's summons in the minefield of densely packed chairs. But when, without warning, he asks for "our thoughts," everyone freezes, frantically looking on both sides of their cards and then wordlessly at each other, unclear if they're actually supposed to give them.

"Jeffrey."

"Yes, Kat?"

"It's over." Finally. "We're going in another direction."

Jeffrey opens his mouth and then closes it.

Guy blanches, "What direction—why?"

"Because Rex is a prick. Because I don't need consultants. You can pass that along for me, can't you?"

"Is this a joke," Guy asks, his forehead glistening.

"*Obscenely* early in the morning for jokes. Just tell Rex he can go fuck himself." A clumsy clamor to hang up is followed by a droning dial tone, cut to silence by Guy slamming his hand down on the dial pad.

Everyone sits perfectly still, their collective breath held.

Suddenly the air is broken by a slap as Guy stands, clapping loudly in sardonic applause. Slap. In Jeffrey's face. Slap. Slap. Out at us. "Way to go, people! Nice work! Really, just *really great work!*" He drops his hands, his face reddening as Jeffrey assumes the amused expression of someone watching a growling puppy. "*I'm* doing everything I can to keep this fucking company *afloat,* and you fucking jerkoffs can't pull it off for *one lousy meeting?!*" he spits in fury. "It's a team effort here, kids. *Get your shit together!*" He storms to his office, slamming the door with such rage the entire wall of glass shakes. Oh-kay.

Everyone looks abashed except Jeffrey, who gently tugs his trousers and takes a seat. Abruptly the door flies open again. "Here's the plan!" Guy bounds back up the center aisle with evangelical conviction. "Folks, I need you all to *hunker down.* We're a consulting company. So act like consultants." He paces back and forth while we, a tech-shop and a feminist, wait for an explanation. "Come up with three new client leads. *At least* three leads—each—and e-mail them to me by the end of the day. I'll give . . . a thousand-dollar bonus to the first lead that goes somewhere." He looks around, wild-eyed. "Stop sitting around waiting for me to fucking fix this! Get on the phone and network! Call your parents, your college roommates, *your fucking camp counselors,* and get me those leads. *Now!!*"

Chairs squeak against the cement as people quickly dart to their desks. "You." Guy points to me with one arm and then extends another at Jeffrey. "And you. And Stacey, in my office."

"Yes, sir. Right away, sir." Jeffrey smiles wryly at Guy's departing back. Stooping to retrieve his briefcase, he clicks it open, slides in his blue binder, then snaps it neatly shut. "After you, mademoiselle." He takes a tiny bow and waves me on. My head throbbing with each step, I follow Stacey into Guy's office.

"Girl, what the *fuck* did you do to *fuck* this up?!"

"Nothing! Guy, nothing. I did *exactly* what you told me to do. I went there. I kept her company—"

"And?!"

"And Muffin made a cogent case for why we were unnecessary."

"And you didn't counter it?!"

Oh, Jesus, that's ridiculous. With what, a blow job? "Guy," I say, fighting not to get sucked into his hysteria. "Rex couldn't be bothered to get out of his chair. Can you really blame her?"

"Come on, Girl, she's a businesswoman," he scoffs. "She doesn't have your pathetic hang-ups. Know what? It doesn't even matter. I just need to get our shit together." He claps his hands as if expecting a huddle. "All right, Girl was too obvious. We'll get *her* all sexed up," Guy says, pointing at Stacey. "Throw her in some of this stuff." He rifles the lacy piles of Bovary samples on his desk. "Kat digs the whole hard-to-get thing."

Stacey steps forward, finally called to arms.

"Sure." Jeffrey glances at his watch and shrugs. "Whatever suits your fancy . . ."

Guy shakes his head in disbelief. "Jeff, man, I gotta tell ya, you're doing a *shit* job. Just an *absolute shit* job." He pops open a can of Coke from his desktop and takes a swig. "Frankly, I didn't really think we needed you, but I've gone along out of respect for Rex." He wipes away the foamy crest from his upper lip. "But you better figure out how you're going to explain what just happened out there, my friend. Step it up or I'm gonna hafta kick you to the curb."

"You arrogant little prick," Jeffrey murmurs. "This was a *tourist trip* for me." He studies his cuticles before looking up with a thin smile. "Your seat is for sale, *my friend.* So you stumbled onto a half-good idea? You're about as equipped to run this launch as she is." He nods at me. True. "If you'd actually gotten Kat's pawprint on the dotted line, who do you think they were lining up for the liftoff? A wet-behind-the-ears junior, two years out of B-school? Really?" Jeffrey straightens his tie. "Please thank Rex for the lovely look round, but I'm going to have to pass." He strides to the doorway. "And, Guy? The cocky thing is adorable, but it's only going to keep you the flavor of the month for so long. I'd learn some manners if I were you."

The three of us watch through the glass as Jeffrey exits MC, Inc. Call me.

I turn back into the room, my eyes landing on Guy's. "Puh," he exhales sharply, forcing a smile. "What a royal asshole." The vein pulsing in his neck, he turns to the windows.

"Guy—"

"Leave."

I follow Stacey down the steps as Rex strides across the company floor toward us.

"Before you go in," I say, reaching out to stop him in a Hail

Mary pass, "we need to talk about this Magdalene donation. MC pledged the money, which means The Bank pledged the money—"

"This isn't appropriate right now." One foot on a stair, he pauses to face me for only the second time since he banished me to The Club's ladies' room. For a moment I balk, feeling the solid force of institution behind him.

"The Bank has to make good on this."

"I just came from a meeting. It's on the table," he says firmly.

"What *exactly* should I tell them?"

"Stall for twenty-four hours."

He reaches for the knob, his broad back filling Guy's doorway to address the wet-behind-the-ears junior. "So, I passed Jeffrey on his way out." I remain rooted for Guy's pending admonishment. "Let's not sweat it. On to Plan B." With a wolfish smile, Rex kicks the door shut with his loafer.

After fifteen hours of dead sleep, I return at nine the next morning with only two hours remaining on Rex's Stall Clock. The phone rings, Julia's number flashing up once more from the caller ID. I remain motionless until it stops. Hello, Vice President of Stalling. *Ring . . . Ring . . . Ring.* Buster's number pops up again—no doubt leaving yet another jovial voice mail. I don't even know what to say to him. I don't even know where to begin.

"Heading to the training? Everyone's gotta be there." Humming, Guy raps his knuckles on my desk as he passes, the apocalypse of yesterday visibly lifted from his shoulders.

"What's this training for? The e-mail was a little vague."

"Jesus, why does everything have to be such a song and dance with you?"

"It doesn't. Is Rex coming in?"

Ignoring me, he bounds away to the horseshoe of chairs, still set up from the aborted 'brainstorming.' I pop two Tums and follow as employees straggle in apprehensively, cups of coffee in hand. Guy takes his place before his congregation, and, one eye on my watch, I slide into a seat. "Hey, folks, good to see you this morning," Guy addresses us with the mellow charm of someone who's just returned from a week in the islands. "I know we had a rough ride yesterday, and I've heard that some of you are having concerns about our future. The truth is, you have *nothing* to worry about. I'm telling you My Company will be *just fine*. I *promise*. We're *family!* We *fight* like family. I had a rough day, but I know you'll give me rope, just like I give it to you."

A hand darts up.

"Yeah?"

"We were wondering if the lead bonus still stands?"

"The what?" Guy squints.

"Yesterday you said that there'd be a thousand dollars for the first lead that turns up business," a second voice adds.

"Yeah, the thing is, Stan, I don't really feel all that comfortable paying you extra for work that isn't extra. Drumming up leads is what consultants do. So, enough heavy stuff! Okay—"

"Then you're not still giving the bonus?" another voice pipes from the back.

"No. I don't know. Whatever, let's move on. So I'm going to hand it over to Lyle and Lynn." Guy claps his hands together with a big smile before retreating to a table at the back.

Lyle and Lynn, presumably the Duke and Duchess of Plan B, take the floor, both dressed in similarly bland gray suits. Lyle clears his throat and gestures stiffly to himself. "Yes, hello. I'm Lyle, and this is Lynn. And some of you may know us or have seen us around. We're My Company's legal counsel"—Our what?—"And we've come to train you today about something that affects us all." Schizophrenic management? Client deficit? Tanking morale? "Sexual harassment." Of course. "It's been decided that this is an issue that requires immediate attention. I want to apologize in advance, as we usually hire out these sorts of trainings, but it was very short notice, so Lynn will be doing the honors today."

Lynn smiles, her blunt wedge cut boxing in her face as she picks up her materials. "What *is* sexual harassment? How do you know if you are *being* harassed *or* if *you* are harassing *somebody else?*" Her eyes pop for emphasis as she proclaims from her manual, "What are your *rights?* And what are your *wrongs?*" She locks the manual against her chest to pump air question marks. "All of these questions and more will be answered in the next five hours and forty-five minutes that we'll be together." While my colleagues suppress groans of misery, her eyes shine with enthusiasm. Evidently, sexual harassment training is Lynn's turn in the spotlight. "Now, there are a *number* of myths about sexual harassment. How many of you think you have to be a *woman* to be harassed?" She looks out with the expectant smile of a kindergarten teacher. At least fifteen hands shoot up. Kill me.

"Well, you're wrong. *Multiple* cases have recently come to light that reveal this crime has *noth-ing whatsoever* to do with gender." Care to rephrase? "That's right. It's a crime committed by men *and* women. Today we're going to talk about what to do if your boss harasses you. If he *or* she harasses you." A number of hairy crossed arms relax as she continues to read, her script riddled with he*or*shes, him*or*hers, man*or*womans.

Antsy, I keep my eye on the double doors, scanning for Rex's arrival. Glancing back at the table, my eyes land on a dark brunette in her late thirties seated next to Guy. Their heads tilted together, he nods along to something she's whispering.

"Next, we're going to work in *small groups*, so turn your chairs in with *four* of your neighbors and discuss the scenarios Lyle is passing out. Now this is a *shared* exercise, so everyone needs to get their chairs as *close* as possible!" Trapped, I reposition myself as instructed—intimately—with a group from the tech department. I think. Despite my three-month tenure, I still couldn't name more than three other employees if you put an electric stapler to my head. We're handed scripts with num-bered paragraphs. Lynn reads along out loud, just in case.

"You have been introduced to a *buxom* college graduate, who has arrived at her first day on the job wearing *inappropriately re-vealing clothing*. She leans across your boss's desk. What advice would *you* give her to *protect* herself from *sexual harassment?* Dis-cuss in your groups."

A programmer nods his blond dreadlocks and taps his soul patch. "I think boobs are an advantage—you know—like a competitive advantage." Unable to resist this golden opportu-nity to publicly air his revelation, he raises his hand.

"Yes! Yes!" Lynn waves encouragingly for him to speak.

"My group here, well, we were just talking about how maybe this graduate could be harassing the guys she works with, be-cause maybe her boobs could get her a raise. Doesn't that make her a criminal?"

"Well . . ." Lynn looks baffled. *"Yes!"* She nods enthusiasti-cally, and I imagine her training guide containing only two words: BE SUPPORTIVE. *"People* with exposed *body parts* may make others *uncomfortable*. Say that Pat had something on hisorher body that made hisorher coworker, Alex, *uncomfortable*. Then *Pat* might be harassing *Alex*—"

The programmer scoots back from our fivesome and strides up to Lynn. "I just want to share how when I worked at this tech shop, out in Seattle, there was this chick who always wore these real thin tank tops. One time, it must have been, like, Novem-ber . . . maybe December? Anyway it was cold as balls and . . ." SHUT UP! SHUT UP! SHUT UP! But he gabs on, his experi-ence sparking a lively debate about whether or not it's appropri-ate to compliment "someone" on hisorher haircut. "What, so if I tell Sally she has nice hair, you're gonna arrest me?"

"Yes!" I pop up, done. "Yes! That's *exactly* it. Could someone get him a mike, please? Because I know *I* can't get enough."

"Role-play time!" Lynn cuts me off.

I make a beeline for Guy. "Where's Rex?" I tap my hands on the thick documents stacked high at his table. Looking down over the piles, I see that his companion is a good six months pregnant.

"He's on his way. Sign this." Guy thrusts something in triplicate at me along with a pen. I read RELEASE OF ALL CLAIMS printed in bold across the top.

"I'd prefer to take this home and—"

"Sign it," Guy repeats, smacking the papers with his pen. "It's just to verify that you attended the training."

I power-scroll through the boilerplate that essentially absolves MC of *all* responsibility should I feel uncomfortable 'as a result of my gender in this environment.' "This is ridiculous," I mutter. "I'm not signing it."

"Here we go," he says, rolling his eyes at his brunette companion.

"Guy, what am I supposed to take away from this?" I whisper furiously, flinging my arm to encompass the sing-along Lynn is now leading. "That *I* can harass *you?*" I stab the tip of my pen in his direction, and he leans back ever so slightly. "How is it effective to indulge in an hour-long debate over whether or not it's *legal* to compliment a colleague on a haircut? Isn't that just a *tad* off point? Aren't we kind of *obscuring* the whole issue here?" I look into his obtuse face. Over it with a capital O.

"And what *is* the whole issue?" the woman asks in a nasal Scarsdale twang, her dark eyes glinting.

"That somehow people manage not to harass *up* the chain of command. It's not nuclear physics. If you wouldn't say it, show it, or share it with your grandma, don't say it, show it, or share it at work. As far as the complexities involved in even needing something like this . . . this . . ." I shake the stupid document. "I can't even . . . Look, Guy, the minute Rex gets here we need to formulate a plan to address the money that we don't have, that

I promised on your behalf. We can't, *can't* leave Julia Gilman and Magdalene hanging any longer."

"You're Girl." She gives me a reserved smile. "I don't think Rex'll be here anytime soon, but I can fill you in on the funding."

"You can? I'm sorry, I missed your name."

"Manley." She extends her small swollen hand to me as I return the form to the pile. "Okay, then I think everything is finally under control here." She heaves her petite, encumbered frame out of the folding chair. "Don't let anyone else leave without signing that. Guy?" She snaps her fingers in the direction of her mustard yellow Birkin on the floor, and after a moment's incomprehension, he bends to retrieve it.

"What about hers?" he asks, tapping the unsigned document.

"She doesn't have to sign it now." Manley winks at me. "I'm ravenous. Girl, care to join me?"

"Sure . . ."

"Good." Without further good-byes, she starts for the door. Despite the disproportionate weight in front of her, she huffs on, her tailored blouse falling smartly around her. "Have these people never heard of walls? Open plans don't make employees more productive at anything other than faking it."

I hold the door for Manley at Bella Russe, the doorman seemingly gone the way of the lavish floral arrangements after only a few short months of itness. "My husband and I have been meaning to drive down and try it," she says, doing a quick inventory. "Looks like we missed it."

"Can I help you?" the hostess asks, smiling graciously, all but one table behind her sitting forlornly empty.

"Snacks," Manley says. We're shown to what once must have been the prime spot, beneath the floating bust of Trotsky, and the surplus of underutilized waitstaff descends.

"So, I read your proposal," she says once the waiter slides a tasting platter of tartares onto our table. "Actually I've read all your materials. Your ideas for feminist modifications of the site were spot-on. Too bad he couldn't be bothered to implement them. What a fucking circus." She rolls her eyes as she pops a raw steak tartlet in her mouth.

"How did you get my material?" And who are you?

"I asked. Anyway, aside from the fact that Guy was clearly yanking you twelve ways from Sunday, you did good work." She takes another tartlet, going into the same paroxysms of ecstasy.

"Thank you. Are you with the company now?"

"The board's brought me in. Tuna?" She pushes the dish of pink cubes toward me. "I'm not supposed to eat this, either." She spoons a dollop on a sliver of baguette. "Rex talked The Bank into letting Guy take this place in a harebrained direction. Rex's track record was impeccable, so, of course, they indulged him. But Guy neglected to put any resources into shoring up relations with the magazines." She gestures indignantly with her spoon as she swallows. "Or improving the technological offerings. He just hemorrhaged money wooing Bovary. That's no way to run a lemonade stand." She fixes herself another slice. "Anyway, I've committed to getting The Bank's investment back in the black inside two months."

"Can that be done?"

"I wouldn't have promised if it couldn't."

"Right, of course."

"So." She pours herself another large glass of Fiji. "I wanted to talk to you about your role moving forward. Thanks to Guy's profligate spending, we're in no position to hire externally, so people are going to be asked to fill roles outside their original job descriptions."

"I never had one."

"Not surprising." She smiles at me before taking a sip. "The next month is going to be challenging, and there's a surplus of cowboy energy up there. I want you to work with me as we get our costs down and our revenue up. I like your assessment of that less-than-stellar sexual harassment training. I like your report. You have a good head on your shoulders, and that's what I need by my side. Okay?" She rubs her hands gently over her protruding stomach as I stare at her, taking in her frank request.

"I'm sorry," I begin, working through my wariness. "It's just that it's really been, well, as you said, a lot of cowboy stuff and I'm feeling a little burned about . . ." She stares at me patiently. "Sorry, I've become unaccustomed to finishing my thoughts."

"I understand you've committed a million dollars."

"I have, I was told to."

"The company intends to come through on that promise, but responsibly to its own welfare. We'll be making one hundred thousand available to Magdalene in the next seventy-two hours, the balance to be delivered, should we meet our objectives, in no later than a month."

"Just like that?" I ask.

She snorts, "You *are* shell-shocked. We can't afford bad publicity right now. So you have my word." She waves for the check. "Can we move forward?"

"Yes, this is great. I'm going to call Julia Gilman." I pull out my cell. "She's the—"

"I know. Will you ask for the check while I go to the bathroom? The peeing—not a myth. Be in by seven tomorrow. We have a big day ahead of us."

As I stagger bewilderedly off the elevator, pulling out my keys, I'm in hope. Conservative, impartial, just-here-for-the-paycheck hope. I will not love her, I will not hate her, I will just work for her.

Using my hip to push open the front door, my grocery bags fall heavily against my ankles. "What the—" I'm greeted by the sound of the evening news broadcasting from my living room. "Hello?" I call out, holding the door open.

"Hey." The TV clicks off, and Buster walks into the entry-way, stopping a few feet from me.

I let out an audible breath, closing the door. "Hi." My body pulses to hug him, but I don't.

He smiles sheepishly. "So I guess we need to talk." He presents a fresh bouquet of white tulips from behind his back.

I cringe at the repeated gesture.

"I've been trying to reach you."

"I know."

He clears his throat. "So, is this over?"

I look at him, unsure. "What was that?" I ask. His face is un-readable. "In bed. What was that?"

He shrugs, his eyes on the floor.

"It just . . ." I struggle to describe the encounter. "It felt like you were with someone else."

"What're you talking about?" he asks blankly.

"Buster, you checked out."

"I woke up and you were so into me and so sexy." His face darkens. "I can't believe this. You're the one out at some orgy, you didn't want to talk, you couldn't get my shorts off fast enough."

"I know." I put my hand up to stop him, my stomach tight-ening around the memory of the dance floor.

"I thought we were both into it," he says. "You were laughing."

"Buster, it was . . . it felt like . . ." I feel the chill of his disap-pearance afresh. "You were pissed at me." He tinges crimson. "Are you? Pissed at me?"

"No!" he protests. "What do I have to be pissed at you about?"

"I don't know. It just seemed like—felt like—you were."

"God, G," he explodes in frustration. "I watch every word I say around you, everything I do—my friends are giving me shit—you need to cut me some fucking slack!"

We stare at each other, strangers again. "How did we get here?" I ask, tears wetting my eyes.

His head drops. "I'm just tired, Girl. I'm really tired."

"Okay . . ." I say, a spike of anger drying my eyes. "I don't know what to do with that."

"It's just frustrating."

"Okay, so . . . we're in a relationship where you're going to arbitrarily work your frustration out on my ass."

His eyes meet mine. "Okay, maybe, *maybe* there was some of that going on, but you gotta acknowledge that you were working something out, too."

"I do. I was." I release a long breath. "But then you passed out, and I cried in the bathroom."

"Shit." Regret twists his features. "I didn't know. I'm sorry."

"I'm not trying to change you, Buster. But if we're gonna do this . . . I have to know that you'll talk to me and not ever let it get to a point that's so . . . volatile."

"Yes. I mean, I love you—" his voice catches. "It doesn't make this mess go away, but . . ."

"No, it doesn't." I take him in, his ruffled hair, his bitten lip, the flowers. "It doesn't, but I want it to." I reach to take the bouquet from him, but he maintains his grasp, pulling me into him. I let my weight rest fully against his frame.

At six-thirty the next morning, I'm halfway across the floor of MC, Inc. before I realize that the dawn light has been blocked by the addition of opaque gray curtains drawn across the glass wall of Guy's office. A stark ray of sunshine escapes through a narrow crack, throwing the honeycomb of empty desks into chiaroscuro.

"Good morning." I step up through Guy's door and nearly topple over the displaced pony-skin chaise.

"Yeah." Sleeves rolled, Guy shoves his chair away from a brand-new floor-to-ceiling partition cleaving his palace in two, his toys now chaotically crowded into half of their former space.

"What's going on?" I ask as he straightens up, red-faced from his exertion.

"These yours?" Manley appears at the partition door, a cardboard box topped with a Nerf ball balanced on her bulging belly.

"Yup." Guy, surprisingly jovial, maneuvers in the cramped room to retrieve it.

"Oh, morning, Girl." She gestures behind her. "Take a seat inside. Guy, get settled later."

" 'Kay, sure." He squeezes around his uprooted desk to follow us into the other side, the half with the private washroom. Transformed overnight into Manley's office, additional gray curtains are drawn across the windows, and a series of graphs and charts have been laid out on the walls. Her desk neatly tucked in one corner and a worktable coolly lit in the center reveal an organizational logic new to these parts.

"Let's take a seat, then." We all pull out chairs. She lowers herself in at the table and turns to me. "So that you're aware, Guy has been privy to prior discussions about the topic at hand. I'll now fully apprise you of our task within the bounds of what I'm allowed by the board. And I'll have a doughnut." She flops back the lid on a box of Krispy Kremes and takes three big bites of a classic glazed before dropping it back. "Those *What to Expect* women are sugar Nazis." Licking her lips clean, she tucks her conservative brown bob behind her ear. "Now I'll share what's pertinent to your role."

"Okay." I grin as she pushes aside the Krispy Kreme box to reveal a yellow legal pad of her own, densely covered in a tight cursive. Guy drums his fingers, oblivious to our shared preference for 'school paper.'

"So, we have a pretty significant reorg ahead of us—"

"Sorry?" I pause her. "Sorry, I'm not familiar with 'reorg.' "

"Don't apologize. Questions are good." Manley flips the box

lid and retrieves her doughnut stub, popping it into her mouth. "Reorganization. We're redesigning this company to streamline its efficiency; our current staffing model is completely out-moded." She squeezes a napkin with her sticky fingers as if it were a stress ball. "Essentially conducting a layoff."

"Oh."

"I'm not going to lie to you. It's substantial. And one hundred percent necessary." Guy's jaw clenches. "You'll be working together to make plans, but I'm looking to you, Girl, to execute the event."

"Me?"

"You've been working independently, an ideal position in re-lation to the floor, and you're capable of it. We'd have looked to your human resource group," she snorts, "but Guy saw fit to dis-mantle them." He clenches again.

"So when is this supposed to happen?" I ask, trying to grasp what she's asking me to do.

"I can't reveal that right now. We've got quite a few other reorg ducks to get in a row first."

"How many people?"

"That either." Oh-kay. She flips the well-chewed end of her pen out from between her teeth. "MC, Inc. is on the brink of a major transition. We can't run the risk of being publicly linked to a large-scale reduction in force, so *everyone* is on a need-to-know basis. I promise you'll have all the information you need to execute this task to the best of your abilities. But the board wants this rolled out stealthily."

"Stealthily, of course," Guy affirms, jolting the table with his palms. Our very own Grand Poobah of Stealth.

"Now I'll be getting everything prepared for the subsequent relaunch so you two can work from Guy's office. And Stacey's not to be involved in this. Questions?"

"Yes," I speak up. "I really appreciate your confidence. But my experience with firing—"

"Rightsizing," Manley interjects.

"Rightsizing—is really very limited." Fuck you very much, Doris. "And I guess I have reservations about the responsibility."

"Guy, we need a moment."

He looks from one of us to the other before standing and running his hands through his hair. "Such a fucking downer," he mutters as he tugs the door shut behind him.

Manley slides the Krispy Kremes over to me with the tip of her pen. "What's wrong?"

"I want to be honest. I really don't have any training for something of this nature and Guy and I, well . . ." I pause, glancing with concern at the partition wall.

"It's soundproof."

"Guy doesn't like me very much."

She smiles as if I've told her a joke. "Are you kidding me?"

"No."

"Who cares?" she snorts. "Girl, *who cares?* I don't care. You definitely shouldn't care." She pushes herself up to stand, still grinning. "Doesn't like you," she says with a laugh, waddling over to the garbage and letting the box drop in. "Get over that, Girl. It'll sink you."

I redden. "Thank you."

"Sure." She laughs again. "So we'll be calling it 'The Project,' and I'd like you both to set to work on a rollout plan immediately." She walks back to her desk and picks up the phone. "Doesn't like you," she replays to herself, as I let myself out into Guy's maze of condensed grandeur.

"So we're working on this together." I close her door behind me.

"Yeah. You can set up, uh, over there." He tosses a Nerf football by way of direction, bouncing it off the chaise.

I squeeze over to it, my knees jammed against his desk. "Maybe we should start by moving some of this furniture out so we can be a bit more mobile in here?"

"Maybe *you* should start by remembering your fucking *place*," he scowls, jerking his chair around to face the window. Oy.

"Why are you out here?"

Having retreated to my old desk by the next morning, I peer over my laptop screen to Manley, her hand on one pregnancy-obscured hip. "Oh, it just seemed a more productive spot than the chaise. It's okay—I'm keeping everything covered and nobody really wanders over here anyways. I prefer it, actually." I affect what I hope to be a preferring smile.

She arches an eyebrow and steps up to Guy's closed door. "Get your laptop and come with me." Reluctantly, I unplug the cord and follow. Manley locks in on Guy. "Is there a problem here?"

He immediately drops the *Harvard Business Review* into his lap. "Not at all, just killing a few minutes before the meeting."

"This desk is big enough for two, understood?"

"Yeah, of course!" he beams. "She wanted to work out there."

"Uh-huh." Manley points me to the other side of his desk. "What do you two have so far?"

Guy gestures my way.

"Well." I slide my laptop gingerly onto the far corner. "I've been researching what support materials companies are giving to their fire—rightsized employees. Information from Unemployment, placement counselors—"

"Oof." Manley's hands fly to her jostled abdomen. "That's fine, Girl, but our priority is strategy."

"Well, I thought you'd probably want to bring each person into Guy's office and talk through letting them go." Guy's eyes lower just enough to continue reading his magazine.

"Nope—can't afford to roll it out that way. We need this planned to the minute." Manley grimaces again, her hand rubbing her stomach. "All right, that's the board." She cocks her head at the advancing stream of white-haired men visible through the open door. They file in behind Rex, as if he's leading a field trip from The Club. Guy stands, his magazine slapping the floor as the space fills like a Metro-North bar car at rush hour, packed shoulder to shoulder in summer-weight woolens.

Smooshed flat to the wall, I hear Rex's familiar boom, "You all know Guy." There's an indistinct murmur from the board.

He clears his throat. "Hi, everyone!"

"And," Rex continues, "most important, for those of you who haven't had the pleasure, this is Manley, who'll be getting us back in the black with our new little subdivision. Gentlemen, I advise you to pay close attention. She can teach us a thing or two."

"Please," she demurs. "Gentlemen, it's a pleasure. Step into my office, and we'll get started."

Guy moves to follow and all eyes look to Rex. "Hey, better to sit this one out."

"Oh, okay." Guy puts up his palms, acquiescing a bit too good-naturedly. "I'll be here if you need me." He reclaims the helm of his desk.

Manley peers through the felt door. "Girl, get together a rough agenda for The Project in the next hour, please." And the divider closes. I resume my post on the pony chaise. Opening a blank page on the screen, I conjure that day with Doris, making a list of the worst parts of the experience and then outlining what she could have done to minimize the humiliation. 1. Drop dead.

Within an hour, I've handed the document off to Manley in exchange for neatly noted bullets on yellow paper. "These are the Affected."

"Okay." I gently close the door while looking down at the names.

And names, and names.

And names.

I run my finger down the first column and then flip it over to count . . . four, five, six columns. Times twenty-four—that's, that's . . . one hundred forty-four people 'affected.'

"One hundred forty-four?!" I gasp. *"One hundred forty-four?"*

"Don't do that," Guy hisses.

"How can we possibly?" I turn to him. "Do that many people even *work* here?"

"We've got a hundred sixty-two on staff." He retreats to his magazine.

I sink down into the chaise, staring at the drawn curtain, behind which sits a world we are—I am—about to obliterate. "Guy, this is practically the whole company. I thought we were talking fifteen, maybe twenty people. *But one hundred forty-four? I* can't possibly—"

"How the hell do you think this is for *me,* Girl?" Guy bolts up and strides to the curtain. "That's my *family* out there." He yanks it back, throwing his arms out in an encompassing circle, eliciting stares from the floor. "These people look to me for leadership, and I have to *cut them off,* I have to *sever* their faith in me. I feel like a total ass about this so just, just—" He turns to me, his eyes wild. "Just stop saying that fucking number."

I chew the inside of my cheeks, reading through the short list of Unaffected beneath my name. Then I reread it.

"Stacey. You're firing Stacey."

"If she's on the Affected list." He bristles. "Don't look at me like that—I inherited her. It's not like she was my hire."

"Aren't you keeping any women other than me?" I stand.

"What're you talking about?"

"There're no other women's names on the Unaffected list." I thrust it at him.

The door swings open and Manley emerges. "Okay, they want it executed in less than an hour, first thing in the morning, and no contact between Affected and Unaffected. Girl, we need something real." She tosses my initial suggestions back at me and disappears.

I spin to Guy. "No contact? How are we going to—there are no walls here."

"I don't know, we'll just, ah . . . hand out tickets, you know." He snaps his fingers. "Red and blue and then we can send an e-mail telling the blue people to go to a meeting in my office and tell the red people to go home and we'll call them later and then when the blue people leave, call the red people . . ."

I tune him out, staring at Stacey shuffling from the kitchen, her soda carefully balanced atop her Tupperware container as she weaves back to her desk. "Guy, I don't think we can do it like that, with tickets. I think it's better to be up front."

Door opens. "They want it on the roof." Manley sticks her head out. "No opportunity to e-mail, reduces risk of getting in the papers." Door shuts.

"The tickets will say 'roof' or 'not roof,' maybe, instead of the color, or maybe do both," Guy continues, pacing back and forth.

Door opens. "They want cell phones confiscated before the roof. Run a strategy for end of day instead; don't want the morning news traffic helicopters picking it up." Door shuts.

"We could say it's a communications check!" Guy jerks his golf club out of his toybox and swings, nearly hitting the glass. "If it's at the end of the day, we could take 'em in the afternoon and say we're wiring new technology into the phones."

"Do they do that?" I ask quietly. "Wire new technology into phones?"

"Does it matter?" Guy's glow is returning to his cheeks. "We can freeze the computers the night before, say it's a bug or something."

"These are technically savvy people. They might suspect something."

Door opens. "They want you to send out an invitation to an

awards ceremony—you know Best Programmer, that kind of thing." Closes. Opens. "Before the roof, they want you to get signatures releasing us from claims, leverage severance as a threat if they don't." Closes. Opens. "They want to make sure there's security." Closes. Opens. "They want 'em to take the stairs up. Too much talking if they have to wait for the elevators, too many little groups plotting." Closes. Opens. "They want Unaffecteds on the roof while we clear out Affecteds and then bring Unaffecteds to the basement—"

Guy beams. "That's great! That'll work great with the blue and red tickets—then the red can say 'roof' and the blue can say 'basement.' We'll have 'em wait in the basement—if it's darker they'll be calmer—"

"Or we could just gas them."

"Problem, Girl?" Manley steps inside, closing the door on the din of men's voices behind her. Guy leans back on his desk, squeezing the club between his feet.

I look into her expectant face. "I can't do this."

The creases deepen between her eyebrows, conveying the absurdity of my misgiving. "Of course you can."

"Well, these plans seem really . . . extreme to me. I just think it makes more sense if Rex, or Guy—someone who had a role in bringing them into the company—would be better suited for this—"

"Guy?"

"Yeah?"

"We need the room."

"Well." He tosses the club up and catches it. "I'm good with all of this. Check, check, and check. I've got the whole ticket thing worked out, so just give me a wave when you're ready."

"Right."

Guy hops around the boxes and leaves. Crowded into the narrow lacuna by the partition door, Manley takes my hand and cups it in both her palms, which are almost feverishly warm.

"Look, I'm not going to bullshit you. We're amputating to save the patient. MC isn't evaluating personalities or character. This is solely about skill sets that meet business needs or don't. It's not about being liked. For them or us." Her deep brown eyes are fixed on me. "I picked you for a reason, Girl. This is a huge growth opportunity for you managerially. And I really want us to be able to give Magdalene that money. Big picture, Girl. Trust me on this." She drops my hand and extends her arm ceiling-ward to get a firm grip on the curtains. Facing the floor of Affecteds, she nods out at Stacey, who darts her gaze back to her screen. "You don't want to be sitting in that seat for the rest of your days, do you?"

"No," I say, unable to discern if it's a question or threat.

Manley yanks the drapes closed, then checks her watch again, holding it for a moment on her wrist. "Look, this meeting's going to run all day. Accounting has the check for Ms. Gilman. Go run it over to them, clear your head, and be back by two."

Door closes.

One of Julia's assistants ushers me into Magdalene's new home. Wet to the bone, I shake off my already broken umbrella, purchased five minutes and fifty gallons too late from a street vendor on Fulton as I searched through the downpour for the boarded-up storefront across from Trinity Church.

"Thank you. It's really coming down. Is Julia here?"

"Girl!" I follow her voice across the ash-shrouded skeleton of the former Wholesale Liquidator's Warehouse to where Julia's perched atop an industrial ladder. In jeans and a flannel shirt, she waves me over to her with one rubber-gloved hand. "Just clearing the dust!" she says cheerfully, tapping her sponge against one of the long, flat light fixtures that hang like baking sheets from the ceiling.

"This place is great!" I exclaim, my heels leaving muddy

prints on the linoleum floor as I cross to her. "Oh, no, I'm not helping. Sorry!"

"God, don't worry." Julia abandons her bucket on the top rung and climbs down. "This whole place needs to be hosed off. Thankfully, everyone will be pitching in starting tomorrow, so that should make it go faster." Smiling, she wipes her hair off her shining face with the back of her wrist, sponge in hand. "But it's going to be wonderful. Would you like the tour?"

"Absolutely!" I nod.

"Well, first we're going to clear out those," she says, swirling her sponge in the direction of the few remaining display cases. "And that." She points up at the shredded store sign. "Downstairs needs to be reventilated, which will be the big investment." Her eyes dart to mine. "But then it'll only take a few coats of cheery paint to make it a wonderful large-capacity dormitory. This level will be divided into a communal area." She indicates the far wall like an airplane marshaller waving landing batons. "Classrooms, offices." She indicates the periphery of the space, "*And* . . . if we can find the money"—her eyes dart again—"I'd love to have our own room for check-ups on-site. And . . . tah-dah!" She holds her arms out in a gesture of finale, her optimism radiant against the matte backdrop of detritus and debris. "So, whaddya think?"

"Julia, it's amazing." Her contagious thrill gives me a long-absent swell of pride. "What a difference you're going to make."

"*We're* going to make!" She peels off her gloves. "What's amazing is the rent, which, thanks to your donation, we can just manage. With the EPA still hemming and hawing about the air, the landlord was thrilled to find a group ready to overlook a little asbestos. Magdalene does have its priorities," she says, laughing.

I hear the sound of sighing stairs, and the young man, Julia's other assistant, appears on the floor, a box of paper towels in his arms. "Julia, you need fresh gloves?" he asks.

"I think this pair is holding up. How are we fixed for Ajax?"

"Half a carton left," he reports, carrying his haul back to where the young women scrape paint off the alley-side windows.

"So, do you have it on you?" Julia asks, reaching for a bottle of water and taking a quick sip.

"Yes! Here you go." I pull the envelope from my purse.

She kisses it. "I'm *so* relieved to see this."

"So am I."

She waves it above her head, calling, "Everybody! The hundred thousand's here!"

"Yay!" the man and woman cheer from the back. "Woo-hoo!"

"Keep an ear out for the locksmith, I'm taking it over to the bank." They give her an acknowledging thumbs-up before resuming their scraping. "Thanks for bringing it, Girl, especially in this weather." She pulls her raincoat from atop a stack of boxes by the entrance, which is still flanked by the plastic security gates.

"Of course. I'm sorry it's taken this long—"

"Not your fault, I'm sure." Julia slides on her trench, its crisp tailoring disguising her scrub clothes. Pushing into the door, she opens her golf umbrella.

"Can I walk you?" I ask, as the warm, damp air blows into the musky space. She waves me in under her Philip Morris–emblazoned awning.

We pick our way through the puddles in silence, Julia holding my waist. "Watch it!" She pulls me back from the brown arc of water sprayed by a passing cab. "The subway's just up there."

I peer out from under the umbrella, making out the glowing green orbs of the entrance to the 4, 5. Dreading the return to the MC bunker, my feet are unwilling to step away. "They're firing almost everyone," it comes out in a rush.

"Are they closing their doors?" Her eyes widen. "What about our funding?"

"No, they have a new manager, a real manager. She's going to have them in the black in two months. I'm sure they'll make good on the rest of your donation."

"Oh God—are *you* on the chopping block?"

"No. But . . . they want me to do it. Fire everyone."

She tightens her grip on my elbow to propel me across the flooding street. "What percent?"

"About eighty-five."

"Whew," she whistles. "Well, then, at least their letting Moldova go wasn't a reflection on her attitude."

"They fired Moldova?"

"A few days ago. And then we had it out over her wanting me to pay for a computer degree." She shakes her head. "I know it sounds cliché, but I've got to draw the line. I've mortgaged my home, for God's sakes." She switches the umbrella to the other hand. "And, of course, I'm sick about it. None of the others seem to have a contact number for her. It's unfortunate, but I can only help those who . . . blah blah blah."

"And you are."

"As long as there's money," her voice rises. "Okay, well, no need to panic yet. They've put you in charge of this, so that's a good sign. Very impressive."

"Not impressive," I say, uncomfortable with the compliment. "They say I'm the one best positioned because I don't know any of them."

"They have a point."

"Julia, I can't be the face these people—*the Affected*—" I pump my fingers. "See at four in the morning when they wake up wanting to kill someone."

She turns from me, and we're quiet for a few steps as we shuffle in tandem, trying to keep ourselves evenly paced. I look down at my water-stained heels. "Well," Julia says, "I always buoyed myself with the knowledge that six months after a layoff finds the majority of those let go in better-suited positions."

"In this economy?" Large drops plop onto my exposed shoulder.

"Girl, they're going to do it with or without you."

"I know that," I say testily, feeling as if I'm sharing the umbrella with Grace.

Julia stops, the dome tilting backwards, the runoff trailing down my exposed front. "If you push back any more on this, you stand a strong chance of being fired yourself."

"Believe me, I get that."

"Well? Do you plan to?"

"Yes. No—I don't know."

"Would you really put Magdalene in jeopardy?" Her blue eyes hold mine, the wall of the downpour solid around us.

"You can't think my presence at MC is that influential over your funding."

"They've entrusted you with a substantial responsibility. They clearly see you as a pivotal member."

My stomach sours as the rain renews its force, coming down again in thick sheets, pounding the umbrella and dousing our legs. "There are one hundred forty-four lives involved here, Julia."

"Who will be let go with or without you."

"Yes, you said that," my voice rises. "Listen, I shouldn't have told you. It's supposed to be confidential."

"Well, I appreciate the heads up." Julia takes a deep breath, then tries to soften her expression. "I know it feels awful, but it's just part of the corporate life cycle. Okay, Saint Joan?"

"Okay." I muster a smile in return.

"At least they're all U.S. citizens, with high school diplomas, and probably much more—families to lean on, families who aren't buying human meat at the hospital just to keep their children alive. *They'll* get unemployment. *They'll* get through this. Remember who you're helping here."

"Yes."

"So you won't risk it for us?"

"I won't."

"Now run and catch your train before we both get pneumonia and are of no use to anyone."

For two anxious, utterly stultifying weeks, I balance at the end of Guy's desk as we both await a 'go' from Manley. He reads voraciously, alternating national and local newspapers with shiny software magazines, occasionally jerking out his BlackBerry to make notes. Mostly it's the monotonous slide of his Coke can lifting up and down off the metal desktop that marks time. Manley checks in routinely, but the "new rollout" is under wraps until the "project" is "greenlit," so the meetings are brief and unprecedently efficient. I occupy myself by staring, either at the three pages of the minute-to-minute firing schedule or at a framed photo of Guy and Rex on a golf course, until Rex's toothy grin blurs with the rest of the stuffy office.

The phone rings, startling us.

"Yeah? . . . Hang on." Guy passes me the receiver, stretching the curled cord taut, and I grab the soda can before it's toppled.

"Hello?"

"How's it going, Terminator?" Buster asks, affecting Schwarzenegger. I glance over at Guy.

"Can I call you back in a minute?"

"I'm leaving to swing by the Atari party."

"One minute." I reach the phone back to Guy. "I'm going to use my old phone."

"*Total* confidentiality, Girl," he intones.

"Of course. No, that's my boyfriend."

"Is he a journalist?"

Yeah, he's a journalist and this has all been a big setup for *The Wall Street Journal*'s Year-End Fifty Biggest Assholes Edition. "No."

One nod and Guy's paper wall is resurrected. I close his door and step out into the sun-deprived office, a mass of heads turning apprehensively in my direction as I scuttle over to my old desk. Ducking down, I reach for the phone and dial.

"Hi, sorry about that. Guy was sitting on top of me—"

"Figuratively, I hope, or I'll have to pound him."

"I hate this," I whisper, pretending not to see the Affecteds pretending not to see me. "That woman from marketing cornered me in the bathroom *again* yesterday, demanding to know if she should close on her apartment. And this place is making a liar out of me every fucking minute I'm here. I don't think I can stand it much longer."

"Monday's Memorial Day. They must be waiting till Tuesday."

A bass beat erupts behind him, and I hear voices singing to the tune of Shaft, "Who's the man with the plan? *Buster!*"

"I better get back."

"Dudes—two minutes!" He laughs before returning to me. "Okay, so I'm going to swing out to this Atari shindig—they're really rollin' out the red carpet for us. Then I'll come over—maybe around five?"

"Sure. That sounds good."

"We should do something fun!"

"Yeah," I say distractedly, as I realize that the closest cluster has pushed Stacey out as an emissary, sending her on a tense leisurely stroll in my direction.

"Something fun," he repeats. "So any ideas?"

"I don't know, maybe there's fireworks or something."

"Cool, and we can swing by Sam's party after." Stacey inches closer.

"Buster, I gotta go."

"See you tonight!"

I return the phone to its cradle.

"Hi." Stacey hovers, the long sleeves of her sweater brushing my forearm.

"Hi!" I stand up, but she doesn't step back, leaving her flushed face only inches from mine.

"How are things going in there? You seem really busy," she says furtively.

"Yeah, Manley has a lot of stuff that she needs help with." I move to step around her.

"Should I be worried?" She moves with me.

"Why? No," I instinctively rush to reassure her.

"Girl. Should I be worried?"

"No, no, I . . ." hate myself. "Have you talked to Guy?"

"He's reassigned me to reception. I know we haven't exactly been friendly—"

"Stacey, it's not about that."

"Please, just a straight answer."

I stare at her hard, willing the intensity of my tone to communicate what my words can't. "I'm not allowed to give you that—"

Guy's door swings open, and he appears behind her, his expression electrified. I meet his eyes, my breath catches. "Liftoff," he says.

Stacey backs away.

"I'm sorry."

"Girl."

I jog up the steps, and we're in motion. From Guy's desk, I hit *send* on the 'awards ceremony' e-mail, while he rounds up the fifteen Unaffecteds and asks them to migrate surreptitiously into his office and stuff themselves in the refuge behind the curtain.

As the Unaffecteds start to arrive, the door to Manley's heretofore locked office opens, and a dozen off-duty policemen, who must've been waiting since dawn, pour out.

"Girl, you're up," Guy returns. "Go."

I cross to the entrance as people reticently stand from their monitors. "Okay, everyone, please take your purses and follow me!" Fighting my gagging reflex every step, I lead all one hundred forty-four employees out the double doors, around the loading dock, and up the decrepit factory stairwell.

Steadily we climb the five steep flights in silence, the air thick with dust. Reaching the fire door to the roof, I push against it, but it doesn't budge. Looking down, I realize the door is bolted shut with an industrial padlock. Oh dear God. I bang it against the exit bar—*Clank! Clank! Clank!*—but it's sealed with a century's worth of rust. I turn around on the small landing. "Um," I call over the heads of those just behind me, my voice echoing down the shaft. "Sorry, I'm sorry, the roof is closed, so we're going to, ah . . . have to have the, um, ceremony here."

"I knew it," murmurs a woman next to me, panic flaring across her face, setting off a chain reaction down the steps, anguished and enraged expressions illuminated by bare twitching bulbs.

Squeezing over to the railing, I shakily lift my paper. "On behalf of My Company management, I would like to thank you for your service—"

"CAN'T HEAR YOU!"

"SPEAK UP!"

I take a shaky breath and start again, "On behalf of My Company management, I would like to thank you for your service. We greatly appreciate your work—" My voice falters, and I struggle to get through Manley's script. "It is my duty to inform you that we will no longer be requiring your services, effective immediately. You will be afforded two weeks' severance in return for your signature on a letter of release that is waiting in the lobby. I must also inform you that your experiences while at MC, Inc. are the property of MC, Inc. and that includes this one." I raise my eyes from the page, and they land on the marketing woman from the ladies' room, tears rolling down her cheeks as she looks up in disbelief. "We will not hesitate to pursue you to the full extent of the law should you violate our confidentiality in this manner. We wish you every success as you continue in your careers. There is no reentry on ten. Please proceed down the stairs to the lobby. For those signing the release, your personal effects will be boxed up and available for your pickup in the lobby starting tomorrow." I fold the sheet, dizzy. "Please, you can go down now," I say, my voice small. "I'm so sorry."

For a moment everyone's perfectly still, and in the near darkness, I question if I've read the statement at all. But then movement begins as the steady tread of descending feet clatters below us. I wait at the top with the others, who manage to recoil from me, despite the tightly confined space. When their former colleagues finally clear the path, I follow down all fifteen flights.

In the jarringly bright lobby, there's already an efficient flow of departures as the phalanx of burly policemen hand off nondisclosure forms, patting each ex-employee down as if processing them at an arrest. Faces taut with humiliation, they're moved toward the doors.

"Thanks, everyone!" And there's Guy, against Manley's strict instructions, blocking the exit, forcing a handshake and patted hug on each person as they try to leave. "Thanks for everything. This is *really* hard on me, having to say good-bye like this. I *hate* this whole thing. It just *sucks*. But you gotta remember, we took a chance, right? You gotta gamble in this business, and that's got its own risks. *Dammit,* I hate this." I watch as he dismisses people onto the sidewalk, one woman holding a middle finger up above his oblivious head.

Eyes cast down, I walk swiftly against the exodus.

"Hey, lady, where do you think you're going?!" a cop calls after me.

"I'm on the list." I turn, handing over my ID.

"Elevator's locked for security. Have to walk up."

"Thanks," I mutter, spinning back around.

"Watch out!"

I collide into the marketing woman, her purse upending and files scattering across the floor.

"I'm so sorry." I crouch to help her collect her belongings, picking up children's finger-paintings and a list of notes under the heading 'Orthodontists—Upper West Side.' She grimaces. "I'm sorry, God, I'm sorry, but they're not going to let you take this if it's in folders," I say as we stand up together, and she tugs the papers out of my hands.

"Why didn't you just tell me when I asked you?" She folds the color-daubed pages swiftly and tucks them under her blazer.

"I couldn't—" I begin to offer a futile explanation, but she turns dismissively to join the march toward the guarded exit.

I'm bumped again from behind and carom into Stacey, her cheeks splotched. "What do you even *do* here, anyway?"

"I—I—"

"Forget it. I don't care." She gets in line to be searched.

I chug up the ten flights, my labored breathing echoing in the now-empty shaft. Outside MC's deserted entrance stands yet another security guard. "Blue ticket?" he asks suspiciously.

He lets me through to the barren offices where the few Unaffecteds, all techies and accountants, wordlessly shuffle from desk to desk, packing their fired colleagues' belongings into labeled boxes, Filofaxes, alumni mugs, wedding pictures. The freight-entrance door opens, and a team of movers in orange jumpsuits begins loading the cleared desks onto dollies. Rex strolls in, his hands tucked into the back of his belt, like a farmer surveying his crop.

"All right, folks! Folks, listen up!" I turn at the sound of Guy's exhortation. "I am *very* psyched to be moving forward with you," he cheers, barely winded from his own ten-flight jog. And I just want to reassure you that you all have *nothing whatsoever* to worry about. You should be relieved to know that *you* are *unaffected*, absolutely *unaffected* by this morning's event." He beams, unaware that his use of our 'project' lingo has a less-than-soothing impact on those remaining. An accountant loses his shaky grip on an Affected colleague's makeup bag, a birth-control-pill pack clattering across the floor to Guy's feet, exactly, I'm sure, where she'd have wanted it. "Let's finish this up quickly. And when you're done, empty your own desks. We'll be moving our operation to a new location in Long Island City! Okay? But before anything else, I need everyone to come over and fill out these nondisclosures here. Everybody got that? Great!"

I dodge movers already unloading Guy's office to stuff my few remaining belongings in my purse. My cell rings. "Hello?"

"Oh good, I found you. How'd it go?" Manley asks.

"They were pretty devastated." I rub my forehead, watching as the Unaffected line up to sign Guy's form.

"They'll get over it."

"I hope. So, we're moving?" The ridiculous pony chaise is carried down the steps.

"We didn't need such expensive real estate. Don't worry—I've built a car service into your new compensation package. Now, a small favor. In the rush this morning, I forgot to clear out a few things from the bathroom in my office. Think you can throw 'em in your box?"

"Sure." Whatever.

"I hope you're ready to play a significant part in our new venture. We launched last night and, Girl, early numbers look *fantastic*. There should be a car waiting for you downstairs. Try to hurry—the kickoff party's just getting started."

I cringe, hot needles pricking the backs of my eyes, forecasting a migraine. "I don't really feel up to a party. If it's okay with you, I think I'll just go home and see you Tuesday morning."

"No, no, this'll cheer you up. And you need to meet the new team, so we can hit the ground running after the holiday. I'll expect you in about forty minutes, okay?"

I reach for an empty box. "Okay."

Rex passes me as I head over, one of the pink nondisclosures in hand. "Hey, Guy!" he calls across the floor. "Let's have you sign one of these babies while we're at it."

I enter Manley's emptied office and cross to the granite washroom that was once Guy's eminent domain. Shutting the door behind me, I feel the sudden relief of no longer being watched. I let my shoulders drop and find my face starting to crumple, warm tears breaking. I lock the door and drop onto the toilet lid, soaking my palms as the last hours, days, months catch up with me.

"Guyser, get in here for a second—" Rex calls from the other side of the bathroom door. I hold my breath. "Close it, would ya?" Manley's office door clicks shut.

"I know I wasn't supposed to be here, but man, Rex—I had to. I mean those were my people out there, you know? I just had to see this thing through. Just like you taught me."

"Yes. Can I have the form?"

"Sure. Here. I'm so psyched for what's next. I'm really amped. You know, Bovary fucked us—so we tried, we learned, but it was worth the gamble, right? You gotta take those risks—"

"Guy, I'm letting you go." My eyes bulge in the silence. "Don't look at me like that. You know the board's been at me for weeks. You asked for this shot, we gave it to you, and it fell through. I have every confidence in you, Guyser. You'll land on your feet."

"But you're gonna hook me up?" Guy's voice is faint.

"Well . . . look, I think it's best if we put some distance between us for a while."

"I see."

"You know how it is, Guy. This has been a bit of an embarrassment for me with The Bank. We just need a cooling-off period."

"Right."

"Don't look so down, buddy. You're the idea man. Something's going to hit, just need to keep shooting."

"Yeah, no, you're right. Well, at least let me take you out for a drink—"

"I've got to get going. I'll call you, though."

"I'm going to be out on the island over the weekend. I'll stop by—"

"We'll be busy." I feel the rush of air over my feet as Manley's door reopens. "We good? . . . Guy?"

"What? Yeah, Rex, definitely . . . good."

I sit and wait.

And wait. And wait. Listening with every ounce of attention. I give it ten minutes, and then, just to be safe, fifteen. Grabbing Manley's toiletries, I tense every muscle before unclicking the lever and opening the bathroom door.

"Fuck. You've been in there this whole time?"

"What? No. Yes." Guy is slumped against the window, elbows propped on bent knees, his skin matching his pale-green shirt. "Yes, sorry, Manley asked me to get her things so—"

"You must really be enjoying this." Stunned that I'm not, I grip the box, trying to nail down what I'm feeling. Exhaustion, mostly.

"Not really."

"Right."

"I'm not, Guy. It's sad." I nod out at the emptying office. "This whole thing is just sad."

He pushes himself up to standing. "Don't be so fucking sanctimonious."

"I wasn't—"

"You were. It's your thing. You reek of it."

I start for the door.

"Don't judge me," he growls after me. "You don't know a single fucking thing about running a business."

"Nor was I supposed to—that wasn't my responsibility." I dig my fingernails into the cardboard. "I wasn't the CEO."

"Exactly—and you never will be. Underneath all that uppity bullshit, you're totally useless." Light streams in the cracks of the blinds behind him, turning the gray in his hair a spectral white. "You don't take direction, follow through, or deliver what's asked for. You have no imagination, no respect, and absolutely no fucking guts. You're a *shit* team player."

"Oh! Oh, sorry, there was a *team*? There was direction? It wasn't just—" I drop the box and flail my arms to the left. "Over there. Or, oh no, wait. How about over here." I flail to the right. "I've just been so busy 'not thinking' I must've missed it. I know, why don't you break into my house when I'm naked and we can have an *inappropriate* conversation about it in the dark! Or, hey! I could just fire everybody for you—either one! Anything you need, Guy. It's all about you."

He glowers with sunken eyes. "Whatever."

"Right." I heft the box into my arms. "Look, Guy, you were supposed to give information and clear directions. You were supposed to motivate, with consistency, and courtesy—be a role model."

"Jesus, Girl, you're *deeply* fucked up."

"No." Standing in my power heels, I stare at him, eye to eye. "What I am . . . is employed." I stride out with Manley's panty liners.

CHAPTER TWELVE

Oh Yeah, Baby, Don't Stop, Don't Stop, Don't Stop!

The limousine pulls up in a row of parked limousines outside a warehouse in a neighborhood of warehouses, and I eagerly hop out, a million-pounds-of-crappy-boss lighter. I breathe in the warm air, the intense reflection from the white sidewalk feeling deliciously beachlike as I scan the glimmering tin buildings for the entrance to a new era.

MC board members tread from their cars, one slapping his palm against a garage door. It flies up, icy air rushing out of the darkness as I follow them under a CONGRATULATIONS banner. It takes a moment for my eyes to adjust before I can make out the cavernous black ceiling arching a good thirty feet above, while a long center passageway rolls out before me, flanked by glassed-in offices. Manley was right; the new-carpet smell mixed with the lingering hint of fresh paint buoys my spirits even further.

"Champagne?" a gracious voice offers, and I reach around the nearest board member, my hand accidentally brushing bare skin. I lean past a seersucker shoulder to find a topless—top-*less*—server handing off flutes from a tray painted to look like a yellow legal pad.

"Sorry, I seem to be in the wrong place. Do you know which building My Company is in—"

"Whoops! Be careful, there, sweetie." I spin to face another half-naked server, steadying the flutes she carries on her own legal pad tray.

"I'm looking for My Company."

"Hush," a man addresses me as he helps himself to a drink. "We're not calling it that anymore."

"This is *Fun* Company," the waitress offers.

Her clones flank us, all sporting identical glasses, buns, pencil skirts, and pumps, all offering hors d'ouevres and cocktails from legal pads, their young hair liberally sprayed a silvery gray.

Confused, to say the least, I head down the glass-walled aisle, hunting for Manley in the flanking empty offices, conference rooms, copy rooms, and kitchen.

Suddenly a school bell clangs. The doors spring open in the back of each of the rooms, and a professionally clad man and woman enter. They freeze in artificial mid-workday positions, like Office Kens and Barbies. The men are young, the women made up to look older, much older. Some sort of party entertainment? Some training group Manley's brought in? I scan along the windows as a second bell sends the women into fits of contrived gesticulated yelling at their male counterparts. In the kitchen, a woman lectures a young man by the coffee urn when, out of nowhere, he hauls off and backhands her. I twist away from the window, only to catch sight of the woman in the boardroom across the aisle reeling over the conference table. She lands against the wall, the wind knocked out of her. The man unzips his fly.

"It's completely interactive," an elderly board member explains to his colleagues, tugging the handkerchief from his breast pocket to pat his freckled brow. "The user just clicks on whichever one looks most like his boss, how he wants her done, and the actor takes over." Office Ken rips Office Barbie's clothes off on the conference table, penetrating her with an assaulting level of force, her head knocking into the wood laminate. She turns her face away from him, and we lock eyes, her Slavic features coming into focus.

"Watch your step, dear." He extends his freckled hand, as I struggle to remain upright.

"Girl, there you are. Great work this afternoon." Manley rounds the corner holding champagne, her free hand patting her pregnant belly beneath her beige linen shift. I blink at her utterly, utterly— "We're having a problem with the air," she announces flatly. "Too warm and the nipples won't stay hard, too cold and they get gooseflesh, which reads on camera." She grimaces. "I'm learning. Haven't they offered you a drink yet? The waitresses should be circulating back here, too." She scowls past me at the servers.

"How did you—how did she—" I point to Moldova, a trickle of blood escaping from her nostril.

"Guy discovered her. What a pistol. Been at it since we went live last night—great work ethic."

"Manley, she came here in a *cargo container*—"

"And now she's making a fortune," she says with a smile. "American dream, isn't it?"

"No! I don't—What *is* this? I mean I know what it is, but what—"

"Cash cow." She takes my elbow and leads me away. "Six aisles going from soft to hard core. We're finding our users progressing through the site much faster than we anticipated, so we'll have to ratchet up the content. But we don't have to worry about that till Tuesday."

"Tuesday?" I repeat stupidly.

"Today we're celebrating. I wasn't planning on taking you through all the boring details, so you could just relax over the holiday." Fat. Fucking. Chance. She takes me in from shaking head to toe. "Or we can talk now, if you'd prefer." She drains her glass and sets it on a passing steno pad.

"Yes. I would."

Manley takes me through a door marked MANAGEMENT, and we're suddenly vacuum-sealed in her office. With its gray drapes and crisp charts, it's an identical replica of her space at MC. "First, here's the thirty-day bonus check Guy promised you." She puts the folded green paper in my numb hands. "Have a seat." She indicates the worktable once again spotlit in the center of the room.

I don't move.

"Well, I'm sitting." She lowers herself into a gray chair and rests a swollen hand on her abdomen. "Girl, I'm greatly impressed by the organizational skills you brought to the reorg. I think you have tremendous potential, and I'd like to offer you my right-hand position, effective Tuesday. That's a one-hundred-percent increase in salary and an annual bonus based on gross profits, which are looking good." She beams expectantly. I shut my eyes, willing anything else to be waiting for me, Jeffrey, Kat—even Doris.

"Girl."

I open them. "You . . . want me to run a porn site."

"Oh, not run. Not yet. Don't worry, I fully expect a learning curve, but I'll be here to manage your transition until I go on maternity leave and even then I'll be available by ph—"

"A porn site?"

She wiggles a plump finger. "Adult entertainment, Girl—we don't use the P word—generates more revenue than all pro football, baseball, and basketball franchises combined. It's a *twelve-billion*-dollar industry, which, to my eye, could greatly benefit from stronger female managerial involvement."

"There's a woman outside that door getting her skull knocked—"

"Girl, seventy percent of porn traffic occurs from nine to five—make the leap—we're servicing an untapped corner of the marketplace—"

"And that makes it *okay?*"

She sighs, rubbing her belly. "The Greeks put it on urns; we put it on the Net."

"But I'm . . . a feminist" is all I come up with.

"So am I," she says, her palms opened to me. "We're women employing women. What isn't feminist about that? And employing them well, I might add. Everyone on the floor is getting full benefits and an unparalleled pay scale for barely passing their GEDs. Girl, I'm giving you the chance to be the boss—"

"Pimp."

"Not pimp." Her eyes well. "Ugh, the hormones." She runs a quick finger under her lower lashes. "I'm launching a national corporation with a targeted eight-figure revenue. These women," she says, gesticulating to the outer room, *"deserve* good management." She pulls her purse from her desktop, truffling around in it until she withdraws gloss, which she applies with a detectable tremor. "This is a huge opportunity," she seemingly reminds herself, as she traces her stretched lips.

"This is huge *bullshit*," I explode. "This is the lazy choice, Manley. With your skills you could be making money *and* a difference at any number of places." I shrug. "Sure they deserve good management; so did the slaves."

"Come on now." She throws her hands up, intolerant of my sophistry. "These women are working for me of their own free will."

"Oh yeah. Following safe childhoods and top-notch educations, it was this or med school."

She slaps her hand down on the desk, the gloss tin making a hollow pang. "What do you think, Girl? That if I shut our doors, they'll apply for that Rhodes they've been putting off, they'll have the childhood someone neglected to give them? No. They'll end up flashing their twats at the strip club down the block. At best." She points the gloss tin at me accusatorily. "Meanwhile you're standing there arrogantly throwing away the opportunity to become successful, independent, and unequivocally rich before the age of twenty-five."

"Off *this?*" I shake my head. "Off *them?*" I struggle for civility. "Off the myth that this is a workforce of hyper-sexed employees who grow up to find the *perfect job.* Manley, you could have a daughter inside you right now."

"I do."

"Would you wish *that,*" I say, pointing at the door. "On her?"

She crosses her arms over her stomach. "Fine. Waste the next fifteen years coffee-fetching and ethical waffling—"

"I'm not waffling! *This is my line.*"

"*Oh, this* is your line?" she hoots sarcastically. "But pimping yourself to Bovary, writing a how-to manual on do-me feminism, all for one fat paycheck, *that* was just peachy-keen." She stands, narrowing her eyes to deliver a final summation. "You're going to look back on this and kick yourself."

"For turning down being President of The Bank's Porn Site Where We Beat and Rape Women? I doubt it."

"*Not* The Bank. Fun Company," she corrects me sternly, inadvertently conveying the stakes. "The Bank has nothing to do with this."

"Why, Manley? If it's such a 'cash cow,' what's to be ashamed of?" I ask, savoring that she's backed herself into her own corner.

"The Bank can't be associated with it because it's immoral." She smiles, matching my smug tone. "Viewing it, using it, running it. Thank God. Take away the taboo, and you take away the profit. So long as the Catholic Church and Right Wing keep condemning us, and the ACLU keeps defending us, adult entertainment thrives. To be against porn is to be anti-American, puritanical, repressed, and just plain hung-up. So, go ahead, judge it—judge me, it's money in my pocket."

Chilled air starts to move through the ducts above, filling the room with a low mechanical hum. Dumbfounded by her comfort, I stare at her, plumbing our hours together to find the kernel of what is true between us. "Manley, it must have been an unimaginably rough ride to get here. I can only guess how many Guys and Rexes you've had to stomach." She nods in spite of herself. "And I have to tell you, I've only worked with you for a few weeks, but you're the best manager I've ever had." Her face softens slightly, the color returning as I take in her crisp linen shift, framed by her crisp surroundings. "You're clear, organized, efficient," I continue honestly. "And you've obviously accomplished an enormous amount in your career. I was really looking forward to learning from you. And *that's* what's hard to walk away from. But I quit. I have to. And I have to believe you'll respect me for it."

"Sign your nondisclosure," her voice catches me before I reach the door.

"No."

"Then *you* can tell Julia Gilman you cost her the nine hundred thousand."

I turn back.

She shrugs, pushing the paper toward me. "Real world."

"I need time—"

"No. I have to get back to the party. Make a decision."

I stare at the form. And the cashier's check for nine hundred thousand she lays beside it.

"Don't be an asshole, Girl. However you feel about me or this business, don't take this funding away from them. It's selfish, and you know it."

I do.

I sign it.

Take the cashier's check.

And leave.

"Wait," Julia cuts me off. "Let's discuss this in private. There's a lot going on here, and the walls aren't soundproof." I become aware of women chatting, phones ringing, and the distinct staple pound of carpet being installed. "Sorry, yes." My mind still sprinting, I follow her down the thin aisle between cellophane-wrapped desks to a more secluded corner of Magdalene.

Pulling up the knees of her suit, she sits on a bag of cement, a small puff of powdery dust rising.

My forehead prickling with anxious sweat, I continue, "So now it's a porn site and Moldova . . ." Julia goes pale. "And they threatened me with a nondisclosure or they wouldn't give you the rest of the money—"

"Which you signed."

"What? Yes. Which I signed. So, should we consult a lawyer? Or do you have a contact who could call the press?"

"Do you have it now, the rest of the money?"

"Yes. Here." I've barely pulled the check from my pocket before she swiftly takes it. She opens the green paper across her knee, a flush spreading over her hollow cheeks.

"Julia, Moldova is getting fucked senseless to earn you that money."

She stands, wiping off the back of her trousers. "Don't oversimplify. This money is for fifty women upstairs who need it. Desperately."

"Doesn't it just cancel itself out?"

"We're not going to turn this into a moral exercise, Girl. This money is from The Bank."

"That's not what the check says."

She glances at the Fun Company imprint, her expression stolid. "My not taking this money won't shut down their site. Which you understand, or you wouldn't have signed the nondisclosure." The crease between her brow deepens. "So why are you now trying to make it seem like this is mine to resolve?"

"I'm not trying to make it *seem* like anything." I steady my voice. "I feel disgusting about this, Julia. I hoped, at minimum, you'd legitimize that. At least *acknowledge* that this," I point at the check, "is shitty. That how that money is being made is shitty. That the fact that you have to take it, is shitty. That I had to compromise pretty much everything I believe in to stand here, is shitty. I hoped that you'd, I don't know, be a mentor or a—"

"I'm not your mother, Girl."

"I know that," I say quietly, taken aback.

"Do you? Because you seem to be looking for some kind of absolution here that I can't give."

"What I was looking for is honesty. And support. And . . ." I gaze down at the raw flooring, briskly wiping away tears. "A job." I exhale. "I don't know what to do with this."

"I'm sorry it's been so hard on you." She slips the check in her pocket. "Don't beat yourself up about the nondisclosure. There isn't an audience for what you have to share." She bends to retrieve an abandoned paper cup, recalling Moldova sweeping to retrieve Julia's coat from the park pavement, her childlike hands gripping the wool with all her thwarted tenacity.

"That's heartening."

"No, that's *honesty*. I'm soliciting for funding every day—no one wants to hear anything about the sex industry that isn't sexy." She pulls back her blazer to check her watch. "Which reminds me, I'm sorry, but I really must—"

"Right." I nod.

She takes my elbow to lead me back through the hum and bustle of her fledgling community. "So, keep in touch, okay?" she says, unlocking the front door.

"Of course," I answer automatically. "I'll try."

Holding the heavy glass open for me, she squints in the sunshine, deepening the creases around her eyes, scars from decades of smiling her way through. "I'm proud of you, if that's worth anything."

"No, it is." Something, but not everything, and the fact that I can even make the distinction propels me forward.

Home, I'm greeted by the sound of a running shower and Buster's overnight bag nestled in the front hall. Kicking off my shoes, I flip through my mail, ripping open a Chatsworth envelope and pulling out a folded piece of newsprint. Jack stands in his soccer uniform with one cleat perched on a ball, Grace's red pen circling the caption, LOCAL HIGH SCHOOL STUDENT AGITATES TO START STUDENT-RUN LEAGUE. I smile deeply, tugging off my blouse and sliding on a clean tank.

I open the door to the bathroom, steam billowing out into the hallway. "Honey, I'm home," I announce to the curtain as I slide my back along the damp tiles to the floor.

"Hey," Buster calls from under the showerhead. "Before I forget again, Kira called this morning. Said she's getting into JFK at eight."

"Really? She's not supposed to be home for another month."

"Yeah, she sounded pretty bummed. Something about engineers and bureaucrats and not being able to dig the well."

"Ugh, that sucks. Did she say anything else?"

"Nah. That's it."

"Cool." I look at my watch, unable to believe she's really getting closer by the minute. "Very cool. So . . . have any projects you might need help with? You know, like, photos put into albums or CDs to alphabetize?" I tie my hair up into a ponytail. "If you need anyone fired, I'll have some free time."

"What are you talking about?" The faucet squeaks as he turns off the water.

"I quit." I breathe in the soap-scented steam.

"You quit," Buster echoes, yanking back the curtain.

"Yup." I stretch my legs along the floor, pushing the bathmat toward him with my toe as he steps out. "I did."

He reaches for a towel, rubbing it briskly over his hair before looking at me. "I thought we agreed you were gonna stick with this."

I push myself up, wrapping my arms around his terry-clothed waist. "Well, the situation changed. Big-time." I put my lips close to his ear. "I signed a nondisclosure, though, so you can't tell anyone." He nods as he walks out to the bedroom. "Anyone," I call.

"Okay, yes, I get it," he says, pulling on shorts.

I pause in the doorway, my arms in a V against the frame. "They wanted me to run—wait for it . . . a porn site."

"Run?" He swipes on deodorant. "That's a huge promotion."

"That's what Mengele said," I mug.

"This is hardly the Third Reich."

"It's hardly Disney."

He sits on the bed, his back against the wall. "I think you're being kind of hasty."

I stand over him, staring in confusion. "Hasty?"

"You should at least try it out for a few months. You could be the next Christy Hefner." He takes my hand and tugs me toward his wet torso, leaning up for a kiss.

I look in his green eyes, our lips close. "Are you serious?"

"Sure." He slides his free hand up my thigh.

I tug my fingertips from his and step back, his hand thudding against the frame. "Why?"

"Because there are no jobs, remember?" He rubs his red knuckles. "Luke had to move home, and you're just arbitrarily declining an amazing opportunity."

"Have I not made clear what I've just come from?" I pick up the towel dampening the comforter.

"How about what *I* just came from?" he scowls. "A bunch of Atari corporate fucks talking to me about getting on the ball with my 'market-share generation' and 'dividend creation' and, oh, next time, could I wear a suit?"

"Oh, Buster." I soften, reaching down to squeeze his ankle. "You must be so pissed—"

"It's all turning into that—into suits, and it fucking sucks."

"There must still be smaller game companies. I'm sure we can find one you'd like better. You have some money saved. If you really hate it, then you should leave—"

"*I* don't want to be unemployed." He stands in the tight space between the bed and the closet.

My face stings. "Buster, this isn't me freaking out about wearing a suit—those women are supposed to be getting raped—"

"Raped?" He shakes his head in frustration, droplets splattering me. "Your perspective on porn is so fucked up—it's so easy for you to judge everything."

"No." I step back from him. "What's *easy* is sticking money in her G-string right along with you. Pretending it's just one big happy, sexy economy for us to earn an honest dollar in."

"I'm so tired of this shit." He rubs his face. "I've never had to work this hard for anybody."

"You're tired?! This is the third conversation I've had about this in as many hours. Buster, you asked me to give you the chance not to be 'that boy.' Well, this, right here"—I circle my palms in the space between us—"is growing. And it's messy and complex and confusing. And you're either up for it or you aren't."

"I want that," he says quietly.

"But are you up for it? I can't keep getting stuck here from fear of exhausting you." My eyes catch the bedside clock, a plan forming. "I'm going to the airport." I walk to the door, dropping keys and Jack's clipping in my purse.

"When will you be back?" He leans against the bedroom door frame.

"I don't know." I slide on my sandals.

"Look, if you need to quit this job—"

"Buster," I cut him off.

His eyes meet mine as I open the door. "I think I'm up for it."

"I only have room for sure."

Kira rests her head on my shoulder as we stare out at the row houses along the Grand Central Parkway inching by. Squeezed between her swollen rucksack and a wood fertility statue wrapped in a week's worth of newspaper, I hold her hand, African dirt still under her nails. "You must be in serious culture shock."

"My six-hour layover gave me some time to acclimate, but, yeah," she says, sighing, "I am."

I touch the sliver tear in her jeans just above the knee, exposing the scar beneath. "War wounds?"

"Shovel injury." She pats my Gucci bag. "Remunerations?"

"That, and this." I pull out my bonus check.

"Whew," she whistles.

"Seed money," I say, folding it back in my wallet.

She pokes me in the shoulder. "You could start *your own* porn site. Actually kill the women."

"Genius—have you considered business school?"

"G, I can't even dig a hole." The cab lurches forward, finding an opening, and we speed all of forty feet before stalling once more behind a Trailways bus. "Is that what you're going to do?" she asks, her lids drifting shut. "Start your own thing?"

"Don't know yet, I can't even free one woman from white slavery. Hey, is there a shortcut?" I call up through the scratched plastic to the driver.

"Nah, lady. Just sit tight. Holiday traffic." We're quiet as we inch onto the ramp for the Triboro Bridge in stops and starts.

"G?" Her voice thickens with tears. "Is it going to keep being this hard?"

"Oh, God, no, no," I rush to comfort her. "Well, maybe, yeah." I pull her into me. "And then it won't be," I say into her hair. "At least, that's what I've heard."

"From who? Your fairy role model?"

"Yeah." I laugh. "Didn't you get one?"

"Hold on, ladies." And all at once the traffic breaks open and we're flying into the Manhattan skyline, the wheels thudding rhythmically over the bridge joints, as the Citicorp and Chrysler buildings come into view, the distinctive toothed silhouette of our little island home.

"I'm gonna close my eyes." Kira nestles against her rucksack, fully succumbing to jetlag. The cab abruptly changes lanes, tipping me into the statue as my Palm Pilot thuds to the floor. I reach down to retrieve it, struck by the satisfying image of it tumbling, end over silvery end, into the East River.

I lower the window. The warm salt air whips the hair off our faces, bringing with it the promise of summer and more flights landing, more compatriots returning, the city once again infused with amity and opportunity, because we're only twenty-four for fuck's sake.

I tuck my Palm safely back in my purse, one souvenir housing another. Suddenly the dark sky is ablaze with Memorial Day fireworks, a glorious burst of pyrotechnics shimmering over the water, making a blurred rainbow as we barrel over the patched tar. I nudge Kira awake. "Look." She grins, the lanes clear before us as we accelerate.

ACKNOWLEDGMENTS

We are utterly indebted to . . .

Our phenomenally dedicated, 'a-rainstorm-gets-your-clothes-clean' Team Girl for their faith in this project and over-time ad infinitum on its behalf: Suzanne Gluck, Erin Malone, Alicia Gordon, Betsy Rapoport, Brenda Copeland, Elisa Shokoff, Judith Curr, everyone at Atria, and Ken Weinrib.

Our parents, Peter & Evelyn, Joan & David, John & Janet, and Joel & Nora, for being our formidable, yet loving, moral compass. Professor Janet Gezari, for so gracefully modeling what is possible in art, life, and feminism. And, of course, Emma's husband, Joel, for being inexhaustible.

Finally, and with full hearts, Nicki's grandmother, Xandy, the original C.G.

1. Discuss the literary device of using proper nouns to stand in for traditional names. How does this device inform and shape the story?

2. Do you think Girl's experiences are typical of a recent college graduate? What about her perception of the working world reflects her age and/or inexperience?

3. Girl's job search leads her to "My Company." What does she find appealing about working there? How much of her desire to work there is influenced by her alternatives? Do you think it would have held the same appeal under different circumstances?

4. Feminism is a constant theme throughout the novel. Discuss how it is presented through the story, the peripheral characters, and through Girl and her encounters.

5. What are your initial impressions of Guy and Rex? What are the main aspects of their personalities? Does your perception of these characters change by the end of the novel?

6. Why does Girl feel it is important to seem complacent, even as her situation and conflict reach higher levels? Do you think Girl's willingness to cooperate in order to salvage her job is justifiable?

7. Discuss Buster's character. Is he portrayed as different or similar to the other male characters in the novel? What are some of the main conflicts between Buster and Girl?

8. The novel provides several different female characters. Who are the most extreme characters? Of these extreme characters, which characteristics are most emphasized? What does Girl ultimately

learn from these other women? Which female characters provide role models for Girl?

9. What is the significance of Manley's name? What are the contradictions in her character that both confuse and anger Girl? Compare her character with the men of the novel. What are the similarities and differences?

10. Girl is consistently trying to balance her values with the overwhelming demands of her employment. Do you think this is a possibility in the type of situation and work environment she consistently finds herself in? What are some of the examples from the book of other characters compromising or finding a type of balance?